SOME DAY
Somebody

La Fleur de Love: Book One

By
LORI LEGER

Copyright © 2011 by Lori Leger

ISBN-10:1940305225
ISBN-13:978-1-940305-22-6
(Cajunflair Publishing: Third Edition)

www.lorilegerauthor.com

This story is a complete work of fiction. Names, characters, places, and incidents are either products of the author's imagination or used fictitiously. Any resemblance to actual events, locales, or persons, living or dead, is entirely coincidental.

All rights reserved.

No part of this publication can be recorded, reproduced, or transmitted in any form or by any means, electronic, mechanical, or audial without permission in writing from Lori Leger.

ACKNOWLEDGMENT

Cover art by Lori Leger

I want to thank my husband, Michael, who has done more than his fair share of the housework and cooking, all for the sake of my second full time, non-paying job.

And my mom, who began introducing me as her 'daughter, the author', as soon as she read the awful first draft of this manuscript. I miss you dearly, Mom.

To my children and grandchildren, who've had to share me with my laptop for the last few years. My family members, co-workers, and friends, both on-line and otherwise, who've proven to be excellent critique partners and editors. My Angels…you know who you are, for being the best support group a girl could ask for.

Thank you, Joan Granger of Simple Memories Photography for my author photo...if only I woke up looking that good every morning!

DEDICATION

This book is dedicated to anyone who has ever had to start their life over for one reason or another. I started mine over at thirty-five and it worked out nicely.

Be strong.

If your life isn't going as you'd planned, you can always change direction. Just remember, second chances are for making wiser choices, not to repeat the same stupid mistakes over and over again.

Map of South Louisiana
Real and *Fictional* towns in book

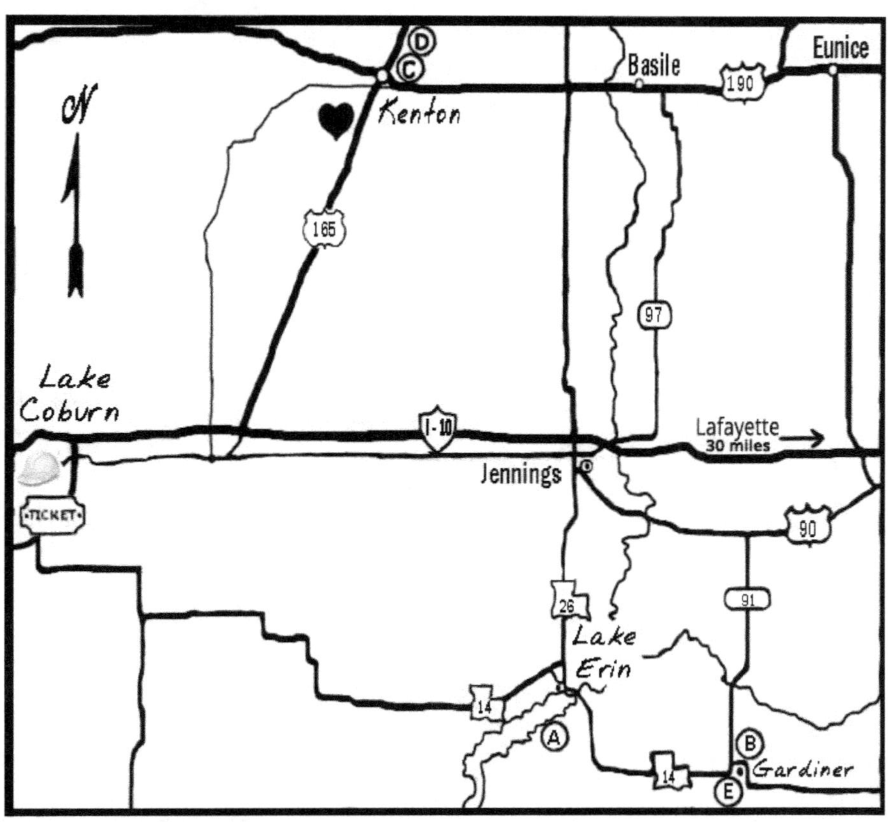

LEGEND:

Ⓐ Carrie's old home (Lakeview)

Ⓑ Christie & Max's home

Ⓒ Sam's home

Ⓓ Carrie's rent house

Ⓔ Elaine's house

Carrie and Sam's Workplace

♥ 1st Date (Kenton Steakhouse)

TICKET 2nd Half of 1st Date (Theater)

Prologue

Late July, 2000
Lafayette, Louisiana
The woman approached from the sidewalk, unaware she'd peaked his interest. He'd been observing her for weeks now. Early to mid-thirties, five-foot-five, 125 pounds, he'd guess. He gave her plenty of room to pass, only turning his head at the last second to catch her scent. Eyes closed behind his shades, he breathed her in, absorbed her aroma into his lungs.
Nice.

He wasn't familiar with the scent, but he knew it was the blend of whatever perfume she wore with her own unique essence. He ground his teeth in an effort to stem the urge threatening to overwhelm him—dark and primal, begging to be released. It had been too damn long since it had seen the light of day.

He was close, dangerously close to seeing his latest plan put into action. He'd chosen this next victim carefully, solely because of her condition. He realized her senses would be heightened, and that intrigued him, made him wish for the days to fly by so he could get to it. By the time she realized her life was in danger, he'd already have her isolated. He loved being alone with them. Loved having the freedom to do whatever he wanted. For a short while, he was their Lord and Master. They did his bidding for a chance to live.

To date, none had survived.

Chapter One

Two days later,
Gardiner, Louisiana

Damn the bad luck.
Carrie Jeansonne groaned at the sight of her soon-to-be ex-husband.

There he stood in all his conceited glory, the dark-eyed Cajun boy she'd been fool enough to fall for. He leaned casually against her car door, smirking and smug, like he didn't have one thing better to do than bug the hell out of her. His tight jeans hugged lean hips while his T-shirt—tight, white, and two sizes too small—outlined the perfect torso he was so damned proud of.

She clenched her teeth and groaned inwardly. "I don't have time for your crap today, Dave." She shifted her armload of groceries, clutched her keys in one hand like she'd learned in self-defense class, in case she'd need to knock some sense into him. He didn't move a muscle.

She struggled not to smash the bread, while trying to keep the contents of her purse from spilling onto concrete hot enough to blister bare feet. "What do you want?" She tapped the toe of her low-heeled pumps, falling into rhythm with an old Zeppelin tune blasting from the sound system of a passing car.

Silence.

Carrie hefted one bag in an awkward attempt to check her watch. "Look, I hate to interrupt your dramatic pause-for-effect, but I have to pick up our daughters before I can go home to cook." Keys jingled from one finger as she shifted her bags from one aching arm to another.

God's gift to women graced her with words. "We need to talk, Babe."

Carrie's stomach soured at the sound of the endearment aimed at her. "I don't have time, and I'm *not* your babe." She wiped the sweat already forming on her forehead. In less than a minute, she'd migrated from air-conditioned-comfortable to hot-as-hell. It didn't take long for her fair skin to betray her by turning sun-kissed pink. Heat and humidity were not her friends. "I need to go."

"You *need* to rethink this divorce." He glared at her from lowered lids, his black eyes daring her to talk back. "You know you can't do this on your own."

She sent up a silent prayer for a sensible way out as an older couple approached. The old man, who had served during WWII alongside her father, stopped to stare, seeming to assess the situation. She watched him nod as his wife quietly reminded him of Carrie's parentage.

He raised an eyebrow that could have doubled as a fuzzy caterpillar. "Is there a problem here, young lady?"

Dave spoke, his voice tight and contained. "I'm speaking to my *wife*."

The man shot a hard glare in Dave's direction. "Are you a young lady?"

"No, sir."

"Then I wasn't talking to you, was I?"

Dave leaned in close to Carrie, his breath hot on her face, and spoke in a steely whisper. "Don't you do it."

Carrie anchored her gaze on Dave as she spoke, too apprehensive of the consequences to lose sight of him. "Mr. Bubby, could you ask someone to call the police for me?"

The man grunted while leaning on his walking cane. "If I were twenty years younger I'd take care of him for you myself, hon." He grabbed hold of the door and turned to shake his cane at Dave. "You're lucky her dad isn't still around. In his younger days, he would have whipped your ass good, boy."

Carrie grinned, watching the old man disappear into the store, before Dave's comment jarred her to the present.

"You bitch."

She gave her soon-to-be-ex-husband a smug look, part satisfaction, part justified anger, bordering on devilish amusement. "That's what happens when you go public with private business." Carrie heard the *pop* of his jaw as it tightened, then saw him relax in reluctant acceptance.

Dave took a step back and gave her appearance a prolonged perusal. "Why didn't you look this good when we were married?"

"Why are you still an idiot?" Her tone, dry as a piece of unbuttered toast.

"You're looking hot these days, Carrie."

"I look the same, Dave. It's just that I'm the shiny toy dangling just out of your reach." Carrie leaned forward to invade his space. "You're the dog who always wants what he can't have."

His dark eyes narrowed. "Are you screwing around already?"

Her eyes sparkled with amusement. "You're kidding, right?"

"You're looking good for somebody; it sure as hell ain't me. Besides, you must want it by now," he goaded, casting a lustful gaze over her ample curves.

"It?"

He nodded.

"Trust me, David, whatever *it* is that you think I want, you don't have."

"Who does?"

"Not your business."

He closed in on her, hot breath in her face once more, his tone low and dangerous. "You'll never know another man, if I can help it."

She jerked away, overpowered by a repulsive mixture of cologne, cigarette smoke, and beer. "Get away from me. You smell like a bar, and I'm not afraid of your threats anymore."

He cupped her chin roughly. "More of a promise than a threat."

Carrie shied from his touch, ignoring the chill his words caused. She clucked her tongue as one of the town's black and white units made a U-turn on the boulevard and hit the lights. "They're hee-erre." She stood her ground until the cruiser carrying two Gardiner policemen pulled up to the store.

The Chief of Police hitched his jeans and *harrumphed*, sounding somewhat like an outboard boat motor. Rob LeDoux stood an impressive six-feet-two inches and, even in his mid-forties, came across as solid as a brick wall. In his prime he had been a hell of a linebacker for Gardiner High.

He made one final adjustment to his navy blue cap and approached. "Carrie." He gave her a light nod.

"Hey, Rob. I see you survived the slumber party. I'm on my way to pick up Lauren and Gretchen from your place." She smiled at the Chief, whose daughter had been friends with her girls since first grade.

Rob glanced at his watch. "Yep, they might be awake by now. When I called at noon, Mona said Abbie and your twins were still asleep." He focused a scowl on Dave. "So what's the problem?"

Carrie jerked her head toward Dave. "He won't let me by."

"We need to talk," Dave growled.

"We're done talking."

Before Dave could respond, the big man in uniform clasped his shoulder in an iron grip, giving him a back-the-hell-off glare only a fool would ignore. "Get her statement, Tim."

The younger officer accompanying Rob stayed behind to question her. He relieved her of the grocery bags. "Ma'am, are you hurt?"

Carrie unlocked her car and popped the trunk. "Just inconvenienced."

The officer placed the bags into the trunk and slammed it shut. "What's his excuse for bothering you?"

"Our divorce is finalizing soon, and he's not happy about it." She peered around the guy's well-developed biceps to keep an eye on Dave.

"Maybe he thinks marriage is too important to walk away so easily."

Carrie whipped her head around to face the officer, a good-looking guy in his late twenties to early thirties, well-groomed and muscular. His hunky looks did nothing to quell her irritation at his judgmental comment. "You're not from around here, are you?"

"No, ma'am."

"If you were, you'd know how many times he's walked away in the last eighteen years."

The officer turned to scrutinize Dave. Carrie could tell the moment his opinion morphed from desperate husband to perpetrator. He faced her again. "I'm sorry, ma'am. Maybe you're better off without him."

Carrie didn't falter, still too full of heart-pumping adrenaline to back down from anyone. "Maybe you'd be better off not jumping to conclusions before you get the whole story."

He smiled, cocked his head slightly before giving her a quick nod. "You may be right."

A slamming truck door had her pulling her attention from the young officer's gaze to see Dave tear out of the parking lot as if he was late for a fire sale at a whorehouse.

Chief Rob approached her. "He won't give you any more trouble."

She raised her hand to block the sun's glare from her eyes and squinted up at her old friend. "You don't really believe that, do you?"

The chief pulled a plastic wrapped toothpick from his shirt pocket. "If he does inside city limits, I'll find his ass." He popped the pick in his mouth then pulled a business card out of his wallet to write something on the back before handing it to her. "As soon as I get back to my desk, I'll call the Sheriff's office and fill them in. You call this guy if you have any trouble outside of town."

Carrie glanced at the card then put it in her wallet. "Thanks, Rob, and—" She turned to squint at the other officer's nametag. "Mr. Hardin."

The younger officer touched the tip of his cap and gave a little nod, like he knew her. "That'd be Tim, ma'am."

She cringed in mock horror at the label. "I wish you'd quit calling me that. I'm not a ma'am. My *mother* is a ma'am."

His gaze grew somber. "It's not an age thing, but a gender thing for me, I assure you."

"It still makes me feel old." She thanked them both and stepped into her car.

She parked her sedan in front of a wood-frame home and tapped on her horn.

Mona LeDoux came to the door and waved, calling to her from the front door. "I'll send them out."

Carrie nodded, then settled back to wait for her girls. She stared out at Mona Ledoux's collection of garden gnomes. What in hell would she have to look forward to for the rest of her life? No husband to bring her down for a start. She'd have sole responsibility for herself and her kids--nobody to blame but herself if things didn't work out.

She allowed her head to rest on the back of the seat and closed her eyes for a moment to consider the 'Dave situation'. Over the past six months of their separation, he'd made some half-hearted attempts to get her back, but she'd heard all his empty promises before. He'd still be the unfaithful, controlling, unsatisfied man he'd always been. Would he continue to cause trouble for her once the divorce was final? Her rental would be ready to move into January first and she was primed to be on her own.

She wasn't afraid of him. For all his bluster, Dave was harmless, but she was tired of trying to avoid him. She wanted to fast forward a few months to when he'd already have someone else so he'd leave her the hell alone.

It had her wondering what she'd be doing six months from now. She adjusted the rear-view so she could see herself. Carrie grimaced as she wiped a smudge of mascara from the corner of one eye. "I won't be with a man, that's for damn sure. Dave cured me of that for good."

What baffled her was the way her almost-ex had fought this divorce every step of the way. His attempts to win her back had grown more desperate.

Carrie rubbed her eyes, exhausted from the hour commute after a long workday. She yawned, wishing there were good job opportunities closer to home for computer drafters. As long as she lived in Gardiner, it was a given that she'd be stuck on the road two hours a day, five days a week, for decades to come. It exhausted her just thinking about it. Her mother had suggested that she move closer to her work, but how could she uproot her kids in the midst of a divorce? Her mom's words from their last discussion came back to her. *"Carrie, children are resilient. We relocated twice when you kids were young, and you all survived."*

"But our parent's weren't going through a divorce." She shook her head, readjusting her mirror.

Carrie tightened her grip on the steering wheel, recalling her husband's hateful words. *"You know you can't do this on your own."* The comment ate at her, made long-dormant feelings of inadequacy rise to the surface like dead fish in a stagnant pond. Feelings she thought she'd buried once she'd received her college degree. She'd earned it, fought for it by defying Dave's demands she stay home and be *just* a wife and mother. He'd always said it like there was no effort involved. As though the years she spent raising children and tending to the household took little effort—but all she could handle.

Bitterness and resentment rose from the pit of her stomach to sour in her mouth. She sought the image of the middle-aged stranger staring back at her in the rear-view mirror. She raised a finger to the worry lines creasing her forehead. "What makes you think you can do this, you stupid, *stupid* woman?"

Carrie inhaled a deep, cleansing breath before side stepping the self-doubt. "What you should be asking is what made you think you couldn't? Or who?" She shook her head forcefully, disgusted she'd let him get to her. "Damn you, Dave."

Long after Gretchen and Lauren joined her in the car, she continued to launch low curses targeted at her ex.

"Mom?" Gretchen asked, interrupting Carrie's personal rant.

"Hmmm?"

"Are you okay?"

"Yeah, you look kind of mad," Lauren chimed in.

Carrie gazed back at the looks of concern on her twins' faces, determined to conquer her fears. Years from now, she wanted her kids to remember she was strong when she needed to be.

"I was, but I'm over it." She shifted her gaze back on the roadway.

"At Dad?" Lauren asked.

"I was more afraid than angry—my fault for letting him get to me."

Gretchen turned in the front seat to face her. "Are you still afraid?"

Carrie reached out and brushed Gretchen's golden brown curls back from her face, then smiled at Lauren in the rear-view mirror. "Not anymore."

The next morning's two a.m. phone call had her reassessing her opinion. The caller spoke no words, made no sounds other than light breathing, but she sensed the threat, more dangerous because of its ominous silence. She suspected Dave but couldn't be certain.

You'll never know another man, if I can help it.

His threat haunted her, kept her awake, tossing and turning until the five a.m. alarm sounded for work.

One week later
Lafayette, Louisiana

The young woman's sightless eyes fixed on the ceiling, her face void of expression, as though she'd taken herself far from the tiny apartment.

He stared, pleased with the effects of their latest session. Vivid, red whelps combined with the pattern of purple, black, and blue, mimicking the patchwork quilt draped across the back of her couch.

He leaned closer and whispered, watching for any reaction from her. "You're tough, I'll give you that."

He fastened the sturdy, square buckle and threaded his belt through its last loop. Recalling the sharp *whack* of smooth leather meeting her skin made him long to hear it again. No time for another round with her. Several weeks of careful planning had culminated in three glorious days of self-indulgent pleasure.

His motivation to maintain the carefully structured schedule had been the same for nearly a decade. Freedom to play, without having to pay.

He pulled on his boots and straightened, studying her one last time. "Maybe that mulish pride will keep you fighting long enough to survive." He paused to brush the back of his hand down the length of her face and neck. "If you do, maybe I'll pay you another visit one day soon." He frowned, mildly disappointed his threat hadn't produced fear in eyes that were otherwise useless. Some would consider her unlucky for being blind since birth, but he knew the truth, and so did she. No sight, no way to identify him—a chance to live. An uncharacteristic show of mercy on his part, but what the hell, he was feeling generous today.

Early August
Kenton, Louisiana

Damn, my life sucks.

Sam Langley gazed up at the August evening sky from the front porch of his home. Today marked the unwelcome anniversary of his first year as a single man—middle aged, divorced, and not enjoying it in the least. Funny the divorce should finalize on the exact same day.

God, it was hot. The dog days of summer were upon them, with no relief in sight for at least another month, maybe even two. July had broken records for heat and humidity levels, causing temperatures to rise into triple digits. He braced both hands on the porch rails and breathed in air that was hot and dense with moisture. Nothing compared to summertime in south Louisiana.

As fast as it got here, it'd be gone. Before long, he'd be surrounded by the sights, sounds, and smells of Fall: parents calling kids inside for meals, homework, and baths; music and cadences drifting over from the stadium as the high school marching band practiced routines for Friday night's games; the smell of leaves burning, or the occasional lit fireplace as someone took advantage of the first cool snap. Fall meant lower temps and drier air as humidity levels dropped, causing the entire population to breathe a collective sigh of relief.

Normally, he'd welcome the sights and sounds of the fall months. It meant the reddish gold of leaves as they turned, and the calls of Speckle Bellied, Snow and Blue geese flying in from the north, precise in their V-formations. Unfortunately, along with football season, the fall season would also bring shorter days and the long, lonely nights he dreaded.

He walked inside to answer his ringing phone, thankful for the interruption to his personal pity party. A smile crossed his face as he recognized his married daughter's number on the caller ID, no doubt calling to check up on her old man again.

"Hey, Pop, how you doing tonight?"

"I'm okay, Amanda. You and Joe just making it back from your mom's?"

"Uh huh, just calling to let you know we made it home."

"I'm glad you did. Is your brother walking home?"

"One of Nick's buddies picked him up. He asked me to let you know he'll be riding around for an hour or so."

"Okay, hon." He paused. "How's your mom and everyone on that end?"

"Everyone's okay."

Sam heard a catch in her voice and her hesitance to continue. "What?"

"Why didn't you tell us the divorce went through, Pop?"

He clenched his jaw and took the phone out to the porch with him. "I didn't want to involve you in our mess."

Amanda spoke quietly. "I would rather have heard the news while I was home, so I could mope in private."

"I'm sorry." He released his breath in a long, slow hiss. "One year ago, I never would have believed I'd be facing another summer—another fall, and all of those damn holidays—alone again." Being single for the holidays was number one on his list of least favorite things.

"You have us."

"I know. I appreciate having you kids around, too." *That won't put a damper on those long, lonely winter nights.*

Sam stood still and listened to the sounds of small-town life. The young mother from next-door, pleading with her husband to help get their two rowdy boys settled; a barking dog down the street; the slow steady rhythm of the train's freight cars clattering along the rail six blocks to the west. "When your mother left me a year ago, I really believed she'd be back by the end of the month." *Like all the other times she left in our twenty-one year marriage.*

"We all thought the same thing, but I guess Mom had other plans."

Sam grunted in agreement, as he heard Amanda cover the phone and speak to someone else in a muffled voice.

"I need to go now, Daddy. You gonna be okay?"

Sam smiled at the label that called to mind images from years past. His little girl, with banged up knees, big brown eyes, a constant pixie grin, and long, black pigtails—now twenty years old with a husband of her own. "You go on and get back to Joe. Don't worry about me."

"Love you."

"Love you too, baby girl."

Sam ended the call and stood there, remembering the day Linda left. How the first month's confidence in her return had slowly disintegrated when two months stretched into three, then four. The loneliness had eaten at him, eventually forcing him to accept the death of his marriage. It ended the only life he'd known for over two decades, with the only woman he'd ever known, in the biblical sense, anyway.

He found himself twisting the plain, gold wedding band he'd continued to wear, even though Linda had discarded hers immediately.

He pulled off his ring and raised it skyward to telescopically view the partial moon through the circle of gold. Sam palmed the ring before walking to the end of the sidewalk then out to the middle of the street. Without another glance, he wound up and pitched the ring as far as he could into the night. He never heard it land but knew it was gone, long gone, like his wife and marriage.

Heat enveloped him as he made his way back to the porch. Sam dropped heavily onto the top step, feeling the residual warmth from the cement. As hot and miserable as it was out here, he dreaded going back inside.

He gazed up at the star-studded sky, amazed at how much he sucked at going solo. He would've at least thought he'd enjoy being able to watch what he wanted on television, but he didn't. He hated being alone, hated shopping for groceries alone, and hated not having a reason to shave. Scratching at his three-day growth of beard, he thought of his king-size bed, and how much he hated sleeping alone. It wasn't even the sex, although he missed that, too. It was being in that big old bed with nobody to talk to at night.

Sam wiped a hand roughly over his eyes. Nothing to look forward to. He stood up slowly and shoved his hands deep into the pockets of his denim shorts. He looked up at the sky as though he were talking to God. "So what the hell do I do now, huh? What do you have in store for this old man?"

Old man? He shifted uneasily at the thought of his birthday around the corner. Being thirty-nine and single hadn't done much for his mood at work. He doubted moving into the fourth decade of his life would be any better. He'd transformed from the office clown to "*Oscar the Grouch*" the past year.

God must have one hell of a sense of humor.

Chapter Two

Mid-August
Lake Coburn, Louisiana

Carrie followed her new supervisor around the office as he gave her the grand tour.

Dale spoke in a quiet drawl, typical of people raised in the northern parishes of Louisiana. "Counting you, we have five designers and a five-man survey party. That's headed by Sam Langley." He pointed to someone just walking into the front door. "Nice of you to join us, Langley. You want to introduce Carrie to your bunch?"

Carrie turned and found herself facing a big, barrel chest covered in a blue chambray work shirt. She lifted her gaze up, up to the tall, broad-shouldered man standing before her. Striking blue eyes, nearly the same color as his shirt, held her attention as he gave her a scrutinizing stare.

The fair-haired man nodded and introduced each of his crewmembers in a business-like manner before retreating into a nearby office.

Carrie watched him walk away, wondering if she had done something to offend him.

The only other woman in the office walked by with a mug of coffee and extended her hand. "Hey, I'm Roxanne, but everyone calls me Roxie. Don't pay any attention to Oscar."

Carrie's gaze danced from one stranger to the next. "I don't remember meeting an Oscar."

Roxie sipped her coffee and motioned toward the office where Mister Big, Blonde, and Blue-eyed had disappeared. "Sam, also known as *Oscar the Grouch.*"

"He seems a tad serious."

"He's been cranky since his wife left him over a year ago," Roxie explained.

Carrie sucked in her breath and grimaced. "I know the feeling. I'm waiting for my divorce to finalize any day now."

Roxie wiggled the fingers of her left hand to flash her wedding ring. "I've been through it, too. I'm on my third husband."

Carrie cringed at the woman's confession. "Jesus—do you walk on broken glass for kicks?"

Roxie put her head back and laughed. “Men! Can’t live with ‘em, too damn broke to live without ‘em.”

The days rushed by in a whir of activity. Before Carrie knew it, she’d been at her job for two weeks. She enjoyed the relaxed work environment and had already formed lasting friendships with her co-workers—or most of them, anyway.

On the second day of September, she glanced up from her studying when members of the office carpool entered from the back door, as usual, nearly ten minutes late. From her own brief experience with the carpool, she was well aware who was to blame.

She’d never forget the embarrassment of being fifteen minutes late her second day on the job because of Sam. She’d sat in that truck with the others, waiting for Sam and seething at his tardiness. The driver, a member of his survey crew, refused to leave without him, so they'd waited at his designated pick-up spot until he'd finally arrived, fifteen minutes later than he should have. Once he’d taken his sweet time to settle himself in his front seat place of honor, she’d given him a verbal chew-out he’d accepted with pure indignation. Since then, anytime they were in the vicinity of each other, the room temperature dropped to match her icy disregard for her co-worker.

She briefly met Sam’s gaze as he dropped coins into the soft drink machine, before returning her attention to her study guide.

“Look at you, hard at it this early in the morning. I’m so impressed.”

Carrie responded in a dry monotone. “Goody. I can sleep at night.” She knew little about the man, other than the fact that *Oscar* seemed to be in a perpetual bad mood.

He folded his long body over to retrieve his can of Coke, then walked slowly toward her desk. “What’cha got there?”

“A study guide.” She returned to her book. The sooner she could get a couple of certifications under her belt, the better. Certifications plus time meant a raise in pay, and boy did she need that. She’d just tanked up her car for the second time since dropping out of the carpool. With the price of gas, her paychecks wouldn’t go far.

He popped the lid on his drink and grunted. “All you ever do is study. What’s the hurry? If you needed the money, you’d still be in the carpool.”

She stared at the man, shocked at his nerve. “If you’ll think back, genius, I tried that.”

“Uh huh, you got all uppity with me, then dropped out after one day.”

Carrie pointed at the large wall clock next to the entrance. “I can’t get to work late on a new job. Do you even *know* the meaning of probationary period?”

“Aw, five minutes here and there won’t hurt anyone.” His tone was a mixture of teasing and serious-as-a-heart-attack.

She blew out a frustrated breath. "Whatever, Sam." She returned her attention to her studies and flipped her notebook to a fresh sheet with a snap of her wrist.

"It's not whatever, it's what *is*."

When she ignored his overly confident comment, Sam would have been smarter to walk away. Instead, he leaned one elbow on her desk, as though daring her to confront him.

Bantering with seven siblings and a nearly ex-husband had left Carrie sharp-tongued, sharp-witted, and itching to put him in his place. Being the new girl, however, she thought it safer to ignore his taunt, lest her position of "Last Hired" become "Next Fired".

She tapped the eraser of her mechanical pencil in time to Toby Keith's *Should Have Been a Cowboy* coming from the piped in speaker system. She tried to concentrate on the text in front of her, an impossible feat when she could feel Sam's blue-eyed gaze tracking her every movement.

"Carrie . . ." His tone issued a challenge.

"Go away, Sam."

"Uh unh, you want to fight. I can see it in your face." He stepped back from the desk and picked up his fists, assuming a playful fighting posture. "Come on, Carrie. Let's fight."

She spun on her stool to meet his gaze. "What's in it for me? Besides getting fired, I mean."

Sam's brow furrowed, his hands fell to his sides. "Is that what you're afraid of?"

She raised an eyebrow in answer.

His rumble of laughter filled the air between them. "You'd practically have to kill someone to get fired from this place."

Dale spoke from behind her. "That could happen sooner than you think, if you don't leave her the hell alone, Langley."

He released a low snort. "I ain't afraid of her. If she had the gumption, she'd have done something about it by now."

Carrie released an irritated sigh and slammed her book closed. She stepped down from the stool at her desk and walked up to Sam, meeting his amused gaze with a sober one of her own. "You've got nerve, you know that, Sam?"

The office buzzed like opening night of a Broadway musical, as co-workers gathered in anticipation of a verbal throw-down. Dale spoke from his spot behind her. "Get him, Carrie. That ornery son-of-a-gun has had it comin' fer over a year now."

Her mouth tightened to suppress a grin at her supervisor's vote of confidence. She focused her attention completely on Sam, and, though she stretched to her full height, still had to look up to face the irritating giant of a man.

She nearly laughed when Sam put up his dukes, ready for a fight. She placed one finger on his broad chest, and gave him a light shove. "Who the hell are *you* to make that carpool late every morning?"

He dropped his fist to his sides. "It's not every morn-"

"*Every* morning." She poked his chest to make her point. "You made me fifteen minutes late my second day on the job." She watched as Sam took a step back and stared down his nose at her.

"Do you have two different colored eyes?"

Her gaze narrowed suspiciously. "Don't try to change the subject, you big Redneck."

"Do you?"

"Yes, but what does that have to do with anything?"

"That's weird."

"*You're* weird."

He cocked his head slightly to the side, as one corner of his mouth lifted in a lopsided grin. "Aw, is that the best you can do?"

"And you're inconsiderate. Despite what your mommy must have raised you to believe, the world does not revolve around you."

"Maybe it should," he added, grinning down at her.

She straightened her shoulders and closed the distance between them. "You're like one of those bullies in elementary school. Just because you're the biggest kid on the playground, you think you can get away with anything."

From her desk in the corner of the room, Roxie threw her head back in laughter. "Boy, does she have you pegged."

"I'm not a bully."

Carrie dismissed his denial with a flippant wave of her hand. "I say you are."

It didn't take long for Sam to retaliate. "You don't know a damn thing about me, lady. I am *not* a bully."

She turned away, giving him an insignificant shrug, and climbed back on her stool. "I bet you were a spoiled brat."

Members of his crew doubled over with laughter, until Sam aimed a glare in their direction and pointed to the back exit. "We have five miles of roadway to survey by the end of the day. Your asses better be in that truck by the time I walk out of here."

The men attempted to wipe the grins from their faces as they grabbed equipment and headed for the door.

Carrie clucked her tongue. "Aw, Sammy, don't take it out on the guys just because you lost an argument with a woman."

Roxanne snorted from her desk. "Yeah, *Baby Sam.* You know he's the baby of the family and the only boy."

Carrie chuckled at the tidbit of information. "Now *that* explains a lot. Do they still call you that?" Her gaze followed Sam as he exited his office with a clipboard tucked under one arm.

He stopped in front of her desk. "Didn't I hear you tell Roxie you have seven brothers and sisters?"

"I sure do," she admitted.

"Then I guess you can't help being jealous of the way I was raised. You being from of a litter of eight and all."

Her eyebrows arched in shock. "Oh, my God, they still call you that, don't they, Baby Sam?" She slapped her hand on her book. "Of *course* they do. By the way, I'm *glad* I came from a large family. At least I wasn't spoiled rotten."

From her desk in the corner, Roxie snorted with laughter again.

Sam threw a glare in her direction. "Hey, Rox, just sit there with your little crossword and be quiet."

Carrie watched as Roxie waved off Sam's comment in silence. "You're not going to let him get away with that, are you?"

Roxie gave her a brief nod. "I just ignore him. He's been useless around here for the last year anyway."

Sam gave a grunt of dismissal before he turned to walk away. He had no idea his comment had put the challenge back into her cause. "Sam, I think you owe her an apology."

"She called me useless. I don't owe her anything."

"I think you're an inconsiderate, spoiled, bully and you owe her an apology."

Sam scowled and settled back on his heels, arms crossed defiantly.

His stubborn display had her recalling Roxie's first comment to her about Sam. *"He's been cranky since his wife left him."* Maybe she'd get better results from her grumpy co-worker if she showed some empathy for his situation. Suddenly, she remembered her mother's advice on handling an annoying classmate in high school. *You'll always attract more flies with honey than vinegar.* Maybe this plan called for a revision.

She made a slight adjustment and tilted her head to scrutinize the man who stood well over six feet tall. She'd always been attracted to big men, and Sam made quite an attractive package with his blondish hair and crystal blue eyes. Her gaze lowered to encompass long legs covered in work-faded denim that fit snugly across slim hips and lean thighs. *He filled out a pair of jeans nicely, that's for sure.* The jeans ended at a pair of scuffed but clean work boots—at least three sizes larger than anything that had ever graced Dave's size ten.

Her brows lifted curiously. Big boots for a big man. She couldn't help but wonder if the size of a man's foot *really* had anything to do with the size of other parts of his anatomy?

She shook off the thought. The last thing she needed was the complication of a man in her life.

He stood stock still, his arms crossed tightly over his chest. His tone reeked of smugness. "Like what you see?"

As she watched Sam's cheek tighten to form a hint of a half dimple, one corner of Carrie's cheek lifted in a partial smile. Adorable. She found herself wondering again how someone so attracted to tall men with blue eyes had ended up married to a man with Dave's dark looks and short, compact stature. She shrugged off the internal interrogation and gave her shoulder length waves a quick flip with her hand. "Curious, I guess."

He stared down his nose at her. "About what?"

"My daddy always said it takes a big man to admit he's wrong. I'm just wandering if you're big enough." She paused when their gazes clashed. "Are you, Sam?"

⚜

Sam stared into the gorgeous, multi-hued eyes that sparkled with curiosity as well as the slightest hint of devilish amusement. He swallowed hard, wondering if that brazen curiosity of hers would extend to the bedroom as well. Sleeping alone for over a year made a man entertain some crazy thoughts.

His affinity for his Cajun roots had him labeling her *tracas*, with a capital *T*. Regardless of whatever qualities she possessed, he didn't need her kind of *Trouble*.

Sam sensed the occupants in the room holding their collective breath and made a strategically sound decision to surrender with dignity. He'd already given his traitorous co-workers enough to fuel the gossip fires for months.

Sam took a deep breath and released it before turning toward Roxie. "Sorry."

Carrie's brow furrowed as though she strained to hear. "What was that?"

Sam clenched his jaw with a snap. She sure liked to push it. He faced his co-worker, placing his right hand over his chest and bowed from the waist. "From the bottom of my heart, Roxie, I apologize."

Roxie's eyes widened. "You do?"

"Yes, I do." Sam turned toward Carrie. "And I'm sorry I made you late the other day. I was w-wrong and I won't do it again." He chanced a look into her eyes, and nearly lost his breath at the sight of her dimpled smile directed solely at him. That was *lagniappe* – a little something extra.

"Thanks, Sam. I appreciate that."

"And you should start riding with us in the mornings again." It was high time he started coming to work on time. Time to stop using depression as an excuse for being a lousy role model for his crew.

Carrie nodded. "I'll take that into consideration."

The crowd dispersed, and Sam took a few moments to watch Carrie as she stared at an empty spot on her desktop. She looked lost in thought—totally focused on something, or someone, far removed from this office.

He paused to lower the timbre of his voice before he spoke. "Satisfied now?"

"Not for a long time."

"Oh?"

His one-word comeback seemed to snap her from her musings. Her eyes widened, and a slow blush crept up from the base of her neck, infusing her fair skin with the most becoming shade of pink he'd seen on a woman in a long time. He thought of the approaching winter nights he dreaded so much. Long, lonely nights filled with emptiness. He wondered, for the first time, what it would be like to have a woman like this—Holy Hell, he may as well admit it—to have *this* woman warm his bed at night.

Determined to push the thought from his mind, he clamped down on his jaw and, once more, paid for his rashness by biting down on the side of tongue. His breath rushed out in a hiss of pain. Sam winced, slapping his hand over his cheek and jaw. He barely managed to suppress the string of curses his crew called his *OSHA* orange streak, in honor of their bright orange safety equipment.

Served him right for dreaming.

Sam positioned himself so he could watch her, unobserved. Everything about the woman screamed difficult, from her outspoken ways to her eagerness for confrontation. After today's confrontation, he expected she'd be even more blatant with her comments and opinions. He liked things neat, simple, and uncomplicated.

Touche pas, old boy. Don't touch. Even as the command bounced around in his brain, he found himself wanting to do exactly opposite of that—to touch her, to study her, to examine every inch of her.

Sam smiled as Carrie mumbled something incoherent and retreated to the women's restroom, still blushing in a way that beckoned him to get up close and personal.

He sauntered over to the back exit, wondering how he could so obviously lose an argument but still walk away feeling like a winner.

Chapter Three

Early November

Carrie sat at her desk, staring into her compact at the dark circles under her eyes. She'd just applied a touch more concealer when Sam appeared next to her.

"Damn, girl. You look dog-tired."

She snapped the compact closed. "Thanks, Sam. You always know just what to say to make a girl feel special."

"You know what I mean. You've been tense and short-tempered lately. Anything you want to talk about?"

"Nope." Raw with on-the-edge emotional baggage, she grabbed her coffee mug and escaped to the kitchen. If he didn't follow her, maybe she could avoid the display of waterworks about to erupt at any moment. The latest in a long line of two a.m. *anonymous* phone calls she'd received over the last two months had left her exhausted and edgy. She filled her cup with hot, steaming, dark roast as she revisited the terror of the latest call. Too little money, a new job, and the responsibility of three teenagers wasn't enough to deal with. Throw in a series of phone calls from what may or may not be a crazy ex, and she had more trouble than your average newly-divorced, single mom could handle.

Carrie jumped at the sound of Sam's voice and turned to see him staring at her, his mouth tight with concern.

"You'll feel better if you talk about it, you know."

"I did some tossing and turning instead of sleeping last night, that's all."

"Is it your ex? Because you're one of us now, and we're touchy when it comes to people messing with one of our own."

She leaned her hips against the kitchen's base cabinets and hugged her mug of coffee with both hands. It seemed easier to discuss her failed marriage with someone who'd been through it recently. "My divorce came through yesterday." She glanced up at him, then shifted her gaze down to her mug. "I wanted the divorce, and I'm glad it's over, don't get me wrong." She paused to wipe the corner of her eye and took a deep breath. "It doesn't stop me from feeling like a failure. I'm just another statistic."

Sam's mouth tightened in a grim line. "Hmm-boy, I remember well. How'd old Dave take it?"

Carrie shook her head and gave him a half laugh. "He was shocked, of course. He's been sleeping with any woman who'd have him since the day we separated and long before, if truth be told. He couldn't believe I went through with it. I swear, what that man lacks in size, he makes up for in nerve."

Sam chuckled. “He’s not a big man, is he? He can’t be more than five-foot-eight or so.”

Her gaze met his above the rim of her coffee mug. “When have you ever seen him?”

“I saw him the day he came to switch out your car for that diesel truck of his.”

“He always told me he was five nine.”

“Yeah, right. He’s got a serious case of ‘Little Man Syndrome’, or what I like to call the ‘Tee-Boy Blues'.”

Carrie broke into a wide grin. “Yeah, when he’d complain about my weight, I told him I could lose weight, but he’d always be too damn short.”

Sam guffawed loudly. “Double or nothing he wasn’t happy with that.”

“Nope.” That argument had led to Dave spending two nights with another woman to “get his head straight”.

“How are your kids taking the divorce?”

“Grant and Gretchen are okay, but Lauren’s having a rough time of it.” She smiled as she pictured Grant and the twins, Gretchen and Lauren. “At least I’ll walk away with *something* good from that marriage.”

“That and your house, I’m sure.”

Her mouth tightened. “My kids will always have a place there with Dave, but it’s part of his family’s estate. I’m only there until I save up enough money for three months of rent and deposits by January. That’s when my rent house will be vacant.” She raised her mug to her lips, then paused. “Not as easy as I thought it’d be.”

Since their confrontation back in August, Sam and Carrie’s truce had evolved into an unexpected camaraderie. She’d been surprised to discover his wicked sense of humor, had been reduced by it to helpless fits of laughter on several occasions. He was intelligent—Carrie had tagged him “the walking encyclopedia of useless information”—and easy to talk to. She still didn’t know much about his personal life, had been reluctant to ask more than he volunteered. Roxie had mentioned he liked to keep private matters private, but considering their latest direction of dialogue, she couldn’t stop her curiosity from taking control of her tongue.

“You can tell me to mind my own business if you want, Sam, but I’d like to know what brought on your divorce. Did you sleep around on your wife? Did you hit on her or drink too much?”

He settled slim hips against the counter and crossed his arms. “Now, why would you assume I’m to blame?”

She shrugged, not bothering to apologize. “Just drawing from my own well of experience with men, I guess.”

“Well then, no, no, and no. Look, just because Dave was a dog, you shouldn’t assume all men are like him.” He crossed one booted ankle over the other in a relaxed manner. “But I’ll admit I made my share of mistakes.”

Carrie’s gaze never wavered from his as she waited for him to continue.

“Linda, my wife, accused me of being controlling. And I was a little.”

Her breath hissed as she sucked it in. "That can be a death sentence for a marriage."

"I know that now," he agreed. "I've learned from my mistakes, and believe me when I tell you she made several of her own."

"Any chance of reconciliation?"

"Nope." He held up his left hand. "I didn't take off my wedding ring until the divorce finalized. Then I chucked that son of a gun." He leaned his elbow against the counter top. "It came through September eighth—on a Friday."

"I started here three days later, on the eleventh."

"Yep. I came in to work late on Monday, and you were here already."

"No!" Her gaze widened in mock astonishment. "*You* came in late? I don't believe it."

"Okay, smart ass. I was depressed. I'd had a hell of a year, you know."

His pained expression made her swallow the sharp comeback simmering just out of reach. She wasn't the only one with problems. "I understand, and I'm sorry." He nodded in mute agreement, making her hate being the one to make his painful memories resurface. "We could always exchange horror stories."

"Or compare our divorce documents," he pitched in.

"Or settlement options."

He grinned down at her. "Did you make out okay? Will you get compensated for losing your home?"

Carrie's brow creased in concentration. "At first, I wanted to prove to Dave I could do it on my own *without* any help from him. But my lawyer convinced me not to let my independent spirit get in the way of common sense."

"Smart, for a lawyer, I mean."

"I expected nothing less. *She's* the best around."

"Well, that explains it then."

She gave him a nod and a half smile, thinking they'd come a long way. "I just wish I hadn't wasted my best years on a man who never wanted me. I don't think he'd ever been happy with me as his wife."

Sam grunted his disapproval. "It always amazes me how some people have everything they need to be happy and aren't, while others can have nothing and be perfectly satisfied. I've heard some of your horror stories, Carrie. I don't know how you put up with it."

She lifted her gaze to meet his. "Do you think I got what I deserved for staying?"

"Nobody deserves that."

Carrie gathered her thoughts while the kitchen's electric wall clock droned with a low hum. "For years, when Dave would leave us, I'd be stuck alone with the kids. I'd always end up terrified and lonely, and I'd start to think anything was better than being alone. At some point, I realized it wasn't so bad. I guess I had to learn to like myself enough to be alone with me. That's when he'd come crawling home." She raised her mug. "Not sure how I'll like being alone for the rest of my life, though."

Sam shifted, rearranging his long legs. "Just because you're alone now doesn't mean you'll stay that way."

Carrie chuckled in disagreement. "Come on, Sam. I'll be thirty-six years old in two seconds, and I have three teenagers. If my body were a roadway, I'd have to post WATCH FOR POTHOLES signs on my midsection and butt. I'm not exactly what guys are looking for."

Sam straightened to his full height. "You're kidding, right? You're a kind, decent lady—"

"And one day someone will come along who'll really appreciate my *qualities,*" she interrupted. "That's a classic 'throw-the-dog-a-bone' line if I ever heard one."

Sam raised his hand and spoke firmly. "I wasn't finished—and you're a good looking woman, as well."

Carrie rolled her eyes and turned to stare at the dismally depressing morning outside the kitchen's single window. Gloomy, rainy, and cool, it felt like an anchor, weighing down her spirit. "You're only saying that to be nice."

J.C. stepped into the kitchen with his usual flair for making an entrance and headed for the coffee pot. "Dat's the biggest bunch of bullshit I ever heard. Sam Langley never says *anything* just to be nice."

"You tell her, JC." Sam encouraged.

"He might say somethin' to piss you off, or prove what a monumental jack ass he is, but he won't ever say it just to be *nice*."

"Yeah! Wait. What?" A veil of confusion slowly settled over Sam's previous look of confidence.

J.C. continued. "I mean, we all know what a grouchy ole son of a gun he can be."

Sam's brow furrowed with deep frown lines. "All right, that's enough."

"He didn't get the name Oscar de Grouch for no good reason."

"Julian." Sam's warning sounded more like a growl.

"He sure can be a crusty son of a bit—"

"*Julian Alcide Carter!*"

A moment of stunned silence permeated the kitchen, until Carrie finally spoke.

"Julian Alcide?" Carrie suddenly understood J.C.'s preference for initials.

J.C.'s eyes snapped with mischief as he glared up at the big man. "You stump jumpin' old son of a bitch. I could kick your ass for dat, yeah!"

Sam gave his vertically challenged buddy a friendly shove. "You'd have to be able to reach it first, short shit."

Carrie chuckled at the good-natured teasing between the two men. She stepped between them and gave J.C. a gentle nudge. "Go to your corner, Killer." She turned to Sam and stuck a finger in his face. "And *you!* Go pick on somebody your own size." She walked out of the room mumbling, "Julian Alcide—I never would have guessed that."

From the doorway, Sam watched Carrie return to her desk. Gradually, he realized J.C. had spoken to him and pivoted to face his friend. "Sorry, did you say something?"

J.C. grinned. "I said *she's* closer to your size. Maybe you oughta go pick on her."

"*Bouche ta gueule,* J.C."

"Don't tell me to shut up. I know what I'm talking about here, dammit. You two would be good together."

"It ain't happening."

"Why not? You're divorced, and now she is too. You know you want her, man."

"*Arret ca*, Julian. Just stop it."

The shorter man poked Sam's chest with his stubby finger. "Look, Jackass. You need to quit calling me dat." He turned and walked toward the door.

"It's a good name—"

J.C. turned and pointed to him. "Den *you* take it."

"Come on, J.C.," Sam pleaded, as the other man left the room without looking back. "It's a good name."

Sam crossed his arms and looked out the window, surprised at how empty the room felt without Carrie's presence. He pictured her the way he'd seen her at various times. With her head back and laughing at his impersonation of an old co-worker, or in profile as she bent over her desk to study a set of plans. The smell of her perfume lingered in the air. He breathed deeply, remembering the effect it had on him the day before as he'd leaned over her shoulder to explain a field book drawing.

Sam hit the building's back exit with an inward groan, as chilled air from the recent cold front surrounded him. He walked around the survey truck and collapsed against the rear bumper. His breath rushed out in a low grunt, as the cold metal penetrated through his jeans to shrink his boys into oblivion.

He leaned forward to rest his hands on his knees and shook his head in an effort to deal with the sudden awareness of his feelings. He stood and leaned far enough to get a glimpse through the window by her desk. There she was, a perfectly framed scene from a movie projecting out into the dreariness of the overcast morning. He sucked in his breath, as Carrie laughed at something else J.C. told her, then groaned out loud at the ache brought on by a woman he used to think was a huge pain in the ass.

Sam stood suddenly and jerked open the work van's rear doors, determined to find something to keep his mind occupied. He thumbed through the stack of survey books, collected the trash, and rearranged the equipment.

He replayed their conversation in his mind, revisiting her fear of ending up alone.

"Not if I can help it."

Why would she want you?

"I'm better than what she had."

Hell, that doesn't take much.

He rearranged the stack of survey books filled with his own neat, hand-written field notes and precisely drawn details. Once more, he tossed them back into the box he kept them in and slammed the truck door harder than he'd meant to.

Sam tried not to stare up at the window, but the sight of her profile lured him. He was a big fat robin and she was a live cricket. She threw her head back and laughed at something JC said. He smiled, imagining the sparkle in those two different colored eyes of hers, the ones she claimed were "really just a birth defect." Birth defect or not, they sure added to the package. Those luminous eyes that sparkled green one moment, blue the next, accompanied by hair that shimmered with golden-red highlights in the afternoon sun. All of those luscious curves that accompanied the full-bodied woman, damned-well-proportioned on her five-foot-seven inch frame, just right for a man of his height. The sudden tightening in his groin area made him grimace with need again.

You want that.

"Not too surprising for a guy who's as horny as a three-balled tomcat."

You want her.

"It'd be too freaking complicated," he continued, trying to convince his inner voice. Sam gazed up at her profile and watched her lean back in her chair and stretch in an alluring arch.

He forced himself to turn away from her, wanting to avoid the tried and true method of *ass on an ice-cold bumper* to diffuse his single man's affliction. Try as he might, he couldn't get the image of her out of his mind. A minute later, he returned to the dreaded bumper and plopped down on the frigid metal. He searched the area, praying nobody had seen his solo performance, stellar enough to earn him a one-way trip to the psyche ward.

He wiped his face and groaned. "Women are just good to make you crazy." Crazy or not, he couldn't talk himself out of wanting to explore every inch of her body at his leisure. He stood, approached the window, watching a moment longer before spinning away, determined to put her out of his mind. He didn't have anything to offer someone like her. More importantly, if he went out on that limb and she rejected him . . .

Holy crap, how much was one man supposed to take?

Chapter Four

November, four days before Thanksgiving

Carrie pulled the pillow over her head, trying to block out the noise. Toto's frantic alto yipping joined with the deep bass barks and low growls from Lucas in a dreadful harmony to further deprive her of sleep. Two a.m. on the final Monday before Thanksgiving, and she had barely gotten any rest. Determined to get at least a couple of hours, she left her bed in an attempt to shush her dogs.

She unbolted the door and stepped out onto the back porch, crossing her arms against the damp chill in the air. The waxing gibbous Moon would normally have given her a full view of the backyard and fenced pasture. Dense cloud coverage blocked visibility by half. "Lucas! Toto! Come!" She whistled, and Toto ran immediately to heel at her side. Lucas ran halfway, then stopped for a fresh round of ominous growling.

Carrie took a few steps into the backyard and squinted to a spot just beyond the huge dog in the center of the pasture. She stood, waiting for her eyes to adjust to the dark until a form—a bit darker than the surrounding blackness—began to take shape. She stared hard at it, watched and waited, for what, she didn't know. She suspected it was a stray dog or a coyote roaming unaccustomedly close. Lucas continued with his low snarls, growls, and the occasional bark. She called to him again, and he finally came to her. She returned to the porch accompanied by both dogs. Something, some pinprick of fear, had her turning back just in time to see the dark form moving off toward the stand of trees near the road. Her dogs watched too, their low growls never abating.

The hair on the back of her neck stood up as a frisson of terror crept over her. "Stay." Thankfully, the dogs obeyed, both setting up guard duty at the back door. "Good boys." She locked herself in the house, tried to close her eyes and put the incident out of her mind. Not so easy when one thought repeated in her mind like a radar loop of a weather report.

From her observation, if that was a dog in the back pasture, the son of a gun walked off on its hind legs—and it was as tall as a grown man.

Sam locked his truck and zipped up the all-weather work jacket while waiting patiently at the carpool's pick-up spot. His heart pumped furiously at the approach of Carrie's gray sedan. Sam wiped his hands on his jeans, hands as clammy as a twelve-year-old boy playing touchy-feely with the preacher's daughter. "Get a grip, you big dumbass."

His heart dropped to his toes when he saw Cory, the youngest member of his survey crew, sleeping comfortably in the front bucket seat next to the driver. Sam's only option was to crawl into the Escort's cramped back seat.

"Pull up that seat, Cory," Sam groaned, trying to stretch his long legs to a less cramped position. "My knees are touching my chin back here. You know," he added, thinking he had nothing to lose. "If you *really* wanted to score points with your boss, you'd switch seats with me."

Cory gave a sleepy groan and moved to open the car door, until Carrie placed a restraining hand on his forearm.

"Don't you *dare.*" She shot a glare in Sam's direction. "It won't kill you to sit back there for a change."

"But my legs are a lot longer than hi—"

"You need your diaper changed too, you big baby?" Her car threw gravel as she peeled out of the parking lot to get back onto the highway.

"You offering?" Expecting a comeback, he glanced in her direction. One look told him she wasn't in a mood for jokes. Instead of a grin and dimples, he encountered a worried brow and a frown. She steered with her right hand in a white knuckled grip while the left supported her forehead. Only a fool would ignore those crystal-clear signs of a woman on the verge of a major "open-your-mouth-and-I'll-tear-you-a-new-one" melt down. He settled into the back seat without another word.

Ten minutes later, Sam staked out his crew's darkened office. "Where the hell are Craig and Dan today?"

"They both called in sick," Dale added from across the room. "They got the flu, out the rest of the week."

Sam slapped his cap against his thigh. "That's just great. How am I supposed to work with half a crew when you need that survey finished by the end of this week?"

"It's kinda slow. We can spare somebody from the office," Dale suggested.

J.C. jumped out of his seat. "I'll go!" He sent a hopeful look at Carrie. "Why don't you come too? We need two people to work da chain."

Carrie sent J.C. a look that would have scared the crap out of a lesser man. "I swear to God, if that's man-code for something disgusting, I may have to kill you."

J.C. shook his head and clucked his tongue in disapproval. "Listen to you, wit your mind in da gutter. It takes two people to work the hundred foot chain for stationing the roadway."

Sam joined in with J.C.'s laughter. "We'll show you how. Come on, you'll have a chance to go outside and get some fresh air and sunshine. It's gonna be a nice day." He turned to their supervisor. "How about it Dale, can we borrow these two today?"

Dale lifted his gaze from one of several letter-size sets of plans cluttering his desk. "Get her a vest and a hard hat."

"Yes, sir. We'll pick 'em up on the way out."

Carrie looked uncertain. "I don't know what to do out there."

Roxie gave her a reassuring pat on the shoulder. "It's easy. I started out with the crew, you know. Once I got to be seven months pregnant with my last daughter, Sam wouldn't take me out anymore. He said none of them could stomach delivering my baby in the back of that old van we used to drive."

Sam walked out of his office with a clipboard in one hand and his pencil and calculator in the other. "Damn straight. I didn't know nothin' bout birthin' no babies, Miss Scarlett, and I sure as hell didn't want to learn on Roxie."

Carrie smiled. "You're not very convincing as Butterfly McQueen."

Sam's eyes sparkled with laughter. "Now wouldn't it be sad if I had been?"

Dale stopped at Carrie's desk. "How about it? You wanta go see how it's done?"

She shrugged. "It can't hurt."

Dale gave a grunt of approval and waved a hand at Sam. "She's all yours."

Sam walked away, wearing an ear-to-ear grin on his face. *If only it were that easy.*

Wednesday morning, the work day started with a light fog and damp chill in the air. Every morning, Sam rode with James, Cory, and Carrie to a section of roadway just north of Kenton to survey the area that would eventually be widened for a turn lane. The fresh air seemed to improve Carrie's mood. She'd laughed as J.C. had bounced out of the truck that first day, insisting he'd acted like her family's dogs when anyone released them from their kennels. On this, her third day with the crew, Carrie's enthusiasm matched J.C.'s. By the time the four of them piled into a burger joint for lunch, the sun's appearance had transformed the unpleasant morning into a beautiful day.

Sam's suggestion to get their meals to go and eat in the city park was met with a round of agreement.

Carrie balled up the bag from her lunch and sunk it into the trashcan about eight feet away from their picnic table. "How long are we going to be here?"

Sam glanced down at his watch. "Another fifteen minutes, then it's back to work."

She stretched and jutted her chin toward the park. "I think I'll make a round on that walking track." She left the group with a *Terminator* worthy "I'll be back."

Sam jumped slightly when J.C. appeared at his right elbow.

"Maybe you ought to join her, Sam."

Sam tore his gaze from her retreating form. "I think she wants to be left alone."

"I don't think she does, man. I think she needs to talk to someone about what's going on in her life. And I think it ought to be you."

Sam turned his gaze on J.C. "What do you think is going on?"

"I don't know. But something's bugging the hell out of her. I think you'd earn some points by acting concerned."

"It wouldn't be an act. I am concerned."

J.C. grunted. "You're probably more than concerned, but you're too dense to tell her."

Sam bit back the *kiss my ass* comment he had ready once he realized his buddy was sincere.

"Don't try to deny it, Sam. And I still think you ought to go for it."

"That so?"

"Yep, and don't act like you hadn't thought about dat already, no. 'Cause I've seen you watching her. You look like a man who's starvin' to death in a face off wit' a big bowl of seafood gumbo."

She looked good every day, but working with the crew seemed to agree with her. She seemed happier being outside and away from her troubles. He could think of a couple of more places she'd look damn good. In his arms. In his bed. *In his life?*

He gave a slow nod as he watched her progress down the track. Thoughts of her had steadily infiltrated his mind, betraying him, breaking down his resistance until he could barely think of anything else, whether she was near or not. He knew he was in serious trouble as the thoughts gradually turned from plain old man-in-need, to wanting nothing more than to care for her, protect her, be in her presence.

In three months he'd transformed from 'Oscar the Grouch' to his former 'Office Clown' glory. If his crew was grateful to have him back, he was downright ecstatic to be back. It felt good to want to get out of bed in the morning. It felt extraordinary to be able to see her at the office five days a week. His world had turned ass-backwards, as he'd grown to hate Fridays and long for Monday mornings.

There wasn't a doubt that Carrie was responsible for the new/old him. It was time to pull the pork off the pit, because he was done. He couldn't deny his feelings for her any longer. He was head over heels crazy about the lady.

Without another word, he took the shortcut path. He paced his long strides and intersected with Carrie at the first turn.

"Mind if I join you?"

She graced him with a smile, her cheeks pink from the exertion of her brisk pace. "Not at all."

They slowed to an easy gait, making small talk, until they made it halfway around the track. Carrie stopped to investigate a decked gazebo with rails and built-in seating around the perimeter.

"What a great place to bring kids." She climbed up the wooden steps to walk through the gated doorway, turning in a slow circle to view the park from a different perspective. "This is perfect for small children and frazzled moms. It's like a giant outdoor playpen."

Sam followed her up the steps and chose a seat across from where she'd parked herself. "Yeah, it's my favorite design yet." He couldn't hold back the pride in his voice.

Carrie jerked her gaze around to peer up at him. "You designed this?"

"Designed and built it on commission. I live a few blocks to the east of this place."

"I didn't know you lived in Kenton."

"I call it God's country."

Her low chuckle sounded over the rustling of leaves. "And I sure didn't know you were a carpenter."

"I like working with wood—lumber too," he added, cracking a grin.

Carrie's eyes sparkled with silent laughter. "Don't ever stop trying to be funny, Sam. One day you'll get it right."

"I'm forty years old." He continued in an exaggerated twang. "If it ain't happened yet, chances are it ain't gonna."

"You big Redneck."

"Watch who you call a Redneck, Coon-Ass."

Carrie twisted her features in distaste. "Call me Cajun all day long, but never Coon-ass. Do you know the origin of that word?"

He nodded. "It's from the word *conasse*, a derogatory word the French used to describe people of a lower culture."

Carrie's mouth opened in surprise. "I'm doubly impressed, Mr. Langley. With this," she said, indicating the gazebo, "and the fact that you're the first person since my dad to have answered correctly."

"Do I get an A?"

She tapped her chin with her forefinger. "Let's see. I may have to grade on a curve."

"How about a date?"

"Maybe a B plus—" She stopped suddenly. "What did you say?"

"I asked you for a date. You know, my reward for answering correctly." He stood and walked over to take a seat beside her. "How about it, Carrie? Is it worth dinner and a movie?"

Carrie gazed at the sincerity in his face. "Oh—I—Ah," she stammered, trying to shake off her surprise as her brain shifted into overdrive. All the reasons she shouldn't flooded her mind, doing battle with her desire to say yes. Everything she'd seen of this man in the last few months told her Sam would be a good risk. Every thump of her heart reverberated in her chest, mimicking the four-pitch drums she used to play in high school.

Sam raised his hand, his features tight. "Forget I said anything. I had no business thinking you'd be interested."

She reached out to lower his hand, her voice strong and steady as she spoke. "Sam, look at me." She waited until he lifted his gaze to meet hers. "It's not that I'm not interested, but, there are things going on in my life right now that—"

"No is good enough, Carrie. You don't have to make excuses."

"I'm not making excuses, but your timing sucks."

Sam propped his elbows on his knees and clasped his hands together. "That's a given."

She leaned forward until she could see his face. "My daughter, Lauren, is depressed about the divorce, and I'm worried about her. She's been visiting the school counselor regularly, but between that and those damn phone calls—"

"What phone calls?"

"I'm sure it's nothing . . ."

"Is your ex threatening you?"

"I don't think it's Dave. I'm not sure who it is. He never says anything. In fact, I don't even know if it's a he. I just know that . . ." Carrie's voice trailed off as she remembered her latest early morning non-conversation with the mysterious caller.

"It scares you?"

"It does. And then, after the call…" She paused, not wanting to discuss this morning's incident.

"What?" Sam asked, stiff-backed and attentive.

"Maybe it was coincidence, but our two dogs went crazy around two o'clock this morning, barking and snarling. I went out to check, thinking they had a raccoon or something cornered." She ran her hands over her arms, trying to shake off the chill at the memory. "I felt like someone was out there, watching me."

Sam opened his mouth to speak then closed it again. He pulled off his cap and ran a hand through his hair. "Well hell, I don't know about you, but that sounds potentially dangerous. Maybe you need to get the hell out of there. I know that road you live on. We surveyed that son of a gun several years back. It's out there in the vicinity of nowhere and B.F. Egypt."

"I'm surrounded by family—"

"*Whose* family?"

"I can count on any of my in-laws to help me if I need—"

"Then why weren't they with you?"

"Because I didn't call any—"

"Why the hell not?"

"And tell them what?" She tried to keep her voice calm. "Help! My dogs are barking?" Her eyes narrowed in confusion. "What's wrong with you, Sam?"

He shoved off impatiently from his seat next to her. "I wish you'd be more careful. You shouldn't have gone outside. Surely, you heard about that poor blind woman from Lafayette that some animal raped and beat for three days. The scumbag left her to die, as if she was nothing. As far as you know it could be the same guy!"

"I had the dogs with me—"

"Yeah, yeah, Toto and Lucas. What are they? Chihuahuas, Poodles, or some other useless little dog?"

She blinked twice and once more before she found her voice. "Toto's a standard white, poodle-terrier mix, but Lucas is a four-year-old Chesapeake with a head the size of a basketball." She shifted her stance and cocked her head toward him. "Anything else?"

"Yeah."

"What?"

Sam took a deep breath and let it ease out slowly, before placing one hand on the back of his neck. "I hear myself being a dumbass, and I apologize, but dammit, I'm in—I'm—I'm worried about you."

Carrie stared up at the man who'd slowly turned into someone she looked forward to seeing every day. She'd grown used to Sam the grouch, the clown, the tease, and finally, the friend. She wasn't accustomed to hearing this level of passion in his voice, or seeing the raw emotion revealed in his face. *He cares about me.*

"Look, if anything like that happens again, I won't go outside."

He rubbed roughly at his face with one hand and nodded. "Fair enough, but you should have called someone."

"You know if I called any of my in-laws, they'd probably send Dave to check it out." Carrie laughed as he grunted his disapproval. "Come on, jerk. Let's go meet the guys."

Once they were back on the walking track, Carrie caught Sam glancing over at her. "What?"

"Can I ask you something? You can tell me to eat shit if you want to."

She smiled. "That's always a possibility. Go ahead."

"You said you and Dave were separated several times. Why'd you take him back all those times? What did *he* have that made you want to keep trying?"

Carrie's steps slowed as she considered her answer. "I was stuck. No education, no job, no way to support my kids. That's when I decided I needed a plan. So, I went back to school." She kicked a small pinecone off the track. "You know, Sam, I dropped out of my first semester of college when I married Dave. At eighteen, I went from my parents' household to Dave's. Being out there alone and responsible for myself and my kids is a huge step for me. At times, it's overwhelming." She scuffed the toe of her shoe uneasily on the asphalt.

"What if you weren't alone?"

Carrie plucked at a stray thread on the hem of her shirtsleeve. "What do you mean?"

"I mean, what if there was someone around to help, offer support?"

She waited several seconds before speaking again. "What kind of support?"

Sam fidgeted before he continued. "Emotional support, or more, if you wanted it, from someone like me. I mean from me."

Sam shifted, unable to meet her gaze. The wind picked up, sending the dry leaves of the park's water oaks and silver leaf maples dancing around their feet. It whistled through the pine grove surrounding the park grounds as the taller, older trees swayed and creaked in the strong wind.

"Listen, Sam. I'm newly-divorced, and I've got three kids to think about. If you're just looking for someone to take to bed—"

His hand flew up to stop her mid-sentence. "That's *not* what this is about. I'm not interested in a fling. I think you're a brave, beautiful lady, and I'm impressed as hell at what you've accomplished." He shoved his hands deep into his pockets and tapped the heel of his work boot on the asphalt track. "I'll be honest with you," he said, his voice steady. "I never thought I'd have the heart to try this again. But there's something about you that makes me want to risk it."

She stared at him, wide-eyed. "You have no idea what you'd be getting yourself into."

"I know *you*," he admitted. "I know your favorite food in the world is boiled crawfish, your favorite dessert is homemade banana pudding. You despise daylight savings time. Your favorite color is burgundy, and you look good in it, but you look even better in forest green. I know you used to cry when you heard the song *Hold On* by Wilson Phillips, because you felt like they wrote it for you. Every Christmas you make it a point to watch *A Christmas Story, It's a Wonderful Life*, and the fifties version of *A Christmas Carol* with Alistair Sim." He pulled his hands from his pockets and grabbed the back of his neck, elbows forward, as he released his breath in a long, slow hiss. "I'm screwing this up, I know I am."

Carrie stepped forward to place a hand on his arm. "No, you're not, and I'm flattered, and maybe once I'm in my new place I can think about it. My life is too complicated right now. Too many unanswered questions to take a step like that. I need to learn to be alone with me for a while."

She lifted her hands and dropped them to her sides again. "All I can do is to ask you to be patient." She stared up him, her pulse quickening, as the drums re-established the rhythm in her ears. She had to dig deep for the courage to continue, but she couldn't stop now. "And if—if you find someone else before then, I'd understand if you didn't want to wait around until I'm ready," she finished in a whisper.

She watched, nervous as a crawfish next to a pot of boiling water, as Sam pulled himself up to his full height. She sucked in her breath and held it. *He's going to say he can't waste his time waiting on me.* She heard him take a deep breath, as though to calm himself. He couldn't possibly be as nervous as she was. *Could he?*

Finally, he spoke. "You know, Carrie . . ." He drew out the four syllables in a slow, seductive manner. "I haven't always been a patient man—"

She nearly fainted as Sam stretched out his arm to place a light touch on the tip of her nose.

"—but something tells me you'd be worth the wait."

The breath whooshed out of her lungs in a rush. Vibrating with nervous tension, she put her hand up to stop him when he tried to say more.

"Don't," she said, shaking her head slowly. "There's *nothing* you could possibly say to top that." Carrie backed carefully away from the man, wishing for once she could afford to let go of her inhibitions. His one-sided grin caused that single "almost" dimple to reappear, making her want to cover it with a slow, lingering kiss. She turned away from the man who stood staring down at her as though she were the best thing since chicken and biscuits.

At the end of the workday, Carrie glanced up as Sam paused before her desk. She sent him a self-conscious smile and retrieved her car keys from the bottomless pit of her purse. The long Thanksgiving weekend would normally be a pleasant respite—no driving, sleeping in, visits with family members. Somehow, the thought of not seeing Sam until next Tuesday put a definite kink in its appeal.

Sam twirled his keys around his finger as he leaned against her desk. "You got big plans for the long weekend?"

"Just a get-together with my family." She lifted her gaze to meet his. "You know, my mom and what's left of her *litter* of eight kids."

"What's left?"

"I lost a brother to bone cancer a few years back, but two of his kids will be there. How about you?"

"Oh. Sorry to hear that." He gave her a non-committal shrug. "My kids and I are supposed to spend it at my sister's place this year. My folks will both be there too." He leaned over on her desk, tapping his key on the surface. "Hope you don't have any run-ins with your ex over the weekend."

"I shouldn't." She snapped her purse shut.

"You need to turn him in to the Sheriff's department for making those phone calls, you know."

His acidic tone made her drop her purse on her desk as she faced him once more. "I said I have doubts it's him making the calls."

"Come on, Carrie. Of course it is."

"It must be nice to be so sure about things. Exactly when did you find the proof?"

"I don't need any proof. I know it's him, and *you—"* He pointed at her for emphasis. "Need to do something about it."

"That's what I need, huh?" She made her tone sweet as honey, luring him like a fly to tacky tape. "Maybe I need a big, strong man to take care of me over the holidays too."

He puffed up noticeably and pulled out his wallet. He handed her his business card. "My home number's on there if you decide to follow through on that."

Carrie smiled and glanced around the office to make sure everyone else had left the building. She tore the card in half, and stepped forward to tuck the pieces into his shirt pocket. "I don't think I'll need this after all." She patted his pocket, the smile still in place. "It took me eighteen years to get rid of one controlling man. There'll be blizzards in hell before I let another man dictate how to run my life." She grabbed her purse and walked toward the door with one backward glance, determined not to waste another minute thinking about old blue eyes.

Chapter Five

Monday, 2:00 a.m.

The smile broke over his face as she answered the phone, her voice grumpy with sleepiness.

"Come on. Don't you ever get tired of this?"

No chance, lady.

"Who's there?"

I'm here.

"Okay, asshole. You've had your little fun for the night."

He frowned as he heard the distinct *click* when she disconnected. Three sentences from her sleepy lips wouldn't do it for him tonight. He hit redial, feeling tremendously rewarded a moment later when she answered, her voice a mixture of disbelief and anger. Her answer made him smile.

"You've got to be kidding me," she croaked.

Afraid not, sweetness.

"I tell you what. Just for tonight, let's pretend you're not a selfish jerk and let me get some sleep."

Or not.

"I'm hanging up now."

I'll call back. And he did—repeatedly. A dozen times—just to hear the sound of her voice grow increasingly more fearful, though she tried not to show it. He'd done his research. Her mother was in a Lafayette hospital with a severe case of bronchitis. No way would she take the phone off the hook, good daughter that she was. He was more than happy to use it against her.

Her final salutation nearly did him in. She answered, unafraid and pissed off enough to taunt him.

"Why don't you say something, you chicken-shit son of a bitch? What, did you get tired of drowning kittens and killing baby birds?"

He smiled. *Small stuff. Microscopic.*

"You don't scare me, you know."

That's not what the tremor in your voice is telling me.

"I'm taking the phone off the hook, now."

"Carrie." Her name rolled off his lips in a tantalizing whisper. Her sharply released gasp told him she'd heard. He smiled, imagining the look of shock on her face, and laughed after she slammed the phone down, breaking the connection. He hit redial, ready to raise the stakes and tell her he was coming for her. Not tonight, but she wouldn't know that, of course. Just a ploy to raise the terror factor. When he called back, he got a busy signal.

"No, no, no. Not now!" His voice—a prolonged, deep growl—resonated throughout the deserted back alley of the local bar.

He hit redial. Busy signal. Again...again...and again.

A low snarl accompanied the loud *crack* as his cell phone hit the twelve-inch-thick cinder block wall.

After five days with no sign of Sam, Carrie was surprisingly glad to see him waiting at his carpool pick-up spot. Instead of sitting in his normal spot in the front of the work truck, he opened the back door, forcing her to slide to the middle when he climbed in next to her. She tried to concentrate on her latest library book, a thriller by a cop turned crime writer. Unfortunately, having Sam near enough to brush his arm against hers, to smell his cologne, sense his need to be near her—it all turned her concentration to mush as she read and re-read the same page. By the time they pulled up to the office, she'd neared her breaking point.

Dan vacated the seat to her left, Carrie slid across the bench seat toward the door. Before she could slip out, a gentle tug at her wrist stopped her.

"Please, stay."

She kept her silence until each of their co-workers entered the building through the back door. As the door slammed closed, she turned on him.

"You were right, and I'm sorry." His apology was out before she could open her mouth. "I'm worried about you, but that doesn't give me the right to tell you how to handle your problems. It's your life and you're a smart, self-reliant woman, fully capable of making your own decisions."

"It's not Dave."

"If you believe that, then I trust your judgment."

"No. Really. It isn't Dave. I got the Sheriff's department to trace the call yesterday morning."

His face paled visibly. "What happened?"

She rubbed at her tired eyes. "He wouldn't stop. He kept calling and calling. I didn't want to take the phone off the hook because of mom being in the hospital. But, finally, I had to."

"So they know who it is now?"

She shook her head. "It traced to one of those prepaid cell phones. Whoever he was, bought the phone in Jennings and paid cash five minutes before he called me. Dave was asleep at his mom's last night."

"You're positive about that?"

She nodded. "I called Ruby's myself to make sure."

"So, if it's not Dave, then who the hell is it?"

"I don't know. And that's what really scares me. As long as there was a possibility it could be Dave, I could dismiss it. Now . . ." Her voice trailed off as she played with the buckle of her leather purse.

"Now you're as worried as I am."

She cocked her head slightly. "Maybe not that much."

"Well, hell. Maybe, it's time *somebody* worried about you, Carrie." He reached out to touch her hand.

She stared at the seat where his hand covered hers. "Somebody," she whispered.

He leaned closer. "What was that?"

"Nothing." She pulled her hand back as she stepped out of the truck.

Sam hurried around to meet her at the door. "You never said. Am I forgiven?"

"You are, but don't let it happen again, please."

He shook his head. "It won't. I got a lot of thinking done over the past five days. I'm determined to change, Carrie. Whether it's for you or just for myself, I'm trying to be a better man."

She scraped her lower lip with her teeth and nodded, afraid to say anything more.

⚜

At seven-thirty the next morning, Carrie walked into the office and intercepted Sam's look of worry.

"I know," she muttered. "I'm late, and I look like crap."

"No you don't" he countered. "Craig said you called to let him know you wouldn't make the carpool. Anything you want to talk about?"

She opened her compact and groaned at her reflection. "I threw on a little war paint during the drive over here, but Max Factor is a poor substitution for sleep." She snapped the compact closed and dropped it in her purse before facing him. His smile had her stomach flipping in nervous anticipation. Jesus, what was it about the man that made her feel like a gawky, inexperienced teenager? She forced her thoughts away from the co-worker who seemed to grow on her more every day.

"Another phone call?"

"Several."

"Maybe it's only a prank. You know, some kid who dialed a number at random and remembered it to keep jerking your chain."

"Whoever he is, he knows my name, because he whispered it to me." She stopped Sam from asking the obvious question. "I couldn't tell who it was." She shivered. "At least the dogs didn't go nuts afterwards so I don't think he came snooping around. I think I'd have had a stroke."

Carrie approached the snack machine for a breakfast bar, then the kitchen, where the aroma of freshly brewed coffee called to her.

Sam followed, leaning his long torso against the doorjamb. "Anything else you can remember about the calls?"

Carrie prepared her coffee and propped herself against the cabinet. "They're always disturbing, but the fact that he wouldn't stop made it creepier. You know, this would be so much easier if it was Dave, but he's obviously moved on."

"Can I say one more time what a fool your ex was?"

She bit back a smile, marveling at how a single comment from him could totally lift her spirits. "I appreciate that, Sam. When I think back on the person I used to be before I met him, and remember how I was when I was with him, I can't figure out when the old me disappeared. I don't believe my children have ever met her."

"Maybe it's time to introduce them."

She sipped her coffee, lowered the cup. "I will, as soon as I find her again." They both turned toward the door as J.C. walked into the kitchen, fairly growling.

"What's going on in here?"

"Sam's letting me vent."

J.C. raised one eyebrow. "Is your ex still dropping by unannounced?"

She gave him a half-hearted shrug and nodded. "Not as often. He just wants me out of the house. Staying at his mom's must be putting a serious cramp in his single life."

J.C.'s eyes glittered with excitement. "You want me to whip his ass for you?"

Carrie laughed at her friend. "Don't offer if you're not willing to follow through."

Sam crossed one booted foot over another. "Yeah, don't let your mouth write checks your ass ain't willing to cash."

J.C. chuckled as he refilled his coffee cup. "Isn't he about my height?"

Carrie grinned at her friend. "Yeah, but I think you could take him. You're probably one of those Crazy Cajuns who jumps into bayous to wrestle alligators with a knife."

J.C. gave her a disgruntled look. "I do not. You'd have to be an idiot to do something that stupid." He pointed a finger at his chest and put on a thicker than normal Cajun accent. "Mais sha, I went to college too, yeah."

Carrie laughed and came back with her own homegrown accent. "Mais, I'm sorry if you got da wrong *imprassion*. I wouldn't do dat, no, me bein' from dat petit, tiny town of Gardiner. You know, we can parlais de Cajun French purty damn good over dere, too, yeah."

J.C's. chest rumbled with laughter. "And can I jus' say dat you do it justice, my fran."

Carrie gave him an exaggerated curtsey. "*Merci beaucoup*, Monsieur Carter."

"You're welcome." He left the room with his mug full of wake-him-up.

Sam shifted and cleared his throat. "So, once you move to Gardiner how much farther will it be to drive to work?"

"About ten miles and twice a day."

"Times five is a hundred miles per week, four hundred miles a month, and about five thousand miles a year. I know. That's what I save by carpooling."

"That's in addition to the two thousand miles I drive every month. My paycheck's already stretched too thin."

"The divorce settlement should help you out, though."

Carrie's laugh reverberated through the room. "*If* Dave's payments come like they're supposed to, my car note and school loan will be taken care of. Rent, food, fuel, and utilities will eat up the rest of my income. You have to understand that during the wintertime, plant work can get kind of lean, so it may affect his payments. I'm scratching to make ends meet now, and I'll be scratching even more if I can ever move out."

"Well, if he skips a note, throw his ass in jail."

"Yeah, that'd go over big with my kids."

"I'd do it."

Carrie frowned and pushed away from the counter. "That's because they're not your kids. Besides, none of this is your concern, is it?"

She rolled to a stop in front of her mailbox, groaning at the sight of Dave's truck parked in the drive.

By the time she'd parked the car, hauled her things inside, and exchanged her shoes for a pair of warm, fuzzy slippers she kept at the door, she was shivering. Rather than raise the thermostat, she shuffled into her bedroom for a sweater to throw over her shirt—and still no visual on Dave.

She listened at the twins' door and heard the steady beat of a pop tune from inside the room. She knocked once, then poked her head inside.

Gretchen sat propped up against her headboard, reading a library book, while Lauren lay on her stomach atop her bedspread, doing math homework.

"Hey, Mom." As usual, their voices synchronized for a single comment.

Carrie smiled and walked into the room, searching for any hints of disturbance from her daughters. "Everything all right?"

Gretchen looked up, her demeanor indicating nothing but total relaxation. "Everything's fine."

Carrie gave her a quick nod and turned to Lauren, whose body language betrayed her frame of mind. Pencil clenched tightly in her right hand, forehead resting on the open palm of her left, she bit down on her lower lip.

"Lauren?" Carrie's daughter turned her huge brown eyes, so like her father's, and lifted one shoulder in a half-hearted shrug.

"Are you upset about something?" Carrie stepped over to sit on her daughter's bed.

Without saying a word, Lauren closed her eyes and dropped her forehead on Carrie's shoulder. A sound from the doorway alerted Carrie to Dave's presence.

"Of course she's upset. You broke up the family."

Carrie wrapped her daughter in a hug, but ignored his calculated words. "It'll be fine, Lauren. How'd your appointment with the school counselor go this morning?"

Lauren sniffed and wiped her eyes. "It was okay. She said lots of kids feel like this when their parents get divorced. But Gretchen and Grant don't."

"No two people handle situations the same way, but you'll be fine. I'm here if you want to talk."

Lauren made a half-hearted attempt to smile.

Carrie rose from the bed and turned toward the doorway where Dave stood, arms crossed stubbornly over his chest. She stepped around him and pulled her daughters' bedroom door shut on her way to the kitchen.

"You heard any more about that rental in Gardiner?"

She stopped and threw back an annoyed look. "It's *still* not available until January fifteenth."

He sent her a scathing look. "Well, I thought you'd have had your family trying to pull some strings to get you in there sooner. I know they all hate me."

She walked into the kitchen to start supper. "They don't hate you, Dave." Within two minutes, she had a package of thawed ground round frying, a pot of water heating for pasta, and two jars of spaghetti sauce sitting on the counter, ready to add to the meat.

Dave looked over her shoulder. "What are you cooking?"

She quirked one brow at her ex. "Are you really that dense, or just making an attempt at polite conversation?"

He laughed—*that* laugh—the one that made the nerves and muscles at the base of her skull spasm with irritation. She clenched her jaw and arched her neck slightly.

"I can see you're making spaghetti, so polite conversation it is."

Carrie glanced at the twins' bedroom door, hesitant to cause a scene that would only upset Lauren more than she already was. She grabbed a large spoon and concentrated on breaking up the ground meat as it cooked. Tired of having Dave watch her every move, she banged the spoon loudly against the side of the pot and dropped it with a clatter onto the spoon rest. "Look, I said you could see the kids anytime you want, but if you come just to upset our daughter, I'll put a stop to it."

"I thought maybe you'd let me stay for supper."

She kept her voice low and even. "Why would you think that?"

He shrugged. "Mom spent the day in Lafayette at the doctor's."

"And what did you do today?"

"I went hunting this morning. I shot my limit too."

"Did you clean the birds yourself or leave them for your mom to clean after she'd been to the doctor and driving all day?"

He glared at her. "I cleaned them myself."

"Did you clean up her kitchen when you were done?"

"Yes, I did, as a matter of fact."

Carrie spoke in a tight voice. "You should have cooked supper for your mom when you finished. You know how tired she is after her appointments, especially when she has a stress test scheduled, like she did today."

Dave's eyes narrowed angrily. He straightened and stalked over to the door before swinging around to point at her. "You've got until the end of next week to get your shit out here. After that, I'm moving back in, whether you like it or not."

She turned her attention to the meat frying in the pan. "The end of next week. I'll be out."

He stalked out the front door, slamming it shut behind him.

Carrie grinned as she stirred the pot. "Don't go away mad. Just go away."

Carrie stopped loading the dishwasher to answer the phone.

"Hey." Dave's tone was considerably more subdued. "You don't have to move out until your place is ready."

"What happened? Ruby chewed you out?"

"Shut the hell up."

Carrie laughed. "Your mom loves me, jerk."

He snorted. "Yeah, she does. All my family loves you, but your mom hates me."

"She doesn't hate you, although you've given her plenty of reasons to."

"What about you?"

She closed the door of the dishwasher and set it to start. "She doesn't hate me either."

"Always the smart ass."

Carrie wiped at the kitchen counter. "I don't hate you either, Dave, but I need to get out of here before I do." She thought of the early morning phone calls, thinking again how she'd feel safer if Dave was making them. An old quote she'd had to memorize in the sixth grade came to mind. *Greater is our terror of the unknown.* No kidding.

"Carrie—"

"G'night, Dave." She ended the call quickly. "It's too damn late for heart to hearts," she muttered, before locking up the house and flipping off the kitchen light.

Carrie opened her eyes but didn't move another muscle. She stared at the bleary glow of red digital numbers coming from the nightstand; blinked them into focus, as four eleven turned to four twelve. Rain pelted the window, overflowed the gutters as thunder rumbled, low and threatening, from miles away.

She lay tense and frozen, certain of one thing. Something had awakened her. A sound? A stir in the air? A sense of not being alone?

Whatever it was had been strong enough to cut her dream short, only her second about her father since his death thirteen years earlier. She'd been having a cup of coffee with him at her kitchen table, while he said how proud he was of her for going to college—for getting away from Dave.

She felt the drip of water on her forehead a millisecond before he whispered her name.

She jerked away from the sound, fully awake now, as her tension-filled body responded to the intrusion. Willing her eyes to adjust to the dark, she finally recognized the outline of Dave's face, mere inches from her own. She smelled his rain soaked hair, beer on his breath, and cigarette smoke from whatever bar he'd come from, as well as a telltale trace of perfume.

"What the hell, Dave?"

"I'm coming home."

Her heart pounded from a massive rush of adrenaline. "I changed the locks. How the hell did you get inside?"

He answered in a low, hoarse whisper. "You can't keep me out of here. This is my home. I built it, and I need to be back in it with my kids."

"Asshole!" Furious with him, she pushed him away and threw the covers off to sit up. "Get off me. It's barely four o'clock, Dave."

"It couldn't wait. I'm losing my mind at Mom's."

"Oh, please. It's too damn early in the morning for dramatics." She got out of bed and grabbed her phone.

"Who the hell are you calling at this hour? Your boyfriend?" His tone dripped with bitterness and anger.

Carrie jabbed at the dial pad, glaring at Dave as she waited. After a few seconds, she spoke calmly into the phone.

"Hey, sweetie, I'm sorry as hell to wake you up like this, but my ex-asshole isn't giving me much of a choice. Would it be okay if the kids and I stayed at your place just until the middle of January? I'll be able to move into my rent house then. It is? Thanks babe. I'll come here straight from work and pick up a few things, and we'll be there later this afternoon. What's that? No, I don't mind sharing the bed with you. Thanks again and sorry for waking you up so early. Wouldn't have done it if I'd had any other *choice.*"

She ended the call and locked herself inside her master bath to get ready for work. Dave's muffled voice carried from beyond the bathroom door.

"Who'd you call?" he asked, keeping his voice low for a change.

Carrie thought of all the phone calls he'd made from her home to other women. All those numbers he hadn't been able to explain away. One in particular came to mind. One number she'd dared to call back.

A woman had answered, her tone low and seductive. *"You'd freak if you could see what I'm wearing now, baby."*

She'd answered dryly. "I'm sure it's just what I'd be expecting someone like you to wear. Which slut of the month are you? This is his wife, by the way. You know, the woman who's wasted her youth on a man who doesn't give a damn about her or their three kids?"

She'd relived it countless times—both the conversation and the reverberating echo of that 'other woman' slamming the phone down.

Dave muttered a foul curse from the other side of the door, as Carrie beamed back at her reflection in the bathroom mirror. She didn't get to turn it around on him often, but her sense of victory provided a cheery start to this dismally wet and gloomy day.

Chapter Six

December 21st

Carrie pushed open the back door of the office and shook out her umbrella. Dale paused in front of her holding a steaming mug of coffee. “All this crappy weather, and you’re still early. You’re such a dedicated employee.”

She chuckled, thanking God once more for her easy-going boss. “I had a little inspiration this morning.”

Roxie joined them, empty cup in hand. “What kind of inspiration?”

“I got a four a.m. ultimatum from my ex.” She deposited her purse at her desk and followed Roxie into the kitchen. She’d just finished telling Roxie about her close encounter of the ugly kind when someone pushed open the door, stomping and swearing.

Roxie stepped back to see who else had braved the weather to come in. “Look who’s here. I see you didn’t melt in this rain, Sam. You must have floated in, like a turd.”

Sam pulled a bandana from his pocket and wiped the moisture from his hands and face. “I know it’s a stretch for you, Rox, but could you at least *try* to be a lady?”

She answered with a snort on the way to her desk.

Sam nodded to Carrie. “That must have been a hell of a drive all the way from your place this morning. It’s really coming down out there.”

“It wasn’t too bad. I left early enough, thank God.”

“No,” Roxie added. “Thank *Dave*.”

Carrie intercepted Sam’s curious gaze. “He woke me up early this morning, that’s all.”

She flipped open a set of plans, smiling as she heard Dale rib Sam about being at the office so early, especially in rain that should last all day, according to weather reports.

“Your crew took the whole two weeks off, Sam. Hell, if Carrie wasn’t here, you’d have kept your ass at home.”

Sam’s obvious attraction to Carrie was a commonly discussed subject around the office—so common that both had become immune to their co-workers’ teasing. Carrie would only admit it was good for her ego.

Sam scratched at his neatly trimmed goatee. “All I have to do is show up to get paid. It’s money in the bank.” He paused at Carrie’s desk to pick up a large rubber band and looped it around his fingers. “What’cha doing today?” He aimed it at her, ready to launch.

She lifted one finger in warning. “Don’t even think about it.”

He chuckled and launched the band to the other side of the room instead. "You studying for another certification?"

"Yep."

"You study too much. Why don't you take a break?"

"If I wait too long, I'll forget the math I re-learned in technical college."

"But it's raining outside. There are only a few of us here today."

She flipped to a clean sheet on her engineering tablet. "I need to pass these tests, Sam. It'll take a couple of promotions before my salary rises above the poverty level."

Carrie tried to smother her grin as Sam turned away, looking every bit as deprived as her girls when she said no to sleepovers. Despite the weather, and her rude awakening, she was in a great mood. As Sam disappeared into his office, she couldn't help but wonder if he was the cause.

Carrie slipped her mechanical pencil inside the book and slammed it shut. She stood up to stretch her back and legs, then grabbed her coffee cup. "Looks like I'll be hauling clothes to my sister's place in the rain this afternoon."

"You have someone to help you?" Roxie said.

"I don't need help. I told the kids to bring enough to last for the rest of the week. We'll get more this weekend."

Roxie followed her into the kitchen. "I bet you're looking forward to moving into your own place."

"I can't wait. I moved straight out of my parent's home and into a house with Dave when I was eighteen. This will be my place, with my rules." She washed her coffee mug and dropped it into the drain rack, turning as she heard a noise behind her.

Sam leaned against the doorway and cleared his throat. "Hey." He shoved his hands into his pockets. He was nervous about something.

"Hello again. What's on your mind, Langley?"

"Maybe you're looking at the wrong town to relocate to. Have you thought about moving closer to work? Fuel costs will only get worse."

"My kids go to school in Gardiner, Sam. I can't ask them to move if I don't have to."

"It makes more sense than being on the road two hours a day."

"Is your ex living in the same town as you?"

"No, she's about forty-five miles away."

"And where's Nick?"

"He's with me."

"So he stayed with you because he didn't want to switch schools, right?"

"Well, yeah. I guess."

"Then I don't see why you'd be so shocked that I'd want to stay in the same town as my kids. The last thing I'd want is for them to live with their dad without me around to supervise."

"Because it's twice the distance," he blurted out.

"It's twice the distance as *what*?" Carrie watched, fascinated by the slow flush infusing Sam's face. Her gaze trailed him as he spun around and left the room. *What the hell?*

Carrie left the kitchen to check out the office's huge wall map of Louisiana. With her fingertip, she traced the highway leading north up to Kenton, Sam's hometown. She measured the difference between Kenton and Gardiner, and smiled when she put it together. The drive from Gardiner to Lake Coburn was twice the distance as it was from Kenton.

She turned toward the double glass doors and rested both arms on the push-bar to stare out at the heaviest rainfall of the year. Rainwater splashed from the overtaxed gutter system onto the paved parking lot. A woman tiptoed in a ludicrous dance through water six inches deep to get from her car to the front door of the neighboring business.

Headlights glowed eerily through the frigid, sogginess of the winter afternoon. The dreary, saturated day should have been reason enough to depress Carrie. Instead, a lovely feeling of warmth radiated throughout her chest, filling her with something she hadn't felt in years.

Hope.

Before she could soak in the glow, the reality of her situation hit her: three kids, school in Gardiner, work in Lake Coburn, an ex-husband, the almost certain disapproval from Lauren if she even looked at another man, not enough money, and never enough time. No way could she throw in a relationship with a co-worker. No amount of re-calculating could solve this formula.

Carrie turned away from the door with a heavy sigh, resigned to the fact that nothing would change anytime soon.

Sam plopped down in his rickety desk chair and dropped his forehead into his hands.

"Something got you down, Sambo?"

The query from Jeff, his office mate, had him shaking his head. "Nope, not me." He pulled a stack of survey books from his desk drawer and slammed the drawer shut with his knee. He opened the top book, stared blindly at the pages, unable to see anything but the confused look on Carrie's face as she'd asked, *"It's twice the distance as what?"* Sam snorted and shook his head, drawing a curious sideways look from Jeff. He pretended to look for something as he busily flipped pages in the book, all the while silently cursing himself for the idiot he was. He'd made a complete fool of himself with his comment. Then he'd topped it off by reddening like a school boy in front of the first and only woman who'd turned his head since Linda left.

"Way to go, dumbass." His low mutter of self-accusation had Jeff grumbling from his desk.

"What the hell did I do to you?"

Sam closed one book and opened another. "I'm not talking to you."

Carrie loaded the last of the suitcases and shut the trunk. Rain fell in heavy gray sheets, drenching everything it touched, obliterating the landscape. The yellow glow of the carport barely pierced the darkness surrounding them.

She leaned over to look inside the car. "Y'all ready to get wet?" she yelled over the sound of water splashing out of the gutters onto the sidewalks.

"Sure." Gretchen's answer came from the backseat while Lauren remained silent in the front passenger side.

Carrie straightened and pulled Grant close for a hug.

"Be careful driving in this stuff, Mom."

Carrie bit her lower lip hard to keep from crying. "I will, son. Are you sure you don't want to come with us?"

"Naw, I'll be fine. I don't want him to be alone. Besides—" He shot a look at his sisters. "It'll be nice to get the bathroom all to myself for a change."

She kissed her son soundly on the cheek. "Listen, if he gives you any grief, you call me and I'll come get you right away." Carrie climbed into the driver's seat and buckled up. "Love you." She blew him a kiss as she started the car and backed into the storm.

Miraculously, the rain let up just long enough to unload their suitcases into Christie's small home. As soon as they'd emptied the car, the deluge started again.

Christie lugged a large duffle into her son Max's room. "I emptied out this chest of drawers so you won't have to live out of a suitcase for the next several days."

Carrie started unpacking the duffle to place items into drawers. "I really hate to put you and poor Max out like this, even for a short while."

"No problem, sis. I know what it's like to be displaced, thanks to my ex."

"I know, but he sure helped you make a good-looking little boy, didn't he?" She grabbed the towheaded two-year-old and lifted him, making the toddler squeal with delight. "Hey, little man, is it okay if Aunt Carrie sleeps in your bed?"

"Yeth!" he lisped through his big, cheesy grin.

"You're a man of few words, Max—just what Aunt Carrie likes." Max ran off and Carrie sat down on the edge of the bed to nest empty suitcases as Christie pushed them under the bed.

"Yeah, and uh, speaking of what Aunt Carrie likes, how are things at work?" Christie asked her older sister.

"Things are great at work. I'm almost finished with the training to get my second certification."

"That is not what I'm talking about and you know it."

Carrie shook her head. "I knew I shouldn't have told you about him last night." She checked to see if her daughters were near.

"They're in the living room with Max," Christie answered her unspoken question as she got up to close the bedroom door for more privacy. "Now, what's going on in that office of yours with Mr. Six Foot Two, Eyes of Blue?"

Carrie rolled her eyes. "He's closer to six three, but you need to stop, okay? I've only been divorced a few months. If anyone gets wind of this, I'll go from divorcee to tramp in one night."

Christie waved off her comment. "That's crazy."

Carrie placed her hair supplies and make up in the drawer of the nightstand. "You know how people around here will twist this like an old dishrag until they've wrung out the last microbe of truth. When they're done, I'll be the old dishrag."

She sighed and dropped onto the bed, emotionally drained. "It's not fair, Chris. As nice as it is to feel wanted by another man, the timing is so unbelievably off. Lauren would freak if I started dating now."

"Are you thinking about it?"

Carrie flopped back on the bed and threw her arm over her eyes. "I try not to, but I can't help thinking about him. Some of the things he's said to me—"

"Give it up, girl!" Chris plopped down on the bed next to her sister. "What kind of things?"

Carrie ran her hands through her dampened hair, her curls tightened from the rain. As she related Sam's comment about her being worth the wait, and Kenton's proximity to Lake Coburn, a smile spread across her sister's face.

"Oh, God, that's so sweet. And he wants you to be closer to him," she whispered. "You should think about it."

Carrie raised herself to one elbow. "I can't do that."

"Why not? We all know how two hours on the road every day is eating you up. Mom's worried sick you'll get in a wreck. If this is what you want as a career, it's craziness to face that drive for the rest of your life."

Carrie traced a finger around the robot-shaped figure on Max's quilt. "I can't ask the kids to switch schools."

"Mom and Dad moved us to another state, and we adjusted."

Carried sat up to rub her eyes and face, as a wave of exhaustion washed over her. "Sometimes I wonder if any of us will adjust." She dropped her hands and stared at them. "This whole situation with Sam scares the crap out of me."

"Really? Hell, I didn't think you were afraid of anything."

"I'm afraid of everything. Of moving too fast with Sam or anyone else, or not moving fast enough. Of losing my kids or their respect and losing my family's respect." She fell back against the mattress. "Then again, I'm getting older. How many chances at this will I get in one lifetime?" She gazed over at her sister. "You know, the last time I went on a date, I didn't have stretch marks from carrying a set of twins."

"I hear that," Christie agreed.

"Whatever I decide to do, I need to be careful, Chris. My kids need at least one of their parents to act like an adult."

Chapter Seven

December 22nd

The skies opened up the next day, drenching the city of Lake Coburn with another day of rain. The local weatherman spouted more bad news from the country radio station blasting from Carrie's car speakers.

"Well, folks, the weather doesn't care that it's the last work day before your Christmas holidays. It's more rain throughout the weekend."

"Great." She pulled up to the building. Since the carpool was down to her and Sam, she'd decided it would be better to drive their own vehicles until everyone else returned after the holidays. She regretted it now, remembering how Sam had dropped her off at the front door one day last week so she wouldn't get wet. She stepped out of her car, right into a puddle of ankle deep water, immediately soaking her shoes, socks, and hem of her jeans. Carrie hurried inside to her desk, cursing with every squish of her saturated footwear.

"Take your socks and shoes off," Roxie suggested.

Carrie squished over to her locker and pulled out the leather work shoes she kept there in case the crew needed an extra hand. She walked into the kitchen and propped one foot on the plastic chair seat to try to loosen her knotted laces. As she struggled with the tangled mass of cold, wet strings, she heard a low groan from the doorway. She peered up to catch Sam standing in the doorway, his gaze lowered to her neckline. She looked down at her cleavage, visible due to the gaping neck of her wet shirt and her awkward position. Carrie raised her gaze to Sam, who still stared, seemingly mesmerized by the sight of her bosom.

"Like what you see, Sam?"

Startled, he turned to leave the kitchen.

She stopped him with one word. "Hey!"

He turned back, his gaze on his boots. "Yes?"

"Think you could help me with these wet laces?"

"Guess I could try. Can you slip your shoes off?"

"I tried that already. My socks are wet, and I laced my shoes really tight this morning." She waved her long nails, recently polished. "I don't want to break a nail, but I can't stand my feet wet."

After a slight adjustment to his jeans, Sam sat down on the chair across from her. He tapped the seat, signaling her to put one shoe up on the seat between his legs.

Carrie propped her right foot on the chair seat and settled back to watch him fight the laces.

Sam grunted as he worked at the tangle. "These damn things get hard to manipulate once they're wet. They swell."

Carrie kept her silence, pursing her lips as she waited for him to ponder his comment. His hands froze mid-air when the double entendre finally hit him.

He lifted his gaze to meet her amused expression, then went back to his task, jerking hard on her strings. “Look, I’ve lived like a freaking monk for over a year now. Cut me some slack, okay?”

“My momma taught me it was rude to stare. All you had to do was look away.”

Sam met her gaze head on. “Now why would I want to deprive myself of the best thing I’ve laid eyes on in ages?”

His hands kept working, as their gazes remained locked for several seconds. He looked away, finally loosened the lace enough to remove her shoe.

Carrie held her breath as he slowly peeled off her wet sock. When he rubbed the arch of her foot with his work-roughened thumb, the skin-to-skin contact broke her trance.

He stopped her when she tried to pull her foot out of his hands. “Hold on, now.” His devilish grin exposed that one adorable dimple. “What’s this?” He bent to examine her polished hot pink toenails.

She jerked her foot out of his grip and placed the other shoed foot on the chair between them. “My girls practiced on mine and Christie’s toes last night.”

He got the next one untied with no trouble and removed her shoe, along with the second sock. “You have nice feet.” He lightly caressed her foot.

“I have big feet. None of the other women in my family have feet as big as mine. I’m a size nine and a half in a family of size sevens.”

Carrie pulled her foot away and slipped her feet into her dry work shoes. She shivered as her bare skin touched the cold leather.

Sam rose, unfolding his long body from the chair. “Wait here. I have something I think you’ll appreciate.”

Carrie appreciated the sight of his rear end exiting the room. In less than a minute, he came back with a pair of new tube socks.

“I always keep a couple of extra pair in my work bag. You never know what’s going to happen when you work like we do.”

“Oh, yeah,” Carrie purred, as she slid the comfortably dry tube socks onto her ice cold feet. “That feels delicious.”

“Have I redeemed myself?”

She slipped her socked feet into her shoes. “I can forgive anything if my feet are warm and dry.”

Sam gazed down at her shoes. “I’ve got an extra pair of work boots, too, if you need `em. They’re only a size thirteen.”

“Thirteen, huh?”

“Yep, and you know what they say about men who wear big shoes, don’t you?”

Carrie swallowed, silently waiting to hear his answer.

"They have big feet."

She laughed and stood up. "You're so bad."

He chuckled as she walked out of the door. "Get your mid out of the gutter, Carrie."

Around noon, Dale stood and stretched before addressing the skeleton crew. "Roxie and I are going to lunch. Anybody else coming with us?"

Sam loomed in his office doorway. "I guess I'll have to go."

"Me too," J.C. told Dale.

Carrie shook her head. "Not me, I brought leftovers. I have enough gumbo for two heating in the kitchen if anyone else wants some."

J.C. stood to get his cap and jacket. "I'll pass. I had gumbo last night, but I bet Sam wants some."

"Hell yeah, if you're sure you don't mind," Sam admitted.

Carrie headed for the kitchen. "I wouldn't have offered, otherwise." She stirred the pot containing the steaming brew and sensed Sam's presence in the kitchen before he spoke. He approached her from behind and she tried not to fidget at his close proximity.

"God that smells good."

"Gumbo's always better the next day." She doled out portions of freshly cooked rice into two bowls.

"The food smells good too, but *what* is that perfume you wear?"

She struggled to keep her hands from shaking as she ladled hot gumbo over the rice. "Um, it's Ob-Obsession."

"Obsession." He whispered the word, so close his breath stirred the tendrils of hair at the back of her neck.

She pulled her shoulders back and turned, lifting one bowl to form a barrier of stoneware. Swirling ribbons of steam rose from the gumbo to heat the air between them. Or was it Sam's nearness raising the temperature in the room?

Carrie's breath caught in her throat as he reached out to cover her hands with his own. Her pulse quickened as he lowered the bowl, allowing her to pull her hands back. Her stomach fluttered at the clean, masculine scent rolling off of the man before her. She lifted her gaze to his broad chest, reached out a shaky hand, overcome by the urge to touch the silky, golden chest hair just visible above his collar. Carrie's hand hovered below his top button for several moments before she pulled it back toward her.

She turned away to pick up her own bowl of gumbo then scooted around him to the kitchen's exit.

"Carrie."

Frozen in place at the sound of his voice, she remained silent.

"I didn't mean to upset you."

Her head fell forward. "I'm not upset. Not with you."

"At what, then?"

"Myself, I guess." She wiped one sweaty palm on the front of her jeans. "I'm as terrified to pass up a chance with you as I am of rushing into something too soon."

"You'll have to explain that one to me." He sounded puzzled.

"I don't want to send you the wrong signals."

"I don't know if you've noticed or not, but I'm a big boy, and I can handle myself."

I've noticed. She released a low burst of nervous laughter. "Like I told Christie last night, my biggest concern is losing my children's respect."

"You discussed me with your sister?"

Carrie squeezed her eyes shut. "I may have mentioned you, in passing." She glanced his direction, scowling at his smug expression, before escaping with her food to sit at her desk. Thankfully, Sam remained in the kitchen to finish his meal.

After a while, the sound of running water and the clatter of dishes in the sink caught her attention. Several minutes later, he walked past her desk at a leisurely pace.

"Give my compliments to the chef." His voice dipped to a low, sexy rumble that made Carrie wish *she'd* been the chef.

She spoke quietly, keeping her eyes lowered. "I will, and thanks for washing the pots."

"Yes, ma'am. My daughter has this magnet on her fridge that says 'Love a man with dishpan hands.' See?" He raised both hands.

Carrie glanced up, wondering what else those hands could do besides wash dishes.

"I'm going into my office now, Carrie. You can study to your heart's content." He grinned before disappearing into his office.

She observed silently, as he pulled files from a cabinet in his office. At last, he settled into his squeaky desk chair, just out of her visual range.

Carrie tried to concentrate on her study manual. Instead, she envisioned a broad chest. She squeezed her eyes shut, trying to block out the sight of Sam and his healthy display of golden chest hair, something she'd always admired in men. Even though she knew one had nothing to do with the other, she'd always equated Dave's bare chest to his immature actions, and the Peter-Pan-Persona he seemed to glorify. What would it be like to be with a man with the physical traits she'd always associated with a mature man? She wasn't talking Grizzly Adams, but someone who could grow a beard that didn't make him look like he had a serious case of mange. A man willing to stay home where he belonged, one who knew how to keep a job and dedicate his life to his family?

A man like Sam?

She sighed and stared out the window as the rain increased to a deafening roar. *It's going to be a long day.*

Sam sat at his desk and gloated. *She told her sister about me.* He understood her uneasiness with the timing, but he had to wonder how many chances he had left in this life. He tried to concentrate on anything other than the woman in the next room, but finally got up and walked to the door of his office.

"Hey." He spoke loud enough for her to hear him over the din of rain beating down on the building's metal awning. "I always take two weeks off between Christmas and New Year's."

"Oh, yeah?"

He nodded. Was that a hint of disappointment he heard in her voice? *God, I hope so.* "Would you want to catch a movie or dinner sometime in the next couple of weeks?"

She looked him squarely in the eyes. "With you?"

Sam blinked once. "Well, yeah, that's the general idea."

Carrie blushed and gave him a half-hearted laugh. "Sorry, I'm not handling this very well. The truth is I'll have to get back to you on that."

"It's okay."

She must have sensed his disappointment, because she rushed to explain. "My daughter is still in counseling over the divorce. I don't want to rush into anything."

"Oh, I see. I thought maybe I could call you during our time off to see if you're okay, or just to talk, if *that's* okay with you?" He thought his heart would explode in the time it took her to finally answer with a smile.

"I think that would be a good way to learn more about each other."

"And, if something happens, and you're able to move into your rent house a little early, I'd be available to help you out with that." He raised his hands, to defend his suggestion. "Just as a friend, of course."

"You'd do that?"

He gave her a quick nod. "We do things like that for each other around here." He pulled a business card from his wallet and met her at her desk. "I wrote my home number on the back." As she reached for it, he pulled it back. "You're not going to tear it up are you?"

He watched Carrie smile and held it in one hand as she scribbled something on a note pad. She tore the page from the pad and slipped it into his shirt pocket before returning to her studies.

Sam waited until he sat at his own desk before reaching for the paper. Not only had she given him Christie's number, but her mom's phone number as well.

He tucked the paper into his wallet. "Yesirree, that'll do."

Sam glanced up from the stack of field books on his desk as J.C. entered his office. "Did you get wet out there?"

"Yeah, but that shrimp platter was worth it." He leaned over and added in a whisper. "We stayed away as long as we could to give y'all some time to talk."

"I asked her out, but I'll have to settle for a phone call instead, not that I'm complaining."

"You never know, Sam. Baby Jesus might send you something—or somebody—special for Christmas this year."

Sam's chuckle filled the room. "*De ta joule a le orrais du le Bon Dieu.*"

J.C. sent him a blank stare. "I didn't get any of that."

"From your mouth to the good Lord's ears," Sam translated.

By 3:30 that afternoon, everyone had cleared out of the office except for Carrie and Sam. She gathered her things as he approached. "Thanks again for the socks. I'll get them back to you after the holidays."

He ducked his head sheepishly. "I'll let you keep `em if I can call you tonight."

She tapped her chin thoughtfully. "Tube socks as a bribe. That's original."

"You want boiled crawfish instead?"

"Not in season."

"Chocolate? I know you like your chocolate."

Carrie looped her purse strap over her shoulder and laughed at his offer. "I don't accept bribes, but you can call me anyway. My kids will be gone for the next two nights."

Sam's face twisted as though he were in pain. "Mine, too. That house of mine feels too empty without my son around. Holidays kind of suck."

"I know, but what am I going to do? Dave's family is coming in tonight. Mine won't be in until Christmas Day. My kids need to see their cousins. What do you do, Sam? Where do you go when Nick's not around?"

"My folks live one street over and I usually end up there for a visit and a meal. Pop keeps a running tab on things they need help with around the house. They're both closing in on eighty years old," he explained. "Anything beats being alone."

She scraped her teeth on her lower lip at his comment. "I used to think that; then I learned better."

"So, you'll be alone?"

"Yeah, Christie and Max, my nephew, are spending the night at her ex-mother-in-law's place."

Sam inched closer. "Is eight o'clock a good time to call?"

Carrie's curiosity ran wild as she breathed him in. Her lids drooped as her thoughts wandered. *What would it feel like to have him wrap her in his arms?* The deep timbre of his voice broke into her reflections.

"Eight?" he repeated.

She blinked then lifted her lids in one languid motion. "Eight is good."

They stood awkwardly, both needing to leave, neither wanting to walk out first.

Sam cleared his throat. "Well, I guess this is it, then. Merry Christmas, Carrie."

"Merry Christmas to you too, Sam—and I hope you have a wonderful New Year." *No Sam until after New Year's.*

"It will be if you're a part of it."

Her heart pounded. "What did you say?"

Sam took a step closer and rested his hands upon her upper arms. "At some point, I'd like you to become a major part of my life in the next year. Do you see that happening?"

Carrie struggled to answer. "Possibly," she squeaked, in a voice hoarse and full of nervous energy.

Sam leaned over slowly and kissed her on the cheek, lingering beside her long after the kiss was over.

Just as he began to pull away, Carrie turned toward him until her cheek made a gentle, but electrifying contact with his. She lowered her lids and lifted her chin, strengthening the skin-to-skin connection. She heard the low moan, realizing too late that it came from her own parted lips. Powerless to move, she felt him pull away before caressing her face in his large hands.

"Open your eyes, Carrie," he whispered.

Her lids opened heavily as she focused on his lips, mere inches away, and lifted her hands to cover his.

"I'll apologize for this later, but I want you to remember me over the next two weeks." He lowered his mouth gently onto hers.

The first kiss was to taste, light and teasing, a little unsure. Carrie felt him draw away but she stayed put, hoping he'd get the message.

I want more.

He got it. The second kiss was firmer, more confident, from a self-assured man who knew what he wanted. By the time he pulled away, Carrie could barely stand on her own two legs. She leaned into him for support, her hands spread out against his broad chest until she regained her balance.

"I'm sorry, but I had to know." He kissed her lightly again. "How you tasted. I've wanted to do that ever since the first time I made you laugh," he admitted. "If that's all it takes to keep you happy, I might have a shot."

She gazed up at him, slightly dazed. Her head tilted forward, then back in a distracted nod.

Sam grinned. "So, all I have to do is be my charming, funny self to earn your undying love?"

She repeated the nod once more before straightening, coming to her senses. "No."

He laughed. "I thought I was getting off too easy." He reached out and ran his forefinger gently along her jaw line. "Focus now, Carrie. What else?"

It was difficult to breathe, to concentrate, with him so near and touching her that way.

He brushed a stray lock hair from her face. "What else would it take to make you mine?"

Carrie shivered at his touch and covered his hand with her own. She attempted to clear her throat, as well as her head. "I can't take being hurt again."

"I won't hurt you."

"Just words—how do I know I can trust you?"

"I'm nothing like your ex."

"How do I know that?"

"Because I'm *telling* you I'm not," he insisted. "But feel free to ask anyone."

She studied him, watching for signs of discomfort, fear of revealed secrets, but she saw nothing.

"Lots of people thought Dave was a 'good ole' boy'. They didn't know what he was doing behind my back."

Sam lifted both hands, as though his patience was at an end. "Okay, then. *You* tell me what you want in a man."

"I don't know what I want in a man," she said. "But thanks to Dave, I damn sure know what I don't want."

"Then tell me. What *don't* you want in a man?"

She took two steps toward the door then turned back toward him. "I *don't* want a man I can't trust, or one who'll push me or my kids around. I *don't* want someone I'm afraid to relax around." Her gaze locked on his. "I can't live like that again."

She held her breath as he walked over to brush a kiss upon her lips.

"In twenty-one years of marriage, I was never unfaithful, and I never laid a hand on her." He pulled her closer for another light kiss. "I've been with the same company for twenty years, and I'll retire from here. I've lived in the same house for the same amount of time. I'm steady as a slab of granite. I love kids, and I promise that neither you, nor your kids will ever have to be afraid of me."

Carrie sighed as Sam left a trail of gentle kisses along her jaw line.

"I'm no stud. My hair is thinning, my mid-section isn't. I live a dull life and I don't have a lot of money to spare." He shifted and continued kissing the other side of her jaw. "If you're looking for non-stop excitement and someone to buy you a lot of gifts, I'm not your man, but I'd find other ways to spoil you."

One side of his lip curled adorably alongside his dimple as she lifted one curious brow.

"Ah, the lady wants to know how I'd spoil her," he mused. "Okay. Let's negotiate."

Sam rattled off a list she'd never again have to do for herself, from car maintenance to yard work, to bringing her coffee in bed and letting her have control of the remote. "I'll buy your favorite perfume for your birthdays, and never give you silk bikinis rolled up like a rose for Valentine's Day."

"It was nylon, not even silk."

"Then neither." He placed his hands on her waist and pulled her even closer. "Besides," he added, "J.C. says we look good together."

Carrie met his gaze, caressed by the warmth in his eyes. "He does?"

"Yep." He bent his head for another kiss.

She placed both hands on his chest and gave him a gentle push. "Have you been talking to people about me?"

"J.C. spoke up one day and told me I should ask you out because we make a good-looking pair," he explained. "That's all."

I've always wanted tall, dependable, and faithful. She thought how wonderful it would be to have a life without worry, without the constant existence of stress and strain she had as Dave's wife. Wouldn't it be wonderful to trust again? It would be so easy to say she wanted him in her life. *But the time wasn't quite right, yet.* She stepped away and stared out at the compound's water covered parking lot. "I need to go before the skies open up again."

"You be careful going home, Carrie."

She adjusted her shoulder strap as he pushed the door open for her. "You too, Sam."

Sam reached out and gently took hold of her arm to stop her before she walked through the door. "Listen, if you have to see your ex, make sure you're never alone with him."

"I'll be careful."

"Don't let him talk you into anything."

Carrie froze in her tracks as a low rumble of thunder echoed ominously in the distance. She gazed out at the gathering of black clouds and suddenly felt the dreariness of the rain-sodden surroundings creep into her soul. "What kind of *anything* are you talking about?"

Sam closed his eyes and sighed. "Never mind."

Carrie turned slowly to face him. "Are you afraid I'll fall into bed with him?"

Sam's tone turned defensive. "I only meant that he might try to talk you into taking him back. You said he could be persuasive."

Carrie tried to remain calm, told herself not to over-react. "Dave could persuade the old me to do a lot of stupid things, Sam. I'm stronger now. The new me can handle him."

"I sure as hell hope so. I just don't want anything like that to happen before—"

"Before *what?*"

"Well, before you, before we . . ." Sam's comment trailed off.

"You mean before I've slept with *you*?" Carrie waited for him to correct her. Hoped—*prayed* she'd assumed wrong. Her heart sank when he remained silent. Unable to speak for the lump in her throat, she turned and ran out into the rain.

Chapter Eight

Sam stood by, still in shock, as Carrie's car started and then pulled out of the parking lot. How the hell had the best five minutes of his entire year turned FUBAR in a matter of seconds? Moving in a mechanical daze, he didn't bother to put on his coat before trudging out to his truck. By the time he pulled his door closed he was soaked, cold to the bone, and disgusted with himself. His truck started with a roar, but he sat and stared out the window until his heater warmed the interior and defogged the windshield.

"Dumbass," he muttered, gazing at his reflection in the rear-view. "You couldn't let her walk out the door and trust her?" He knew Carrie wouldn't do anything as stupid as to take Dave back. She'd worked too damn hard for her independence. He shook his head, disappointed in his own insecurities.

Never again would he let fears bred from his own marriage control his tongue. Starting now, he'd put everything behind him and be a better man for the woman he...what? Loved? Did he love her? He liked her courage, her determination to have a better life, to provide her children with a chance for a better future. He admired every intelligent, sensitive, stubborn inch of her, from her glossy curls to her dimples, to her hot pink and polished toes. He welcomed her ability to hold her own in an argument with him or anyone else, man or woman. Reveled that she didn't back down from a challenge. But did he love her?

The only thing he knew for sure was that he needed to apologize.

Sam threw his truck in gear. He'd give her an hour and a half to get back to Gardiner before calling to tell her he was sorry. That should be easy enough

Swish-swash . . . swish-swash . . . swish-swash . . . The hypnotic rhythm of the wipers did nothing to ease the tension in Carrie's shoulders as she hugged the steering wheel to get a better view of the roadway. Even set at the highest speed, her wipers couldn't keep up with the torrential rain.

"Folks, if you can hear my voice, you'll be seeing this super heavy precipitation for the rest of the afternoon and night. If you're driving in Lake Coburn today, here are some areas for potential flash flooding . . ."

She groaned at the weatherman's words, thinking about the shopping she needed to do before driving to Christie's place. Disappointed in the way she and Sam had ended their conversation, she drove on, feeling down and depressed.

Two hours after leaving the office, she fell into the doorway of Christie's kitchen door, kicked off her shoes, and hauled the three dripping bags of groceries to the sink to drain. She went to the bathroom and slipped out of her drenched clothes, placing them straight into the washer and starting the cycle.

She pulled on a pair of dry jeans and a sweatshirt and pushed her feet into her fuzzy slippers. The shrill ring of the phone sliced through the metallic ping of raindrops hitting the aluminum-covered carport. She ran to answer it, determined that if it was Sam, she'd give him a chance to explain. She answered, fully expecting to hear the deep, sexy, bass of the voice she loved.

"Hey," she said, breathlessly.

"Where've you been?" a hoarse voice whispered.

She passed her hand over the curls plastered to her wet cheeks, wishing she'd remembered to pick up her umbrella this morning. "Excuse me?" She wasn't altogether certain she'd heard him correctly.

"Where've you been, Carrie?"

"Who is this?" Terror gripped at her. "Who are you?"

"You'll learn soon enough, sweetness. Just like you'll learn you can't move to get rid of me. I'll always find you."

"What do you want from me?" She waited, her breath coming in shallow, frantic puffs. In the next several seconds of jaw clenching silence, she'd almost begun to believe he'd hung up.

The voice answered, in a slow, evil sounding hiss that made her skin crawl.

"Everything."

She wrenched the phone away as though it scorched her ear.

By eight o'clock, Sam had dialed the number at least a hundred times. Finally hearing something other than the dreaded busy signal, he waited with bated breath for the sound of her voice. Hell, at this point, he'd take anyone's voice telling him she'd made it home safely. His imagination had gone wild, creating all kinds of tragic scenarios caused by the weather conditions and her frame of mind when she'd left. He'd mentally kicked his own ass seven kinds of ways since then, wondering when he'd ever learn to keep his big mouth shut.

Carrie stared at the ringing telephone. Her head throbbed, and her stomach had long ago morphed from mildly upset to a lump of dread and queasiness. She grabbed the phone off the coffee table and gave the answer button a hesitant press. She spoke, her voice barely above a whisper. "Hello?"

The short silence on the other end of the line finally produced a nervous clearing of a throat. "Is that you, Carrie?"

Carrie clapped her hand over her eyes. "Sam?"

"Yes, finally! I'm a dumb son of a bitch, Carrie. I'm sorry. I know you must be tired of hearing me say that, and thinking I must be a hell of a slow learner, but if you give me one more chance, I promise you won't be sorry."

"Sam!" Relief washed over her in waves at the sound of Sam's voice. She wiped at a trickle of tears from the corner of one eye. "I wanted to call you back, but I washed your card in the pocket of my jeans and I couldn't read it anymore."

"The number's been busy, Carrie. Did you take the phone off the—"

"He called again. And he spoke to me, and the things he said to me. I-I don't know how he got this number. How'd he know I wasn't at my old house anymore? He said there's no place I could go where he wouldn't find me."

"Jesus, Carr—"

"So I called the police department and they called the sheriff's department, and just like before, it's the pre-paid cell and they don't know who's calling, but this time—this time he was close. He was just ten miles away from me."

"Oh, God."

"And I *know* he knows where I am. I'm afraid, Sam. There's a cop parked outside the house, but I'm still afraid."

"God, Carrie, what can I—"

"And I washed the card with your number on it, and I tried to get it. I checked the phone directory and called information trying to find your number."

"I'm not listed—"

"I was afraid you'd think I didn't want to talk to you, but I did. I really d—"

"Carrie, stop," Sam cut in. "Are you okay? Tell me you're okay."

Something about the sound of his voice made her give in to the rush of emotions that bubbled to the surface. "Yes. No. Oh, hell, I don't know!"

Tears flowed, hot and heavy, down her cheeks, as she paced back and forth, trying to calm herself. It didn't help. Nothing helped, and before she knew it, she was blubbering into the phone like a two year old.

The hammering in Sam's chest increased as his panic level rose. "Listen to me, Carrie. Everything will be okay." His voice sounded calmer than he felt. If only he knew whose sick ass to kick for this. "Can you hear me?"

"Y-yes."

"I'll be there in an hour or less. I'll leave this minute."

"I-I d-don't know, S-Sam."

"Let me come over, Carrie. I only want to help." Sam paced his living room, one hand clutched at the back of his neck as the other pressed the phone close to his ear. He felt the strongest need to help her, to hold her as she cried. "How do I get there once I get into Gardiner, Carrie? Give me some directions." His heart broke at the sound of soft sobbing.

Finally, she sputtered, "I'll b-be o-ok-kay. M-my n-nerves are shot, th-that's all."

He continued to speak in soothing tones. "I want to go to you, Carrie. Tell me how to get there."

"Oh, God, this is so hu-m-miliating," she stammered. "And my head is k-killing m-me."

"Do you have any aspirin in the house? Maybe a shot of whiskey?"

"I don't know, g-give me your number again and I'll c-call you back in a while."

Sam hated to end the connection with her. "Please, let me go to you, Carrie."

"I c-can't let you do that, Sam," she said. "I'll call you. Give me your number."

He sighed, praying it wasn't a line. He called out the digits, then cleared his throat. "Maybe you should take your phone off the hook until you're ready to call back."

"You b-bet you're a-ass, I will."

He smiled at her return of spirit. "Promise you'll call me back?"

"I p-promise, Sam."

"Okay." He hit the disconnect button and set the phone down on the counter.

Sam paced back and forth in his small living room. A room that, until one week ago, held nothing but a sofa, recliner, console television set, and a space heater against one wall. Now it boasted a seven-foot tall, fresh-cut Christmas tree in the corner by the windows. Every pass of his body sent the smell of pine wafting through the air.

The full tree, sparsely decorated with a handful of wooden ornaments he'd found in a discarded box and some colored lights, mirrored the room's emptiness—both victims of the death of a marriage.

He waited a full forty-five minutes before breaking down to call her back. By then it was nearly nine p.m.

"Hey, Sam." She sounded stronger, although still somewhat hesitant.

"You sound better. Are you okay?"

"I'm embarrassed."

"You should be. You broke your promise."

"I'm sorry, Sam. I'm mortified at falling apart like that. I just couldn't make myself call."

"Don't feel that way with me, Carrie." He stopped pacing as silence filled the airwaves. "Are you there?" His shoulders drooped in relief at the sound of her slow, but audible, exhale.

"I'm here. I swear I was fine until I heard your voice."

"Well, hell, that can't be good."

"Actually, it is," she began. "It's like talking to my mom when I'm upset but trying to hold it together. If I hear her voice, it's over with. I fall apart. She makes me feel secure enough to let go."

Another silent pause filled the airwaves, as Sam let her comment sink in. "I'm taking that as a compliment."

"You should."

He stood in front of a grouping of various-sized framed mirrors, one of the few things Linda had left when she walked out. His smile at her comment reflected back in multiples. "So, can I go to you?"

"Sam—"

"Just say the word, Carrie."

"Thanks for offering, but I can't ask you to do that. Tomorrow is a busy day for me," she said. "I've got to help my mom with some baking for Christmas Eve. I'm sure you have some last-minute shopping and other things to do."

"I'm actually done with my Christmas shopping."

"No last minute food preparation?"

Sam chuckled. "Nope. I only have the one big meal with my family and kids on Sunday, and leftovers for lunch on Christmas Day. I'm a poor bachelor, so they don't ask me to bring anything but my bright, shining countenance."

"Of course. I'd forgotten how shamelessly your mom and sisters spoil you, Baby Sam. "

Ever since the day she'd heard about his nickname, he'd had to put up with her merciless teasing. "I bet you look good in envy green."

"Bright, shining countenance, my ass," she grumbled.

Sam chuckled. "Hey, I figure as long as they don't ask for my *incontinence*, I'm okay."

Her laughter rang out, sounding light-hearted and sincere. "How do you do that?"

"Do what?" He remembered how it felt to hold her face in his hands earlier—wished he could do it again.

"Take me from feeling really crappy to laughing so quickly."

"I'm glad I could help you out." *Damn this feels right.*

Another hour of phone talk revealed a wealth of information about each other. As ten o'clock neared, Sam heard Carrie's failed attempt to suppress a yawn.

"I'd better let you go, lady."

"Yeah, I'm tired," she admitted. "But your phone call saved the evening for me."

He gave one loud 'ahem' to brace himself. "Here's the thing, Carrie. I tell myself to go slow with you, so I don't scare you off. I mean, hell, I've been single a lot longer than you have, and I'm ready to move on with my life. But you may not be ready yet."

"Mentally or physically," she added. "I've had three kids, two of them a set of twins. Big twins. God, I was huge. My body, Sam. It's-I-I don't look like I did the last time I dated."

He identified with the self-doubt in her voice. "You think I do? Do you honestly think I don't have all the same insecurities as you?" He waited out her prolonged pause at his question. She finally responded with a lowly spoken comment.

"I haven't had sex in over a year."

"That long?"

She gave a sudden gasp. "Sweet Jesus, did I say that out loud?"

"Either that or I'm incredibly adept at reading your mind."

"I have to go now," she groaned.

"Carrie, wait."

"Goodbye Sa—"

He cut off her words. "Listen to me. All I'm trying to say is that maybe we could allow ourselves the chance to be happy again." When she didn't end the call, he lowered his tone, hoping to comfort and encourage her. "I care about you, Carrie, and I won't hurt you the way he did."

Her sniff had him worrying she was crying again. "Are you all right?"

"I'm okay. It's just that you make me feel special."

"You are special."

Several seconds passed before she spoke again. "Thank you."

"Yes, ma'am, I aim to please."

"Good night, Sam."

"Good night, Carrie."

Sam dropped the phone on the sofa and walked over to the large, sparsely-decorated tree. He watched the multi-colored lights twinkle in the semi-darkness of his living room and wondered what Carrie would think of this place. He'd called this simple wood structure home for two decades. He'd always thought it was good enough. But would she?

He gave it a slow walk-through, taking mental notes of things he could change to make it more appealing. New carpets, paint, fancier trims, and built-ins. Would it matter to her?

He walked onto the front porch and gazed out at the houses up and down his street, most decorated and ready for Christmas. What would she think of this town? His ties were here, but hers were in Gardiner. Would she be willing to pull up roots if they ended up together? *If.* He didn't want to think about the shape he'd be in *if* this didn't work out.

He remembered the day J.C. caught him watching Carrie at the office. His co-worker had given him a hearty slap on the back. *"You're a goner, man. Don't even try to deny it, it's written all over your face."*

A noise from the vacant rent house on the corner lured him out to the end of the sidewalk. He saw the owner, and old classmate of his, struggling to unload a washer from his truck. Sam hurried over to help, arriving just as one corner of the washer tilted dangerously off the bed of the pick-up.

"I got it, Len." He shifted the weight of the appliance to his shoulder. "Damn buddy, next time come ask me for help before you try to do something like this."

The small framed man peered around the corner of the washer. "Thanks, Sam. Ten years ago, I could have handled this son of a bitch by myself. Now I'm glad for the help."

Within ten minutes, the two men had both the washer and dryer placed in the home's utility room.

Sam brushed his hands on his jeans and stepped back to look around. "You've got this place looking good, man. I hadn't been in it since old man

Bordelon lived here." He squatted to pass his hand over the glossy floors. "New oak flooring in a rent house?" His low whistle pierced the air. "Business must be good."

Len muttered a string of curses under his breath. "Those last renters had two dogs in here—big dogs—Rottweiler breed. I had to replace every floor in here. I figured I'll put this in and I'll be finished for a while."

"Until the next pet-owning renter comes along."

"Nope. No more animals. That's what the fenced in backyard is for."

Sam checked out the neat three-bedroom home and turned to the other man. "Who's my new neighbor?"

Len hooked his thumbs on the loops of his carpenter jeans. "I don't have anyone yet. I was so disgusted at the shape of this place, I nearly sold it." He released a deep sigh as he scanned the surroundings. "But, it was Gayle's mom and dad's old place." He paused for a few seconds to clear his throat. "Before she died, she told me to hang on to it for Scott. I figured I'd rent it out and any money I make goes into my boy's college fund account." He nodded and blinked a couple of times. "That's a better start than I ever had."

Sam kept quiet, leaving his friend to his thoughts. He knew Gayle had suffered for two years battling ovarian cancer and that Len and Scott suffered every day they lived without her.

"We sure miss her, Sam."

"I know you do, buddy. Makes you wonder sometimes, with all the awful people walking this earth."

"Anyway." Len's voice boomed, belying his small stature, "Know anybody decent who needs a rent house?"

Sam cocked his head to the side and looked down at the man. "I know somebody I'd sure as hell like to see in here, but I bet it's too steep for her, even if I could convince her to move from Gardiner. Divorced, raising three teenagers, and she has dog's but she's mentioned them being outside pets."

"Is she a friend of yours or something more?"

"A friend, but I'm hoping for more," he admitted, giving his old buddy an ear-splitting grin.

Len nodded. "Good for you, Sam. I'd let her have it cheap. Two hundred a month and I could easily get six for this place. All appliances included, even a new washer and dryer. If you can vouch for her, it'd be worth it to me to have someone in here that won't trash the place."

Hours later, Sam lay in bed, wide-awake and imagining what it would be like if Carrie lived a few houses down from him. He mentally prepared a list of *pros* to use in his favor next time he spoke to her and slipped in a quick wish for the cons to take care of themselves. Though he considered himself more of a 'have a chat with the man upstairs' type of guy than a praying man, he added something a little more specific tonight.

All I want for Christmas is Carrie. Please, keep her safe and let her come to me.

Chapter Nine

The day before Christmas Eve proved to be uneventful for Sam. Perusing the local pharmacy for some OTC meds for Nick's lingering cold, he stopped at the greeting card section on his way to checkout.

A holiday card *To the One I Love* caught his attention and he picked it up. He scanned it, along with a few others, and returned them to the slots, knowing he wouldn't find anything appropriate. He settled for a blank card with a beautiful Christmas Village scene and paid for his purchases. It wouldn't hurt to jot down a few thoughts for the next time he saw her.

On his way out, he stopped at the display of animated toys—singing Santa's, Dancing Reindeer, and a dog that barked *Here Comes Santa Claus*. Just as he was about to leave, he found something at the back of the tallest shelf. Grinning at how right it was for the situation, he walked back to the counter to pay for it. *Just in case.* He walked out of the store, as pleased as a first grader bringing a gift home to his mother.

Carrie's day was going quite differently. She'd awakened with a stress/crying/alcohol-induced headache, but at least the puffy eyes were minimal, thanks to Sam. Her thoughts lingered on him as she paused from filling a box with baking supplies. One corner of her lip curved at the heady excitement of possibilities. She caught sight of her reflection in one of the glass-inset doors of Christie's upper cabinets.

"Stop it," she chided herself, forcing the silly grin from her face. No way would she get her hopes up. She'd concentrate on getting her own place and leave her friendship with Sam at that.

They'd learned a lot about each other during that marathon phone call, and he'd asked again to take her to dinner and a movie. Again, she'd refused, afraid to upset her kids. She could take losing anyone's respect but her children's. *How did Dave do it? How could he do the things he did and not worry what their kids thought of him?*

She loaded the box in the backseat of her car. By the time she went back to get her purse, she had to stop to answer the phone, tensing only slightly as she waited for an answer.

"Hey, Sis!"

Tension rolled off Carrie's shoulders as she heard Christie's voice, thankful it wasn't *his*. "Are you and Max back in town?"

"No, and it turns out I won't be leaving until tomorrow. I want to give Max more time with his dad. I should be back at Mom's for lunch though. I tried to call you last night, but I think the phone was off the hook, because I kept getting a busy signal."

Carrie was quiet for a minute trying to decide how to break the news to her sister. "It was off the hook until nine, and then I was talking to Sam for an hour."

"Sam—from work? What did y'all talk about?"

"I'm warning you now, Chris, this is one of those drag-me-to-hell-and-back stories that'll make you want to pop a Prozac."

"I've got time. What's going on?"

Carrie filled her in on the events of the previous evening.

"So, you're telling me that guy not only knows my phone number, but also where I live, and he's getting closer all the time?"

"Afraid so, Sis. In addition, I feel like I brought it all on you myself. I need to find another place to stay."

"Where could you go, Carrie? You shouldn't be alone."

"Are you saying I should have my kids with me when this guy shows up? Or how about you and Max, would that be better?" Carrie's voice rose to a level of near hysteria. Silence on the other end of the phone told her the reality of the situation had finally sunk in. "The longer I stay here, the more danger I put you and Max in, Chris."

"But what will you do? Where will you go?"

"I have no idea, but I sure don't want to drag anyone else in my family into this situation. Since you're not coming back tonight, I guess I don't have to worry about it until tomorrow. Rob said he'd post someone outside the house again tonight. I'm just glad I had Sam to talk to last night."

"Is this Sam guy *really* that nice, or is your judgment impaired because of HWS?"

"What the hell is HWS?"

"A little condition I call *Horny Woman Syndrome*."

The small living room echoed with Carrie's laughter. "As it happens, I'm quite familiar with the condition, but I really think he is that nice, Chris. He's funny too. He had me laughing so hard I choked on my drink. Trust me, Southern Comfort is smooth going down, but it bites like hell when it comes up through your nose."

Christie's laugh rang across the phone line. "Was that *my* Southern Comfort?"

"Not anymore, but I'll buy you some more."

"Don't worry about it, but I tell you what. You arrange for me to meet Mr. Sam Langley, and I'll let you know if your *condition* isn't making you biased. A woman will allow some crazy things when she's gone without it for a while."

"It?" Carrie asked, anxious to hear what her sister would add.

"Yes, *it*...and I'm not just talking about sex. I'm talking about all the other stuff that can't be replaced by silicone and batteries."

"You're a sick puppy."

"Uh huh, wait and see."

Carrie chuckled into the phone. "You could be right, you know. Everyone's on their best behavior when they first meet. Sure, he may *look* normal, but how do I know he doesn't have a closet full of black leather, whips, and ball gags?"

"Ew!" Christie groaned. "Who's the sick puppy now?"

Carrie's mom, Elaine Hebert, met her at the front door of her home, three miles south of town. "Hey, darlin', how are you?"

Carrie bent at the waist to hug the woman who'd given birth to eight children in fourteen years. "I'm good, Mom."

Elaine studied her daughter's face. "You've been crying, haven't you? What did Dave do?"

Carrie smiled at her mother. "Nothing, but I thought I did a good job of getting rid of the puffiness."

Elaine reached up to touch her daughter's cheek below one eye. "Just a touch around the eyes. Now, what happened?"

"I wish it was just Dave, Mom." Carrie sat with her mother as she explained the situation.

"You need to move in here with me."

"Absolutely not."

"Why not? Your brother Mack is right next door."

"Yeah, along with his pregnant wife and child. Nope, I'm not going to do that."

"What will you do then, if you don't want to stay with me or Christie?"

"Well, I was thinking maybe I'd call Dave and ask him to stay in the house until this situation is behind me."

Elaine stared at her daughter, then got up to jerk open the door of her fridge. She reached inside for the massive turkey. "Surely we can think of a better solution than that."

Carrie maneuvered her mother gently out of the way to lift the bird from the fridge and placed it in the stainless steel sink. "I don't see anything else to do right now, Mom."

"Maybe it's Dave making the phone calls to get you to do exactly this."

Carrie turned to stare at her mother. "Oh, my God, you sound like Sam."

"Sam who?"

Carrie closed her eyes and sighed. "Somebody I work with. It doesn't matter, because you're both on the wrong track."

"So, the phone was off the hook, and that's why I couldn't get hold of you last night. I nearly called Kathleen to go check on you."

"Kathleen? Oh, Rob LeDoux's mom. I keep forgetting she lives next door to Christie." She sucked in her breath, suddenly feeling guilty for making her mom worry. "Glad you didn't do that. I was fine." Carrie placed her hand on her mother's shoulder. "I'd like your opinion on something."

Elaine filled two stoneware mugs with steaming coffee and placed them on the table before seating herself. "What's going on?"

Carrie stared into her mother's eyes, wishing she knew beforehand what her reaction would be. "The phone wasn't off the hook the entire time last night. I was talking to a friend of mine."

Elaine's mouth opened and she nodded, giving Carrie her classic I'm-not-surprised look. "Was it Sam, the guy you work with?"

"Uh, yes it was. How'd you know?"

"Just a feeling, dear," Elaine said. "So, it's happened."

Carrie's mouth snapped closed. "What's happened?"

"You've found someone new."

Her mother poured creamer into her coffee, acting as calmly as though her daughter—*this* daughter—found a new man every other week. "Well, Sam and I are friends, but that's as far as it's gone." She faltered and gazed down at the table, turning her cup nervously until the hot liquid splashed over the top. "He's asked, but I haven't accepted any dates from him."

Elaine raised her cup to her mouth, one brow lifting noticeably. "Why not? Don't you like him?"

"I like him a lot."

"Is he married?"

"Divorced."

"Is he a criminal?"

"No." Carrie bit on her lower lip to keep a straight face, torn between wanting to and *not* wanting to tell Sam about this conversation.

Elaine brought her cup to her lips and paused. "What's your dilemma?"

"It's too soon to date. I've only been divorced four months. I'm afraid my kids would have a fit. I don't think Lauren could handle this now—"

"Good Lord, it sounds like you're reading from one of Letterman's Lists." She splayed her hands up as though she were framing a marquis. "The Top Ten Reasons Carrie Should Never Date Again."

Carrie released a tortured sigh as she gazed across at her mother. "It's too soon for me to date . . . isn't it?"

Elaine lifted her mug. "I don't know. Are you grieving over the divorce?"

"God, no."

"Is he a good man?"

"I think so."

"Then he probably is. You'd know all the danger signals, thanks to the father of my three gorgeous grandchildren." She sipped her coffee and threw in the traditional southern accompaniment to any insult. "Bless his heart."

"Jesus, Mom. I thought for sure you'd give me the old 'find yourself first' speech."

"Are you lost?"

"No, I don't think so."

Elaine's laughter echoed through the cozy kitchen. "Well, I'd think you'd know if you were."

Carrie blinked several times in an effort to process this conversation.

Elaine covered her daughter's hand. "Look, Honey, I'm over seventy years old, and if there's one thing I've learned over the years it's this: It's never too late or too *soon* to find joy in your life. If you think you need some time alone to 'find yourself,' then take that time. If not, go for it. *You* make the rules now, remember?"

Carrie's worried brow lifted. "I do, don't I?" She gazed into the eyes of the woman who'd doled out unconditional love to eight children. "But, *you're* happy alone."

"I am. If I want to read until five o'clock in the morning and sleep until noon, there's no one to stop me, except maybe someone from the Garden Club Committee."

"Or the Museum Committee," Carrie added.

"Or the Ladies' Altar Society."

Carrie smiled at her mother. "The point is, maybe I should be more like you."

"You mean alone for the rest of your life?" Elaine asked. "Why the hell would you want to do that? Your dad and I were married over forty years when he died."

"You could have remarried. Remember when Mr. Potier called you for a date a few years back?"

"He was an old man then, and he's even older now." She waved her hands before her. "I've had my great love. I married your father when he was young, gorgeous, and in his prime. It took years to train him the little I could. I have no desire to start whipping another old man into shape at my age." She patted Carrie's hand. "You're too young to give up on finding love again."

"But the kids—"

"Will go to college, leave home, and have families of their own one day." She caught Carrie's hand in her own. "And it'll happen sooner than you care to admit. Do you want to be alone when that happens?"

Carrie studied her mother's face, still beautiful for a woman her age. "I don't want to hurt them."

"You're a good mother, and your children love you. They'll adjust to any changes you make right now. This is *your* time, Carrie—your time to make the changes that will affect the rest of your lives. They'll have their time later."

She passed her hands through hair white as a cotton ball. "I can't tell you what you should or shouldn't do. I just want to see you happy for a change. If you can do that alone, fine. But if finding a good man who you can be happy and grow old with makes it easier for you, that's fine too." Elaine sat back and relaxed in her chair. "So, tell me about this Sam who wants to date you."

"Sam Langley is from Kenton." She placed one hand on her stomach to calm the butterflies she felt just from speaking his name. Carrie gave her the low down on Sam then lifted her gaze to meet her mothers. "He makes me laugh."

Elaine's face creased with a knowing smile. "And those are all qualities you want in a man, but does he melt your butter?"

Carrie's mouth fell open at her mother's frankness. "Ew—I so don't want to have this conversation with you."

Her mother's eyes twinkled with mischievous laughter. "Well, he sure has put a smile on your face and a sparkle back in your eye. As your *mother,"* Elaine said the word with emphasis, "I can tell you it's been too damn long since I've seen you like this. Will you see him over the holidays?"

"I wasn't planning to."

"Didn't you say Grant and the twins would be with Dave tonight and tomorrow night?"

Carrie used a paper towel to wipe up her coffee spill from the table. "Yes, so they can visit with their Texas cousins, but they'll be here tomorrow for lunch."

"Does Sam have plans tonight?"

"No, he's alone tonight too." Carrie drained her cup and set it in the sink. "His kids have something with their mom tonight and tomorrow. Where's the pan for the turkey?"

Elaine pulled a large aluminum roaster from a bottom shelf and handed it to Carrie. "I don't see a reason in the world why you two can't go on a friendly date. Why don't you go out and have some fun?"

Carrie pulled out what she needed to inject the turkey, then paused as she thought about her mother's comment. "You really think it would be okay?"

"Go on, sweetie. Have some fun while you're young."

Sam studied the number flashing on his phone's screen, recognizing the number Carrie had given him to her mom's place in Gardiner. "Carrie, is everything all right?"

"Everything's fine, Sam. Is this a bad time to call?"

"Not at all. What's up, pretty girl?"

"Christie won't be home until tomorrow, and I don't care to sit at home all night."

Sam held his breath as his heart pounded out the George of the Jungle kettledrum rhythm in his chest.

"So, I was wondering . . . "

God, I want to see her so bad.

"If you don't have anything to do tonight . . ."

"I don't." *Come on baby. Say the words I want to hear.*

"How about we go on that first date?"

He clenched his fist in victory while struggling to keep his voice calm. "Sure. We still talking dinner and a movie?"

"Sounds great."

"What time can I pick you up?"

"Maybe I should meet you in Kenton. There's not much to do here in Gardiner."

Sam glanced around, thinking of everything that he'd need to do before she got here. "I'd love to have you here, but I hate the idea of you driving all the way to Kenton."

"The nearest theater to Gardiner is an hour drive. Besides, I need to get away. I'm on edge over here."

"We'll do whatever you want." He gave her directions, and they ended the call. Sam set down the phone, unable to believe his luck. "Time to crank it up, old boy. You've got a date."

By two o'clock, Carrie and Elaine had finished with the meal preparations. She drove back to town and pulled in at a gift shop boasting a huge sale. Fifteen minutes later, she walked out with a small gift box for Sam, along with a card.

At four-thirty sharp, she slipped into short leather boots and smoothed down a burgundy sweater over black jeans. Trying to ignore the battle of nerves playing out inside her stomach, she applied her favorite perfume and grabbed her purse. Carrie took one last look at the mirror over the entry table and pulled open the front door. Her breath rushed out of her lungs at the sight before her.

Chapter Ten

Dave stood in her doorway, one hand fisted midair in pre-knock position. The other gripped a huge bouquet of red and white roses in a cut crystal vase. His gaze seared her as though she were a piece of meat on a hot grill.

"Where the hell you going looking like that?"

The accusation in his tone turned the ball of nervousness inside her stomach into anger. Instead of trying to come up with a way to defend her actions, she remembered her mother's words from that morning. *You make the rules now.*

She stiffened her spine. "Is there something you need? I'm about to leave."

He shoved the flowers at her. "I brought you these as an early Christmas gift."

Carrie grabbed at the flowers and raised a one brow skeptically. "You never brought me *real* roses in all the years we were together. Why now?"

"Because I want to make amends for all the times I didn't bring you any."

Her eyes narrowed suspiciously. "What are you up to?"

"Nothing. I'm not up to anything."

"Dave—"

"Look, that house just isn't the same without you there, Babe. I want you to come back home."

"So, you're saying you want me to move back home."

His face lit up. "Yes! Exactly."

"And you'll be—where? At your mom's?"

"No, I'll be at the house with you, of course."

"With me. As a couple, you mean?"

"Well, sure, as a couple."

"No, thank you."

His brow furrowed. "You took the roses."

She shoved them back at him, forcing him to take hold of the vase. "No, I didn't."

"You didn't answer my question. Where are you going all dolled up like that?" His tone was hard and edgy.

"I don't believe that's any of your business." She leaned around him, glancing at his pick-up. "Where are the kids?"

He moved to block her view of his truck as well as her path out of the door. "At Mom's. You didn't answer me."

Carrie's mood darkened considerably. "I don't have to answer you."

He leaned in closer. "I asked you a question."

She didn't reply, but tapped her foot and raised her wrist to glance at her watch. "You've got thirty seconds to tell me why you're here." She pushed the sleeves of her sweater up to her elbows. "And then I'm leaving."

"You bitch! I see right through you, you know. Who are you screwing?"

She stuck her finger in his face. "You almost had me going Dave. Who did you get to make those phone calls? Some guy you work with? To think I chewed Sam's butt for accusing you of doing exactly what you did. And Mom agreed with him."

"What the hell are you talking about? What phone calls? And who the hell is Sam?" Dave's face scrunched in a mask of confusion that would have convinced her any other time. Now she knew better than to fall for it.

"I defended you." She shook her head. "I should have known better. God, I'm such an idiot."

Dave splayed one hand. "I don't know wh—"

"Sure you don't, jerk. I'm leaving now." She pushed past him, then closed and locked the door. She'd only taken two steps before he jerked her around by the arm.

"Stop, dammit. I want to talk to you."

The old version of Carrie, the 1.0 version, would have attempted to reason with him. The newer, improved version knew reasoning wouldn't work and had no desire to try. Not with Sam waiting.

Carrie wrenched her arm away and glared at him. "Get your hands off of me." Clutching her keys tightly, she spun around and walked to her car. Just when she thought she'd escape without any further trouble, he pinned her against the car door from behind.

"I want you, Carrie." His breath was hot and moist near her ear. "You know you want me. We were always so damned good together."

Her outrage turned to amusement at his ludicrous proposition. The initial on-set of low chuckles increased in volume, turning into uncontrollable guffaws.

Dave pushed away from her, his foul curses reverberating across the small yard into the quiet neighborhood.

Carrie turned to face him, wiping tears of laughter from her eyes. "Come on, Dave, we're divorced. It's over. Neither of us has wanted the other in years, and we've never been good together. Can't you be honest with yourself?"

He stepped closer and raised his volume a notch. "I've always wanted you."

"Along with any other woman you could get."

"I still want you."

"Uh huh—along with any other woman you can get." She tightened her grip on her car keys and stared him down. "But I don't want you anymore." She got in her car and closed the door. Hoping for the end of the drama, she pressed the automatic lock button.

"Carrie, you have to come home now." His voice was slightly muffled through the closed window.

"Just stop creating a spectacle of yourself and go home to our kids."

"Screw you!" He reared back, and threw the vase of roses into the windshield.

Carrie jumped at the resounding *crack* of glass against glass. The thick vase bounced off and landed with a thud in the grass that lined the driveway. She stared at the fracture line travelling across the upper part of the windshield until it encompassed its entire length. Red and white rose petals littered the glass, along with one snapped bud that settled at the base, jammed inside a wiper blade.

Her heart pounded with a rush of adrenaline as she tried to steady her breathing. She squeezed her eyes shut and took two calming breaths. By the time she opened them, Dave had leaned over to investigate the damage.

"Great. Just great, asshole."

Dave gave her his typical "Yeah, I screwed up, but it's too late to take it back" look, which was about the closest he ever came to a sincere apology. She glared at him through the fractured glass, the jagged lines further proof that divorcing him had been the right thing to do.

Two minutes later, Carrie walked into the police station, shaken, but determined to show Dave she was as strong, if not stronger, than him.

Chief Rob Ledoux glanced at her from his desk, his phone to his ear. He nodded at her while speaking to the person on the phone. "She just walked in, Mom, it's alright. I know, Mom. Yes, ma'am. I'll take care of it right away." Rob hung up the phone and stood to place a comforting hand on her shoulder. "My mother saw the whole thing from her front door. Are you hurt?"

"Damn, I keep forgetting Ms. Kathleen lives next door. I wondered if he'd disturbed any of the neighbors."

"*That* neighbor is quite disturbed and good and pissed at your ex." Rob led Carrie out the door of his office, then told the dispatcher to have someone find Dave and bring him in for questioning. He turned back to Carrie. "Mom told me to 'put that crazy S-O-B in jail and throw away the key.'"

He followed her outside and shook his head as he checked out her windshield. "I'm glad you came by to report this. I've seen too many women ignore situations, when all they had to do was make a report to raise a warning flag. This is the second one, in his case. One more and he'll get jail time." He picked up the red rose bud that had jammed behind the wiper blade. "Didn't like the color?"

Carrie released a disgusted sniff. "Son of a bitch never once gave me roses when we were married."

Rob chuckled at her answer. "I'll talk to him about having this repaired. You shouldn't have to file it with your insurance."

"Thanks. Is it safe to drive until then?"

He examined the break again. "I think so. I hope that we can avoid any further confrontations between you two, but just in case, I want you to be careful, okay? Whatever you do, don't take any threats lightly."

His words reminded Carrie how convenient life in a small town could be when everyone knows everyone else. "Thanks, but it happened just in time. I was really starting to worry about those phone calls. Now that I know it's him, I'm not worried."

"Wait, he confessed to making the calls?"

"No, I know he couldn't have made them, but I also know he put someone up to it."

"How do you know?"

"The timing is too perfect, Rob. He waited until he knew I was good and scared to ask me to move back home with him. He really expected me to say yes."

"That all sounds good, and I hope that's exactly the way it happened. But we don't have any proof, and Dave would be a fool to admit to it. To be safe, I want you to be careful."

"I will, but I'm telling you, it's not necessary."

"Yeah, well, humor me, okay? I'll have someone park at Christie's tonight, just in case."

"I'm about to leave town, and probably won't be back until late. Christie and Max won't be back until tomorrow."

"Well, then, stop at the station on your way home and have the patrolman follow you there."

"All right, if you insist."

They walked back into his office and he pulled out a form. "Now, the fact that he did it while you were sitting behind the window indicates a threat to your person." He handed her the form and a pen. "Here, fill this out, please."

Carrie spent the next few minutes filling out a complaint and pushed the paper at him. Once Rob took pictures of the damage, she was free to go. Just as she opened her car door to leave, Dave drove up in his truck, escorted by a police cruiser. He stepped out of the vehicle, his face a depiction of angry resistance.

Rob pointed at Dave and spoke in a voice booming with authority. "*You!* Stay put until I tell you otherwise." He turned back to Carrie and spoke in a calm manner. "You call if anything else happens."

She nodded. "Thanks, Rob." Determined not to show Dave any fear, she turned to him and pointed to her car window. "And thanks for the early Christmas gift, Dave. This one has you written all over it. I know the kids will appreciate it."

Dave leveled an icy glare in her direction but kept his silence.

As soon as she drove off, Carrie's calm façade fragmented dangerously fast. A strong mixture of waning adrenaline and righteous fury had her struggling to hold back tears. She snapped up a tissue from the box on her console and dabbed at her eyes. If she cried, there went the make-up. "Oh, come on," she spoke to her reflection. "Get pissed if you have to, but do *not* cry. Don't you *dare* cry."

As a distraction, she turned the car radio to a station playing continuous Christmas music. For the entire hour drive to Kenton, Carrie sang along as loud as she could. When she got to Kenton, she pulled out Sam's directions. By the time she saw the big, blue cross in his front yard, she nearly cried out with relief.

Carrie rolled to a stop next to Sam's truck and turned off the ignition. She stepped out of the car and stared at the doorway just opening to reveal his bulk. The crisp, cool air of the December evening restored her, and she managed to get to the porch without falling apart. However, the glare he aimed at the window of her car deflated her reserve as quickly as a ten-penny nail in a bicycle tire. By the time she reached him, she wanted nothing more than to bury her sobs in his embrace.

Sam was so glad to see her he nearly missed the broken window. Once he saw it, a cold fury for the man he knew had to be responsible flooded through his system. He riveted his gaze back to the only important factor. Carrie looked like a lady whose tenuous hold on a wildcat had about broken loose. He brushed his fury aside long enough to open his arms.

They stood on his front porch just outside the doorway of his home, for God and everyone to see, for a full five minutes. He rubbed shoulders that practically vibrated with nervous tension, praying the bastard hadn't touched her. They stood, Carrie's face buried in his chest, her arms wrapped tightly around his waist. He rocked from side to side, keeping his silence until she pushed away with a renewed grip on her emotions.

"You okay?" He didn't trust himself to ask more than that.

She nodded and wiped at the corner of her eye. "I am now, but it was a long drive. Can you show me where your restroom is, please?"

Once she'd stepped into his bathroom, he walked out to get a closer look at her car. His jaw clenched furiously as he examined the jagged crack in the windshield. God, he hoped she wasn't in the driver's seat when that happened.

He walked back into the house to pace impatiently until she rejoined him.

By the time Carrie emerged, looking relatively unscathed, Sam was the one tied in knots.

She approached slowly and lifted her gaze to his. "Hey."

Once more, he reined in his anger for her. "Hey, pretty girl. You ready to talk about it yet?"

She released a trembling breath. "Dave showed up at my door just as I was leaving. If I'd left one minute earlier, I'd have missed him." She lifted one finger. "There is a bright side to this."

Sam shifted uneasily and clasped his hands behind his head, squeezing his elbows together. "I'd love to hear it right about now."

She placed her hand gently on his chest to calm him.

"Go on, tell me the rest."

"I'm sure he's behind the phone calls, Sam. I think you and my mom were both right."

Once he heard everything she and Rob had discussed, he grunted his approval. "It sounds like the Chief's on the ball."

"He is. Now, can we please drop the subject for the rest of the night?"

Sam smiled and stepped back to drink in her appearance. "You always look good, but—wow. Is all this for me?"

She made a show of looking around the room. "Actually, it's for that other guy I saw lounging around here—"

He pulled her close. "Always the smart ass."

"Would you want me any other way?" One delicate brow arched in question.

"Absolutely not."

He locked his arms around her, luxuriating in her warmth, her soft curves, and her smell, spicy and sensual. He felt the rightness of her being here, like some missing piece of his life had fallen neatly into place.

She buried her nose in the front of his shirt and groaned, low and inviting. "God, you smell good."

He rested his chin on the top of her head. "It feels good having you here, Carrie."

"It feels good being here. It's easier than I thought it'd be."

He grinned at the strangeness of her thoughts mirroring his. "Is it?"

She nodded and pulled away from him. "It's too easy."

She looked around, seeming to appraise his home, and he wished again he had more to offer.

"So, I've already seen the bathroom. Want to show me around the rest of your place?"

"It's nothing fancy. I'm a simple man, I guess, but it's been my home-sweet-home for twenty years." He grimaced at painful memories. "Sometimes it was sweet, anyway—other times, not so much." He showed her the living room, kitchen, and small dining area in the back.

"This place has good bones, but it does seem a little bare."

"Linda took a few things with her when she left initially, then a few more things over the last year or so."

She bobbed her head in agreement. "Two bachelors living alone—yeah, it looks a little like a man cave."

"I guess I got used to it. Would you like a beer or something? I've got your favorite."

"Just in case you thought you could get me drunk and have your way with me?" she teased.

"You know I wouldn't do that, don't you?"

Carrie gave him a playful shove on his arm. "I know that. I'll take that beer, thanks." She accepted the long neck bottle from him. "How'd you know this was my favorite beer?"

"I heard you tell J.C. a couple of months ago," he answered.

"You paid attention that long ago?"

He opened a door and nodded. "Here's the spare room . . . and here's my room." He reached out to push open the partially closed door to reveal his California-king-size bed.

Her eyes widened noticeably. "That's a big ole bed."

"Too big, lately," he murmured.

"What?"

"Uh, I'm tall, so I need a big bed." He led her to the back end of the house, where the dining room and second bath were located.

After Carrie admired his various pieces of woodworking, which included the dining room table, she pointed to a doorway at the end of the back hall. "What's through there?"

"Nick's room, and it's not fit for human eyes."

Carrie raised her hand. "Say no more. I don't go into Grant's room unless my tetanus shot is up to date. You keep a neat house, Sam."

He burst into nervous laughter. "It wasn't quite this neat when you called. I mopped and did some laundry."

"Just for me?"

Sam beamed at her and nodded. "You impressed?"

"I am."

He turned, remembering the gift he'd bought her. "Hold on a sec, I got a little something for you." He walked into his bedroom to retrieve the gift. By the time he got back to her, she held a wrapped gift in her hands. "Great minds think alike, I guess." He held a gift bag up to her. "Merry Christmas, Carrie."

She opened the card first and smiled at the Christmas Village scene. She remained silent as she read what he'd written on the blank surface:

Carrie,

Thank you for taking a chance on me. I plan to make sure you don't regret it.

Merry Christmas,

Sam

He watched her blink rapidly, as though to keep tears back.

"Thank you, Sam." She put the card gently aside and turned her attention to the package. She pulled out the sheets of tissue to reveal a stuffed alligator with a wreath around its neck and carrying a sign in its mouth that boasted *Cajun Christmas Greetings.* The bag also contained a package of Magnolia scented potpourri.

A wide smile spread across her face as she looked at the stuffed gator. "How adorable. Thank you, Sam. I love it." She turned around and gave him a hug. "Now, it's your turn." She handed him the box and card.

He read the card first and thanked her, then opened the boxed 'Facts for Fun' note block, each sheet bordered with interesting facts and statements.

"May you never run out of useless information, Sam."

"Man, I love reading stuff like this. Thank You, Carrie."

He leaned toward her, and brushed her lips lightly with a kiss, then backed away. His gaze locked onto hers like a beacon, and within moments he'd pulled Carrie into his arms for another kiss; this one deep, penetrating, and perfect. Sam knew he got it right when she shivered and arched her back like a cat. Tongues softly explored, lips molded, heads tilted ever so slightly to achieve just the right angle for optimum contact. Her arms looped around his neck to cling as tightly as he did. He hadn't experienced a kiss like that in too damn long.

He ended it slowly, pulling away, going back for just one more, then another, then one last taste of softness. Finally, backing off, separating himself from her, denying the contact his body longed for.

A single sigh escaped her lips as she stepped away, squeezing her eyes closed for a moment longer. When she finally met his gaze, he saw his own feelings of need reflecting back. He knew she also felt unsure of him, terrified to take another chance. He stared down at her, feeling lucky, and curious. He couldn't help but wonder what life had in store for them.

She backed away from him and cleared her throat. "So, what's the plan for this evening?" Her voice wavered, revealing her jitters. She walked slowly to the tree, her booted footsteps echoing on the bare wooden floor.

"I thought I'd take you to a restaurant first, then a movie."

"I haven't been to dinner and a movie since the twins were in first grade. Is there a theater around here?"

"No, but I'm only thirty minutes to Lake Coburn. Do you mind getting back on the road?"

"Not if I'm just the passenger. Do you have the internet to check the schedule?"

Sam pulled out the weekly paper and turned to the movie schedule. They bent their heads to study it.

Carrie tapped the paper with her forefinger. "I heard the one with George Clooney was really good."

Sam pointed to the comedy. "I heard the same thing about this one." He laughed at the face she made. "We can see something else."

"How about this one?" she asked, pointing to the last on the list.

Sam sucked in his stomach and puffed out his chest. "You're not going to compare me to Val Kilmer all night, are you?"

"Relax, Big Boy, Val doesn't look like he did in *Top Gun* anymore."

Sam gave her a twisted smile. "Thanks, I feel loads better now."

"Besides, I'm not on a date with Val, am I?" She looked down at the paper again. "There's a feature at eight o'clock and it's a quarter to six. I don't have a problem with fast food for supper."

Sam pushed away from the counter and shook his head. "My mama would slap me good if I took my first date in over twenty years to a burger joint. You want steak or seafood?"

She closed her eyes and sighed. "Mmm, steak. Definitely."

"Beef –it's what's fer supper," he drawled, putting his own twist on Sam Elliot's advertisement. He placed a light kiss on her fingers. "Let's go."

Less than five minutes later, Carrie stepped down from Sam's truck and gave him a tentative smile. "You know, if we were in Gardiner, tongues would be wagging already. You sure you want to do this?"

"I doubt anyone expects me to live the rest of my life like a monk. Besides, I don't mind showing you off." Sam paused at the door of the restaurant, his hand on the knob as he stared down at her.

"What's wrong?" She gave her reflection a self-conscious go-over in the windowpane.

"Not a thing. Have I told you how happy I am you're here with me tonight?"

She lifted a hand to his face for a gentle caress. "I think you just did."

Inside the restaurant, she slipped off her coat and tried to relax. Sam placed a comforting hand on the small of her back as a waitress led them to a table in the corner of the room packed with curious diners. Once they seated themselves, Carrie leaned in close to whisper. "If I had toilet paper trailing from my shoe, you'd tell me, right?"

"It's only a few squares."

Her brow wrinkled in a frown. "There are times I appreciate your humor. Now isn't one of them."

He picked up his menu. "Don't worry, they're just wondering where the hell I found someone as good-looking as you, that's all."

"Yeah, sure they are." She picked up her own menu, glad to have some way to hide the blush she felt creeping up her neck. "So, what do you recommend?"

"I'm partial to the sirloin, but you can't go wrong with a T-bone or rib-eye."

Sam smiled at a young woman approaching their table with two glasses of water. "Hey, Lace. How're you doing?"

She placed water at each of their settings. "I'm good, Mr. Sam. How's Amanda?"

"She's doing great, just got a job at a bank here in town."

Carrie smiled and nodded politely at her, quick to notice the wink of approval she sent Sam's direction.

She took their drink orders and left the table.

"Lacey is a childhood friend of my daughter's," he explained.

Carrie took a sip of water, fidgeting at the curious stares of other diners. "And so it begins..."

"Maybe we should stand up and introduce you."

"Nah. Let's keep `em all guessing awhile longer."

A second waitress, this one closer to their age, brought salads to their table, talking fast and gushing over Sam with obvious gusto.

"Did we order salads yet?" Carrie asked, smiling through the server's exaggerated twang and overzealous attention to Sam's needs. She listened, shocked as the woman attempted to engage him in small talk while sending not so covert glances in her direction. Sam gave her a polite nod of thanks and began preparing his salad. Instead of leaving, she loitered at their table.

Once Carrie realized Sam did not intend to introduce them, her curiosity took over. She offered her hand to the woman. "I'm Carrie Jeansonne, and you are..."

"Bertie Miller," the woman said, countering with what felt to Carrie like a reluctant handshake, before wiping her hands on her apron.

Knowing a snub when she got one, Carrie couldn't resist egging her on. "Birdie? Like a bird?"

"Uh, no, that's with a T."

Carrie stared in disbelief as the woman turned her back to pick up a one-sided conversation with Sam. *Snubbed again.*

"Like I was sayin', Sammy, if you need anythin' at a-all, Sugar, you just let me kna-ow—"

"Oh, Burtie. Like a *man*," Carrie interrupted. "Your parents must have been expecting a son, then. Your father must be a Burt or Robert."

The woman turned to stare at her. "Nooooaah..." she drawled. "B-E-R-T-I-E...as in short for Roberta? Oh, and by the way, I'm a friend of Linda's. You know, Sammy's ex-wa-af? You must not be from around here, you havin' such a *thick* Cajun accent an' all."

Carrie gave the woman a thousand-watt smile as she rested her chin on her clasped hands. "Nooooah, but I lived in East Texas fuh six years of my laf, an' when I get the yearnin', I bet I can lay the twang on *every* bit as good as you . . . *Sugar*." She batted her eyelashes dramatically at Bertie before continuing. "It's been a pleasure, Burt, but I see our *real* waitress is back to take care of my and *Sammy's* needs. Thanks so much for everything."

Their waitress stepped up, effectively cutting off the older woman's contact with Sam until Bertie sulked away.

Lacey gave Carrie a look of pure mortification. "I'm so sorry—I turned my back for a second, and she was out here. She *knows* this is my section."

Carrie pointed to the two vegetable filled plates. "These are someone else's, aren't they, Lacey?"

"Yes, ma'am."

Sam looked up from cutting a cherry tomato in half. "They are?"

"Did we put in our orders, yet, Sam?"

"No, but..."

Carrie cocked her head to the side and lifted her hands, palm side up.

He gazed mournfully at his salad. "Do I have to give it back?

Lacey giggled, shook her head. "Of course not. Y'all ready to order?"

Sam ordered a sirloin, well done, with a side of grilled vegetables and then turned to Carrie.

"I think I'll just have a salad."

"I thought you wanted steak?"

"Not if Bertie is going to be within twenty feet of my food, I don't."

Lacey grinned. "I'll make sure she doesn't go near it, I promise."

Carrie handed her the menu. "Okay, then. But just to be safe, I'll have what he's having, with the same grilled veggies."

"How do you want that cooked?"

"Medium please and could you bring a dish of extra lemon for Sam's iced tea, please?"

Once Lacey left with their order, Sam wiped his mouth on his napkin. "How'd you know I liked extra lemon?"

"You ordered it the day we all went to eat at McKinley's Grill."

"That was less than a month after you came to work with us."

She sliced a cherry tomato in half. "It was the day after my divorce finalized."

"You paid attention to what I said that long ago?"

Carrie ignored the question and changed the subject.

"That Bertie chick may know your *ex-waaf*, but she was certainly no friend of hers."

He grabbed his fork and attacked his salad again. "Used to be, but not for several years."

"What happened? Did Linda figure out that Bertie wanted to *sweeten your tea for you, Sammy*?"

Sam pulled on the collar of his shirt. "Damn, it's hot in here."

"Y'awnt me to call Bertie over here, Saaa-mmy? Bet she can make ya even hotter."

Sam stabbed at a piece of lettuce. "Stop it."

Carrie leaned in closer to tease him. "What happened, Sugar? Did the scary lady make a pass at Sammy Wammy?"

Sam gulped at his tea before answering. "She grabbed my ass when I wasn't looking. Linda saw it all and went over to confront her."

"Oh-oh, did she threaten her?"

"She wouldn't say at first, but a couple of weeks later, during one of our too-frequent arguments, Linda admitted to me what she'd told Bertie." He wiped his mouth with his napkin. "Linda said if she wanted that part of me, Bertie had to promise to take the whole GD package. But, it'd cost half of my retirement, everything we owned, and Bertie had to take the son-pampering mother-in-law too."

Carrie's mouth dropped open. "Oh my God, she really told her that?"

Sam puffed out one cheek before answering. "I don't doubt it for a second."

Carrie brought her straw to her mouth for a drink then pursed her lips. "That's pretty good."

"This time I'm the one asking to change the subject." Sam cleared his throat. "How'd you get into drafting, anyway? Last night you said something about almost becoming a paralegal?"

She used her fork to point at him. “Okay, but only because I owe you one. My two girlfriends, Sharon and Sandy, and I were on our way to a technical college in Lafayette to test for paralegal studies. About halfway there, I had a meltdown and told them I couldn’t work for a lawyer. I had drooled over the drafting technology section in the catalog, but the required math scared the hell out of me. My friends gave me the boost in confidence I needed and convinced me to go for it. I scored in the top three percentile on the school’s technological entrance exam.”

“Not bad for someone who’d been out of school for over a decade.”

She nodded. “Yeah, I guess I remembered more than I gave myself credit for.”

“Why drafting?”

“All my life I’d seen this funny looking, three sided ruler hanging around our home. I remember holding it, examining it, and never being able to figure out how to use two sides of it.”

“A scale?” Sam asked her.

“That’s right. I remember looking for a straight edge to draw a line and I asked if anyone knew where that three sided ruler was.” She laughed at the memory. “My dad, who could draw anything to scale, said, ‘I keep telling you. It’s not a ruler, dammit, it’s a scale! ’ At the time, the only scale I knew about was the kind that weighed things. I didn’t know anything about drafting arms, templates, or CAD programs. I think dad would be proud I chose this career.”

“What does your mom do?”

“She retired as a teacher’s aide, but since Dad’s death, any damn thing she wants to.” Carrie dabbed at her mouth with a napkin. “She loves to work in her garden. I swear that woman could grow a rose bush from a rock. She’s the president of the Garden Club and involved in all kinds of things.”

“Do you like gardening, too?”

She raised her thumb. “Does this digit look green to you?”

“I enjoy gardening.” Sam stacked their empty salad plates as Lacey arrived with their entrees.

“I hate it. I’ve got better things to do with my time.”

“It’s the differences that make life interesting.”

“I guess you’re right.” A trio of women at the entrance grabbed her attention.

“What’s wrong?”

“I think those women are talking about us over there.”

Sam waved her off. “It’s a small town. Tomorrow they’ll be talking about someone else.”

Carrie leaned over to look around him. “I think this is different.”

Sam looked in the direction and groaned. “Aw, hell, damn, and double damn,” he muttered, as one woman walked toward them.

“Who is that?”

Sam sighed, picked up his napkin from his lap and threw it on the table. “My ex.”

Chapter Eleven

The pretty, full-figured woman approached the table wearing a smile mixed with equal parts smirk. "Hey, Sam. Don't get up." She placed a hand familiarly on his shoulder.

"Thanks. I wasn't planning to."

"I'm having supper with Deb and Margaret and wanted to come over and say hello."

Sam clenched and released his jaw several times during her dialogue before he shrugged, then answered in a low growl. "There's a first time for everything, I guess." He sent Carrie an apology-filled plea for patience. "Carrie, this is Linda."

The woman reached over the table to extend her hand.

In Carrie's mind, Linda's bold act of walking over to their table in front of everyone in the dining room implied one of three things: First, Linda considered this *her* territory and Carrie the interloper; second, Sam's ex-wife was an extremely friendly person; or third, Linda was just nosy as hell.

Linda's insincere smile hinted at a mixture of territorial and flat out nosiness. Carrie chose to stand as she clasped hands with the much shorter woman. Linda's smile faded, obviously from shock at the sight of her ex-husband's date smiling *down* at her. "I'm Carrie Jeansonne. Hello, Linda. It's very nice to meet you."

"It's nice to meet you too, Carrie. I didn't realize Sam was seeing anyone—and so young, too."

Carrie intercepted the smug look Linda directed at a tight-lipped Sam. The woman had nerve, for sure, but absolutely no idea who she was messing with. Carrie cocked her head slightly. "People always tell me I look much younger than my age, Linda, but thank you so much for the compliment."

"So, how long have you two been dating?"

Sam rested his elbows on the table, the fingers of both hands interlaced tightly. "Since when do you give a damn about anything I do?"

Carrie reseated herself, leaving Sam's ex standing alone, and covered Sam's clasped hands with her own. He latched onto her fingers with both hands, as though he were a drowning man reaching for a buoy. She answered his questioning gaze with a warm smile. "This is only our first date, but Sam and I work together, and we've been friends for a few months."

Linda blinked once and furrowed her brow. "I thought the company frowned upon co-workers dating."

Carrie gave the woman a bright smile. "Oh, Sam's not my boss. I'm a road-designer, so it's okay."

"You must be new. Roxie's been the only woman in that office for years."

"I've been there for—has it been over four months already, Sam?"

"On the eleventh."

"You remember the day?" She feigned a look of surprise more for the sake of Linda than anything else.

"You know it." He spoke in a low voice, never taking his eyes from her.

Under the circumstances, Carrie decided she could afford to be gracious. "I've seen pictures of your beautiful kids, Linda. Amanda and Nick look a lot like you."

"Oh, uh, thank you. Well, I don't want to keep the two of you from your meal."

Carrie watched as Linda turned abruptly and walked back to her friends. Several other heads watched the woman's hasty retreat back to her own corner of the ring.

Carrie raised her hand to ring an imaginary bell. "Ding! Ding! First round goes to the challenger. The mouthy interloper from Gardiner, Louisiana . . ."

Sam's shoulders shook with laughter at her imitation of a boxing ring announcer. "I believe it did, Slugger."

She settled back in her chair to slice her tender sirloin. "You think she got what she was looking for?"

The remainder of a chuckle rumbled deep in his chest. "Oh, yeah, and so much more." He raised his fork to his mouth and paused. "You know, that's the first time she's initiated a conversation since we split. We normally repel each other like two magnets with the same pole.

Carrie smiled at him as she looked up from cutting her steak. "I figured as much. I guess that was the female version of a pissing contest."

He snorted. "You definitely won."

"You think?"

"I know."

Carrie swallowed her bite of steak and leaned forward to speak. "To the victor go the spoils."

Sam reached over and ran the back of his hand gently along the side of her face as his tone deepened. "This spoil is yours, if you want me."

"I'm considering it," she said, leaning back in her chair. "But first, are there any more exes or wannabe's to contend with, Saa-mmy?"

Sam rubbed at his face. "You don't have to contend with anyone. Bertie's slept with half the men in town but never me. As for Linda—she was just being down-right nosy."

She sipped from her water glass. "She's just curious."

"*C'est tout le meme chose*."

"I guess it is the same thing, isn't it?"

They finished their meal with no more drama and arrived at the theater in plenty of time. Carrie laughed at the previews of two comedies and whispered after one trailer. "Cory said the soundtrack to that movie is outstanding. I'd like to see it."

Sam leaned close to her ear. "How about next weekend?"

"I'd love to go with you next weekend."

He straightened in his seat, his face plastered with an ear-splitting grin. "You're so easy."

"And cheap, too," she added. The two of them faced each other and fell into helpless laughter.

"I meant you're easy to be with, as in comfortable," he explained, as he reached his arm around and pulled her closer.

She smiled, settling into the cozy warmth of his embrace.

Two hours later, Sam reached out from the driver's seat and grabbed Carrie's hand, entwining his fingers through hers. "Did you enjoy the movie?"

"I did. It was no Tombstone, though. I loved Val Kilmer in that one".

"I'm your Huckleberry," he drawled, imitating Val's character, Doc Holiday. He studied Carrie's profile while waiting for a signal light to turn green. "So, what day do you want to go next weekend?"

"I guess we'll have to check the schedule again." She gazed out through his truck window. "But, you don't have to take me out, you know. I'd be just as happy with a home-cooked meal and a rented movie."

Sam nodded. "Whatever you want to do, we'll do." He smiled as she tried to hide a yawn from him. "I need to get you back so you can go home and get some rest. I bet you're tired."

"I am," she agreed. "Mom and I got all the baking done for tomorrow and the next day. I don't want to see an electric mixer or mixing bowls for a while."

"I guess you have big plans with your family and kids tomorrow night?"

Carrie played with the zipper of her purse. "Actually, the kids will be with me all day tomorrow but are going back to their dad's tomorrow night. Christmas Eve night is a big thing at Ruby's." She turned to face him, her gaze filled with curiosity. "How about you?"

"Lunch at my folks. My kids have places to be all day tomorrow and tomorrow night." He turned to her, a hangdog expression on his face. "My sister invited me to her place, but I'd hoped to have other plans for that night."

Carrie raised one brow, her eyes twinkling with amusement. "Poor baby, I'd invite you to my mom's, but I doubt you'd survive it."

He pulled at his collar uncomfortably. "Um, you may be right about that."

"Besides, before anyone in my family can meet you, I'd have to broach the subject of my seeing other people with my kids."

Sam stared straight ahead at the roadway and swallowed hard. "Other *people*?"

"Well, just to see if they'd mind. I mean, this is only our first date."

He swiveled his gaze around to face her. "But, you've already accepted a second date."

She stared ahead, avoiding eye contact with him. "Yes, I did."

"I thought we'd be—that made us—um—that we were . . ." He gave up in frustrated defeat.

Carrie's voice held a hint of laughter. "Sam, are you asking me to go steady?"

He ducked his head. "Go ahead. Laugh at a man who's on his *first* 'first date' in twenty-three years."

Carrie gave a low whistle. "That's nearly a quarter of a century."

"Oh, you're funny."

"So I've been told." She smothered her laughter. "I'm sorry."

"Like hell you are. You enjoy making me squirm."

"I love watching all men squirm, I admit it."

"I keep telling you, we're not all like Dave."

Carrie studied him silently for several seconds before replying. "I'm beginning to accept that."

Sam nodded as he pulled up under the carport next to her sedan. He threw his truck into park and turned off the engine. Dozens of strands of Christmas lights strung along his porch filled the pick-up's cab with a multi-colored glow. He felt her staring at his profile, and resisted the urge to straighten, to make himself look taller. His head nearly touched the liner of his truck's cab as it was.

Carrie reached out with her fingertip to trace the bridge of his nose.

"I know. I have a big nose." He puckered to kiss her fingers.

"I like it. I like your looks, and I love being with such a tall man. But, you know what I like best of all?"

He gathered her fingers in his hand and brought them to his lips for another kiss. "What?"

"I like your character. This is different for me, Sam. This is mature admiration for a man I've worked with for a few months. I *like* you."

He stared at her, as the wind whistled in from the north, audible over the soft clicks of the cooling engine. It buffeted the side of his truck and caused it to rock slightly. The Canadian cold front had moved through, accompanied by icy winds and low humidity sure to dry up water left from two days of drenching rains.

He shook his head before tearing his gaze from hers. "I can't help thinking you could do a lot better than me."

"Sam." She reached out to him with her free hand. "There is no better."

He caught her hand with his own and turned his face to place a gentle kiss on the inside of her palm. "Thank you," he whispered. "Sixteen months of being alone has taught me a lot about myself, things I didn't want to know. I made a lot of mistakes in my marriage."

"It didn't come with an owner's manual, did it?"

"Nope, and neither did the kids."

Carrie laughed softly. "I'd love do-overs with my kids, especially Grant. I was so green when he was born. I'm sure I've scarred him for life." She pulled her coat closer to her body and checked her watch. "It's a quarter to eleven, and I have a busy day ahead of me. This night flew by, didn't it?"

"It's the best night I've had in a long time." Sam glanced sideways at her. "You have time to take a little walk?"

"Will it take long?"

He got out of his truck and walked around to meet her. "Just over there. Come on, the walk will help to wake you up for the drive home." He held out his hand and she took it. He walked with her to the end of the street and crossed the intersection to stop in front of the house on the corner lot.

"Who lives here?"

"No one right now, but I wanted you to see this place. It's for rent—very reasonable, three bedrooms, two baths, all kitchen appliances, along with a brand new washer and dryer. I happen to know the owner personally. He doesn't need the money. Just wants it lived in by someone who won't tear the place up." He turned toward her. "I just thought, since you were about to move, maybe you'd want to get something a little closer to work. You know, less gas, less time on the road—"

"And conveniently close to you," she added, her voice tinged with suspicion.

He reached out to place both hands on her shoulders. "You'd be neighbors with a couple of cops. Doug's across the street. Works for Kenton PD. Ben's a deputy with the Sheriff's Department, and he lives on the opposite end of the block. I admit though, it'd be nice to have you so close."

She smiled sadly up at him. "I told you about my kids wanting to be in Gardiner, Sam. Their friends are all there, and their lives are in enough turmoil as it is."

"They'll make new friends, Carrie. If they're anything like their mom, they'll make friends no matter what school they attend."

Carrie studied the house, as he watched for a reaction. By the time she turned back to face him, his hope had faded. He stared down at his boots and kicked at the cracked edge of the stone walkway. "I'm sorry," he muttered, unable to hide his disappointment. "It's not all selfishness. I worry about you, dammit. Phone calls, barking dogs—" He pointed across the street toward her car. "Not to mention broken windshields from crazy ex-husband's."

She pulled her coat tighter and gave a delicate sniff. "It's all Dave, just Dave, and I can handle him."

"I hate to say this, but what if it's not? What if he really doesn't know anything about the calls?"

"It *is* him," she insisted.

"He didn't admit to it."

"And risk having more ammo for me to use against him? No way would he admit to it. Don't worry about me, Sam. I'll be fine."

He nodded and took her hand. "All right, then. Let's get you back to where it's warm."

As they walked back over to Sam's place, Carrie stopped to breathe out a puff of icy smoke. She squinted into the darkness and reached out her hand. "It's sleeting."

They stood listening to the quiet tick, tick, ticking sounds as the tiny droplets of ice made contact with the street and sidewalk. Carrie hugged her coat tighter to her and turned for the porch. "I need the bathroom first, but then I have to go. I don't want to drive on frozen roads."

He managed to spit out the first part of the warning. "Careful, the steps are starting to fr—" just as her foot slipped on a small patch of ice on the step. Sam caught her, saving her from a painful, butt first landing on the cold, wet sidewalk.

"I've got you," he murmured, his voice husky with concern, as he held tightly to her.

Carrie regained her footing, but remained in his arms, her back to his front. She covered his forearms with her own. "Yes, you do," she murmured, letting her head fall back against his chest.

He heard her soft, satisfied sigh as he tightened his grip on her, before turning her loose with a reluctant groan.

The hallway clock struck eleven as she exited the bathroom. Carrie bit her lower lip, knowing she had to leave, and dreading the next week with no Sam. He stood vigil at the steps and helped her safely down. She lifted her chin, determined to hide the tumultuous range of emotions raging through her. "Merry Christmas, Sam."

He stepped closer and opened his arms. "The same to you, Baby. I had a great time with you tonight."

She snuggled into the comfortable hollow and slipped her arms around his waist. His mouth lowered to hers for one last kiss. She eagerly accepted it, suppressing a groan of pleasure at the serious play of his tongue on hers.

Sam broke the kiss, and gave her a gentle peck on the nose. "You be careful going home, you hear me?"

"I will." Carrie rid her voice of its quaver with a ladylike clearing of the throat. "I guess I'll see you next weekend?"

"If not sooner. Maybe I could only take a couple of days off of work." He gave her a careless shrug. "It'd save me some leave."

"Yeah? I was thinking you don't need to take *any* time off and save more. What is it you're always saying? 'That's money in the bank.'"

His chest rumbled with deep laughter. "You drive a hard bargain, girl. Let's say I don't take any days off. What's in it for me?"

Carrie moved out of his embrace to pull on her gloves. She grabbed the door knob and threw a backwards glance in his direction. "Me, if you play your cards right. Good night, Sam."

She was already out the door and down the steps before he roused himself from his stupor. He hurried outside to stand next to her car. "Call me when you get home?" he called through the window.

"I will."

"And drive safely, watch your speed. When you get home, if *anything* looks suspicious do *not* go into that house. Go to the neighbor so she can call her son."

She nodded again. "I'll talk to you in an hour...and, Sam?"

"Yeah?" he asked, looking like a lost puppy.

"I love it when you call me Baby."

She could still see him smiling as she headed for the highway.

Carrie pushed open the front door and froze. The unmistakable scent of roses assaulted her senses. She stood outside the doorway, trying to ignore the frisson of fear that caused the hair on the back of her neck to stand up.

"Aw, hell." She barely heard her own whispered words over the frantic pounding of her own heart. As her eyes adjusted to the dimness of the house, lit only by one tiny nightlight, she saw the huge bouquet of roses on the dining room table. Minus a few buds and several petals, it was otherwise intact.

Dave was here. Carrie scanned the room quickly, looking for anything broken or out of place, but Sam's words of warning prompted her to back cautiously out the door. The breath she'd been holding released in a loud whoosh, accompanied by a shriek as she backed into a large, solid, body. *Definitely not Dave*. She jumped to the side and pivoted to catch a look at her intruder.

Rob LeDoux stood with his hands up in the air. "Whoa—it's me!"

"Sweet Jesus!" Carrie's hand flew to her chest as she glared up at the mountain of a man. "You scared the crap out of me."

He gave her a sheepish grin. "Sorry, but I've been sitting at Mom's, waiting for you to get home. She called me around nine—said she saw Dave disappear into the back door of the house, then leave after a few minutes."

Carrie closed her eyes as relief flooded through her. "I was on my way to the police station." She pointed to the vase filled with roses. "You'd think he could have found someone else to give those to. By the way, I *know* I locked all the windows and doors. How the hell did he get in?"

"You were *supposed* to stop at the station on the way in." The officer pointed to the kitchen. "He cut the screen on the back door and jimmied the lock. I have a few beers with Christie's landlord every week. I'll talk to him about putting in dead bolts."

Her eyes gravitated to the back door. "Christie's going to be pissed." She turned to Rob again. "Now do you believe it's him behind those calls?"

Rob brushed his thumb and forefinger over his mustache. "I interrogated him a good while about that earlier. He says he didn't have anything to do with them, and I lean toward believing him."

She shook her head. "I still think it's a ploy to get me to move back home. You have to admit the timing is too perfect. Besides, I can't afford for it not to be Dave. Anything else is too terrifying."

He leaned forward and pinned her with a stern look. "What you can't afford is to insist Dave's behind it when he isn't. It's bad enough that whoever it is knows exactly when you moved. That means he's watching you and probably lives in or near Gardiner. We need to figure out a plan of action. Now think, is there any other place you could go?"

"Like where, Rob?" Her voice rose to a hysterical pitch. "I can't stay here and put Christie and Max in danger. I won't go to Mom's and put her in danger. I sure don't want to risk putting my own kids in danger. So what the hell am I supposed to do? Camp out in your jail like the town drunk on the Andy Griffith show?"

"Now there's a thought. We could fix you up with your own cell, just like Otis." Rob didn't even bother trying to hide his grin.

"Seriously, Rob. Where could I go and not put someone I love at risk? I was even considering asking Dave if he'd stay at his mom's, so I could move back in the house for a while, but *that's* out of the question now."

Rob rubbed the back of his neck with his hand. "Were your plans to stay here with Chris for a while?"

"I'm supposed to be renting a house here in town by the middle of January—Mark Dronet's place at the southeast end of town."

He nodded. "I know it. Nice place." He sucked in his breath and grimaced. "Just inside city limits, empty lots, grassy pastures on three sides, and no nosy neighbor."

She blew out an exasperated breath. "I know. The very thing that attracted me most when I first saw it is a big negative now."

Rob gave her shoulder a friendly pat. "We'll think of something, don't worry." He got to the door and waved down the cruiser passing slowly in front of her house, then turned to her. "I'll make sure he stays right out here. You call if you need anything, okay?"

She picked up the roses and met him at the door. "Take these with you please."

His left brown arched. "You mean you don't want them?"

Carrie snorted. "The only rose I ever got from Dave when we were together was one made out of a pair of red nylon panties. I sure as hell don't want any now."

"Are you joking?" Rob smothered a laugh.

"Afraid not. I got that, along with a four inch ceramic bear that had 'I Love You Bear-ry Much' painted on the belly. The panties must have been a size 0." She handed the vase to the laughing Chief of Police. "I called it in to a radio station as the worst Valentine's Day gift I ever got. It won the contest. I got a box of chocolates and a beer coozie from Gator 101."

"Mona would have loaded my ass with buckshot if I'd done that. Can I give these to her?"

"Sure, maybe you'll have better luck than Dave." After he left, she locked the door behind him. As added protection, she wedged a dining room chair under the knob and then did the same to the kitchen door. Carrie placed fingertips to her throbbing temples, one thought running through her mind: A move to Kenton didn't sound so terrible right now.

From his position behind the massive oak across the street, he watched the chief drive away from Carrie's place. Excitement at the thought of her being in that house, alone all night long, made him hard and anxious to have her. His stomach soured when Rob flagged down the cruiser. Damn that guy, and damn these holidays. Christmas festivities were not conducive to his plans for her. Soon, he'd have her all to himself. No protection from Gardiner's finest and no kids around to spoil his one-on-one time.

Ten minutes later, Carrie crawled into bed with the phone. She cringed when Sam answered on the first ring, his voice tight with worry.

"I thought you'd never call. I've been making up all kinds of scenarios in my head." A quick explanation from her had him muttering mild profanities. "I'm tempted to go pick your ass up and lock you in my bedroom where I can keep an eye on you."

Her nails clicked in an impatient rhythm on the handset. "You and what army?" Sam's frustrated groan had her taking pity on him. "For what it's worth, I believe more than ever that Dave's behind this, even though the chief doesn't."

"And if he is, you really don't think he's dangerous?"

"Nope. Just a giant pain in my ass." She frowned when Sam let loose with a string of expletives. "And here I thought you were a gentleman."

"Sorry, babe, but I cuss when I'm feeling helpless, and right now I feel like a castrated bull in a pasture full of heifers." She heard a loud beep from the handset. "Aw hell, somebody's calling. It's probably Mom checking up to see how our date went."

"I'll let you go then. I just wanted to make sure you made it home safely. G'night, Carrie."

"Night, Sam." She pressed the star to speak to the other caller. "Hello?" Dead silence. She imagined Dave gloating about how he could still control her, and it fueled her fury.

"You can stop now. I know Dave put you up to this, numb nuts. The only thing you'll get for your trouble is time in prison." She pressed the phone's speaker button and placed the handset on the unit.

"Carrie…"

For a second she forgot she wasn't showing fear. "What?"

"I want you."

"Sure you do."

"I'm going to have time, but not in prison. Time alone with you. More than enough time to do one of two things. Make you mine, or make you dead."

Any quick comeback she had planned died at her vocal chords. Carrie hit the speaker button and cradled the handset before walking to the door. She flipped the porch light on and off several times to signal the officer.

"But not until we have some fun first."

She pulled the curtain aside to look for whoever was on duty. "Fun for you or for me?"

"Both of us, if you're as smart as I think you are."

The breathing grew labored—heavy—almost as if . . .

"I'm—going—to—have—*you.*"

She spun around, stare in horror at the phone base as his guttural groan filled the air. "Oh, God!" She winced at the sound of his sadistic laughter.

"Was that good for you?"

Footsteps on the wooden porch had her checking the window again. Carrie eased open the door for the officer standing there, and held her finger up to her lips, then pointed at the phone. "You're disgusting! Why don't you just admit Dave put you up to this?" More raucous laughter had her skin crawling.

"This is so much bigger than Dave; he's a fool, and so are you if you think that officer you let inside can stop me if I decide to get at you tonight."

Carrie's breath released in a rush as the officer grabbed his radio with one hand and drew his weapon with the other.

He spun around and called over his shoulder. "Lock up behind me. I'm calling for back up."

"Why'd you have to go and do that? It was just getting interesting."

"Do what?" She tried to keep the quaver from her voice.

"We'll save the rest for later. Sweet dreams, Carrie."

Carrie fell, exhausted, into the bed an hour later. The last officer had just cleared out, leaving one parked out front and another circling the block with a searchlight. She clutched the phone tightly to her chest, fighting the urge to call Sam. A strong, independent woman should be able to take a night alone, without calling a man to talk her through it. She'd spoken to no one but cops for the last hour, not even a family member. Did she still believe the caller was someone Dave had enlisted? As certain as she'd been earlier, she had to admit her opinion faltered considerably after that last call.

Only once did she buckle and dial Sam's number but hung up before it rang. The last thing he needed was her waking his butt up at nearly two in the morning.

The other thing he didn't need was a girlfriend with a psycho after her. Rob was concerned this was somehow connected to that poor girl in Lafayette. She'd given a surprisingly detailed description of a man she'd never seen. About six foot tall, muscular, straight hair, short—military style cut, fanatically clean because he shaved and showered every day of the three days he kept her hostage, and his voice—unnaturally deep, as though he was trying to mask the sound of his real voice. Funny, but the first time her caller spoke, she'd thought the same thing.

Great. Awesome.

A fitful hour of tossing and turning later, she still worried how to keep her kids as far away from this as possible. She finally managed to doze off, her phone clutched to her chest.

Chapter Twelve

Carrie sipped at her coffee and held the phone away from her ear as Sam let loose with another OSHA Orange streak of cussing. Once he eased off, she brought the phone closer. "Got it out of your system yet?" Silence greeted her for several seconds, and she pictured him pacing the floor.

"I wish you'd called me," he growled. "The thought of you, lying there alone in that house, scared and not wanting to *bother* me—it kills me."

"No sense keeping you awake, as well. Besides, I had some thinking to do. The only way I can think of keeping my kids safe from all this is to separate myself from them, just until this is all over with."

"How? Where would you go?"

"I don't know. I feel like I'm being backed into a corner by admitting this, but maybe I should think about the place in Kenton."

"Seriously?"

"It might keep my family safe, but what if it brings danger to you and Nick?"

"I doubt he'd follow you to Kenton."

Carrie rubbed her burning eyes with one hand. "God, Sam. You don't know how much I'm hoping you're right about this."

"I am, you'll see. So, does this mean I can give Len a call about the house? When would you want to come see the place and talk to him?"

She inhaled and held the breath, hoping to slow down the frantic beating of her heart. "You think tonight is too soon?"

"I could call him for you."

"I'd rather speak to him myself if you don't mind. I need to stand on my own two feet, not lean on you. Just give me his number and I'll call you back."

Within ten minutes she'd called Sam back and made plans to meet him at six p.m. She cut it short and dialed her mother-in-law's number. Within seconds, she heard the unmistakable smoker-cough that told her Dave's mom had answered. "Hey, Ruby, it's me."

"Hey, darlin'. Am I going to get to see you for Christmas?"

"I don't know, Rube. I guess that depends on your son."

Once she explained the circumstances, her mother-in-law's fury was substantial. "Wait until I get my hands on that boy of mine."

"I didn't tell you to get him in trouble. I just didn't want you to think I was avoiding you."

"I hope you know me better than that. You know you'll always be my daughter-in-law, whether you're divorced from my foolish son or not."

Carrie squeezed her eyes shut against the tears caused by Ruby's heartfelt confession. "You know how much I love you, right?"

Ruby was quiet for a moment. "No more than I love you. I know you gave it everything you had."

Carrie sniffed and cleared her throat. "Are my kids still there?"

"They left about five minutes ago. They should be getting to your mom's soon."

"Good. Did, uh, did Arlene and Jerry make it in yet?"

"Yep, they got here about thirty minutes ago and she's waiting right here to talk to you."

Carrie drummed her nails on the handset while she heard the phone shuffling from one set of hands to another.

The voice of her old friend—sharp with East Texas twang and demanding—made her jump.

"Where the hell are you?"

"I'm at Christie's, but I'll be leaving to go to my mom's soon. Is Jerry hunting yet?"

Arlene snorted with disgust. "After all these years, you should know better than to ask. I had to drive this morning so he could make sure he didn't need to stop for more damn shells on the way over here. I told him we could fill up the freezer with chicken, pork, and beef with the money he throws away hunting ducks and geese every year."

Carrie cut in with a reply honed from years of practice. "Yeah, yeah—thrill of the hunt, sound of the birds flying over—"

"The excitement he gets when the birds respond to *his* calls and fly right over the duck blind—"

"—showering them with duck doo," Carrie added her perfectly harmonized voice to her soul sister's finale. They'd all had to suffer through years of the Jeansonne men's infamous excuses for spending too much money for a handful of birds every year.

The two women erupted into laughter, but Arlene made a quick recovery. "Just like every year, there's not a man around, and us gals are working our butts off to get dinner ready. So, what'd Dave do that has Ruby so pissed at him?"

As she described the incidents to her friend, she could sense Arlene waiting patiently to add something.

"Bastard!" Arlene spat, her voice filled of venom. "He's with a different woman every week and has the nerve to pull that crap."

"Right? He doesn't even want me. That's why this is so frustrating." Carrie sensed her friend's wind-up for the next question and braced herself.

"Now, Missy, where were you when he broke into Christie's? Your ex said something about you being all 'dolled-up for another man,'" she said, in a perfect imitation of Dave.

"I was on a date."

Arlene's voice lowered considerably, as she pummeled Carrie with questions of who, what, and where.

"Sam Langley, he's a co-worker, and he's settled, dependable, trustworthy."

"Hmmm. Maybe he'll bore you."

"If boredom means being able to relax and let down my guard, then bring it on. Besides…" She paused, wondering how much to say.

"No flipping way do you get to say something like that and not follow through! Give it up, soul sister. Start with the obvious—what he looks like—then work your way up to how you feel when you're with him."

Carrie chuckled into the phone. "I like the way you think, honey." She settled back on the sofa. "He's kind of blond, with light-blue eyes, and he's so funny. God, he makes me laugh." She sighed. "And when he wraps those long arms around me, I melt."

"You really like this guy, don't you?"

Carrie closed her eyes. "I do. But I'm just trying to catch up to how he feels about me."

"So, you think this Sam thing could be serious?"

"It's way too soon to tell."

"Okay, but you always said if you could do it over you'd have chosen someone tall. How tall is he?"

"Nearly six three, and he wears a size *thirteen* shoe." She grinned at her friend's sharp intake of breath.

"Thirteen? I wonder if it's true what they say—"

"I have no idea, but I'll let you know as soon as I do." The two women burst into laughter.

"Oh, God, I miss you, girl, but it was bound to happen sooner or later. We all knew someone would come along and show some appreciation for what Dave took for granted all those years. You took that crap a lot longer than I would have."

"When you don't think you deserve better, you settle for less. Now I know better. I need to go, hon. My kids are bound to be at Mom's by now."

"I want updates on this Sam situation, you hear?"

Carrie promised, ended the call, and locked up before leaving. She hadn't mentioned the possibility of moving, just in case Dave was involved. She realized it would only be a matter of time before the caller tracked her down, but if she could have a week, even, of no calls, it would be worth it.

Five minutes later, she pulled up beside Grant's black Ford pick-up parked in her mother's driveway. Her son straightened up, his arms loaded with wrapped Christmas gifts. His mouth tightened noticeably when he caught sight of the huge crack in her sedan's windshield. She got out of the car and gave her son a kiss on the cheek. "Merry Christmas Eve, Baby Boy."

"You too, Mom." He stared at her windshield and gave his head a slow shake. "*That* looks about ten times worse than what Dad described."

Carrie shrugged, but kept her silence.

"That's not right, Mom."

She opened the gift-filled trunk of her car. "Let's not talk about this now. Are your sisters inside?"

Grant gave a snort. "Yeah, it only took `em two hours to get ready."

Carrie placed her hand on his shoulder and laughed. "You'd understand if you were a woman."

Gretchen bounded out of her Maw Maw Elaine's house, as excited as a young puppy. "It's Christmas Eve, Mom!"

Carrie gave her daughter a big hug. "I know, sweetie."

Lauren rushed out next. "Merry Christmas Eve, Mama." She returned her mother's hug.

"You too, sweet girl."

The twins turned toward the windshield and asked in perfect unison. "What happened to the window?"

The last thing Carrie wanted to do was ruin their holidays. "It was nothing. Come on, grab some things and let's go on inside to help Maw Maw get lunch ready."

Grant spoke up. "Mom, you may as well get it over with." He turned to his sisters. "Dad broke it."

Gretchen's jaw dropped. "Why?"

Carrie's head fell back on her shoulders. "I don't know why, honey. He was angry."

"What does *he* have to be mad about?" Gretchen demanded. "You're the one who should be mad. He gets to stay in our house."

Lauren spoke up, her tone icy. "He did it knowing we have to ride in this car, too."

Carrie grabbed an armload of gifts. "He wasn't thinking straight at the time. Help me get all this inside and then I want to talk to the three of you about something."

Once the car was unloaded, she asked her three teenagers to follow her out to her mom's back deck. There, seated at the large round redwood table, she explained the situation with the house and Sam. She refrained from mentioning the caller or her fears of keeping them safe—they didn't need to hear the ugly details right now.

The solemn, unreceptive faces of her daughters cued her in on the upcoming struggle.

"So, you're dating this guy?" Lauren stared at her, wide-eyed.

Carrie nodded and swallowed. "One date last night."

Gretchen looked up through bangs that needed a good trimming. "What if you get married? Would he want to move over here?"

She opened her mouth to answer, but Lauren's next comment cut her off.

"I don't know why you have to date at all. You're *old!*"

Grant turned to his sister. "You're so stupid."

Lauren glared at him. "Well, she is!"

"No, she's not," Gretchen added. "Brittany's mom is dating again, and she's a lot older than Mom is."

Carrie sucked in her breath, picturing the last time she saw Brittany's mom, sloppy drunk, and dancing on the pool table of the Red Rose in Lake Erin. Any comparison to Mary Ellen Wakely was not good, especially since the woman practically got paid by the men she "dated".

"Look, when I was your age, I'd have thought I was ancient, too. Believe me, you'll be here before you can spit and turn around."

"Ew—that's a long time from now." Lauren's tone held unadulterated horror.

"Not as long as you think. Besides—" She sent Grant a silent plea to understand. "Who I date isn't the real issue here. You all know how far I have to drive to work."

"So do Uncle Cullen and Dad," Lauren added.

"They also earn triple my starting salary, sweetie. I can't afford to have fuel costs eating up that much of my take-home pay."

Gretchen picked at a dried leaf on the table's surface. "But you went to college and got a degree. That's not fair."

Carrie cocked her head and gave her daughter a lopsided grin. "Welcome to my world, Gretch. Life doesn't always guarantee you'll be treated fairly." She placed a hand on her daughter's cheek. "But sometimes it hands you opportunities to help balance things out. I think this is one of those times." Carrie cleared her throat. "I saw a place in Kenton last night for half of what I'd have to pay for the place we're supposed to take in January. It's larger, completely remodeled, in a quiet neighborhood, and I'd be able to move in right away. I've thought about this all night long, but I wanted to talk to all of you first. It's possible I may have to take it." She examined her daughters' expressions.

"I'm not moving to Kenton," Gretchen proclaimed.

"Me either. All my friends are here," Lauren agreed.

Carrie nodded slowly. "I know that, and I wouldn't ask any of you to move now, but I thought maybe when—" She paused, wondering how to finish the statement. *When what? When I don't have a psycho jerking off on the phone while he talks to me?* She took a deep breath and continued. "Maybe sometime in the future you might want to give it a try."

Carrie crossed her arms tightly against the defiance on her daughters' faces and turned to stare out at the back pasture. When had life turned into one major stress-fest? She gazed out at the tall grass, longing for the carefree days when she'd used that patch of land to explore and play all day long. She wiped away a tear forming at the corner of one eye and took a calming breath. She had no other choice. "Nothing has to be decided now, but if the time comes when all this—when everything is settled, I'll expect the both of you to move in with me."

Her twins exchanged silent gazes steeped in stubbornness, and Lauren turned to add her two cents. "We already have a home. You remember. It's the place you helped build with *Dad*. If you'd just move back there, we c—"

Carrie jumped in to cut her off. "Look, I will *always* be thankful that I met your dad. Without him, I wouldn't have the three of you." She focused on Lauren as she continued. "But he and I are finished. You have to accept it, so we can all go on with our lives." When Lauren's face crumbled, Carrie pulled her daughter close for a hug. She smoothed a hand over tawny curls, tangled from the brisk, December wind. "Life is all about growing, changing, and having different people come into our lives at times to help us adapt to those changes. Your lives will be full of new people and new experiences. You'll make new friends, but family will always be our constant. You are my children, and I'll want you with me. All of you, if that's possible."

Lauren pulled away from her mother. "What if we go live with you and those Yankees don't like us?"

Carrie burst out in unexpected laughter. "Yankees?"

"Last year I heard you say how anyone north of I-10 was a Yankee and how they talk funny."

"That was a joke, hon. I'll admit that some people there talk with a twang like your cousins from Lake Coburn, but it's still in Louisiana, even if it is a different Parish. To people from Kenton, we'll be the ones with the accents."

"You see?" Lauren cried. "I don't *want* to be different. I want to be the same as everyone else."

"You don't know what it's like to leave your friends," Gretchen accused.

Carrie's brow lifted. Surely she'd told them about her childhood before. "I don't? My dad moved us from Gardiner to a small town in East Texas when I was in the third grade. I made new friends. Four years later we moved to central Texas. I made new friends. I still have friends I stay in contact with from both places. Besides, we have family ties in Gardiner, so you'll see your friends often."

Gretchen groaned. "What if they don't like us?"

Carrie placed a hand on her daughter's cheek. "They'll love you, sweetie." She realized when the time came, she would have to push the issue. Now wasn't the time. *Forcing* her daughters to move would lead to more complications. Carrie pictured them planting their stubborn size sevens firmly in Dave's camp and blaming her for everything bad happening to them from now until forever.

She stood and wiped her hands on her jeans. "Come on, let's go back inside."

She followed them into her mom's dining room through the patio door, wearing her heaviness of spirit like a bulky overcoat. Her discussion with her children had been eye opening. She knew that any permanent change of location or future relationship with Sam, depended on whether or not her children would be willing to give change a chance.

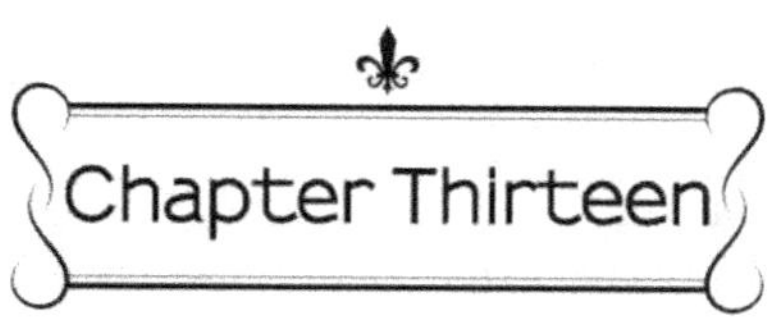

Chapter Thirteen

Carrie stared out of her mother's front door, sipping a cup of coffee. When Christie pulled up into the driveway, she set the cup on her mom's entertainment center and went to help her sister unload the car. "Hey, roomie, I didn't realize you and Max would be back this early."

Christie unbuckled Max from his car seat and set him on the ground. The toddler promptly ran to the front door of his Maw Maw Elaine's and banged on it until someone let him inside.

Carrie watched her nephew's progress, then turned to grab some packages out of her sister's open trunk.

"You want to tell me why the screen on my back door is cut?" Christie asked.

"Dave," she answered, then gave her the abbreviated version of everything that happened.

Christie glared at the windshield. "That son of a bitch!"

"I know, and as bad as that seems, it's not the worst that's happened. She explained about the call and the fact that he'd been watching Christie's house. "I'm considering a move to Kenton instead of the place in Gardiner. I'm going to check it out tonight."

"Really? You'd move to Kenton?"

"I don't know yet. I balked at the idea at first, Chris. But the rent is cheap. Sam assures me the landlord is a great guy and a friend of his. It would cut down on fuel costs and travel time to work. There's a cop right across the street and another at the end of the same block. Sam's place is just across the street." Carrie balanced a third gift on top of the two in Christie's arms. "It sounds…safer, you know?"

"Is this guy really scaring you that much?"

She nodded. "He—he scares me, Chris." Carrie couldn't, didn't want to admit more than that right now. "Enough to make me leave everyone I love behind. I need to know my kids are safe. The fact that I'm staying at your place has only put you and Max in danger."

Christie set the gifts back in her car and turned to hug her. "I'm sorry. I know how difficult this must be for you." She released her and gave a loud sniff before re-arming herself with the gifts. "So you and Sam went out on a real date."

Carrie's jaw dropped at her sister's comment. "After all that, you're worried about my date?"

Christie whipped around to glare at her. "You didn't sleep with him, did you?"

Carrie's jaw shut with a snap. "*That* was a Dave-worthy comment. Of course not."

Christie raised one hand in explanation. "Hey, I told you all about the lack of sex and the horny woman syndrome." She pulled a pack of cigarettes from her purse and lit one up.

Carrie wrinkled her nose in distaste. "I thought you quit smoking."

Chris took a long drag on the cancer stick. "I did, but no way in hell I can give up sex and cigarettes at the same time." She took two more exaggerated drags before putting it out. "See? Just talking about it has me needing a smoke." She grabbed the last of the gifts and closed the trunk. "Have you spoken to your kids about moving to Kenton?"

Carrie grabbed a few more items and groaned. "Yes, and *that* went over like a tent in a hurricane."

"At some point, they need to learn there's a world outside this tiny town."

Carrie led Christie to their mom's front door and paused, her hand on the handle of the full-glass storm door. "I *wish* I knew what the future held for us, Chris—whether or not it'll be worth it to put my kids through this."

"What are your instincts telling you?"

Carrie bit her lower lip. "Honestly? That this is the right thing to do."

Christie gave her a brief nod. "It'll be fine, then."

"Don't tell anyone about the cut screen yet. I don't want anyone talking bad about Dave in front of the kids. It would ruin their Christmas."

"My lips are super-glued."

The rest of the family streamed steadily in until around noon. They feasted on a wild goose and sausage gumbo, cooked by Mack, Carrie's older brother by two years. After lunch, the grandchildren migrated to the front porch to take advantage of the crisp, clean air of the sunny December day. The men, stuffed on good food and desserts, staked out various couches, chairs, and recliners for naps. That left the women of the family seated around the table in the just-cleaned kitchen. The aromas of dark roasted coffee, fresh baked breads, and fig tarts filled the air.

At the first lull in the conversation, Carrie cleared her throat. "I need to get your opinions on something. I've got an opportunity to move to Kenton," she said, as the other women focused their gazes on her.

Her older sister, Jen, looked up from her mug of coffee. "I remember playing Kenton in football. That's about thirty miles north of Jennings, right?"

"Yeah, it's about sixty miles from here, but less than half that to where I work in Lake Coburn."

"That should save you lots of time and fuel," Katie added.

Elaine turned to place a hand on Carrie's arm. "I wanted to tell you that I got a phone call bright and early this morning from Kathleen Ledoux, Rob's mom."

"Oh, hell, I guess she told you everything, didn't she?"

"Well, if everything includes 'Crazy Dave's' antics, from a broken windshield to breaking and entering, then I guess so. She also said something about another threatening phone call early this morning?"

Carrie shushed her while she checked the front porch to make sure her kids were out there. "They know about the windshield, but that's it, and I don't want them to know anything else." She gave the other women a look of warning. "We talked some about me moving when I got here. They think it's just to be closer to work, and Sam, but they're not thrilled, of course."

Katie's blue eyes sparkled with excitement. "Sam? Who's Sam?"

"He's her new boyfriend!" Chris busted out.

Carrie glared at her sister, tight jawed with annoyance. "He's a friend for now, who may or may not turn into something more. Yes, the house I'd be renting happens to be catercornered from his place, but that has nothing to do with anything." She gave an eye roll at the resulting snickers.

Elaine spoke up, putting an end to the teasing. "They'll go with you, Carrie. Maybe not right away, but they'll go. You're a good mother, and they'll miss that if you're not around."

Carrie walked over to the coffee pot for a refill. "I hope you're right, Mom." She turned and leaned against the cabinet and sipped from her mug. "Sam and I have only been on one date, so don't *assume* something is happening that *isn't*." She glared at Christie. "And please don't upset my kids by talking about Dave."

Elaine smiled at the mention of her former son-in-law. "Honey, despite the fact that we all walked on eggshells when he was around, that man did his part to give me three beautiful grandchildren. I'll always be grateful to him for that."

"So," Christie leaned forward in her chair. "When do we get to meet this Sam Langley?"

Carrie sent her sister a bewildered look. "I thought we'd take things slowly. No pressure, you know? I planned for us to get to know each other before I told anyone about him." She eased herself into a chair. "So much for plans."

"When are you going to see him again?" Katie asked.

"Tonight. He's coming with me to meet the landlord and to check out that house. Sam says it's nice, and it's cheap. Apparently, he's had bad renters in the place, recently. He's looking for someone trustworthy. If I do this, I'll need to find a bed. I may be sitting on lawn furniture for a while."

"What about your own stuff?" Susan asked. "You have a right to half of everything."

Carrie nodded. "I know, but I told him he could have the living room furniture. It's shot anyway. I'm taking my small dresser, the freezer, my rocker, and a few other odds and ends. Besides, all three of my kids will be at their dad's at least until the end of the semester and they'll need beds."

Jen leaned forward. "So, tell us more about this co-worker in Kenton."

Carrie spent the next several minutes telling them about Sam and answering whichever questions she could about him.

Elaine hugged her. "Well, *I* can't wait to meet him."

Carrie sent her mom a serious look. "Don't get your hopes up about him, Mom. It's not just about Sam and me; it's about our kids too."

Elaine reached out to cover Carrie's hand with her own. "Don't borrow trouble, sweetie. Just get to know each other, and stop trying to figure out what's going to happen a year from now. God has a way of working things out when you least expect them to."

⚜

By four fifteen, Carrie and her kids pulled up at Christie's place to unload a few gifts. It also gave her the opportunity to change clothes. She discarded her blouse and jeans for her favorite hunter green, V-neck sweater, along with dressy black slacks, and a pair of rarely worn heels that added a good two inches to her height. After refreshing her make-up and dabbing perfume to her wrists, she met her children in the living room.

"You kids ready to go?"

Grant took one look at his mother and whistled. "You look good, Mom."

"Thank you, Grant."

"You sure do," Gretchen told her. "Are you going to check out the rent house dressed like that?"

Carrie nodded in the direction of the car. "Yep, and I have to be there at six, so let's go."

Once they were on the road, Carrie began fielding questions from her curious teens.

"Are you going to see that man again?"

"What's his name?"

"How come he's not married?"

"Does he have any kids?"

"How many?"

"How old are they?"

Carrie cleared her throat and began. "Sam's divorced, like I am. He has two kids, Amanda, who's twenty and is married to Joe. Nick is seventeen and he's a junior. We went out on our very first date last night."

Lauren's head popped over the seat. "You did? A real date? Where'd you go?" She fired the questions in rapid succession.

"Sit back, and buckle your seatbelt, please." She waited until Lauren followed through. "He took me to a restaurant for a steak dinner. Afterward we went to a movie in Lake Coburn, and then we went back to his place so he could show me the house. I was back at Aunt Christie's by midnight."

"Where'd you meet him?" Lauren asked.

"At work. He's head of the survey crew. They go out and collect data along the roadways we use in plans."

Gretchen's next question threw her. "Do you like him a lot, Mom?"

She thought about how to answer that as she drove past the long harvested rice fields lining the highway. "I don't know everything about him, but I like what I've seen so far. He makes me laugh."

"Is he nice?"

She nodded slowly. "He's very nice."

"Have you been on many dates since you and dad split up?"

Carrie stared at Lauren's reflection in her rear-view mirror. "It's the first date I've had with anyone else since I met your dad." Her daughter's shoulders sagged in relief.

Grant stared out the passenger window as he spoke. "It's too bad Dad can't say the same."

Lauren's reply was bitter. "If he could, he and Mom would still be together. Daddy is so stupid."

Carrie's gaze zipped from Grant to her daughters. "You know, now that I'm older, I've come to realize that some people just aren't compatible, no matter how hard they try. I think your dad and I are two of those people. But I don't regret the years we spent together, because it gave us you three."

She slipped off her sunglasses as the winter sun dipped behind the dense cloud coverage. "Your dad may have been the best husband in the world for some other woman, he just wasn't for me." She glanced at Grant, then back at the mirror to his sisters. "We were so young." She sighed and turned her attention back to the road. "If I ever remarry, I'll make wiser choices than I did back then, I promise you."

"So, how do you know this guy's not just putting on a good act for you?" Lauren asked. "Maybe once you fall for him or *marry* him, he'll turn out to be even worse than Dad."

Carrie chanced a look in the rear-view again and her heart sank at the glare of unadulterated disdain coming from her daughter. Her grip on the steering wheel tightened. "You could be right, Lauren. I don't know everything there is to know about Sam, but I believe he's a good man."

"What does he look like, Mom?" Gretchen asked.

"He's very tall, Gretch. Way taller than me, and he just turned forty."

Lauren's face twisted in disgust. "He's *old!*"

"So am I, according to you." Carrie figured it was anger rather than shame causing her daughter to flush a bright red. *She's probably good and pissed at me.*

Gretchen leaned forward in her seat. "Is he good looking?"

Carrie nodded. "He's a nice looking man, but that doesn't count for much, in my opinion." Carrie watched Lauren roll her eyes and turned to stare out the window again. She swallowed her disappointment and plowed ahead. "Look, my primary concern with any other man will be how well he gets along with the three of you." She waited until she caught Lauren's gaze in the mirror. "If Sam's not right for *all* of us, I'll walk away. I promise."

They drove the remainder of the trip to Ruby's in silence, arriving at a quarter to five. Before the kids got out of the car, she turned in her seat to face them. "I love you kids, you know that, don't you?"

One by one, her children said they loved her also.

Carrie got out of the car to give them hugs. "Try not to get in any trouble tonight, and be careful popping fireworks. I'm sure they have tons of them."

She watched them disappear into Ruby's house and waited. As she expected, Arlene appeared at the door to meet her.

"Hey, Ruby wants to know if you want to come in for a cup of coffee and visit for a while."

Carrie shook her head doubtfully. "This is Dave's turf."

"He's not here. He went to your house. I mean his house. Oh, hell!" She bounded down the steps and embraced Carrie in an emotional hug. "I hate this. Holidays around here bite without you!"

Carrie pulled away from her friend. "It's strange not to be a part of this anymore. I miss holidays here, and as much as I'd like to sit down and talk to everyone, I don't have time to stop. I've got to go look at a house I'm thinking about renting in Kenton. The landlord is meeting me at six, and it'll take another fifty minutes to get there." She consulted her watch. "I need to get going."

She opened Ruby's front door long enough to tell everyone Merry Christmas and how much she loved them. By the time she faced Arlene again, she was blinking back tears. "I'm leaving before Ruby comes out here, or I'll fall apart for sure." Carrie buckled herself into her car. She settled her tearful gaze on her friend, who fought her own battle of brimming emotions.

"This is silly. You know that no matter where I live there will always be room for you guys to come and visit. I'll call you when I'm settled."

The other woman wiped her cheeks with the back of her hand and sniffed. "You'd better."

"Love you, soul sister." Carrie blew her a kiss and backed out of the driveway.

Chapter Fourteen

The sharp clip of her heels on the hardwood floor echoed throughout the spacious house, void of anything but kitchen appliances.

"As you can see, it's just been painted and the floors have been replaced. There's new carpet in all three bedrooms and new vinyl in the kitchen and bathrooms. The living room is hardwood. It comes with a gas stove, hood with built-in microwave, and a fridge. I can leave the washer and dryer if you need it."

"I definitely need it," Carrie mumbled.

Sam walked outside to inspect the yard and exterior, while Carrie finished checking out the inside. Signs of recent renovations were everywhere: stickers on newly-installed double-insulated windows, floor surfaces that gleamed as though wet, freshly painted walls and trim in pleasing, muted tones, and a marble counter-top that reflected the glow of shiny new light fixtures. The house was a steal—easily worth three times the rent he was asking, and so much nicer than the place in Gardiner. Could she sell her kids on this?

Once more, she heard her mom's words of wisdom. *You make the rules now, Carrie*. Again she felt it in her gut; the feeling this was where she and her children belonged. This will be good for them.

"If you want to think about it, I'll save it for you until the first." Len's voice cut through her musings.

She reached for her purse and pulled out a checkbook. "I'm making an executive decision. This place is perfect. How much do I make the check for?" She waited, pen in hand, praying Sam hadn't got the price wrong.

"Sam's a good friend and he's vouched for you. A hundred dollar deposit and January's rent of two hundred. As far as I'm concerned, you can move in immediately and the rest of December is free. The backyard is fenced in if you have a dog. No pets in the house—I think you can understand why."

Carrie grinned across at her new landlord, who stood about the same height as she did. "No inside pets. It's bad enough having three teenagers in my house. I did my time when my kids were little—hamsters, puppies, kittens, baby birds, even a baby nutria once."

Len's brows rose in surprise. "That's a new one. How'd that work out?"

She tore out the filled check and handed it to him. "Actually, it was the best behaved and easiest to train out of all of them. I don't think Joey realized he was a nutria."

"You trained him?"

"The kids did. When they called him, he'd waddle right to them to be petted. He'd grunt at the door to go out, and he'd grunt to come back in."

"We had a pet raccoon when I was growing up. He acted just like a dog," Len told her. "My grandmother, a mean old woman, was terrified of him, so we took every opportunity to bring him around when she was at our place."

"Hey, the raccoon lived there—she was just a guest." She laughed at the image.

"That's what I tried to tell the old crone before she nearly twisted my darn ear off." He lifted one finger. "She only caught me once, though. I got faster after that."

Carrie laughed, thrilled to have such a pleasant man for a landlord. "Oh, but you haven't truly lived until your huge pet nutria comes waddling up the front porch steps right in front of a pair of sweet, old, black ladies witnessing Jehovah. I bet those two didn't know they could move so fast."

Len slapped his thigh as he guffawed. "You win with that one." He put the check in his wallet and handed her a business card and a set of keys. "Glad to have you, Ms. Jeansonne. If anything goes wrong in the house, call me, night or day. My numbers are on there."

She took the keys and his card before shaking his hand.

Sam walked inside from the backyard, bringing the smell of brisk winter air with him. "Len, you have some dead limbs overhanging the edge of the house. You may want to get those trimmed soon."

Len gave him a nod. "Got somebody coming to trim those the day after Christmas, Sam, but thanks for the heads-up. Let me know if you catch anything else I might have missed, will you?"

Sam leaned over to shake his hand. "Sure will, buddy." Len walked out, leaving Carrie and Sam alone in the house. "Doesn't he want to lock the place up?"

Carrie dangled the keys in front of him. "I guess he thought I could handle it. So, how do you like me now, neighbor?"

"Seriously?" Sam pulled her into his arms and nuzzled her neck. "I think I like you even more. Can I help move you in tomorrow?"

She giggled, ticklish at his neck nuzzling. "I need something to move first. Mom mentioned that my cousin lives in a huge two-story house and has several sets of living and bedroom furniture, and she said I could borrow a few pieces. It'll hold me until I get some of my own stuff."

"Are your kids okay with this?"

Her throat tightened at the thought of her children. "No. I'm hoping they'll come around. My mom swears they will. She told me to make the change and eventually they'll end up with me."

Sam brushed a finger down one side of her cheek. "Do you believe that?"

"If I didn't, I wouldn't be doing this. I think Grant will want to graduate from Gardiner, though. He's halfway through his junior year. I guess I can't blame him for that." Shaking off the urge to cry, she headed straight for the back door. "Come with me to check out the yard." She walked onto the back porch, which was newly screened in and just right for a bistro-size table and chairs. It boasted a ceiling fan for those hot summer afternoons, as well as plenty of shelter for Toto on cold winter nights.

"Your dogs are outside dogs, right?"

She flipped a light switch, illuminating part of the fully-fenced-in backyard, and nodded. "Oh, I love gardenias," she groaned, seeing several shrubs, along with two huge oak trees. "I'll only have Toto here. He's my dog. Lucas is Dave's hunting dog."

Moonlight filtered through the branches of one oak that had to be at least fifty years old. She raised her arms toward the evening sky and inhaled the cold, crisp air of the late December night. "I don't know about Toto, but I could be very happy here. As long as my kids are here, too," she added in a somber note. "I'll try to hang on until the beginning of the next school year. If they're not here by then . . ." Carrie let the comment trail off, avoiding Sam's gaze.

She pulled her coat tight against the icy wind, and turned to examine the backside of the house. "You can't see inside the bedrooms because of those new blinds. That's good," she mumbled. Her gaze gravitated toward the huge picture window in the dining area that faced the backyard, the only one with no covering. "I'll have to buy drapes for that window. You can see clear into the living room through that thing."

She started for the house, and Sam followed. Once inside, she pulled a pad and ink pen from her purse to begin a list. Sam's comment drew her attention.

"Len did a great job with this place, didn't he?"

"It's a wonderful house," she replied. "The kids will be pleased. I think they believed we'd be stuck in a dump. Not that our house was a mansion or anything, but we were comfortable enough." She stretched her arms out across the massive window. "I wish I had a measuring tape."

Within minutes, Sam had retrieved one for her and she had the measurements she needed. She let the tape snap closed and noticed Sam's ear-to-ear grin. "Have you stopped to consider maybe you won't like having me as a neighbor?"

"I'd be a damn fool not to." He stepped in to close the gap between them. "It'll be a huge relief to have you here."

She blinked several times to stem the tears from forming. "I hope whoever's making those damn calls doesn't follow me here. I won't feel good about this place until my kids are here, permanently. And I know they can't be here until it's safe for them."

"Somebody needs a hug." He rocked her in his arms and whispered. "Have you taken all the notes you need for the night?"

"I think so."

After returning to Sam's driveway, Carrie stopped to retrieve a plastic container from the trunk of her car. "I brought you some goodies."

Once inside, Sam bit into a homemade fig tart, rolling his eyes in blissful appreciation. "Oh, God, that's good. Please tell me you baked these."

"Those are my Mom's specialty. I made the fudge and pralines, though." She turned away when Sam grabbed a praline and held the container out to her. "I'm still too full from lunch. We always have too much food."

Sam rubbed his belly enthusiastically. "Sounds like a good time to me."

She leaned up against his counter and sighed. "And we'll do it all over again tomorrow." She turned to Sam to explain. "My brother, Josh, is coming in from north Texas late tonight. No one's seen him in over a year."

"Your mom's going to have a full house."

"Sometimes it's a challenge to get everybody together at once. I don't get to see some of them as much as I'd like to but we're close for a big family."

Sam and Carrie spent the next hour seated beside each other on his couch, talking. One or the other got up to switch stations on his stereo when the urge hit. They kicked off their shoes, settled in close to each other, the television on but muted, and listened to music.

"Nights like this I miss my old place," Carrie admitted. "The smell of the fireplace on cold, winter nights. The view of the lake from the front porch. It's really pretty out there."

Tight-lipped, Sam left the couch and walked over to his stereo again. Instead of changing the station, he shoved his hands deep into his pockets and turned to her. "Carrie—"

She stretched her arms above her head and yawned. "Hmmm?"

"Is, uh—I mean, would this place—" He stretched out an arm to indicate the living room and beyond. "If you decide you . . ." His voice trailed off, and he released a frustrated sigh. "I don't have a whole hell of a lot to offer you, Carrie." His eyes scanned the place, from his living room and dining area on down to the hallway. "This place is all I've got. It's not fancy, and I don't have a lot of money or material things."

Carrie's breath caught at Sam's heartfelt confession. She rose from the couch and walked over to meet him. "Money and things don't matter to me, Sam. What matters is what's in your heart." She splayed her hand on the center of his broad chest. "I know you've got a good heart."

Sam reached out and gently placed one hand on each side of her face. "Thank you for that. I think you know by now how I feel about you. I just worry that maybe what I have isn't enough."

"It's enough, Sam. If we're meant to be, what you have or don't have materially won't affect my decision, I promise you."

He pulled her close. "I want you to know I'll do everything in my power to get your kids to like me so they'll all want to move here. I know that's what would make you happy, and God knows I want you happy here in Kenton."

She slipped her arms around his waist and gazed up into serious blue eyes. "Be careful, Sam. Talk like that could get you into big, big trouble."

"How so?"

"Talk like that makes me never want to leave here."

"That's what I'm counting on."

"Ah, but I still say once you get to know me you may not want me around." She stood perfectly still as he traced the arch of her brows with one long index finger.

"Bring it on, Baby. I'm dying to get the chance to prove you wrong."

She let him kiss her, clinging to him, her hand pulling his neck, his tangled in her hair. Another long exhibit of wanting and willpower as they both found the strength to separate.

"Dear, God, I love your mouth," he whispered, his voice hoarse with need. She moaned in pleasure, as he buried his face in the crook of her neck. "And you smell so damn good. Is that the same perfume you always wear?"

"Eau de gumbo?" she said, unable to resist. When he responded in a voice deep and raspy with need—half groan, half chuckle—she couldn't find it in her to laugh.

"You have the most remarkable eyes I've ever seen." His finger trailed down the side of her face and across the slope of her jaw line. "And you said it's called Obsessed, or something like that?"

"Obsession." Her lids closed heavily, drugged with a sudden satisfaction that all was as it should be. Her head drooped forward to rest upon his chest as she felt the soft massage of long fingers against her scalp. *Oh. My. God.* She felt him, his breath, his heartbeat, his need for her.

The sudden *BANG* against the wood siding of the house jarred them.

"What the hell?" Sam leaned over to glare through the gaping black hole of the double windows behind the Christmas tree.

Carrie clung too tightly to do anything but move with him. Nothing but darkness, muted by multicolored shadows from the tree lights reflected back at them.

"Stay here, so I can check that out."

"Like hell I will." Her voice, shrill with tension and terror, sounded foreign to her own ears. He tried again to make her stay put, but she refused.

"Okay, but stay close," he warned. Needlessly, as it turned out, since she'd already latched on to him like lint to one of those *as seen on TV* dusters.

Once outside, they investigated the area around the double windows, finding nothing.

"Do you think the wind blew something against the side of the house?"

He nodded. "It's one possibility, I guess—"

"But you don't think so?"

"I didn't say that." He peered into the darkness before draping his arm around Carrie's shoulders. "Come on, let's go back inside."

Once inside, her gaze kept returning to the blackness outside the windows. "Can we close those curtains?"

He released the tiebacks until the drapes fell into place, sealing out the darkness. "Promise me something, baby?"

"Maybe."

"Next time I ask you to stay inside, could you please do that? I mean, considering everything that's happened—"

"No."

"Final word?"

"For now, I feel a lot safer with *you,* even outside."

"Even if you're locked inside?"

"Yep."

Sam's jaw worked. "I could take it as a compliment."

"You could."

Sam gave his eyes a dramatic roll.

"Sam." She lowered her voice. "Look at me." Carrie smiled at the look of resigned worry in his eyes. She brought both hands to the sides of his face and pulled it level to her own. Gazing straight into his eyes, she gave him a tentative smile. "Have I told you how much I love it when you call me Baby?"

Sam cocked his head to the side, and gave her a sheepish grin. "I aim to please."

She looped her arms around his neck as Percy Sledge crooned *Warm and Tender Love* from the speakers. The local radio-station D.J. was smack dab in the middle of another hour of belly-rubbing Swamp Pop from the 60's. They swayed in unison to the music as winds rattled the windows in the small living room. Flames of the gas space heater flickered with the draft, as Sam maneuvered her closer to the warmth.

She flexed her shoulders and groaned as the waves of heated air radiated up her back.

"I know," he muttered. "It gets pretty cold in here when the wind comes in from the north. I plan to change those old windows out." His gaze settled on her. "This place needs some work."

She studied the room as if giving it an appraisal. "It's a nice place."

"I've always thought so, but I've been told that I get too set in my ways and resist change."

"Yeah?" she answered with some amusement. "If I stick around long enough, maybe you'll let me whip you into shape."

He raised one brow. "I'm whip-able, and you're sure as hell welcome to try."

She smiled and put her head on his shoulder, as they continued to dance to the old song. Suddenly, she could picture them dancing just like this, years from now, in this same house, their hair peppered with silver, their faces wrinkled, and surrounded by pictures of grandchildren and great grandchildren.

Instead of comforted by the image, Carrie felt a sudden rush of panic, as though things were moving far too quickly. She cleared her throat and moved away from him, pretending to be calmer than she felt. "I have to go, Sam."

He frowned in disappointment. "So soon?"

"I-I just realized how much I have to do." She pressed one hand against her stomach, queasy with nerves, as she reached for her purse with the other. She opened the front door and turned, letting her gaze settle on him. "Thanks for all your help."

She saw momentary confusion cross his features as he nodded and lowered his head to kiss her good night. Instead of raising her lips to him, she turned so that his mouth grazed her cheek. She gave him a stiff smile and turned to walk out the door.

He caught her wrist, halting her escape. "Don't leave me like this without at least telling me what I did wrong."

The brass handle of the storm door chilled her grip, in sharp contrast to the warmth of his hand on her wrist. “Honestly, you did nothing wrong, Sam. It’s happening too fast, that’s all.” She grasped his hand tightly, and found the courage to face him. “It scares me.”

“What does?”

Carrie scanned his living room, then the porch with brightly colored Christmas lights, and finally landed on the large blue cross on his lawn. “This.” She lifted her hands to indicate all of it. “You. The way you make me feel. It’s wonderful, but I’m afraid I’ll find myself in the same situation, because I let it happen too quickly.”

Sam released her wrist. “I don’t want to pressure you.” One brow lifted cockily. “You know, you *could* let me gloat a little for making you feel that way, even if it scares you.”

“Oh, Lord. I can see your ego inflate as we speak.”

He pulled her close for a hug. “I can’t help it, Carrie. I’m proud as hell that you’d even consider dating me.”

She dropped her head back and groaned. By the time she straightened to kiss him—on the lips this time—she’d accepted her defeat. “All right, Sam, you win, but I really do have to go.” Chills ran up her spine at the chuckle that rumbled deep in his chest.

“And after that, I’ll let you.”

She pulled her hand out of his and walked to her car, smiling to herself.

Sam stood at the end of his sidewalk, watching her taillights disappear around the corner. He gazed up at the clear, star-filled sky, thinking about the day’s events. The sound of a truck’s diesel engine starting up caught his attention. A cold dread crept up his spine, as he watched the pick-up pull out from in front of Carrie’s rental. The two-toned truck drove slowly along his street, then slowed to a near stop directly in front of him. He couldn’t see past the dull glow of the dash lights, but he knew it was Dave—felt the man’s gaze on him.

Sam walked determinedly towards the truck, his hand reaching for the door handle. He slapped the side of the vehicle, swearing loudly as it sped off after Carrie.

Feeling for his keys, he swore again, as he realized they were inside. Sam jumped the steps and ran to the key rack, knowing in his gut they wouldn’t be there. “Shit! Where’d I put the damn things?” He spun around, now in full panic mode, and saw them hanging off the edge of the counter top. In five seconds he was out the door and down his steps. His truck’s engine barely had time to catch before he threw it in reverse and pulled out of his carport. Spinning his tires on the street, he sped off in pursuit of the other two vehicles.

Concern for Carrie overrode his regard for traffic laws or cops, as he prayed he’d catch up to her before her ex did something stupid. His imagination spun out of control as he contemplated all sorts of scenarios, all ugly. What the hell was Dave up to? It wasn’t long before he spied the red taillights of the truck. He passed it easily and concentrated on catching up to Carrie. At 90 miles per hour, it only took another minute to catch her. He flashed his lights a couple of times and turned on his interior light to let her know he wanted her to stop.

Finally, she pulled over to the side of the road and came to a complete stop. Sam pulled up behind her car, was already half-way out of the cab before he threw his truck into park. He grabbed Carrie's hand as she got out of her car and pulled her off the road.

"What's going on?"

"Dave followed you." He pointed to the approaching headlights.

The truck accelerated as it passed them, leaving them standing on the side of the road and staring after it.

Sam pointed at Carrie's sedan. "You can get back in that car and follow me back home. There's no way in hell I'm letting you drive all the way back to Gardiner with him waiting for you. It ain't happening."

"I don't understand. When did you see him?"

"He'd parked in front of the house, Carrie. *Your* house. As soon as you left, he started his truck and passed slowly in front of me. That son of a gun *wanted* me to know it was him." He shook his head, determination guiding is next actions as he took her gently by the arm. "Come on, let's go home."

She pulled out of his grasp. "I think he got what he came for. I'm sure it's fine for me to go back to Christie's."

"It's not fine," he growled. "I'll have to wait and wonder for another hour if he ran you off of the road somewhere and did God knows what to you. I can't let you do that. You're coming home with me." He nudged her gently to her car.

She spun away from him. "I'm thirty-six years old, Sam. Don't tell me what I can and cannot do."

Sam spoke before he thought. "Well, now you're just being silly. Come on, let's go."

She turned an icy glare in his direction. "I didn't leave one controlling man to fall into the arms of another." She stalked off toward her car.

"Dammit, Carrie, don't be hard-headed about this!"

She opened her car door and paused to send him a glare. "You're not making any points. Good night, Sam."

He groaned, frustrated at her lack of concern. If he couldn't reason with her, maybe he could scare her. He walked up to her door before she closed it, and leaned in the window as she buckled herself in. "All right, but I'm following you home."

"You don't have—"

"And when I get there, I'm going to stay parked in your drive. And you can bet your ass before I leave town, I will be talking to someone in the Gardiner police department."

"Sam—"

"And do me a damn favor, would you?" he cut in, his voice rising from his aggravated state. "If you see his truck pulled over somewhere, don't stop to talk to him. If he's in front of you, don't try to pass him. And if he pulls up alongside you, pull into the first driveway you see, all right?" He walked back to his truck, got in, and waited. After almost a minute, she made a u-turn on the highway, and headed back toward Kenton. "I'll be damned," he muttered, as she passed him, keeping her eyes straight ahead. He maneuvered his truck into a one-eighty and followed her.

By the time they made it home, he found himself wondering how Dave would take the news that, thanks to him, he and Carrie were spending the night together. Hell, he may have to shake the bastard's hand before it was over with. He pulled up alongside her under the carport. She got out of her car, looking like she could spit nails. Then again—maybe not.

Sam slammed his truck door, thinking he should try to smooth things over. "Look, you drove all the way over here to see me and that house. It's my responsibility to make sure you're okay." She turned her back on him and walked up the front steps. He followed her inside and locked the doors behind him.

Carrie dropped her purse on the couch and turned to him. "God, you're stubborn!"

"I can be," he admitted, "when it's called for." He hung his keys on the rack and turned to point at her. "And I don't give a rat's ass how pissed you are, as long as you're safe." Sam grinned as she wheeled away from him and muttered a low string of curses that would make any Marine proud. By the time she turned back toward him, he'd wiped all signs of amusement from his face.

"What do we do, now?" She crossed her arms, clearly uncomfortable with the situation.

"You might want to call your sister, if she's waiting at home for you." Sam handed her his cordless and then walked into his bedroom to kick off his shoes. He turned on the king-size electric blanket to high then rummaged through his clothes, trying to find something for her to sleep in. He could hear her on the phone, explaining things to her sister, and saying how she was sure *he'd* overreacted. He snorted to himself. And she called him stubborn? He settled on a long-sleeved flannel shirt, faded and soft from hundreds of washings. He turned, startled, to find Carrie standing, shoving the phone in his face.

"She wants to talk to you."

"What for?"

"I have no idea."

Sam took the phone, holding it as though it could explode any second. "Hello?"

"So, you're Sam."

He resisted wincing at her tone. "That'd be me."

"Are you using this situation as an excuse to get into my sister's pants?"

"What? Hell no!"

"Why not? Are you gay?"

Sam rubbed his hand roughly over his forehead. "Oh, my God."

"Are you?" she repeated.

"Of course not."

"Well, then, let me give you one word of warning. If you hurt my sister, I'm going to find you and give you a world of trouble. I don't care how big you are. You got that?"

Sam's breath rushed out of his gaping mouth.

"Did you hear what I said, Mr. Langley?"

"Uh, yeah. I hear you, and you don't have to worry." He listened as dead silence greeted him. "Are you there?"

"Yeah. Are you sure? Because she's my big sister . . ."

He heard her voice crack and waited for her to finish, realizing they were on the same team.

"And Dave has already put her through too much hell."

"I know, and yeah, I'm sure. I won't hurt her."

"All right then. Put her back on the phone."

Carrie waited until Sam disappeared down the hallway. "Chris?"

"Carrie, you didn't shave your legs, did you?"

"Uh, last night I did, why?"

"Oh, boy," Christie groaned. "For future reference, unshaved legs are the best reason in the world to keep your pants on. Even then, some guys would sleep with a lady Sasquatch to get some. Start carrying condoms at all times."

"Christie!" Carrie hissed.

"You need to know these things if you're going to live as a single woman. There are diseases out there."

Carrie pinched the bridge of her nose. "I don't think that's a concern right now."

"It's always a concern, and don't you forget it. At least you can't get knocked up."

"Hanging up now." She watched Sam's approach.

"Remember! Condo—"

She cut off the conversation and put the cordless on the counter as Sam approached.

"Here, let me know what else you need and I'll scrounge something up."

She took the flannel shirt and toothbrush still in the package that Sam handed her. "Thanks. This'll do. Just get me a pillow and a blanket and I'll take the couch."

"No, you take the bed. I'll sleep on the couch."

Too exhausted to argue with him, she nodded then went into the bathroom. Ten minutes later, she tiptoed out of the room, her face washed free of makeup and her teeth brushed. The tail of Sam's clean flannel shirt trailed all the way to her knees. She didn't see him around, so it was the perfect opportunity to sneak into bed and avoid the embarrassment of him seeing her halfway undressed. She slipped under the covers, immediately enveloped by warmth instead of the expected iciness of cold sheets.

"Mmmm. An electric blanket. Yes!" She burrowed deep, pulling the toasty covers up to her nose in the chilly room.

"Do you need a heater in here?"

She turned toward the sound of Sam's voice. "Nope, this is nice. My nose gets all stuffy if I sleep with the heater on. Thanks for turning on the blanket for me, Sam."

He smiled and took one step inside the room. "You're welcome. You need anything else?"

"I don't think so."

He turned halfway, then paused. "You still mad at me?"

Carrie studied his demeanor, seeing the flash of guilt even though none of this was his fault. She pulled the covers down and reached for him with one hand.

He seated himself on the bed beside her.

"I'm not mad at you, Sam. I'm aggravated with Dave."

He kept his silence.

She attempted to roll up one sleeve without exposing too much of herself to the chilled air. "Somebody's got really long arms."

Without a word, he flipped one cuff into tight, neat rolls, then the other.

She raised her arms, now completely manageable. "Much better."

"You look good in my shirt."

Carrie lowered her arms and caught his heated gaze. "It's soft and cozy. I might have to take it home with me." She raised one sleeve to her nose and sniffed. "It smells like you."

"It's yours." He stood and reached for the lamp on the nightstand. "You want this off?"

She nodded, amazed at how that statement fit so many things. His clothes—her clothes—oh, man. Christie was right. It had been too damn long. She thought about his size thirteen shoes and her face heated immediately.

"You look even better in my bed." A split second later, he clicked off the lamp. "Good night, Babe."

She barely managed to croak a hoarse "Good night."

Sometime during the night, Sam gave up the battle of trying to find a comfortable spot on that old sofa. He crawled into the bed on the opposite side of where Carrie slept soundly. *You stay on your side, and I'll stay on mine.*

Despite the fact that he was dead tired, it still took him a while to fall asleep. The image of Carrie in his flannel shirt *and very little else* planted itself firmly in his mind. By the time he did sleep, he was good and exhausted, and still on his side of the bed.

Chapter Fifteen

Carrie awoke slowly, aware of being wrapped in warmth. *I must get myself an electric blanket.* She lay there, her eyes closed, drowsy from sleeping so hard, and trying to figure out why she was so comfortable.

Sam snorted in his sleep.

Carrie's eyes flew open. *What the hell?* Sam was in bed with her, and somehow they'd both ended up in the middle of that California King—entangled limbs, her head on his chest, his arm wrapped tightly around her. She lifted her head from his chest and tried to inch herself back to her side of the bed. In a flash, Sam's hand came out to grip her forearm, halting her retreat. She looked up, blinking sleep from her eyes, as she met his amused gaze with her own.

"Where you going?" His voice was rough and gravelly.

"I wanted to put some space between us." She moved herself to the far side of the bed. "Why are you here?"

"I live here, what about you?"

She made a face. "Always a smart ass. What, the sofa's not as comfortable as you remembered?"

"I tried babe, I really did. I finally gave it up around three o'clock. How about you? Did you sleep well?"

Carrie nodded. "I did, but I really have to get dressed and go home."

He turned to face her. "Merry Christmas, Carrie."

She smiled. "I'd almost forgotten. Merry Christmas to you, too, Sam."

"Waking up with you in my bed on Christmas morning—this rates number one on the 'best Christmas gift' list." He gave her a crooked, though somewhat sleepy grin.

She blushed and pulled the covers up over her mouth. "I'm a little mortified, if you want to know the truth."

His brow furrowed. "Why?"

The covers over her mouth muffled her reply. "Oh—dragon breath, no make-up, and messy hair. Not how I'd choose you to see me this early in our relationship. My ex didn't even see me like this until after we were married."

"When it was too late to take it back?"

She punched him on the shoulder. "Oh, that's nice."

Sam cracked a wide grin, then farted loudly. "There, that should even things up."

"Ever the charmer," she snorted. "And here I thought it was just a Dave thing."

He laughed and tweaked her nose. "I'd wager it's more of a guy thing. Naw, you look fine to me. As a matter of fact," he drawled, reaching out for her. "I wouldn't mind waking up to this sight every day for the rest of my life."

"Uh uh." She scooted away from him and out of the bed. Carrie stood and pulled at the shirt hem in an unsuccessful effort to make it longer. She grabbed her things and ran quickly into the master bathroom, but not quick enough to keep Sam from getting a good look at the hem of his shirt flapping on bare thighs.

"You look damn good in my shirt!" he called out as the door shut.

She opened the door just a crack. "You'd better be dressed by the time I get out of here."

Carrie exited the bathroom fully dressed, combed, and made-up. The welcome aroma of bacon frying permeated the air, making her mouth water and stomach growl. She stepped into the kitchen, appreciating the rear view of Sam standing in front of the stove. "Mmm, it smells good in here."

He spun around to face her. "Hey, pretty girl, are you hungry? I've got biscuits, bacon, and scrambled eggs coming right up."

"I'm starving." She seated herself in front of the plate of food he placed on the snack bar. "Thanks, Sam."

"It's the least I could do." He shrugged. "Sorry, but I don't own a coffee maker. We could go over to my folks if you want," he suggested. "They're a couple of houses down from me across the backyard."

Carrie cringed and shook her head. "Let's do that when I don't feel awkward about sleeping here all night. I'll be okay until I get back to Christie's."

He nodded as he served a second plate for himself. "What are we going to do about Dave?"

She waited for him to sit beside her. "You mean, what am *I* going to do?"

Sam shook a bottle of hot sauce over his eggs. "The man followed you to *my* turf; I'm directly involved now."

She considered that for a moment. "I guess you're right. I really don't know what I can do other than keep Rob Ledoux informed. He didn't break any laws." She popped a piece of bacon in her mouth and chewed.

"You want juice or milk?"

"Juice, please."

He poured a glass and placed it beside her plate. "Maybe we should tell Doug, my neighbor."

She frowned, giving her head a shake. "Cops talk, Sam. I don't need the whole town knowing about this. Besides," she added. "Maybe now that he's seen you, he'll leave it alone. I promise I'll tell Rob what happened."

His face sobered with concern. "I'd feel a hell of a lot better explaining the situation to Doug. You'll be a citizen of this town soon. It would help if he knew what was going on."

Carrie lowered her head and released a low groan. "Would you at least wait until I'm gone? I can't face anyone this morning, especially knowing what he'll be thinking."

"I hate to ask, but do you have a picture of him? It might help if he could put a face to the name."

Carrie pulled an old family photo from her wallet, folded so that only she and the kids were visible. "God, this is humiliating. Before this is over with everyone in Gardiner and Kenton will know everything about my crazy ex and psycho stalker."

Sam reached for the photo and studied it for a moment. Carrie bit her bottom lip, trying to gauge his reaction as he got his first glimpse of her and Dave as a couple. She tensed, fighting the urge to rip it out of his hands.

He glanced her direction. "You look like a cat ready to bolt, what's wrong?"

She jutted her chin toward the photo in his hands. "I can't explain it, but for some reason I'm uncomfortable with you seeing that."

He smiled as he studied the picture. "That's a good-looking lady."

"Not good enough. He left me for another woman before the proofs came in."

Several creases appeared on Sam's brow as he grunted in disgust. "Can I say again what a fool your ex is?"

By eight a.m., Sam waved Carrie off and walked back inside. He hated the emptiness of his place now that she was gone. He tried to imagine her living here, in this home, giving the place her own personal touch, doing what women do to make a place their own. One thought led to another and soon he was wondering if his kids would accept her as a stepmother. Carrie was right. More than two lives would be affected by their new relationship. It would merge two families—two branches from two separate trees. Would their kids get along—eventually accept each other as siblings? Would they be able to blend as a family?

Suddenly, it hit him. The realization of the enormous sacrifice Carrie and her children would have to make by relocating—if they chose to. They'd go through a tremendous upheaval and a hell of a lot of trouble. *Am I worth it?* It forced him to think about the kind of man, the kind of husband he'd been. The kind of man he was now. He shook his head—there was definitely room for improvement. He vowed then and there that if he ever got the chance to start the new life he wanted with Carrie, he would be a better man and a better husband.

Sam placed the blankets and extra pillow back into his closet, then walked into his master bathroom. He closed his eyes and breathed in her scent, wishing he could keep it with him. He picked up the flannel shirt she'd folded and placed on the side of the tub and held it up to his nose. *That's Carrie*. He buried his face in it, thinking it was a crappy substitute for the real thing. Instead of bringing it to the laundry room to be washed, he folded it, carried it back into his room, then placed it on the foot of his bed. He paused, catching sight of his smugly pleased expression in the mirror. "Shut up." He turned and left the room.

Sam bundled up and went out on his porch to stare at Carrie's rent house. Lost in his own thoughts about the possibilities, he didn't notice Linda pull up to the front of the house until the door opened and Nick spilled out. His gangly son hauled a duffle bag from the back seat, then waved off his mom. Sam didn't even look at the car until the brakes squealed at the intersection. No gut wrenching pain in his stomach, none of the regrets he usually felt around this time. Amazing. He pictured Carrie in his flannel shirt and in his bed first thing this morning. The sound of Nick's throat clearing jolted him into the present.

"Hey, old man, what're you grinning about?"

Sam turned to open the door for his son. "I didn't realize I was, but I guess it's because I feel so good." He hugged Nick, then slapped him heartily on the back. "Merry Christmas, Son."

"You too, Dad."

Sam took his son's shit-eating grin for what it was. "What's on your mind?"

"I heard we're getting a new neighbor soon."

Sam played along, fully suspecting that at least one of Linda's friends had called her already. "Anyone we know?"

"Nobody I know, but I heard you may know her. Some *young* thing, from down around Gardiner," Nick drawled.

Sam gave his son a knowing grin. "Who called her?"

"She wouldn't say, but she heard all about you calling around for deposit info. Whoever called Mom said this woman left her husband for you."

"Bullshit. Carrie was six months separated and waiting on her divorce when I met her. And your mom has met her already. She walked over to our table to check her out at the steak house the other night."

"Uh huh, I heard all about it."

"I'm not going to lie to you, Son. I care for this woman, and I hope she's more than a friend one day." He leaned against a section of the ponderosa pine cabinets he'd built himself and crossed his arms. Sam stared at his son, wondering if his ex-wife had said anything to poison him against Carrie. "Look, I don't know what she told you, *and I don't want to know.*" His tone bordered on forceful. "Carrie's a real nice lady. She's thirty-six and has three teenagers. She's having some trouble with her ex-husband, and I need to let you know what happened here last night before the town gossips get a hold of it." He explained the occurrences of the previous night before leveling a serious look on his son. "To make a long story short, I made her come back to the house with me. I didn't want her running into him down the road. Yes, she spent the night here, but nothing happened."

Nick nodded in understanding. "I get it, Dad. It's not that big a deal."

Sam studied his son. "That's the thing, Nick. She is a big deal to me. I wake up looking forward to the day now. Carrie's done that for me, and I hope you and Amanda can accept that I'm moving on with my life."

Carrie did some serious 'Sam pondering' on the way home. Why did everything about the man make her want to cuddle up close to him, as though he were some big teddy bear? Common sense told her there was no way she could possibly care that much for someone she'd known for such a short time. It scared her as much now as it had last night during the dancing. Waking up in his arms this morning—what a glorious way to start the day. Her face heated when she thought of that big bed with him in it. She'd be in huge trouble unless she found a way to slow things down.

She pulled into Christie's drive and approached the door with keys in hand. She opened the storm door and bent to retrieve a folded slip of paper someone had slipped inside the doorjamb. Carrie unfolded it and read the message written in Dave's scrawl.

Carrie-

I only went to Kenton so I could get a good look at the man who is ruining our second chance to be a family. I stayed in this driveway until five A.M. – where the hell did YOU sleep last night?

Dave

Carrie cursed under her breath, then unlocked the door and walked inside. She'd only had time to set her purse down and kick off her shoes, when she heard the unmistakable sound of Dave's diesel coming down the street. She slammed the door's deadbolt home and hit the speed dial for the Gardiner PD.

Within two minutes, she heard a single siren blast and caught a flash of light from a side window. Pulling the curtain aside, she saw the police cruiser pull up right behind Dave's truck. In the time it took Dave to saunter over to the first cruiser, Rob Ledoux had pulled up alongside.

Carrie turned from the window to face Christie, who entered the room yawning and stretching.

"What the hell's going on in my driveway?"

"A dramatic Dave entrance. He's a little testy from waiting for me in your driveway until five a.m."

"How do you know that?" She read the note Carrie handed her and rolled her eyes. "Oh, come on! You divorced him. Is he insane?"

Carrie turned back to the window to see what was happening. "It's all about putting on a good show, Chris. He doesn't want me any more than I want him." She clucked her tongue. "After this, everyone in town is going to know even more of my business." She watched another few seconds before she slipped back into her shoes and hit the door, grabbing her coat and the letter on her way.

Carrie walked over to Rob and handed him the note, giving him her foulest fed-up-with-the-whole-thing look. "I don't know what he told you, but this was in the door when I got home this morning."

Dave gave her an accusing glare. "Where've you been all night, Carrie?"

She smiled sweetly. "You ought to know. You followed me to Kenton."

Rob got in Dave's face. "Did you follow her all the way to Kenton?"

"Hell yeah, I followed her, but I didn't go near her. There's no law against that. I just wanted to get a good look at that prick."

"The divorce has been final for months."

"In God's eyes, we're still married."

"Don't you *dare* spout that 'holier than thou' crap to me, not after everything you've pulled over the years with a wife and three kids waiting at home." She lowered her lids to half-mast as she remembered the knock on Sam's wall. "It was *you* outside his window last night, wasn't it, Dave?" His silence spoke volumes. Her voice lowered to a tantalizing whisper.

"You shouldn't have run away so fast. Sam was anxious to introduce himself to you."

Rob interrupted. "That's enough, you two." He told the second officer to detain Dave while he got the full story.

Carrie shook her head as T. Hardin "assisted" Dave into the back seat of the patrol car. "Freaking lunatic."

Rob held up the note in front of her as they walked back to Christie's front porch. "Explain this."

"Be glad to." She related the events of the previous night.

Rob nodded. "I would have done the same thing if I were in Sam's shoes. He must care about you some to go chasing you down like that." The big man grinned at her.

"Some," Carrie countered.

He chortled as he placed a hand on her shoulder. "Good for you, girl. I hope he makes you happy."

"A little too soon to tell."

"Hmph, don't know about that. I knew I loved Mona a week after we started dating. My feelings haven't changed a bit in the twenty years we've been married."

She nodded curtly in his direction. "And I'm thrilled for you, but I'm determined not to make the same mistake twice. I moved too fast when I met 'Mr. Fidelity' over there. I'd like to take it slow this time around."

Rob gave her a smug smile. "Just remember, the older you get, the more 'taking your time' can jump up and bite you on the ass. Now, let me see what I can do with 'Crazy Dave', as my mother has dubbed him. You can either stay on the porch or go back inside."

"I'm staying. I want to hear this."

Rob headed back toward her ex and pulled him out of the car to point a finger in his face. "This is just how I wanted to spend my Christmas morning, buddy. You are not making any points with me or my family. What the hell did you think you were doing, when I've already warned you to stay away from her?"

Dave lifted his chin stubbornly. "It's not against the law to drive to Kenton. I never went near her."

"But you're sure as hell here now, aren't you? What if she'd come back to Gardiner last night? What would you have done then?"

Dave shook his head smoothly. "Not a damn thing. I just wanted to see him. But this tramp didn't come home."

Carrie bristled at his words. She walked up as far as Rob would let her go and stared Dave down. "As you well know, I *was* on my way back to Gardiner.

Thanks to you, I ended up spending the night at his place. Turned out to be the best Christmas gift you've ever given me." Her voice took on a sing song southern drawl. "Thanks *ever* so much, David."

Dave sent her a contempt-filled glare. "You bitch."

She sauntered dangerously close and lifted her chin as she addressed him. "Did you get a good look at him, Dave? Did you see the man who appreciates what you never did?"

"Okay, that's enough." Rob grabbed her arm and pulled her back to the porch. "Dammit, Carrie, stop goading him. You already know about his temper."

"Goading him?" She pointed to the man in question. "I go on one date with a man months after I divorce Mr. Man Whore over there, and he's got the nerve to call me names? I'm lucky I never got a disease from that cheating son of a bitch!" She glared in Dave's direction.

Rob nodded. "I know, but go inside or at least stay on the porch so I can finish talking to him. I mean it, Carrie."

Carrie stood there on the porch, mad enough to kick someone, preferably Dave, where it really hurt. She went inside for the phone, remembering she'd forgotten to call Sam, as she'd promised. He answered on the first ring. "I'm home but the cops are here talking to Dave." She filled in the details quickly. "When I heard his truck approaching, I locked the door and called the police."

"You did the right thing. Are they pressing charges?"

"I'm not sure what they can do. He called me a tramp for spending the night in Kenton."

"I made you stay because of him," Sam countered.

"I know, and Rob told me I goaded Dave afterwards, but I swear he had it coming."

Sam groaned. "I have a feeling I'm not going to like what I'm about to hear, but tell me anyway." He waited until she finished before commenting. "I know it must have felt good to throw that in his face, but Rob was right. Is that too much to ask to just walk away for once?"

Carrie was quiet for several seconds. To anyone else, her silence may have been an indication that she'd given up the fight. Those who knew her would recognize her icy muteness as the calm before the storm. She doubted Sam had a clue.

She spoke through jaws clenched tightly enough to crush glass—the ominous undercurrent in her tone came through loud and clear. "Excuse me, but I thought I did that, Sam. *He*. Followed. *Me*. To Kenton. *He* banged on your house after spying on us through *your* window. He drove back here and sat in my sister's driveway. *He* waited until five a.m."

"Carrie, listen—"

"*You* listen! I played that role for too damn long. I was the good wife who sat by for years, while he screwed his way through the phone book, then accused me of things I never did to justify his actions."

"Babe, I know tha—"

"I refuse to hide from him, and I damn sure refuse to stand here quietly while he calls me a bitch."

"Carrie, I'm sor—"

"He's gotten as much slack from me as he's going to get in this lifetime. You know, Sam, if you can't handle this side of me, then maybe you shouldn't handle me at all. *Maybe* I'm not the right woman for you."

Carrie pushed the end call button and stormed into the kitchen for a just-brewed cup of coffee. She poured as Christie stared at her in silence. The phone rang, and she turned off the ringer without answering.

"What is it with men, Christie? I swear, when God creates them he must say to himself, 'This one will grow to be a man someday. I'd better not forget to add that insufferable jerk gene. He'll get lots of use out of that.'"

She paced the kitchen, mumbling to herself. "Maybe it's time to back off of this thing."

Christie stared up from the rim of her mug. "Who are you so pissed at? Dave, Sam, or the mystery man caller?"

"Is there a choice for all of the above?" She turned to her sister, suddenly remembering she should be concerned. "Did you get any phone calls last night?"

"Nope. I slept like a full-bellied baby with a fresh diaper."

"Great, Mr. Man must have seen my car wasn't here. I wonder if that lunatic followed me to Kenton too." She stormed out through the front door again, too angry to give that thought serious consideration.

Rob turned at the sound of the door opening and sent a low growl in her direction. "Oh, crap, here comes trouble."

"Hey, jerk, did you tell your caller to follow me to Kenton too?"

"Look, Carrie, I've told Rob over and over that I didn't have a damn thing to do with that. I swear I didn't. I don't!"

"And you wouldn't lie about something like that, would you, especially with Rob ready to throw your butt in jail." She spun around to face the chief. "What are you going to do about him?"

"Well, do you want to press charges for harassment?"

"Sure, maybe I'll get to enjoy one day of my Christmas vacation without him ruining it for me." She growled the last comment as she turned around to walk back to the house.

Dave took a step forward. "Come on, Carrie, you'd do that to me on Christmas Day?" His voice held a rare note of panic. "Have a heart."

Carrie turned in midstride and stalked angrily up to Dave. "What about you, Dave? How about your heart?" She poked his chest angrily with her finger. "Do you even have one? How about a conscience? How do you even have the nerve to call me names after everything you've done to me? How can you, huh, Dave?" She shoved him back against the police cruiser with all her might. "*Answer me*!" Panting with fury as her heart pounded with the rush of adrenaline, she glared back at the three men who stared, open mouthed, at her.

"You know what? Just forget about it. If I press charges, I'll have to spend another hour of my day in your office filling out paperwork, and he's not worth it." She turned around and stood nose to nose with Dave. "I'm just sick enough of you to do something about it on my own. Go ahead and bother me again. I dare you!" Teeth clenched, she swiveled angrily toward Christie's porch. "Get him the hell out of my sight," she called back, waving her hand and storming back towards the house. She turned around in time to hear Rob's last warning, as he wagged his finger in Dave's face.

"If you give her one more second of grief, she won't have the choice to press charges or not. Your ass is going to jail for no less than forty-eight hours. You got that?"

Dave dropped his head. "Yeah, I got it."

Carrie grunted in satisfaction and went back inside. She fielded Christie's curious look. "I don't want to discuss it right now."

Christie nodded. "Okay then, as soon as I get Max dressed, we're going to Mom's."

"I think I'll take a leisurely soak in the tub. I just need to get back in time to see Katie before she leaves. God, I need more coffee, you want a cup?" Carrie asked.

"I'm good." Christie struggled to get a shirt over Max's head.

"Mo...mmy!" Max's voice sounded muffled from under the shirt. "It's too fit!"

Carrie laughed in spite of her previous aggravation. "It's too fit because of that big head of yours." She tickled her defenseless nephew, turning him into a mass of headless giggling.

Christie gave up trying to get the shirt over her son's head and threw it off to the side. "I tell people not to buy him anything but button down shirts for gifts, but do they listen? Nooo." She dug in Max's closet and pulled out another shirt, this one a long sleeved button-down.

Carrie watched her sister dressing the toddler. Christie was a hard-working single mother whose husband left her for another woman a year earlier. They'd sympathized with each other plenty over the year. She lifted the blind to check if the men were still there. "You know, there's a serious bit of beef cake out there in your driveway right now."

Christie lifted her face curiously. "Oh, yeah?"

Carrie nodded. "I met him a few months ago. His name's Tim Hardin, I think. You might want to go check that out. He seemed like a nice guy when I met him. He figured Dave out pretty quick."

Christie peeked out the window and gave a low whistle of appreciation. "Where the hell did he come from? Look at that body," she groaned. "He must do some serious working out."

"You could always get Rob to introduce y'all. Go on out there right now." She poured herself a cup of coffee.

Christie shook her head. "I'm not ready for that. Besides, he doesn't look the type to be interested in a divorcee with a three year old."

Carrie lounged on the sofa to soak in the lights of Christie's Christmas tree. "I hate to see the Christmas season end. It sucks to see people put their trees to the curb on Christmas afternoon. I always leave mine up until New Year's day."

"Me too," Christie agreed. "Later than that, if I don't have the time to take it down."

The two sisters got quiet for a moment and Carrie sighed. "That rental in Kenton is a steal, Chris. Nice place—the owner obviously doesn't need the money for what he's asking. He could easily get quadruple what he's asking from me, even for a place the size of Kenton. I took it last night. I can move in any time."

"You did? Sam must be thrilled. Is he going to help with the move?"

Carrie picked at her thumbnail. "I'm wondering if it's the right thing to do now."

Christie dropped to the couch beside her. "Talk to me, Sis."

Carrie released an exhausted sigh and then told her about the phone conversation with Sam. "I'm probably being too hard on Sam, but I spent too many years with a controlling husband to have another man tell me what to do. And besides, if we do stay together, how do I know what this wacko caller is going to do? What if he follows me over there and hurts Sam or Nick?"

Christie pointed to the phone. "You know, Sam is probably trying to call back so he can apologize."

"I don't feel like hearing it just yet."

"So, are you moving to Kenton or not?"

Carrie dropped her head back on the couch. "I don't know what to do, Chris; I can't stay here, and I'd save so much money with the move. But, it all fell into place so easily. Maybe it's not supposed to be this easy to start over."

"Give yourself some time to think on it a little longer. The house will still be there, and the one in Gardiner won't be vacant for another couple weeks. You have some time to figure this out."

Carrie ran her hands through her hair, trying to rid herself of the morning's stress. "Maybe you're right."

A knock on the door had her rushing to see who it was. She opened it a crack before turning to Christie. "Stud alert, Sis. Look alive." She pulled open the door. "Hello, Officer Hardin. What can I do for you?" She stepped aside to let him in. "I don't think you've met my sister. This is her place, by the way."

The man nodded and touched the brim of his cap. "Tim Hardin, ma'am. It's nice to meet you."

"You also, Tim. I'm Christie."

Max entered the room at a run. "Mommy, I weady to go to Maw Maw Lains!"

Tim smiled at the child. "And who's this little man?"

"He's my son. Max, can you say hi to Officer Tim?"

Max seemed to study him. "He-wo, ossifuh Tim."

Rather than laugh at Max's speech impediment, Tim knelt before the child, his hand extended. "You know, when real men meet, they shake hands. Like this, Max. Can you give me a good, strong handshake?"

Max complied, his face somber as he concentrated on his task.

"Just like that, Max. You learn quick, little man." Tim stood and faced Christie. "Cute kid, ma'am."

"Ma'am?" Christie spat out, looking every bit as affronted as Carrie had when Officer Beefcake called her that the first time.

Carrie laughed and placed a hand on her sister's arm. "Don't worry, Chris. It's a gender thing, not an age thing, right Officer?"

He graced Christie with a smile, showing off two full rows of perfectly straight, white teeth. "That is correct. Something drilled into me at an early age." He turned his attention to Carrie. "Chief Ledoux asked me to check on you one last time, Ms. Jeansonne. He wanted to make sure you were okay. Personally, I would have liked to see you press charges on your ex, but it's your choice, of course."

Carrie waved him off. "Dave's harmless. Just a pain in the butt, is all. Besides, I've got bigger problems than him, right now."

Tim nodded, looking serious. "The caller, I know. Are you convinced he's someone other than your ex?"

All trace of laughter vanished for her reply. "Unfortunately, I am." Carrie finished the last of her coffee and turned to her sister, her voice lowered. "I'm going to soak in the tub for a bit. Tell Mom I'll be there in time to tell Katie and her bunch goodbye before they leave for Texas."

She left them then, but caught the low murmur of conversation for a few minutes longer. She smiled at the thought of Christie and Officer Tim as a couple. He seemed a little uptight, but if anyone could loosen someone up, it was her sister and her adorable son, Max.

She heard the light tap on the bathroom door, followed by Christie announcing their departure. "I won't be long. Lock up behind you, please."

Carrie showered and shaved her legs, then put the stopper in the tub and poured her favorite scented bath crystals. She lay back in the tub, allowed the luxurious aroma of jasmine, and the sounds of blessed silence work on her frazzled nerves. No phones, no television, no radio, no sound except for an occasional drip from the faucet. Tension eased from her body, and she even dozed for a few minutes.

The water cooled and she roused herself to step out of the tub. Dried and wrapped up in her thick terry robe, she applied her make-up. She entered the living room to retrieve the brush she'd forgotten in her purse.

Another brisk rap at the door had her inching the window's curtain aside to check. Carrie gasped, dropped the curtain, and backed slowly away from the door.

Chapter Sixteen

Tap. Tap. Tap.

"Come on, Carrie. I know you're in there."

Oh, God.

"Come on, please open up."

Carrie finally reached for the locks and opened the door. She stared at Sam, his bulk absolutely filling the space.

"Carrie . . ."

The deep timbre of his voice sent chills down her spine. Her feet could have been planted in cement. She'd lost all capability of speech—couldn't even look away from him. *What the hell is he doing here?* Did it matter? He was here . . . for her.

Sam cleared his throat nervously. "May I come in?"

Carrie fought the urge to throw her arms around him. She forced herself to remain silent as she stepped aside. He walked past her. By the time he turned to face her, she'd already replaced her momentary smile of jubilance with a look of sober composure.

They stood there, neither speaking, but neither willing to break eye contact.

She savored the symptoms of Sam's unease—a nervous tug of his collar, tucking and re-tucking his shirt, and fiddling with the waist of his jeans. Her mind's processor worked at full capacity, trying to find answers to questions. *How did he find his way here?* The phone numbers—he must have called someone in her family. She groaned inwardly as realization hit her. *Mom.*

Of *course*, he'd call her mother. His own had spoiled him rotten. Why wouldn't he expect her mother to bend the rules of family loyalty to help him out? And she did. She totally did. Carrie resisted the urge to laugh. She could just imagine the discussions going on at Mom's this very moment. Even if she was ecstatic to see him here, she wasn't ready to let Sam off the hook so easily. She pursed her lips to keep her grin at bay. *He's cute as hell when he's all contrite and squirmy.*

Sam jerked at his collar again, as though he found the room stifling. He finally seemed to pull himself together and spoke.

"I had to come, Babe. I had to make sure you were okay."

"I'm fine."

"You certainly are. And I can see you're okay too."

Her gaze had all the warmth of a winter day in the Arctic Circle.

Crash—and—burn.

He took a deep breath and released it as sweat beaded on his brow. She expected the poor man to turn tail and run back to Kenton any second now. *You can run but you can't hide, Langley.* His presence here proved one thing—the man was into her something fierce. So much so, he was willing to put up with her wrath, as long as it meant she kept him around. She would, but not without seeing a little fancy footwork. Carrie fought to keep her unaffected gaze in place. *Show me what you've got, Sammy.*

"Carrie, I want to apologize for what I said over the phone. I wasn't angry with you. I was frustrated at not being able to be here with you to protect you."

She frowned. *Why would I care if you were angry? Come on, Mr. Langley, surely you can do better than that.*

"When you told me you'd confronted Dave, all I could think about was how and what he'd do to get back at you, Carrie. I was terrified for you, can you understand that?"

Carrie furrowed her brow even more. *You're disappointing me . . .*

"I swear I wasn't trying to tell you what to do, and I wasn't angry at *you.*"

It's not happening for me, Sam. Her facial expression must have shown her distaste for his last weak effort. His tone altered into something truly desperate.

"Damn it all, Carrie, I'm sorry! I'm sorry I didn't keep my big mouth shut and give you the support you asked for when you called me. I'm sorry I acted like a jerk."

Better.

Sam rubbed his face with one hand. "As soon as I said it, I knew I shouldn't have, I knew I'd screwed myself. I tried to apologize to you, but you hung up before I got a chance. The fact is I can't even imagine a future without you in it."

You're getting there.

"Hell, Carrie, when you made that comment about not being the right woman for me—" He shook his head and muttered a not so mild oath. "That's not true. That couldn't be farther from the truth. You're exactly the kind of woman I want. You are the *only* woman I want. I can take that side of you, Carrie. I love that kick-ass side of you that's willing to stand up for your rights and not back down from anyone. I love that you feel this way, because, from what you've told me, for so long you didn't, and now you do. I can't help but feel proud of that. I'm proud of everything you've accomplished. I'm proud of you, and I'm so proud that you even entertained the thought of spending time with me. Even if you never speak another word to me, Baby—I still—I will *always*—love you."

His proclamation nearly knocked the breath out of her, and she fought to keep the somber expression plastered on her face.

Sam narrowed the distance between them and placed both hands on her shoulders. "Can you forgive me? Can you give us another chance?"

The *tick, tick, tick* of the wall clock counted the passing seconds, as they stood facing each other in the otherwise silence of the room.

Sam searched for the sound and found the clock behind Carrie. He stared at its face, not wanting to see Carrie turn away from him. The clock counted fifteen seconds, then thirty, forty-five. He lost all hope as the second hand neared the one-minute mark.

It's too late.

He was too much of a dumbass to learn from twenty years of mistakes, even with a year of loneliness as the harshest lesson. He turned, took three steps toward the door.

"Sam." She spoke softly.

The single word stopped him in his tracks.

He turned but kept his gaze down. He couldn't bear to watch her lips form the words he did *not* want to hear. Couldn't stand to hear her say he'd blown it.

"Sometimes I just need to vent. It doesn't mean I need you to fix things for me. I'm a big girl, and I can do that for myself. Can you understand that?"

Sam nodded, but still avoided her gaze, looking everywhere but at her. He was too terrified to see something in her eyes that he wouldn't be able to handle. When Carrie walked up to within an arm's reach of him and stopped, he finally lowered his gaze to meet hers. He didn't find the anger and hardness in her eyes that he'd expected to see. He found a soft vulnerability, tempered with a strength and determination. In that moment, he really *saw* the woman he loved . . . and she was beautiful.

Her dark green robe accentuated the specks of hazel in her blue and green irises. He stared at her eyes, then down at the neckline of her robe where he could see her pulse, imagining what she wore—or didn't wear—beneath it. She'd washed her hair obviously. The ends of a snow-white towel had loosened, freeing the soft curls along her neckline. He loved the texture, the color of her hair, loved that she wore it down. He only now realized how much he also loved it pulled away from her lovely neck and beautiful face. Carrie's face—heart shaped with a pronounced 'widow's peak', as his sister's called it.

Drawn to her, he took a step nearer, then placed his hand on her neck to pull her gently toward him. She went to him and turned her head to lay it softly on his chest, as though to hear the beating of his heart. Sam reached up slowly and pulled the towel from her hair, let it fall to the floor. His hands came up to smooth her curls away from her face. He ran his long fingers through her thick, damp hair, gently detangling and smoothing her silky reddish brown tresses. He put both his large hands on the side of her face and raised it slowly to his. Her eyes had been closed, but she opened them wide now as she gazed up at him.

He lowered his mouth to hers and kissed her. Her hands clutched the front of his shirt, bunching the material, as if she was afraid to let go. He wrapped his hands around her waist and pulled her close as she looped her arms around his neck. He held her tight so that he could feel her, every luscious, womanly curve of her.

He broke the silence, his whisper husky and sincere. "I'm sorry."

"I know."

Once again, the clock counted down the seconds as they stood in the center of the room, neither wanting to break the connection.

Her voice, muffled against his chest, sounded as sweet as anything he'd ever heard.

"How'd you get here, Sam?"

He knew what she wanted to know, but his inner comic genius wouldn't give it up that easily. "My truck."

She groaned. "Always the smart ass."

He hugged her tighter and laughed. "Oh, once I realized you'd taken the phone off the hook for good, I swallowed my pride, tucked away my manhood, and called your mom." He could feel her smile through his shirt.

"I knew it."

Sam took a deep breath and continued. "After introducing myself to her, I told her that I'd misjudged the situation and desperately wanted to make amends. I asked if she'd please give me the directions to wherever you were, so that I could spend the rest of my life making it up to you."

Her gaze clashed with his. "You did not say all that."

He grinned. "Oh, but I did. Desperate times—desperate measures, and all that good stuff." Her brow rose and he lowered his head for another kiss. Her words stopped him.

"You realize what you've done, don't you?"

"I'm not sure what you mean." He ran his hands through her hair.

"Christie went over there with the full story. Therefore, everyone is at my mom's talking about this right now. They're all wondering what's going on and what we're doing all by ourselves. You'll have to come with me." She pulled away from him, but stopped when his tug on her belt opened the robe partially.

His face lit up as he caught a good glimpse of her smooth, pale thigh, and bare waistline.

She grabbed the gaping flap and closed it. "Hey!"

"I've been dying to see what you're wearing under that robe." He pulled her close. "And you always smell so good." He buried his face into the side of her neck.

She scrunched her shoulders. "It's jasmine bath crystals." She slapped at his hands as they grabbed for her belt again. "Stop that! You haven't kissed nearly enough butt yet."

He gave her a crooked grin. "If you'd just open up that robe, I'd be glad to take care of that for you right now." He leaned over to slip his hands under the robe, groaning as he made contact with the skin of her thighs. "You're so soft."

Carrie took the time to release a long sigh, before pulling away. "Oh no, any butt-kissing will be done on my terms—not yours. Sit. Over there." She spun him around physically and pushed him in the direction of the sofa. "I'll be ready as soon as I get dressed and blow-dry my hair."

Carrie picked out a pair of jeans and a rust-colored cowl neck sweater to wear, before locking herself in the bathroom. Ten minutes later, she walked out of the bathroom fully dressed and ready to leave. "Ready to face the mob?" She reached for her purse.

He gave her a smug expression. "Do I have a choice?"

Carrie straightened. "Yes, you do. We don't have to do this today, or ever, for that matter." She shrugged carelessly as she picked up her jacket.

Sam gave her a low whistle as he sidled up close to her. "Then I *choose* to be wherever you are today."

She cocked her head slightly. "Weren't you having lunch with your family today?"

He grabbed her hand. "Something more important came up at the last minute." He lowered his forehead to hers. "Did I screw things up? I mean, you're still moving to Kenton, right?"

Her look turned sober. "I don't think I have a choice in moving, but as to whether or not we'll be seeing each other? I think I'll hold off until I see how you handle my family."

He dropped his head. "Aw hell. What if they hate me?"

Carrie giggled. "Relax, Sam. Compared to my ex, you're an ankle-deep wade in the kiddie pool."

"Oooh, high praise."

Carrie laughed as she took his hand. "You want to follow me over there in your truck?"

"I'll drive and bring you home whenever you want." He squeezed her hand.

Five minutes later, Sam pulled into the last remaining spot in front of her mother's home. He exited the truck and gazed at the flat countryside located several miles north of the White Lake Wetlands Conservation area, and another several miles to where it ended at the Gulf of Mexico. He closed his eyes and listened to the call of the geese as well as the distant sounds of cattle in the neighbor's pasture. "Man, I don't hear any of that living in town. Do the geese have a favorite spot around here?"

Carrie pointed in the pasture across the road running in front of her mom's house. They heard the single pop of a gun in the distance and within seconds, hundreds of geese lifted in flight, filling the air with the sound of calls.

"Beautiful." Sam breathed. "I hear Speckle Bellies and Snow Geese."

Carrie watched the sight reverently. "It's something, isn't it?" she murmured. "I'll miss this living in town." She lifted her gaze to Sam and smiled. "You ready for your unveiling?"

As soon as they stepped inside, the sights, sounds, and smells of Carrie's boisterous family bombarded Sam. A football game blared on TV while raucous calls of four men watching from various spots in the small living room joined the cheers of the televised crowd. Breads baking, meats roasting, and the distinctive smell of roux simmering in some kind of gumbo, had his mouth watering and stomach growling with hunger.

Carrie's three brothers-in-law, Tom, Lonnie, and Craig, as well as one brother, Mack, took time out from the game to give Sam hardy handshakes when she introduced them. Sam turned from the last handshake as an older, much shorter version of Carrie entered the room.

"You must be Sam," the woman crooned. "I'm Elaine, and you look exactly the way you did when I dreamed about you." She walked right up to him and gave him a big hug, surprising both Sam and Carrie. One by one, he met her four sisters and one sister-in-law.

Christie introduced herself last, grinning up at him. "It's nice to put a face to that voice of yours, Sam."

"Yours too, Christie." Sam leaned forward to the tow-headed toddler hanging onto Christie's leg. "And this young man must be Max."

"Yeth," Max told Sam, giving him a gap toothed grin. He pointed to Carrie. "That'th Aunt Cawee."

"I sure am, buddy boy," Carrie said, as she scooped him up and kissed him on his neck, until he chortled with glee. "Max, can you shake Sam's hand and tell him hello?"

The toddler reached out to shake hands. "He-wo Tham."

"Hi, Max."

Elaine took his arm and led him to a chair at the kitchen table. "I see you were able to follow my driving directions?"

Sam nodded. "Yes, ma'am, I found her just fine, and thanks again."

"There was something in your voice that made me think you were sincere. To tell you the truth, Carrie's been smiling more in the last couple of weeks than she has in years. I have a feeling you're the reason. Sam, are you hungry? We're about ready to eat."

Sam lifted his nose to breath in the wonderful aromas coming from the kitchen. "My mouth's been watering since I walked inside this place."

Carrie elbowed him as they lined up to fix their plates, buffet style. "Just like you to get an early start on buttering up my mother. She's a sucker for a hungry man."

"I'm a sucker for good cooking, so we should get along fine."

"Butt kisser," she accused.

"Pain in the ass," he countered. "Besides, I needed all the help I could get to find you."

"Yeah, well, I may turn out to be such a big pain in the ass you'll wish you'd kept yours in Kenton."

He slid his hands around her waist and leaned forward to whisper in her ear. "Not in this lifetime, Baby."

The two of them sat in the dining room with several other family members, feasting on the delicious turkey, oven roasted to succulent perfection, various rice and vegetable dishes, as well as wild goose gumbo. Carrie's siblings had lots of questions for Sam about his work, his home, his children, his parents, and the ultimate question, asked by none other than Carrie's mom.

"So, Sam, what are your intentions concerning my daughter?"

Carrie kept her eyes on her plate, obviously not inclined to run interference on this particular subject. Both the dining room and adjoining kitchen grew quiet as everyone stopped to hear his answer.

Sam set down his glass of tea and cleared his throat. "Well, I don't think it's a secret how I feel about her—"

A female voice from the kitchen table interrupted. "Not anymore." Giggles and snorts of all genders accompanied the comment, before someone shushed them all into silence.

Lines from one of Carrie's favorite movies, *It's a Wonderful Life*, filtered through a small television set in a small room off from the kitchen. Jimmy Stewart and Donna Reed sang the last strains of 'Buffalo Gal' as Sam got his thoughts together.

"Ma'am, the ultimate decision is in your daughter's hands, of course." He turned his gaze on Carrie. "But as far as I'm concerned, I'm all in—for good."

Seated next to Sam, Carrie swallowed audibly, then glanced up as all eyes fixated on her. "What?" she said, her eyes wide. "We've only been on one date. I can't help it if he finds me irresistible."

Jen's resounding snort was the first of the onslaught of comments and relentless teasing from her family.

Elaine placed a hand on Carrie's shoulder. "I don't mind telling you the antics of that husband of hers were hard to swallow sometimes. But he did have a hand in giving me three gorgeous grandchildren."

"Okay, y'all need to lay off poor old Dave when he's not around to defend himself," Lonnie chimed in. "You just never appreciated him, Carrie," he added, using the sarcasm he was known for. The statements brought on a chorus of '*Poor Daves'* that ended in laughter.

Sam glanced over at Carrie. "I guess he didn't have time to establish much of a fan base among your family, did he?"

Katie answered for Carrie. "He had plenty of time, just no inclination. Trust me, Sam. That split was a long time coming."

Carrie scanned the room. "I needed a plan, okay? When you have three kids, no education, and no place to go, you have to wait until the time is right. Today's for picking on Sam, not me."

Sam turned on her. "Is that why you brought me here? So they could pick on me?"

Carrie grinned. "Yep, throw you to the wolves, and see if you come out standing like a man, or cowering like a mama's boy. Can you handle the pressure, big boy?"

"Oh, I think I can. The previous competition doesn't appear to have been too stiff." Sam gave them all a devilish grin. "Or maybe he was."

"You must have met old Dave." Susan's comment broke through the round of laughter. "Personally, I've always thought of him as our own Stanley Kowalski. You know, Brando, drunk and yelling 'Stella!' at the window."

He scanned her family as he answered. "I've only seen Dave in passing—" He turned to Carrie and added, "Literally. But I haven't had the particular pleasure of meeting him yet."

"Whatever she's told you about him, it's probably worse than that," Katie said, lowering her voice. "I think little sister kept a lot of what went on in that part of her life to herself."

Carrie cleared her throat. "We're not here to talk about Dave."

Sam pulled at his collar again. "Apparently, we're here to talk about me."

Carrie's siblings spent the next hour or so regaling Sam with hilarious family stories and anecdotes. Carrie's mom told him about the time when two year old Carrie used a stool to climb onto her counter top.

"Did you get a spanking?" he teased Carrie.

"No. Mom was so impressed, she snapped a picture, then moved the stool and walked out of the room—without taking me off the cabinet, mind you. Of course, when I tried to get down without the stool, I fell on my butt."

Sam laughed, then asked the obvious question. "What were you looking for up in that cabinet, Nosy Rosy?"

"Fudge. Mom always kept a plastic container of it on the top shelf."

"She'd hide it from us so we couldn't get to it," Mack added.

"It sounds like she didn't hide it good enough," Sam answered.

"Aw hell, we *all* knew where to go to find the fudge," Christie answered.

"That was my PMS stash, way back before PMS had a name, of course." Elaine laughed as she glanced around the table. "Good Lord, I blamed your father for years!"

"And now you know why the very first thing I learned to cook was fudge," Carrie explained, before turning to face her mother. "It was in self-defense."

Sam laughed along with the others as the stories continued.

After a while, the women got up to clean the kitchen and the guys migrated to the living room to watch some football. Sam hung around the kitchen with Carrie and the women.

Elaine turned to her daughter. "Carrie, before you got here this morning, Ruth called wanting to know when you needed that furniture. She's studying for exams this week but said she'd be free after lunch if you wanted to go look at what she had. I told her I didn't know if the furniture was going to Gardiner or Kenton. "Which is it?"

Carrie chewed her lower lip thoughtfully and dried her hands on a dish towel. She grabbed hold of Sam's belt loop and pulled him gently toward the doorway leading out to the backyard. "Come on, we need to talk."

When they got out to the deck, Carrie released Sam's belt loop. He followed her in silence down the steps and out behind her mom's house for a little privacy. He came to a halt behind her as she stood with her arms crossed tightly across her chest, staring out toward the back pasture. Other than a few muffled thumps coming from inside the house, the only sound came from the north wind rushing over dry, frozen grass.

Carrie emitted a prolonged and majorly glum-sounding sigh. "I don't think I can do this."

Chapter Seventeen

Sam placed his hands on her shoulders, his voice low and pleading. "Come on, Babe, can't we talk about this?"

"There's nothing to talk about, Sam." She turned, gazed into his tortured eyes. "Unless you can tell me right now you're willing to help me move some furniture to my new place in Kenton."

Sam cocked his head slightly. "What did you say?"

Carrie hooked her thumbs in the belt loops of his jeans. "I was wondering if you'd be available to help me pick up some furniture and bring it to my place. You know, that cute little house just across from the cop and his crazy neighbor in Kenton?"

Sam threw his head back with a shout then reached out to pull her close. "Nothing would make me happier right now, except this."

He placed both hands on her face and kissed her long enough and deep enough to make her toes curl.

Back in Elaine's kitchen, every woman in the family was pushing for a space at the only window with a view of the couple.

"Would you look at that," Christie crooned. "Well ladies, it looks like Carrie's moving to Kenton."

"Wow," Jen murmured. "Look at them. I so envy that."

"God, can y'all even remember what that felt like?" Katie added. "When you thought you'd die if you were away from your man for even one night?"

Christie snorted. "Damn! I need a cigarette."

Carrie's younger brother, Josh, who'd snuck in past the snoozing men in the living room, chose that moment to walk in on his sisters. "*What* are y'all looking at?"

Christie jumped the highest, and punched her brother on the arm. "Dammit, Josh! You scared the crap out of me."

Josh cackled gleefully. "I swear some things never change. Whose privacy are you nosy bitches invading now? Hmm . . ." He gave his chin a calculating tap. "By simple process of elimination I suspect it's Carrie." He craned his neck to look out the window. "And there she is."

Susan turned to give her youngest brother a hug. "Carrie's making out with her new boyfriend, Sam Langley. It's good to see you, little brother."

Josh returned her hug. "Merry Christmas, Susie." Once he'd spread around the hugs, he turned his attention to the view out of the window. "Now, who the hell is this Sam Langley character? Doesn't he know he can't suck face with number six until number seven has cleared him?" He banged loudly on the glass pane, getting the prey's attention.

Sam turned at the sound of banging on the kitchen window. A man yelled out a brawny sounding command of, "Get a room!" from inside the kitchen. "Who the hell is that?"

"Little brother Josh just made it in. And it seems we've got an audience. Jesus, nothing changes around here. It always was like living in a freaking fish bowl."

"Hmph . . . more like a fifty gallon aquarium."

She grinned and took his arm. "Let's face the mob."

Sam pulled her back to him. "Not without telling you this, first."

"Sam—" She glanced up at the window where her siblings still watched with keen interest.

He waved off the onlookers. "They've been at that window since we walked out here, and nobody's tried to chase me off with a shotgun yet." He threaded ten fingers through her hair and captured her face between his palms. Lowering his head he gazed into her eyes. "I love you, Carrie."

She clasped her hands over his forearms. "I know you do and I thank you for that."

He gave her another mind-blowing kiss, then lowered his forehead to hers and brushed away a single tear with his thumb. "I understand if it's too soon for you, but are you worried that you can't return the feeling some day?"

"Aw, Sam." Her eyelids drifted closed as she pushed away from him. "It's not that I can't love you, it's that I shouldn't."

"Why not?"

"You know why."

"Clarify it for me."

She lifted her hands and let them fall to her sides. "All of this—everything I'm going through right now—it's more than I should expect any man to handle."

"Why don't you let me decide what I can handle?"

"There are so many things that can go wrong."

"I know, but I'm asking you to let me try, anyway."

She stood back, staring up at him. "God, you're stubborn."

"I already told you I can be, when it's something important to me. And you're pretty damn important to me."

"I don't want to let you down if things don't—"

"Stop," he cut her off. "This is going to happen. We are *going* to be together." He stepped forward and embraced her. "I want to be here for you, Baby. Please." He lowered his forehead to touch hers. "Please, let me be here."

She gave one final sigh and nodded. "All right, Sam." She pointed her finger at him. "But don't say I didn't warn you."

He kissed her on the mouth. "It won't come to that. Can we pick up that furniture today?"

She lifted one shoulder. "We may as well."

Sam gave her a cheesy grin. "Hell, I feel just like that kid who got his BB gun on *The Christmas Story*."

Carrie pushed her windblown hair out of her eyes. "Just don't shoot your eye out, Ralphie. Now come on, you've got another brother to meet. Josh is the one who's thirteen months younger than me."

Sam grinned down at her as they made their way to the backdoor. "Thirteen months. I guess your folks didn't have a television set back then?"

Carrie's eyes crinkled in amusement. "Mom's not a big advocate of the old rhythm method of birth control, but aren't you glad they didn't stop at number five?"

"Thrilled, seeing as how I've grown quite fond of number six."

She smiled and gave him another light kiss. "I may as well warn you. Josh is funny as hell, but extremely obnoxious."

They walked in through the back door of the house to cheers, whistles, and clapping. Carrie bowed regally while Sam gave them his best "*Thank you—thank you very much*" a la Elvis.

"Best show I've seen in years," Josh said, hugging his sister. Then he reached out his hand to Sam and gave him a strong handshake. "Hi, I'm Josh. And in case Carrie hasn't warned you yet, I'm the gay brother." He spoke in an excessively overstated whisper.

Sam chuckled as he returned the handshake. "It's nice to meet you, Josh. No, but she did mention the traits funny and obnoxious."

The look Josh sent Carrie was laden with disappointment. "You told him I was obnoxious, but not *gay*?"

"Extremely obnoxious, if you want the truth," Sam added.

Josh turned to his sister with a dramatic flair. "How could you, Carrie? I'm wounded—Terribly wounded!"

Carrie put her hands on her hips. "And deprive you of all that drama you created by telling him yourself?" She waved her hand with a flourish. "Consider it your Christmas gift."

"You're so sweet. Silly, but sweet," Josh said.

She leaned in closer. "No, really. It's the only gift you're getting from me this year. In case you haven't heard, I'm kind of in dire straits."

"You are?" Sam said. "Man, I *love* that group."

Josh pointed a finger at Sam. "Dude, you stole my line."

"Obviously, it was my line first," Sam bragged.

Josh laughed and broke into a verse from *Money for Nothing*.

"My favorite is *Sultans of Swing*," Sam insisted.

"It's a good one," Josh agreed.

Christie walked up to the trio. "No!" she cried.

"*Walk of Life*," Carrie yelled, pointing at her sister.

"Absolutely," Christie agreed, as they started in on the first verse. Everyone else in the room joined in when they sang the chorus.

Tom chose that moment to poke his head in the kitchen. "What the hell is going on in here? Are y'all insane?"

Josh nodded adamantly at his brother-in-law. "Yes, Tom. Yes, we are. And—"

Sam stepped forward. "And the lunatics are running the asylum!"

Josh turned on him, his face shrouded with unadulterated shock. "Dude, you took my line *again.*" Josh turned to Carrie, his tone filled with disgust. "He's gotta go, sis. You *know* how I hate being upstaged."

Carrie laughed and pushed playfully at her brother. "Sorry, Josh. Looks like you need fresh material. You've got some competition."

Josh put a hand firmly on Sam's shoulder. "Don't get used to wearing that crown, buddy. I'm the only royalty allowed in this house." He turned to Carrie and spoke over the laughter. "So far, he seems like a keeper." Before she could answer, he turned back toward Sam. "So, what's the deal, Sam? Is my sister moving to Kenton or staying in Gardiner?"

Sam raised his chin triumphantly. "She's moving to Kenton."

"Yep," Carrie threw in. "Today. Any of you hard-working, generous people want to help?"

A loud chorus of "*No!*" came at her from all sides.

Her jaw dropped. "That was pretty good. Did y'all rehearse that while we were outside?"

"Yes!" they all chorused again, before everyone in the kitchen dissolved into more laughter.

Tom and Jen came up to Carrie. "We'll help you, Sis," Jen said. "I'm dying to see your new place."

Carrie nodded. "If I could get the heavy furniture moved in by tonight, I could make a few trips in my car over the next couple of days."

"Do your kids know yet?" Jen asked.

"Not yet, but I need to call them. Maybe I can get some free labor out of this. Mom, did Ruth mention if she had any spare beds?"

"We do," Mack told his sister. "We just bought a king-size mattress set and we have a queen set you can have."

"Vivienne McAllister asked me to let you know that she's got two complete sets of bedroom furniture to give you if you need it. They're both standard size beds."

Carrie smiled. "God bless Mrs. Vivienne. I'll call her right now and tell her I can sure use them. I can't be too proud when I'm starting from scratch." She walked into her mother's room and closed the door so she could make a call in private, leaving Sam alone to fend for himself.

Elaine placed her hand on Sam's shoulder. "How much does she need to get set up over there, Sam? Do you know what the deposits are going to run her?"

"I know she wrote a check for three hundred dollars yesterday for the deposit and the first month rent. I also know it'll cost another three hundred to have the utilities put in her name. That's not counting a phone."

"You think she'll get a cell phone now?" Katie asked.

"She said she doesn't want to get locked into a two-year contract and could do without a land line until she can afford to get one."

"How much is the phone deposit, Sam?" Elaine asked. "I'll pay the bill every month if I have to. I can't have her over there without being able to call her."

"It's another hundred bucks," he answered. "I wanted to help, but she said no."

"I should hope she did," Elaine said. "Some things shouldn't be accepted from anyone but family."

Sam sat back and watched as Carrie's mom and siblings each pitched in enough to help her get established.

Elaine placed her hand on Sam's arm. "I feel better knowing she'll be near you, especially with the Dave situation."

Mack's wife, Sharon stepped forward. "As well as a serial rapist/murderer on the loose in this area."

"What?" Katie stepped forward. "I live in Texas. What are you talking about?"

"They linked the torture and rape of that woman in Lafayette to several in Chicago over the last three years and maybe some in Minnesota a couple of years before that. If it turns out to be the same guy, he's only left one woman alive. That's the one in Lafayette, and he let her live because she was blind from birth and couldn't identify him, not from sight anyway," Sharon explained.

Susan joined in on the conversation. "That's right. But it turned out this girl is a master at detecting dialects. She connected him to the Chicago area, and sure enough, there were some unsolved cases with the same MO. She also detected a residual Minnesota accent, and guess what? More unsolved cases and same MO. Not a speck of evidence, but because of one blind woman, they may be close to breaking this case."

"But he's still on the loose? Oh, hell, that's not good," Katie admitted. "How far is her rent house from yours, Sam?"

"One house over and opposite side of the street. We can stand on our front porches and yell at each other."

Josh nudged Sam. "Man, you think you'll be able to stand being that far away from her every night?"

Sam grinned at the man. "Carrie omitted your mastery of sarcasm."

Josh bowed his head in utter defeat. "My finest quality. I've worked decades honing that particular skill. I foresee imminent castigation."

Sam joined in with several other siblings' laughter.

"But seriously, did you have to pull some strings to find a place that close to you?"

Sam recalled the serendipitous chain of events that made this come about. "I've known her landlord for years, but I swear it all just kind of fell in my lap. I'd be a liar if I said I wasn't thrilled at the turn out."

Several minutes later, Carrie burst out of her mother's bedroom, excited and grinning like the cat who just discovered a private stash of canaries. "Grant and the twins are meeting us in Jennings at four o'clock. They're bringing some of my furniture and anything else that can fit in the truck." She clapped her hands together excitedly and beamed at Sam. "They want to spend the night at the new place with me tonight."

Sam reveled at the pure joy in Carrie's face. She practically glowed at the thought of being with her children in their new home for the first time. Praying he could keep that look on her face, he nodded. "I'm ready when you are."

Carrie turned to her mother. "Sorry we have to eat and run like this, Mom."

Everyone crowded around Carrie when Elaine put the money and checks into her hands. "Here, honey. This is to help you get started."

"It's from all of us," Katie explained. "It's a gift, not a loan. Use it however you need it."

Carrie blinked back tears of gratitude as she calculated the results of her family's generosity. "We could get by with a lot less than this."

"If that's true, I could use a couple hundred," Josh said.

"Me too," Mack said, grabbing for the money.

"God, y'all are idiots!" Christie slapped at her brothers' hands. "Just take it, Carrie. We all hope it'll make the transition easier for you and the kids."

Carrie couldn't speak because of the lump in her throat. Finally, she was able to croak out a weak, "Thank you."

Josh lightened the mood by whispering loudly to Carrie. "Hey, sis, about that 'it's a gift—not a loan' comment? I'm sorry, but I need my sixteen dollars and thirty two cents back ASAP."

"Could you possibly be any more obnoxious than you already are?" Christie accentuated the question with several sharp jabs to his shoulder.

Josh gave a deep chuckle. "There's always hope, little sister." He made a show of rubbing his shoulder. "You really need to find another outlet for all that animosity, *Christine*."

"I know," she groaned. "I'm praying it comes in the form of a man."

Sam backed-up his truck to Mack's house next door to Elaine's. Within fifteen minutes, the queen size mattress, headboard, and rails were loaded and tied down in the back of his pick-up.

As Sam waited for Carrie, Mack approached him, his hand extended.

"Thanks for doing this for her, Sam, we appreciate it."

"I'm more than happy to, Mack. I was worried this morning it wouldn't happen."

Mack guffawed loudly. "Yeah, Christie told us all about that. Little sister had you scratching, did she? That's good. It means she's getting some of her old spunk back." He shook his head. "She was a different person with Dave, you know. That son of a bitch did a number on her self-esteem. Make sure you treat her right, okay Sam?"

"You have my word." He started his truck and backed slowly out of the driveway.

Carrie ran out to meet him, brimming with excitement. "You remember my mom mentioning Vivienne McAllister? Her son, Scott, will be meeting us at Christie's. He and his brothers are loading up his trailer with the two sets of bedroom furniture Vivi is giving me. Red's going to follow us to Kenton and after we unload the trailer, he'll head back to LSU."

Sam nodded. "These McAllister's are close friends of the family, I presume?"

"Vivi is my mom's second cousin, actually. I used to babysit for the kids when I was in junior high and high school. You can't ask for nicer people. The kids are all red haired and blue eyed, like their dad, smart as whips, and sweet, all eight of them. They're good people."

Once they got to Christie's, she filled her suitcases with her belongings. The twins had most of their clothes with them at their dad's already. Between Carrie and Sam, they had her car loaded down in thirty minutes. Sam had just closed her trunk, when a full-size truck hauling an enclosed trailer pulled up to the intersection and honked the horn.

Carrie waved at the driver. "Here's Scott."

The truck pulled over next to Christie's drive. Sam watched as a tall, buff young man in his early to mid-twenties jumped out and bounded up to give Carrie a big bear hug.

"God, it's good to see you, Carrie!"

"Scottie!" She hugged him back. "Thank you for going to all this trouble for me."

"No problem. The folks would have emptied out the house for you. Man, they're proud of you." He turned toward Sam. "Hey, I'm Scott McAllister, but my friends call me Red." He pointed to his dark auburn hair. "I don't think it needs any explanation."

Sam laughed and gave the young man a firm handshake. "Sam Langley, Red. It's good to meet you. I've heard good things about you and your family."

Red gave him a broad smile. "Thanks, Sam. We all think the world of Carrie, you know."

When Carrie went inside to make a final run-through of Christie's place, Red turned to Sam. "You plan on treating her right?"

Sam's gaze followed Carrie into the house. "Only for the rest of my life." He turned his gaze to the young man, who stood a couple of inches taller than himself. "I'm crazy about her."

Red flashed him a grin. "So I've heard. How does *she* feel?"

Sam turned as Carrie locked Christie's front door and made her way toward them. "She won't say yet, but I'm working on it."

They drove their vehicles to the small town, where Jen and Tom were waiting for them at Ruth's place.

"Now who lives here?" Sam asked Carrie as they met in front of the large two-story home.

"My cousin, Ruth, lives here with her husband and two kids. Her dad is Donald, my mom's baby brother."

Once Carrie made introductions, Ruth led them to the three extra sets of living room furniture stored in her spacious home.

Carrie stared, dumbfounded, at the choices. "It's like a furniture show room in here. How did you accumulate all this?"

"I keep my ears open," Ruth said. "You'd be surprised how many people get tired of their good quality furniture before it wears out. I've got the room for it, so why not take it? Somebody can always use it."

"I'm glad you do, or we'd be sitting on lawn chairs," Carrie admitted, before choosing a set for her home.

Within thirty minutes, the men had a very nice couch, two matching chairs, and a set of end tables loaded into Red's spacious trailer.

Carrie thanked Ruth once more as they left to meet up with Grant and the twins. By the time they pulled up at the designated area, her kids were waiting with Grant's truck loaded down. Carrie scanned the items in the truck-bed, and gave her kids a big thumbs-up at the sight of her favorite armoire and nightstand.

The caravan of five vehicles drove off in a northerly direction, arriving in Kenton within a half hour.

Grant and the twins piled out of his truck and went straight to their mom for hugs and introductions.

"Hey, Mr. Sam," Grant said, shaking his hand firmly.

"Nice to meet you, Grant." Sam grinned as he checked out Carrie's kids. "I've heard good things about you three."

"Yeah, we've heard some pretty good things about you, too," Grant said.

Gretchen stepped forward. "Are you my mom's boyfriend, or what?"

Sam scratched his chin thoughtfully. "Well, I'd like to say yes, but it kind of depends on you, your sister, and your brother."

Carrie stepped forward, saving Sam from more of Gretchen's outspoken grilling. "Okay, we've got to unload these trucks before dark."

"Yeah, so you can enjoy the first night in your new house with your mom tonight." Sam glanced over at his own house. "Look, it's more free labor." He waved to Nick, who was standing out on the porch. Within seconds, he was making more introductions.

"I wonder if she's planning to bring Toto here."

Sam turned to Carrie's twins and addressed Lauren's comment. "Go check out the backyard." He followed them and pointed out its qualities. "It's fenced in and the screened-in back porch is plenty big enough for him to stay when it's cold and rainy. I could even build him his own dog house to put back there. This place is perfect for Toto."

Lauren nodded. "I guess so, but we'll miss him at Dad's."

He nodded, hoping to score some points. "I bet you will. But just think how much it would mean to have a bit of home here with your mom. And when you're here with her, you'll have Toto, also."

"Yeah, and Dad still has Lucas," Gretchen added. "Toto found Mom when he was a puppy, so it's only fair that she gets to keep him."

Lauren turned away and headed for the back door. "It's not fair."

Gretchen's apologetic gaze landed on Sam. "She's still kind of mad about all this, but she'll get over it." She followed her sister into the house.

Lauren's statement settled on his chest like an anchor, a heavy reminder that nothing had changed. If her children didn't eventually accept this—well, he didn't want to think about the rest of it.

Carrie joined him a moment later, her voice echoing his concern. "I hope the kids will like it here."

He pulled her into his arms for a quick hug. "It'll be fine, you'll see. Now come on inside and show us where you want everything."

By six o'clock, all five vehicles were unloaded and furniture placed where Carrie wanted it. Beds were made and ready to be slept in thanks to extra sets of sheets and blankets Carrie's children had packed. By eight p.m., everything else was unpacked and placed. The extra help left for their own homes, with Carrie's profuse thanks and a promise to cook them a meal at the first opportunity.

The four teenagers sat in the living room, snacking on junk food, comparing schools, teachers, and friends. Sam and Carrie walked from room to room, Carrie with her pad and pen again, adding to her previous list of things she'd need for the house.

"I need so many things. Thank God Len left the utilities on in here," she admitted. "I have four hundred dollars put aside for deposits, but I'll have to hit the stores for a few things tomorrow. The kids thought to bring bedding, towels, and wash cloths. At least we can take baths tonight." She turned to Sam. "Are there any grocery stores open?"

"The convenience stores, but it'd be cheaper to wait and hit Market Basket tomorrow."

"I need to feed my kids some kind of supper. I'm not worried about breakfast. I'll have time to go shopping tomorrow morning before any of them crawl out of bed."

"Why don't y'all come on over and I'll heat up our leftovers," Sam suggested. "I've got enough to feed an army."

She gave him a brief hug. "That'd be nice. Thanks."

After walking over to Sam's, the teens headed to the living room with plates of reheated leftovers to watch MTV, talking and joking like they'd known each other for longer than a few hours. Sam and Carrie settled at the small dining room table to talk quietly among themselves.

She pushed her food around with her fork, too excited to eat. "I feel strange, like I'm living someone else's life."

"It's your life, just different."

Carrie dropped her fork on the paper plate. "I just hope it's better for them." She nodded toward her children.

He placed his hand on hers. "It'll be fine."

"God, I hope so. A week ago, I would never have thought it possible this could be happening tonight."

Within minutes, their kids clambered back into the kitchen with empty plates.

"Mom, is it all right if we go take a spin around town in my truck?" Grant asked. "Nick wants to show us around."

Carrie gave Sam a questioning look and he nodded. "Go ahead, but be careful."

She helped Sam put the food away and pulled out her steadily lengthening list. "Storage containers and bags, a garbage can and liners, soap, dishwashing liquid—at least Dave let one of the TV's go from the house." She looked up at Sam. "I want to go back to my place. Want to come with me?"

"Sure," he said. "Let me get some laundry going, then I'll go meet you."

Carrie closed Sam's door behind her and stepped into the brisk winter air. She walked slowly toward her new place and stopped at the intersection to observe her surroundings. Her place was the one house as far as she could see down both streets without Christmas decorations of some kind. *I'll get a wreath for the door.* She looked at the door in question and couldn't help but smile. "I'll get a wreath for *my* door," she whispered.

The occasional faint boom of bass speakers from highway traffic penetrated the peaceful Christmas evening. Sam was right about it being a quiet neighborhood. The sweet, woodsy aroma of oak logs burning in a fireplace reached her, and she searched the area, wondering which house it came from.

She continued the walk to her new-to-her home, noting the kids had left the lights on in their bedrooms, as usual. Obviously, it was time to reissue the penny-pinching speech. She used her key to unlock the door. As she turned on a lamp, the strangeness of the place hit her full on. Other than a few items from home, nothing seemed familiar.

She searched out those items as she walked through the bedrooms the kids chose for themselves. She peaked inside one, smiling at the familiar mess of a portable boom box with CD's scattered on the dresser, a McAllister donation. She flipped off the light switch and headed into the other room, already littered with posters and scrapbooks, another familiar mess. Grant's old futon was set up in the equally sized office space/bedroom. He'd sworn it was all he needed, along with the computer desk, printer, and PC. She switched off that light, then did a walk-through of the kitchen.

Carrie frowned at her own reflection in the large, bare, glass of the window before reaching over to turn off the light. She stood before it, feeling somewhat less like a mannequin in a storefront window. A slight movement to the left had her body clenching with awareness as a dark shadow took shape, then disappeared, swallowed up by the even darker shadows of the yard. She recoiled from the window, then jumped when Sam stepped through the front door.

"What happened to the lights?"

Her breath rushed out in relief as she switched on the lamp. "I felt like a window display. I turned them off."

"What happened?"

She placed a hand over her pounding heart. "It's nothing, I guess."

He placed both hands on her tension-filled shoulders. "Tell me."

"You didn't go out in the backyard first did you?" She asked anyway, even knowing he couldn't have been two places at once.

His brow darkened. "No. What did you see?"

She waved it off. "I'm sure it's nothing but my paranoia at being in a new place. And that damn window."

Sam searched the darkness, but didn't see anything. "You got anything big enough to cover this one?"

She shook her head. "Not unless I strip a bed."

"I'll be back with something to use until you get curtains for that thing." He turned when he got to the door. "Is *that* on your list?"

She stuck out her tongue at his sarcasm. "Don't knock my list making abilities." She waited by the locked door until Sam returned with a king size flat sheet a few minutes later. Together they tacked it up over the window.

Carrie backed up to observe their handiwork and breathed a sigh of relief. "That's better." She pulled the sheet aside to stare into the darkness. "I sure thought I saw something out there."

"It was probably a stray dog."

"Inside the fenced-in yard? Grant checked it for gaps and said there weren't any, and I latched it myself earlier."

"Let's check again," Sam said, as they headed outside. He raised the closed latch in a smooth, silent motion and lowered it again. "Maybe one of the kids left it open and the wind just blew it closed."

Carrie's nose wrinkled at an odd chemical smell. "Did you oil the latch? It squeaked when I tried it earlier."

"It wasn't me. It must have been Tom or Red before they left."

They walked back inside and Carrie brushed her hands over her arms at the chill in the air.

Sam pulled her close. "Come here and let me warm you up." He rubbed his hands briskly along her arms and back. "How's that?"

"Much better." She snuggled for two seconds before spying a sales catalogue in the stack of mail the kids brought for her. Twisting out of Sam's arms, she reached for it. "Oh, yeah! After Christmas white sales."

Sam snorted with laughter. "Nothing like the thought of shopping to get a woman excited."

"You got that right. I need to find something to put in that window." She stopped suddenly on a page. "Oh, I like that," she said, pointing to a lamp in the catalog. She turned toward her empty end tables. "I could use a pair of lamps." She pulled the list out of her pocket and searched for a pen.

Sam grabbed the list from her hands and slapped it on the snack bar. "No more list. You worked hard. It's time to sit back, relax, and enjoy it for a little while."

As Sam pulled her into his embrace, she put her arms around his waist and lay her head on his chest. “Everyone worked hard. I owe you for this.”

He smiled and kissed the top of her head. “You don’t owe me a thing. I’m glad to help.” He gazed out into the living area. “You got this place pulled together quick, that’s for damn sure.”

“I never could stand to see a box that needed emptying. I like to get it over with as quickly as possible.” She pulled herself out of his embrace.

Sam’s head dropped to his chest as she pulled away. “*Why* do you keep doing that?”

She looked around. “Doing what?”

He wrapped her in his arms again. “You keep pulling away from me.” He nuzzled her as she tilted her head to the side in sweet surrender. He moved her hair with one hand and kissed her neck softly. “Damn, you always smell so good. Make sure you never run out of that stuff.”

Carrie’s eyes rolled back in bliss. “It was a gift,” she murmured. “I can’t afford to buy it for myself.”

“Then I’ll buy it for you. Who makes it?”

“Calvin Klein.”

“Mmm, and where do I find it?”

“Any department store,” she managed to add, as he layered gentle kisses and nips on her neck, creating the most tantalizing sensations. “It used to be a little pricey, but not so much anymore.”

Sam smiled in triumph as a strong shiver ran through her upper body. His words came out in a low growl. “I don’t care…totally worth it.”

She let her head fall back and he was quick to take advantage of her moment of weakness. In seconds she felt his hardness pressing against her.

Carrie moaned as he covered her mouth with his own in a heated kiss, all exploring tongue and soft lips. When it ended, she found the strength to push him away. Her voice husky with need, her core moist with wanting him, she barely managed to speak.

“Stop.”

Chapter Eighteen

His head fell back against his shoulders. "Why?"

"Why not?" She turned to pick up her list again.

Sam reached out and tugged gently at her wrist. "Talk to me."

"Saa-aam," she groaned. "Don't pretend you don't know what's bothering me."

"I know you feel like it's happening a little too quickly."

"A little?" she interjected. "Try a lot. This is happening a lot too fast." She glared at his smug expression, growing more frustrated. "You only make the situation worse."

He lifted his chin and stared down his nose at her. "How?"

"You know how, don't make me say it," she pleaded.

"I swear I don't. How?"

Carrie gave him a hard stare that softened at the genuine expression of concern on his face. She answered in a voice, soft and sincere. "You make me want."

His lip lifted at one edge before he managed to control the smile that lingered there, just out of sight. "Want what?"

"I've told you this before," she whispered. She lifted her hands. "All of this. You—being here with you—all of it. I don't know if it's possible yet."

"But you're here and that's half the battle."

"You think so?" She closed her eyes and turned away from him to gather thoughts that spun around in her mind like a tornado. She'd overheard Lauren's comment about bringing Toto here. She'd seen the look on her face. "I can't lose my kids over you, Sam. They have to come first."

"Lose your kids?" he huffed. "After everything you've told me about Dave's antics, no judge in the world would award custody to him over you."

She shook her head slowly. "I'm not talking about legally. I'm talking emotionally. I don't want them to feel betrayed. I don't want them to feel I'm choosing Kenton over Gardiner, because of you. If they start to feel like that, and I keep seeing you, what kind of message am I sending them? It would be like saying they don't come first. Don't you see that?"

He reached out and took her hand in his own. "I do see how that could be a possibility, but I don't think it'll happen that way. I believe God led us together at this point in our lives for a reason."

She turned her tear-filled eyes up. "How do you know that?"

He smiled and pulled her into his arms. "I have faith, hon." He hugged her then pushed her gently away from him. "But I do understand your fear, and I'll try to be more understanding and less—what's that word you used at your mom's today? Oh, yeah—" He grinned. "Irresistible."

She wiped at her eyes. "You're such a smart ass."

Laughter rumbled deep in his chest. "Get used to it, babe. I come from a long line of smart asses."

"Really? I come from a long line of bitchy women," she volunteered.

"No, you don't," he insisted. "Your mom seems sweet as she can be, and so do you and your sisters."

One brow arched devilishly. "As long as you don't cross us."

He stood in the shadow of the plate glass window and watched through the sliver of space between the sheet and the window jamb. All he needed was a pinhole to see into the entire length of the room, as long as they stayed in the living area. He cursed in a low growl as she moved out his sight and into the kitchen, while the big guy stayed behind to set up her television. At least they weren't hanging all over each other. *That* had nearly driven him over the edge.

What the hell did she see in that guy? She needed someone younger, in better shape. His jealousy boiled into the danger zone, as *Sam* stood to ask her something. He emitted a low guttural sound as Carrie walked over to the television set to meet him.

I know what I want. His smiled stretched over his face. *And if that big old boy knows what's good for him, he'll stay the hell out of my way when I'm ready to go after it.*

Sam stood and stretched his back. "Okay, you've got a signal," he said. "You can thank your landlord for leaving this antenna up. You can catch all the locals—Lake Coburn, Lafayette, Alexandria, and three different PBS channels. It's not cable, but it's better than nothing."

Carrie stopped re-arranging the lower cabinet and sent him a smile. "Thanks, it's good enough for me."

"I wonder how long it takes to get a phone. You sure you won't consider a mobile? You get immediate service."

"I can't be bogged down with a contract. Land line with dial up internet is all I can handle, and that's only because my *mom* insists on paying for half until I get a few promotions under my belt."

"I hate that you'll be cut off from anyone until it's installed."

"As long as I can open a window and scream, I won't be cut off." She watched as Sam's mouth tightened in a grim line. "We'll be fine."

"Wait a minute. I have a set of wireless radios and I can give you one for tonight." A relieved smile erased the lines of worry.

"You mean, like the walkie-talkies we use surveying at work?"

"Yep," he nodded. "And they'll communicate just fine from this distance."

Carrie called to him when he got to the door. "You're spoiling me, you know."

He shrugged. "Just doing what your family asked me to do. I promised them I'd take care of you."

"Did you? So tell me, what else did you people talk about behind my back?"

"Most of it you've already told me yourself. I got a few death threats and a couple 'I know people' speeches if I break your heart. The usual, when I meet a new woman."

"Smart ass!" she called out as he left to get the radios.

She walked out to the back porch, looking out over a nice covered area. It faced the spacious backyard containing at least two huge oaks. The trees would provide abundant escape from summer heat a few months down the road. Heat wasn't an issue tonight, as the temperature had steadily dropped since their arrival. It would be in the lower twenties by midnight, hard freeze weather.

Her breath vaporized into white puffs as it met with the already freezing air temperature. It was dark, but not so dark that she couldn't see. There were no clouds to block the moon, nearly full in its stage of growth. The crystal clear sky glittered with pinpricks of dazzling light from visible stars. She could see all the way back to the west end of the yard, where the hurricane fence separated her lot from the neighboring lot. *My yard.* "Toto's going to love this place," she whispered.

A loud "SNAP" to the left drew her attention. She whipped her head in that direction and caught sight of a dark object disappearing around the corner of the house. A sudden chill swept up the back of her neck, causing her hair to stand on end. Her heart pounded with adrenaline, producing terror as the feeling of being watched increased.

All that brave talk this morning of taking care of Dave herself came to mind. Here, alone in the dark, in a house with no means of communication? Just talk. She felt foolish for being out here alone—and worst of all—she was too terrified to move.

She swallowed, forced herself to speak. "Dave? Is that you?" Of course it was, she thought, trying to work up a healthy dose of anger, which beat the hell out of being scared to death. She forced herself to remain there and breathe deeply. Cigarettes. She smelled cigarettes, but not just any kind. Marlboro—the Reds—the kind her dad had smoked for as long as she could remember. Dave, like her, had never smoked a day in his life. If it wasn't Dave out there, then who the hell was it?

She took another deep breath, wishing like hell she'd thought to have the kids bring Toto here tonight. She controlled her fear enough to call out. "Who's there?"

Another rustle and *snap* to the left had her stifling a scream. She forced herself to back slowly into the house to shut and lock the back door. She tiptoed toward the front door, searching every nook and cranny of the kitchen and living room on her way there. A loud rattle in the kitchen had her whipping around, fully prepared to see someone trying to get in through the back door. By the time she realized the culprit was the fridge's icemaker, she was on the verge of an ear-splitting scream. Carrie spun toward the front door, then recoiled in terror as footsteps pounded up the porch. Her heart nearly exploded with the rush of adrenaline as the door swung wide.

Sam took one look at her face and rushed to her. "What's wrong? Did something happen?"

Her shaking knees nearly gave out as she reached for him. "Please tell me that was you out by the back porch," she gasped.

He shook his head.

"Did you see anyone?"

"Not a soul. What happened?"

"I was standing out on the back porch and I heard a noise, like someone stepped on a twig or something. It was a loud snap."

Sam's jaw clenched visibly.

"I saw a blur of something dark going around the corner of the house. Maybe the phone calls have me paranoid, but I smelled cigarettes—Reds—Marlboro Reds."

"What brand does Dave smoke?"

"He's not a smoker—never has been. Sam, I know you'll think I'm crazy, but it just didn't *feel* like it was Dave out there."

A frisson of pent-up fear worked its way up her neck. She rubbed the goose bumps that appeared on her bare arms, even though the house was warm and toasty.

"Hey, come here." Sam pulled her to him and rubbed his hands up and down her arms and her back. "Those aren't from the cold that's for damn sure. It must be near eighty degrees in here." He craned his head to search the area near the back door. "Okay, babe, I want to go check around the house, and I want you to stay in here."

"Didn't I tell you I wasn't that type of girl?" She threw on her coat and latched onto his arm with both hands.

The two of them walked outside arm-in-arm, circling the house, and found nothing suspicious.

"I'm going to call Len tomorrow and see about a security light." He put his arm around her shoulders. "Come on. Let's go back to my place. When you're ready to come back with the kids, I'll come with you to check it out."

She nodded, got her keys and locked up. During the walk to Sam's, she stopped to look back at her house. "I don't want to say anything to the kids about this, but I'll sure feel better when Toto's here. I'll be fine once he's out there. He's a good watch dog. He'll set off an alarm if anyone's snooping around."

Sam opened his front door. "You must be exhausted. Go stretch out on the sofa until the kids get back."

"I'm too pumped up to sleep. Is there anything good on TV tonight?"

"Let's check it out," he said, sitting down with the remote. Opening credits of *The Christmas Story* flashed on one of the cable networks.

"Ooh, leave it there, please!"

Sam grabbed a knitted afghan and a pillow from a chair, before seating himself on one end of the sofa and propping his feet on an ottoman.

Carrie had nearly dozed off with her head tucked snugly in the crook of Sam's arm, when their four teenagers drove up in Grant's truck. She groaned, giving Sam a look of apology, and moved to the opposite end of the sofa before the kids came bursting through the front door.

Gretchen's face flushed with excitement as well as the cold. "Mom, we met so many people!"

Grant entered next. "They do the same thing here as we do in Gardiner. Ride around and meet up in a store parking lot to talk."

Sam grunted. "One small town is pretty much like any other, Grant."

"There sure are some good looking girls here," Grant added.

Gretchen grinned at her mother. "I saw a couple of cute prospects, too."

Lauren plopped herself down between Carrie and Sam. "I love this movie!"

The others planted themselves in various positions on the living room furniture and even on the floor.

Carrie reached out to touch Lauren's hair. "Did y'all meet any kids your ages?"

"We met our landlord's son. Nick, what's his name? Kyle something?"

"Kyle Martin," Nick told her.

Lauren lifted her face to Carrie's. "He's kind of cute."

Carrie smiled over at her daughter. "I haven't met him, but his dad seems like a nice man."

"Kyle's a good kid, stays out of trouble—" Sam added.

Gretchen laughed. "He must not hang out with you then, huh, Nick?"

Nick gave her a playful shove. "He's two years younger than me, and besides—Shut up, twerp."

Gretchen shoved him back. "Make me, punk."

Sam met Carrie's gaze across the top of Lauren's head. "You know, Kyle lost his mom to cancer a few years ago."

"He did?" Lauren turned to Sam.

Sam nodded. "Yep, it was rough on him—on all of them. She was a real nice lady."

"That's so sad. It must be awful to lose your mom like that." She turned to face the television set, but leaned back to place her head against Carrie's shoulder.

Carrie cradled her daughter with one arm, and placed a kiss on her crown. Nick pulled out a gift canister full of popcorn, and the six of them settled in to watch the movie.

When Lauren vacated her seat to go to the restroom, Carrie took the opportunity to snuggle close to Sam, covering herself with the afghan. When Lauren came back, Carrie pulled her close to share the afghan with her.

After a while, Sam leaned over and whispered in Carrie's ear. "This is nice, isn't it?"

She nodded without lifting her head from his chest. "It is, but it would also be nice to go home, take a hot bath, and go to bed, too."

"But this is on cable and you don't have it," he reminded her. "You wouldn't want to deprive our children of a great Christmas tradition?"

"What tradition?"

"Maybe we could make it our new Christmas tradition," he whispered.

Carrie felt Lauren's arm curl around hers and felt a moment of doubt wiggle its way into the mix. "We'll see."

They watched the rest of the movie, cheering and laughing as they watched Ralphie run from bullies, get caught cussing, decode a message, and finally get his BB gun. They all sang the fa-ra-rah's at the last restaurant scene and applauded as the credits rolled.

Carrie stood, holding back a yawn. "Okay, kids. We've bothered Sam and Nick long enough. It's time to go home."

"At least you don't have far to go," Nick said.

"Sure don't." She slipped on her coat and smiled, as Sam reached for her.

He adjusted her collar. "Y'all are welcome anytime."

"Thanks, Sam."

"Yes, ma'am," he mumbled. "Are you ready to go, pretty girl?"

The twins, who stood off to the side, exchanged tortured looks. "Oh, God, y'all aren't going to get all mushy on us or anything, are you?" Gretchen rolled her eyes.

Carrie grinned at Sam. "Everybody got their coats? It's way below freezing out there." She turned to Nick. "Thanks for showing them around, Nick. See you later."

Grant and the girls told him goodbye and piled out the door to run on ahead.

"Watch those steps!" Sam called to them just as the twins slipped on the already iced over steps and fell into a giggling heap. They recovered quickly and raced to the house on the corner.

As Sam and Carrie approached, she stopped to make sure she hadn't left anything in her car. She locked it and turned to Grant as he spoke, his voice tight with concern.

"Mom, did you see this?"

She walked around to the back of the car, where Grant and a grim-faced Sam stood, staring at the rear windshield. As her gaze fell in line with theirs, her sharp intake of breath made her wince as icy air filled her lungs. In the layer of thick frost, coating the rear windshield, someone had drawn a heart with the word 'CARRIE' in it. Below that, and infinitely more disturbing to her, was the word SAM with a circle and a slash drawn through it, a universal sign for NO.

Carrie's knees grew weak as she took a step back from the windshield and groaned. "Oh, God."

Sam caught her and pulled her close. "This is really starting to piss me off now." He scanned the deserted streets. "I sure wish he'd show himself."

The twins walked up to check out the commotion. Gretchen's jaw slacked. "That's too freaky."

Lauren approached. "That is *not* dad's handwriting."

"She's right," Grant said. "I should know, I write like him."

Carrie stood there shaking her head. "They're right." She turned toward Sam. "What the hell's going on, here?"

"Uh, Mom," Gretchen lifted her face to her. "Do you have a secret admirer?"

Lauren's response was coupled with a derisive snort. "Whoever he is doesn't like Mr. Sam very much."

Carrie was afraid to say anything about what she'd felt earlier. She didn't want to scare her children unnecessarily, but she knew better than to take any situation too lightly. She shook off a chill and stared into the darkness. "I don't think 'Secret Admirer' is quite the phrase I'd use."

"Okay, then. You have a stalker."

Moments later, Doug Courville and his family pulled into their driveway on the opposite corner. Sam called him over. He joined the group gathered around the car, and seconds later Nick joined them too.

Sam made introductions and went on to the problem at hand. "We have a situation here, Doug." Sam had Carrie explain how she'd seen someone in the backyard and felt like she was being watched. "This could only have happened in the last two hours. I walked past that car earlier and there was nothing written on it. *Somebody* was watching her on that back porch, and whoever he was hung around quite a while, until the temp dropped enough to do this."

Doug gave a low whistle. "He obviously doesn't appreciate you being in the picture, Sam. Think it's your ex, Carrie?"

"I thought so at first, but Dave couldn't write that neatly if his life depended on it."

"Do you mind if I call someone over here to get a picture?"

"Go ahead." She lifted her hands helplessly. "I don't know what else to do."

"Try not to worry, we'll take care of this," Doug told her. "Let me check the house and yard, and I'll make that call."

Carrie locked tight onto Sam's arm. "I want to go in, Sam. I don't feel comfortable out here," she whispered.

Sam nodded, and began herding the kids toward the door. "Let's all go inside."

They walked in as a group, turning on every light in the house. Sam and Doug checked out every room, every closet, and every space that anyone could possibly fit. When Doug left to put a call in to the station, Sam checked to make sure they'd locked every window.

Carrie stood in the middle of the living room, her gaze following Sam's movements around the house. She fought back tears, wondering how a place could go from cozy to foreboding so quickly. She placed a hand on her stomach, fighting off queasiness. "Grant, would you pick Toto up for me tomorrow if I give you gas money?"

"Sure will, Mom. Toto may not be much for hunting, but he's a good watch dog."

When Doug knocked on the door a few minutes later, Sam opened up for him along with two on duty officers for the Kenton PD. One officer asked questions to verify everyone's whereabouts over the last two hours, while a second took pictures of the windshield. Sam, Carrie and the kids had all been together during the only time it could have occurred, and none of them had heard or seen anything.

"We'll send patrols by at least once every hour."

"Thank you." Carrie stood with Sam on the front porch to see them off. Enveloped by the quiet of the deserted street, Carrie frowned into the darkness.

Sam placed his hand on her arm. "What is it? Do you see something?"

She shook her head. "I don't see anything. It's just this feeling I have—and there's a smell." She scanned the area in all directions and settled her gaze on the house just north of hers. She pointed toward the house. "Someone's there."

"Stay here, while I—" The look Carrie gave Sam as she gripped his arm stopped him mid-sentence. "We'll both go. I know the family is out of town for the week."

Carrie loosened her grip and walked to the back corner of the house. "Can you smell that?" She sniffed the air.

Sam did the same. "I don't smell anything."

"I smell cigarette smoke," she explained. "Marlboro Reds, just like before."

"Sorry, babe, I don't smell it," he told her again.

"It's here," she insisted. "He stood right here and smoked. You have a flashlight?"

He took out his penlight key chain, a Christmas gift from Nick, and used it to light the area where they stood.

"There!" Carrie said, after a few moments of searching. She bent down to pick up a butt that was still smoldering. She straightened up and held the butt under the light for a closer look. "I told you. It's the only kind my dad ever smoked. I'd recognize that smell anywhere."

Sam uttered a low curse. "I'll never doubt you again, babe. I can't believe you could smell that. In this cold, I can barely smell anything."

"It's just the opposite for me. Smells get sharper when it's cold. But he's gone now," Carrie said, pulling on Sam's arm. "Come on, the kids will be worried."

As soon as they hit the porch, the door opened.

"Did you see anything?" Grant and Nick asked.

Sam held up the cigarette butt and related the story of Carrie's expert sense of smell.

Nick stood up. "Someone really was out there?"

"Yep, we just don't know who or why." Sam adjusted the blind in the living room window and pulled Carrie into her room to speak in private. "Are you all right?"

She walked over to the bed and tugged nervously on the blanket to smooth it. "I'm exhausted, Sam. I'd love to take a long soak in the tub and hit the sack." She picked up the radio he'd given her and walked back over to the door. Pausing, she heard her kids talking in low tones, and motioned Sam over to listen.

"It's true," Grant said. "Nobody else could tell if I'd been smoking, but Mom always knew, even hours later. She's got an unbelievable sense of smell."

"Yeah," Gretchen agreed. "We can't get away with anything. She always catches us."

"I swear, it's like she has eyes in the back of her head, or something," Lauren added.

Carrie tapped the side of her head and grinned. "Secret Parental Superpowers," she whispered.

Sam gave a low chuckle. "All teenagers think they invented sneaking around behind their parents' backs. If only they knew we did it first."

"That's why we know what to watch for," she added.

He placed his hands on her shoulders. "I don't want to leave you alone. Nick and I could bunk down here. Your couch looks comfortable enough."

"Nope, we'll be fine. Go on now. Take Nick home."

Sam groaned on his way out to the living area. "Come on Nick, it's time to go."

Gretchen's eyes grew wide with panic as she turned to Sam. "You're leaving us here alone? With no phone? What if that stalker comes back when you aren't around?"

Sam raised his hands. "I offered for Nick and me to stay. I could sleep on the—"

"We are not inconveniencing you boys tonight. Besides, we've got Sam's two way radios," Carrie cut in.

"There you go, that's as good as a telephone," Grant said, sounding impressed.

Carrie followed Sam and Nick out to the porch. "I don't know how to thank you for everything you've done for us today."

"It makes me feel good that I could help."

She managed a tired smile as she perused the area. "I don't think he'll be back tonight. Don't ask me how I know, it's just a feeling."

"Yeah, well. Don't turn that radio off until morning. As soon as I get home, I'll switch mine on."

Carrie placed one hand on Sam's chest then took hold of his coat and drew him closer. She gave him a feather-light kiss on the lips, held it for a few seconds, before placing her hand gently on his face. "I'll see you tomorrow morning. And call me later." She held up the radio.

"Yes, ma'am, I will." Sam backed slowly off the porch and waited until she closed and locked the door. He met Nick in her driveway, slinging his arm loosely around his son's shoulder as they began the walk home. "It's been a strange day, Nick. Good, but strange."

"Things are about to change for us, huh, Dad?"

"It's possible. We'll see how it all turns out. What do you think of Carrie and her bunch?"

"They're okay," he said. "They're fun to be around. Except they talk funny."

Sam grinned, knowing that was a brilliant review for a seventeen-year-old kid who didn't volunteer much information. "Yeah, well, if you ask them, they'll say it's us that talk funny. Carrie's always calling me a big Redneck. Did they talk about their dad or the divorce? Are they mad at their mom?"

"Grant says she should have done it years ago. They're all real proud of Carrie. And the twins—" He shrugged. "They just don't want to move."

"She feels guilty for asking them to, but this is much closer to her work." He saw his son's grin. "Okay, I'll admit it's convenient as hell for me." He gave his son a playful shove. "Give your old man a break, will you kid?"

Nick laughed. "Merry Christmas, Dad."

"Merry Christmas, Son." The two walked into their home and closed the door against the chill of the cold, winter night.

The truck's beefed-up engine started on the first crank. He waited a few seconds before throwing it into drive and hitting the highway. *Damn, but that was close.* He'd high-tailed it to his truck, parked two streets over, to avoid getting caught. How the hell did she know he was there? How was she able to pinpoint the exact spot he'd been standing?

He stared at the dimly lit roadway, allowing himself to latch on to what he wanted to believe. *We're connected. We're bound by some invisible tether shared by two people who are meant to be together. For a little while, anyway.*

His truck hit an icy patch on the road and he fought to keep from skidding off into the ditch. Once he'd cleared the danger, he stared soberly at his image in the rear-view.

"Pay attention, buddy. All you need is to get caught in Kenton, three parishes and sixty miles from where you're supposed to be tonight."

Carrie soaked in the tub long enough to let the tension ease from her body. Later, she emerged from her bathroom, dressed in her warmest pajamas, thick robe, and terry cloth slippers. She roamed the house and checked first on Grant sleeping on his futon.

The second bedroom remained empty, the sheets and blankets still neatly spread over the mattress. Gretchen's room, everything placed just so, not a speck of dust anywhere on the bedroom set from the McAllister family. She definitely owed them a visit.

The third bedroom, Lauren's room, looked like a closet had exploded. Both twins sound asleep, sprawled out on the second McAllister donation. Carrie smiled to herself, knowing she'd hear complaining in the morning. Lauren would be stuck picking up her room with no help from her sister.

Gretchen was good at making messes for everyone else to clean. Throughout their entire oh-so-dramatic lives, they'd fussed about having to share *everything*. Yet, here they were, sharing a space when they didn't have to.

Carrie walked into her bedroom and closed the door before crawling under the covers. She picked up the two-way radio, pressed the call button once as Sam showed her. Within seconds, she heard Sam's voice coming through the transmitter.

"Everything okay over there? Over."

She smiled, knowing he must have been waiting for her call. "Everything's fine. My kids are with me, and that makes all the difference in the world. Over."

"I know it does, Babe, and I'm praying they make Kenton their home. It was a good day, wasn't it? Over."

"It was," she agreed, and waited. "Oh. I forgot. Over."

"Are they asleep? Over."

"Yeah, we worked them pretty hard today. Over."

"Yeah, Nick went right to bed too. I hurried up with my shower, and I've been waiting for your call. I swear you've got me walking around here like I'm a teenager again. Over."

Carrie smiled to herself. "Yeah, but I bet you weren't the one waiting on phone calls back then. Guys never waited on calls." She waited. "Oh. Over, dammit!" She heard Sam lose it on the other end and had to laugh too. "This takes some getting used to, doesn't it?"

"Over?" Sam added, with a distinct chuckle.

"Yeah. Bite me, Langley. Over."

"It does at that," he said, laughing even harder. "Over."

"Hey, if you're gonna make fun of my radio skills maybe I won't invite you to come shopping with me tomorrow...*over,*" she added.

"Love to. And I'd never make fun of the woman I love...over."

She paused, wondering if what she felt for this man was love. Possibly. Even if it was, she sure as hell wouldn't proclaim it for the first time over a friggin walkie-talkie. She jumped as Sam's voice cut in on her thoughts.

"You there...over?"

"I'm here. Just thinking how sweet you are...over."

"Thanks, Babe. Get some sleep. Over."

"I will. Come meet me for breakfast at eight? Over."

"I'll be there. Good night, Baby. Because this ole redneck knows how much you love it when I call you that."

She paused. "I do. I definitely do...and, uh, how do we end this? Over."

"Love you a lot...Over and out."

"Over and out."

Carrie placed the radio on her nightstand and stared at it until her vision blurred. She sniffed several times, trying to hold back what she couldn't. She finally gave in and cried, letting the tears cleanse her of the emotional stress of the day. Letting it ease the tightness caused by fear and anxiousness of so many unknowns.

Had she really expected her children to pull up roots and relocate to a place where they knew a handful of people? Yes, she had. Should she expect that after tonight? Gretchen had come out and said the word: stalker.

"Oh, God," she groaned. "What the hell is going on, here?" Women like her didn't have stalkers. Actresses, models, beautiful people had stalkers, not below-poverty-level divorcees with three kids.

She cried some more, knowing this would be so much less complicated if it *had* been Dave, instead of some mysterious Marlboro smoking man with good handwriting. Dave, she could handle. She never could count on the son of a bitch to come through when she needed him. Why should now be any different?

Ten minutes later, she dried her tears, telling herself to quit being a big baby. She'd handle this. If she could put up with 'Crazy Dave' for nearly two decades, she could handle anything.

Carrie picked up the radio, longing for the comfort of strong arms, a big barrel chest, and that oh-so-enticing smell he wore so well. "Sam," she groaned, wishing she could hear just one word from that resonating base. She wanted so badly to feel even one touch from his gentle hands. "Sam," Carrie repeated, in a whisper this time. She pressed the 'push to talk' button ever so softly. "I think I love you," she whispered, and released it—while Sam slept soundly.

⚜

It was two a.m. before he trusted the situation enough to enter the house. He did it quietly, so quietly that no one noticed. One day soon, she'd realize that no locks could keep him out. He'd started to go home, but once he'd realized he wasn't being followed, he'd talked himself into going back. Now was the time to watch and learn about her likes and dislikes by checking around the house and going through her personal things.

He'd learned to move stealthily and with deadly precision as a soldier. He was trained for night patrols during the Gulf War. Compared to that, this was nothing—and everything. He watched Carrie sleeping, dreaming about who knew what. If only he could get her to dream about him. He got near enough to feel her breath on his skin and fought the urge to touch her. Not tonight. "Soon, Carrie." The words, spoken a decibel below a whisper as he watched her in her sleep. "I'll have you soon." As an after-thought he reached for the wireless radio on the night stand, depressed the talk button. "She's mine, Sam," he whispered into the microphone.

Chapter Nineteen

Carrie rose at six-thirty, made her morning preparations, and was ready to hit the local grocery store by seven o'clock. Her three teens still slept, but Carrie woke Grant gently to let him know she was headed to the store. She grabbed her purse and keys and quietly slipped out of the house, locking the door behind her. The offensive message had been scraped from her car's rear windshield. Sam? She didn't doubt it for a minute.

She was inside the toasty warm Market Basket three blocks away in two minutes. "I could get used to this," she said, thinking of the ten-minute drive to a grocery store from her old house. Her mouth watered from the smell of freshly brewed coffee. She followed her nose to the bakery section, knowing that's where she'd find the complimentary coffee. After helping herself to a large cup, she took her first sip and closed her eyes in pure bliss.

"Is it that good?"

She opened her eyes, and stared at her and Sam's policeman neighbor. "Good morning, Doug." She lifted her cup. "I usually try not to talk to anyone before the first cup, but I'll make an exception." She glanced at his basket and grinned. "I always wondered if the cops and donuts thing was true."

"My turn to buy for the office," he said. "They're good here, if you're interested."

"I better not. I need to buy some real groceries, and Sam's coming for breakfast. Enjoy them, though, and thanks for helping last night."

He shrugged. "That's what we do. See ya, neighbor."

Thirty minutes later, Carrie had the oven preheating as she unloaded several bags of groceries. The kids had brought her set of cookware and one pizza pan, so she was able to bake biscuits while frying up bacon and eggs.

She removed the pan of scrambled eggs from the burner just as Sam knocked on the door.

He walked in when she opened the door for him and raised his nose to the air. "Mm, I smell biscuits and bacon—the breakfast of champions." He leaned to give her a kiss. "Good morning, pretty girl. Did you sleep well?"

She returned his kiss eagerly. "I did, thanks, and breakfast is ready." She handed him an empty plate. "Serve yourself." She brought him a glass of milk and served her own plate. They stood at the snack bar to eat their breakfast and talked quietly about the day's plans.

"I got a phone call bright and early this morning from my mom." He gave her a conspiratorial grin. "The town gossips have been hard at it, Babe. They've already heard about you, and she and Pop would like to meet you when you're up to it. Want to go after breakfast?"

"I guess we could." She couldn't help but feel a little nervous. Suddenly, she developed a new appreciation for Sam's composure during his harrowing meet-the-family experience a day earlier.

Sam lifted a finger in warning. "Remember, Pop may speak to you in a mixture of French and English."

"He'll probably sound a lot like my Grandpa Hebert, my dad's dad," she said. "He used to mix both languages when he cussed."

"Go on, give me an example," he goaded. "You know you want to."

She gave him a playful shove. "*Fils de Putin, de la merde, de son of a bitch!'* That was like, *his* thing...*his* infamous string of French/English cuss words."

Sam threw his head back and laughed. "Now that sounds like my old man. He loves to cuss in French."

"We lived next door to Papa, and there were eight of us, so one of us was always getting into something we shouldn't have been."

"Even you?"

"Oui, Sam. Moi aussi." Her chest bubbled with laughter. "Even me. Usually jumping off bales of hay in the barn, or stealing one of his empty barrels to have races. Sometimes we'd have wars with berries from the big old China Ball tree in front of dad's work shop."

"You played war with your grandpa?"

"No, but sometimes he got caught in the crossfire. He'd let it rip, and we'd fly in all directions."

Sam helped Carrie clean up, and within a few minutes, they'd arrived at Sam's parents' place.

"Hey, Mom, Pop." He spoke to the two older people who met them at the door. "I've got someone I'd like you to meet. Carrie Jeansonne, this is my mom, Lucia Langley."

Sam's mother surprised Carrie by giving her a big hug. "It's nice to meet you, Carrie. Come on in." Her accent was thick and Cajun, and Carrie fell in love with it immediately. "You're taller than I thought you'd be. About the same height I used to be before I got old and shrunk," his mom assured her, her green eyes sparkling with laughter.

"Yes, ma'am, I see where Sam gets his height. It's wonderful to meet you," Carrie said.

Sam's father, a much shorter man than Sam, stood quietly to the side with his hands in the pockets of his jacket. Carrie smiled and held out her hand. "*Comment ca va*, Mr. Fred?"

The old gentleman smiled broadly, obviously pleased by her effort. "*Ca va bien! Ca va bien!*"

She nodded. "*Bon! Je m'appelle Carrie Jeansonne.*"

He nodded. "*Tu parle francaise?*"

"*Petit-peu parle francaise*," she answered, and held up her fingers to indicate a *little bit.*

The old man laughed and pulled a chair out for Carrie. "*Ca c'est bon. Sit tois.*"

Sam's mom stepped forward, indicating the coffee pot. "Carrie, would you like some coffee?"

Carrie turned to her. "Yes, please. *Mais oui, sil vous plait*." Once she'd prepared her cup, she took a sip and closed her eyes in appreciation. "It's strong like my mama's. *Ca c'est du bon café'*."

The four of them passed a pleasant half hour as Carrie practiced her limited, but much appreciated vocabulary of Cajun French words and phrases. After her second cup, Carrie turned to Sam and reminded him of the busy day ahead of her. She thanked the older couple and promised to visit them again.

After using Sam's phone to set up her utilities accounts, she walked back to her own place. She entered and smiled at Grant, who sat at the snack bar eating breakfast. "We'll have the phone by tomorrow morning."

Grant gave her a brief nod before licking his finger. "Good food, Mom."

"Thanks, Son. Hey, I have to go into Lake Coburn to do some shopping. Please don't forget to bring Toto back with you tonight."

"I won't. Anything else you want us to bring from the house?"

Carrie shrugged. "Bring whatever your dad is willing to part with. He needs it too, and there's nothing there that's worth fighting over."

"You said something about gas money?"

She pulled two twenties from her wallet. "That's a tank up with some left over. Lock up before you leave and drive carefully." She gave him a hug and drove over to meet Sam.

He met her at the door with good news. "I found you a windshield and they can replace it today if you leave your car with them. I can take you shopping, and my pickup will hold a lot more than your car. I've seen that list of yours."

A few hours later, Carrie pulled her car and its sparkling new windshield into her driveway. Sam parked his truck beside her to help her unload the groceries and household items she'd dropped a bundle on. By that afternoon, all of Carrie's purchases were unpacked and placed, giving the place a much homier feel.

Carrie stretched on her toes to hang the last curtain rod in its bracket, then stepped back to get a look at the large window, now completely covered by curtains. She nodded in satisfaction, as Sam walked up behind her and slipped his arms around her waist. "The place looks great. How about I take us all to supper to celebrate?"

She leaned back and rested her head on his chest. "That would be nice. I'm too tired to cook. Is it okay if I call my kids from your phone?"

"Sure." They walked over to his place.

Carrie dialed her old number and stiffened when Dave answered. "Hello, David."

"Look, before you start raggin' my ass, I was at the bar with Jay last night when all that stuff happened. I didn't do it," Dave insisted.

"I know that."

"Good."

"But you could have put someone else up to it."

"I didn't, and as a gesture of good will, I'm sending Grant over there with five hundred dollars to fix your windshield. I know it won't cost that much, but just keep anything that's left over. I owe you." His voice sounded heavy with remorse.

"Yes, you do, but thanks. Now if the kids are still there I need to speak to Grant, please."

When Grant got on the line, she told him about their plans for supper and reminded him to pick up dog food on the way home.

Carrie ended the call and stretched to get the kinks out of her back. She faced Sam. "I'm going back to my place to relax for a while. I'll see you later?"

He kissed her. "Just try and stop me."

Carrie walked the short distance home and unlocked her door. She stood just inside, awed by everything she'd accomplished with the help of her family and Sam. She could appreciate it now in the daylight, with no one watching from the shadows. Daylight made all the difference.

She walked into her bedroom and stood in front of the mirror to gaze at her reflection. Was this really her, with a new home, a career, a new man, in a new town? With a whole new life? Carrie closed her eyes and sent up a silent prayer. *Please, God, let this be the right choice for me. Somehow . . . some way . . . please let this work out.* She pinned up her hair before she slipped into the tub to soak her tiredness away.

Two hours later, she'd finished a leisurely bath and spent extra time on her make-up and hair. She wanted to look special tonight, so she pulled a figure-flattering dress from the rarely-worn section of her closet. The extra effort turned out to be worth it. When Carrie opened the door to Sam, he pursed his lips in a low whistle as one brow lifted, obviously pleased with what he saw. The man could make her feel pretty without uttering a syllable.

He had to clear his throat twice before he finally managed to speak. "You look . . . really . . . *really* great in that dress." He paused, and shook his head, as though to focus his thoughts. *"Ma belle fille* . . . my pretty girl."

She blushed at his heartfelt compliment and stepped aside before murmuring a polite "Thank you." He stared at her long enough for her to wave an arm toward the living room. "Are you coming in?" He brushed by her, disturbing the air with his masculine scent. She closed her eyes and breathed deeply, savoring whatever scent he was wearing. Once she'd closed the door, she turned to him. "Of course you already know that I don't wake up looking like this. It takes some effort, and, unfortunately, the older I get, the more effort it takes."

A growl deep in Sam's chest resonated in the open space, as he closed the gap between them. "Knowing you did this for me—Damn, it makes me feel good."

She looped her arms around his neck and he cupped his hands around her butt to pull her against him. Carrie groaned, feeling how hard he was. He planted his mouth on hers, kissed her long and hard, letting it linger—one of those kisses that, when paired with an embrace, left nothing, absolutely *nothing*, to the imagination.

Sam pulled away and spoke in a gravelly whisper. “Carrie . . .”

When he tried to step back, she pulled him forward by one belt loop, curved one arm possessively around his neck to nibble on his earlobe. “Yes?”

He groaned, as though struggling for control, when her lips moved from his earlobe to his neck. “Not that this isn’t nice, but . . .” his voice trailed off.

She scraped her teeth gently along his neck, smiled with satisfaction when he didn’t even attempt to stifle the next groan. She lifted her mouth to his ear. “You started it,” she breathed, before catching his earlobe between her teeth, giving it a gentle tug. “Want me to stop?”

“He-ellll no. You can do this all night if you want to.”

She gave him a seductive smile. “We’ll have to wait on that all night thing.”

“I’m begging you, Babe. If you’re gonna do things like this to me, please don’t make me wait too long for that.”

“Haven’t you heard that saying ‘the longer the waiting, the sweeter the kiss?’” she whispered into one ear. She kissed him gently on the mouth then moved to his other ear. “Or how about ‘good things come to those who wait?’”

He shuddered at her nip, then pulled her close. “If you don’t stop, I won’t be able to wait for a damn thing.”

“You’ll have to. The kids will be here soon.”

He shook his head and pulled her hips forward against his erection. “Not that soon, Babe. You need to trust me on this.” He threw his head back as she nipped at his neck again.

Carrie pulled away from him and took his hand. She walked slowly over to the stereo system and pressed the play button. The soft sounds of Wilson Phillips singing “Hold On” came through the speakers. Carrie lifted her eyes to his. “*Danse avec moi*, Sam?”

He held tightly to her, as they swayed and moved to the song. Before the chorus began, she gazed up at him. “Listen,” she whispered, as the trio crooned that one day somebody special would make them turn around and say good bye to their old life.

“*You* are *my* ‘somebody’, Sam.” She spoke in a voice hoarse with emotion. “I’m willing to walk away from everything I’ve ever known for you. No matter how much I try to claim this move was for sound financial reasons, I have to admit that you’re at the crux of it. I’m here, because you’re here.” His gaze pierced through her blur of tears, and she could see the second he believed her.

He pulled her closer, and held on tight. They swayed as one through the second chorus. Fingers interlaced, bodies molded tightly against each other, two hearts beating frantically, as heat radiated to regions too-long neglected. He held her closer, if that was possible, kissed her throughout the third chorus. As the last notes drifted off into silence, he pulled away just enough to speak in a raspy whisper. “You have no idea how proud I am to be that for you, Carrie.”

"You have changed my life, I can feel it," she murmured against his mouth.

He rested his forehead against hers. "I can't imagine what kind of Christmas I'd be having if you weren't a part of it."

She leaned back, somehow managing to find a sliver of humor in her situation. "No cigarette smoking stalker proclaiming his hatred for you on a windshield."

He brushed several heated kisses along the soft curve of her neck, pulled her hair aside to move to the sensitive spot behind her ear. "Sounds boring as hell. My God, you smell good enough to eat. Remind me to buy you a gallon of this stuff."

"Really? I was thinking maybe it's time to try something else."

He buried his face in her neck again. "Don't you dare."

She tilted her head to allow him easy access. "I didn't know you liked it that much."

"Liar."

She smiled. "And you, what is that? Davidoff?" She trailed her nose along his neckline, inhaling his clean scent.

"Amanda and Joe's Christmas gift. Like it?"

"Uh huh—clean, fresh, and just a hint of spice. I have very sharp sense of smell, and this…" She nipped one ear. "…on you…" She nipped the other, as she sucked in her breath. "…is a very big turn on."

"I aim to please," he murmured.

"Just me, I hope. I've been down that other road before, and it kinda sucks."

He cupped her face in his hands and met her gaze. "Just you, Carrie. Only you, always. If you believe only one thing about me, you can believe that."

She searched his eyes. "I believe you, Sam." She closed her eyes, laid her head onto his chest again.

"So, this being your '*somebody'*, what exactly does that entail?"

Carrie listened to the steady rhythm of this big man's soft heart. "It means that, at this moment, I can't see anyone else in my future besides you. It means that I'd love to see us make a life together—blend our two families into one. Even though I don't know if I'm in love with you right now, there's nobody else that I'd rather say those words to." She raised her head to meet his intense gaze. "Is that enough for now?"

Sam responded with a kiss that made her toes curl and her back arch.

"It is for now." He cradled her face in his hands. "God knows I'm nuts about you."

She raised her hand to caress the side of his face. A tentative knock sounded from the door. Carrie took a few seconds to fan her face and straighten her clothes before opening the door to find Nick standing there.

She waved him inside, thankful for the save. "The kids should be back from Gardiner any minute."

"Man, you got a lot done today." Nick stood there, looking around. "This place looks great."

"Thanks, and we even have food and drinks in the house now. Would you like a Coke or Dr. Pepper, maybe?"

"No, that's okay. I'll wait until we go to the restaurant and make Dad pay for it. Where are we going anyway? Amanda and Joe called wanting to know. They should be meeting us here any minute."

"I've already taken her to the steak house, so, seafood?"

Carrie opened the door as Grant's truck pulled into the driveway. "Sounds good to me." The girls got out, each grabbing armloads of stuff to bring in.

Grant walked around to the back of his truck and dropped the tailgate. A medium-sized dog with white, curly fur jumped out and ran to Carrie.

"What kind of dog is *that*?" Nick asked.

"He's a fluffy, lovable mutt, aren't you, Toto? Did you miss me, boy?" Carrie scratched his head and scruff, as he wagged his tail happily. "Let's see how you take to your new home, and whether or not that fence will hold you." She walked him into the backyard and closed the gate. Toto explored his new domain, marking his territory every chance he got.

She gave a lighthearted chuckle. "Just like a man."

"So that's the infamous Toto," Sam commented from the back porch, as the dog ran back to Carrie. "I thought he'd be bigger."

Carrie put her hands over the dog's floppy, fluffy ears. "Don't hurt his feelings. He's been a member of the family for a long, long time, and he's big enough when it comes to raising a ruckus, you'll see. Did you remember his favorite dog food, Grant?"

"Yes, ma'am, and a water bowl and food dish, too," Gretchen replied. "Toto's a good hunter, Mr. Sam. He kills mice, rats, and we've even rescued a few rabbits from him. He barks at anything, so he should let us know if anyone's around."

"Hey, Mom," Lauren said as she walked out to the back porch to meet them. "We told dad you didn't have cable so he gave us the DVD player from the living room. Grant's hooking it up right now."

"That was nice of him." She filled the new bowls with dog food and fresh water.

Lauren turned to Sam. "I'm hungry, Mr. Sam. Where are we going to eat?"

"The seafood place here in town. We can go as soon as my daughter and son-in-law get here."

Grant came around the back with a large cushioned pet bed in his hands. "Hey, Mom, I bought Toto a bed for the porch. Sheltered from the wind and rain, he should be real comfortable back here." He placed the padded bed on one side of the porch next to his food and water. Within seconds, the dog jumped up the steps and sniffed at it before curling up inside. "He must like it."

Carrie smiled at Grant. "You got everything you need to hook up that DVD player?"

"Yep, it's ready to go."

"If you want, we'll go rent a couple of movies after we eat," Sam suggested.

They walked into the kitchen just as Amanda and Joe knocked at the front door. Lauren let them in for another round of introductions.

Amanda looked around the house in appreciation. "I can't believe you just moved in yesterday."

"We had a lot of help, including your dad and Nick."

Grant and Nick unloaded several more items Dave had been willing to part with. Carrie placed them immediately, making her new home feel even more complete.

Carrie grabbed her keys. "Let's go eat," she announced, as the house emptied and she locked both doors behind her. They all piled into two vehicles, the two boys riding with Amanda and Joe and the twins riding with Carrie and Sam in her car.

"You got the window fixed," Lauren said.

"Yeah, Sam and I went shopping in his truck this morning so I could leave my car at the glass place here in town." She cast a smile in Sam's direction. "By the time we got back, it was done."

Gretchen spoke up. "That was cool of you, Mr. Sam."

"Anything to help, girls." He smiled at them.

"Mom, Daddy said to tell you he's sorry about doing that. He said he was real upset with you at first, but he's starting to get over it and he wants you to be happy. We told him it looks like you are, or you would be, if all of this other stuff wasn't going on," Gretchen added.

Lauren turned from the window. "He swears it wasn't him that wrote that on your windshield, and Uncle Jay said he was with him last night, so I believe him."

"I believe him too, Sweetie." Carrie's answer was tinged with trepidation. There it was again. She met Sam's serious gaze, knowing they were both thinking the same thing. *If it's not Dave, then who the hell is it?*

They walked into the restaurant, chattering excitedly. The group of eight drew as many stares from the onlookers as Carrie and Sam had on their previous outing to the steak house. The waitress seated them at a large table in the back dining room, and they discussed what to order. Carrie liked both Amanda and Joe immediately, and the young married couple made sure to include all four of the teens in their conversations. Carrie smiled as she watched her and Sam's children interacting.

Sam reached for Carrie's hand under the table and squeezed it tightly. She turned to him and met his gaze as their fingers interlocked.

"Look at them," he said quietly. "That could be our new family, if we can make a go of this."

She nodded, answered in a reverent whisper. "That's what I was thinking."

"I love you, Carrie," he whispered in her ear.

"I know you do, Babe. Thank you."

One hour and eight full bellies later, everyone ended up back at Carrie's place. Amanda and Joe dropped the two boys off and went home to prepare for work the next morning. The four teens piled into Carrie's car to find a movie to rent for the night. Sam told Nick to put a couple on his account until Carrie opened one for her family.

Sam walked up behind Carrie, who stood at the kitchen sink, and wrapped both arms around her waist. She turned to let him cradle her protectively and buried her face in his chest. "I could cry," she said, the words muffled against his chest.

"Why? What's wrong?"

She cupped his cheek for reassurance. "Happy tears, Sam. It's a woman thing."

He kissed the inside of her palm and placed it over his beating heart but remained silent.

"Did you *see* them?" She lifted her gaze to meet his. "Am I reading too much into this, or did they seem amazing together?"

Sam gave her a satisfied smile. "I know what you mean. It's like I could see them ten or twenty years from now, all married with children of their own—surrounding us with grandchildren."

"It's crazy to think this way when we've just started dating, but it feels inevitable somehow." She laid her head on his chest again. "When I think of the paths we both took to find our way to each other, it's astonishing. It's almost like we were meant to be." Sam rested his chin on the top of Carrie's head. "Maybe God knows what he's doing when he throws certain people together. Maybe I was meant to be your 'somebody' all along."

He parked his truck a block down from Carrie's and took his time walking the distance to her place. Her move to Kenton meant some extra effort on his part, but it was better for him in the long run. No one knew him here.

He walked alone in the pitch black, relying on his keen night vision and letting his highly developed sense of navigation help him to avoid objects and ditches. He embraced the darkness. It was the perfect companion for his intentions. In Iraq and Afghanistan, he didn't need the night vision goggles, preferring to use his other highly sharpened senses to find his enemies—always hiding, waiting like cowards, to end his life. He always got to them first.

He raised his face to the thick layer of clouds blocking out any light from the moon's glow, thanking his luck. It sure as hell wasn't God. He'd long ago abandoned that fairy tale.

The side window over-looking the kitchen sink was completely covered. He couldn't see a thing, but heard them talking, Carrie and the old guy, Sam. That fool had no idea he was about to lose her. He smiled, hoping Sam would dare to interfere with his plans. He didn't usually veer from the planned strategies, but if it was called for, he complied.

He walked around the back of the yard where it was darkest, thanks to the huge evergreen shade trees. There was no gate back here, no need for his lubricating spray to silence any squeaks. He placed one hand on a vertical post and leapt effortlessly into the yard. Covered in dark clothing from head to toe, he blended into the black, invisible to the naked eye. He made his way to the window with the best view, pulling up short before it. Dammit, she'd put up curtains there, too. *Why'd you have to do that, Carrie?* Again, it was an inconvenience, but of no serious consequence.

He didn't need an unlocked door to get into that house, and he sure as hell didn't need an open curtain to see her. All he needed to do was sit here and wait for *Sam* to leave, and for her to go to bed. He saw her car was missing. That meant her kids must be in it. Her boy, Grant, was a driver. He'd thought for sure they'd be at their asshole father's tonight, another minor hurdle. It simply meant waiting until they were all asleep. The pitch black hid his smile. This would be worth the wait.

He closed his eyes and settled back, remembering the feeling of being inside her house the night before, among her things, as she and her children slept. What a turn on. Just thinking about it made him hard, made him want her more. Once he'd satisfied his need to watch her in her own bed, he'd checked out every lock on every door and window. All were easy to bypass for someone with his skills.

I need a smoke. Smoking, his one vice. He pulled a cig out of the protective hard case. No drinking, drugs, and absolutely no sex without a condom. He definitely wouldn't leave that evidence behind. He exercised as if his life depended on it, got enough sleep, and ate all of the right kinds of foods.

Giving up cigs—that's another story. He'd started the habit when he was thirteen, too young and stupid to know any better, and couldn't kick it. In his opinion, the only thing better than a deep pull on a Marlboro Red was the fear in a woman's eyes as she begged for her life. He closed his eyes, lifting one corner of his mouth in sadistic pleasure. That's what did it for him, even though the sound of a woman begging disgusted him. He hated the whining and pleading—hated the sound of them choking on tears of pain and terror. The thought caused memories to wash over him—unwanted memories from his so-called childhood. If that's what anyone would call the years of twisted abusiveness.

He'd never begged. Not once, in all the years that whore beat him within an inch of needing medical attention. His jaw tightened as he heard her voice in his head, gravelly from alcohol and cigarettes.

"That's the trick, sweetness. No marks on the face and limbs, and no trips to the hospital." It had taken years for that bitch to get what she deserved. His only regret being that it hadn't come from him. Some John deprived him of his revenge. He would have loved to hear her beg as he slowly tortured the life out of her. Her death should have been a welcomed relief; instead he'd fallen through the cracks of the system—from one foster home to another, then on to

a juvenile detention center, where he'd experienced more neglect, more abuse from those he should have been able to trust. He'd grown angry, forged his determination, and strengthened his will to survive. He'd escaped as soon as he could manage and lived on his own until he was old enough to join the military. There he learned the skills he craved—the skills to survive and, more importantly, to kill with his bare hands.

The thought snapped him back to the present. On the rare occasion when he found a woman who wouldn't beg for her life, he considered letting her live. There were always extenuating circumstances, reasons he couldn't, or wouldn't let it happen. Except for that last one he'd left alive, barely, believing she had no way to identify him.

He should have known better. Blind as a newborn pup, she'd still managed to link him to those women in Chicago and Minnesota. By his accent, she'd said. What accent? He worked for months clearing his speech of any residual dialects. Again, all part of the plan. Now he had to come up with some reason to disappear that wouldn't bring up any suspicion. *My screw up, but it won't happen again.*

Would Carrie beg for mercy and, ultimately, her life? Nah, not her. He'd bet his own life on it. He'd familiarized himself with her background. When people talked, he paid attention, and in small towns they talked plenty.

He walked around to the other side of the house, back by the porch that was closed off on the north side. He finally pulled the lighter out of his pocket, tamped the cigarette on the back of his hand, and flicked his lighter. The cigarette tip glowed as he pulled on it, took the first welcome drag—deep into his sinus cavity and lungs. He put his head back before expelling the smoke slowly through his nostrils. He took another deep tug on the cigarette—and froze.

One low growl was the only warning. It preceded a sequence of hysterical barking, loud enough to wake the dead, then a lunge for the screened door, accompanied by scratching and growling until the damn thing flew open.

He ran through the dark backyard with that ball of fur hot on his ass. With less effort than previously, he jumped the fence, leaving the snarling, scruffy white mutt behind. He hit the back alley at full speed, not stopping until safely in his truck. He cranked it up, threw the truck into gear and peeled out, nearly hitting a car when he ran the stop sign at the intersection. It took a moment to realize it was Carrie's car. Luckily, her boy slammed on the breaks to avoid a collision.

He laughed maniacally, calling himself lucky. Again. Until he realized how dangerously careless he'd been. Shit! Civilian life had dulled his edge.

Toto's barking began suddenly, with a frantic snapping and snarling.

Sam ran to the back door, Carrie close on his heels. "It's got to be him. Stay here!" He threw open the door and took the steps at a flying jump.

Carrie followed, of course, just in time to hear more than see someone hit the fence at a full-out run. She knew the intruder had cleared the fence when

Toto ran to the corner of the yard, barking until whoever he was disappeared from Toto's domain.

"Here, boy!" Carrie called to her pet, waited until the dog came to her. She showered him with praise, and straightened as Toto ran over to examine something on the ground. She walked over to the still glowing cigarette and held it up for Sam to see. "Looks like he'd just lit up when Toto surprised him." She leaned over to scratch the dog's ears again. "Good boy," she crooned.

Sam's shoulders stiffened angrily as he shook his head. "That son of a bitch! Tomorrow I'm installing a security light in this yard. Maybe even two of them," he growled. "This really chaps my ass."

She stared into the darkness and nodded. "He's got some balls, doesn't he?" She attempted to hide her concern at this guy's brazenness—doubted seriously Sam bought the act.

He took one look at her and swore again. "I need to tell Doug about this, Carrie."

Grant pulled into the driveway and the twins stumbled out of the car at a run. Lauren reached Carrie first. "Mom, we almost got hit!"

"But it wouldn't have been Grant's fault," Gretchen finished for her. "Some dude in a big truck."

"He ran the stop sign on the corner over there." Lauren pointed just west of their street.

Sam turned to his son, his face wreathed in concern. "Which street, Nick?"

"It was Second Avenue and Tenth Street, Dad. That guy almost plowed into us. It would have been bad if Grant hadn't slammed on his brakes when he did."

"Did anybody recognize the truck or driver?"

Grant spoke first. "I've seen that truck somewhere, Mom. It has to be from the Gardiner or Lake Erin area. What happened?"

Carrie held up the cigarette. "He was here again. This time Toto surprised him and chased him off. That guy jumped the back fence to get away from Vicious here." She turned to Sam. "You think it's the same guy?"

Sam nodded slowly. "Could be. That's just one block over. If he's in decent shape, he could easily have run that distance in the time we've been out here."

"And Toto chased him off." Lauren bent down to hug the dog.

"Good boy!" Gretchen lavished praise onto the ecstatic animal.

"What kind of truck was it? Can any of you describe it?" Sam directed his question mainly toward the boys.

"Chevy Z-seventy-one. Newer model with lots of chrome," Nick said.

"Big tires and V-eight engine, by the size and sound of it. Like Nick said, lots of accessories," Grant added. "The truck was either Navy blue or black, but our lights reflected off of all that chrome."

"I didn't see any kind of custom paint job, did you, Grant?" Nick threw in, as Grant shook his head.

"Did it have a tool box or anything else in the back of it?" Sam asked.

The two young men looked at each other and shook their heads. "Nope," they answered in unison.

"The inside of the truck was dark. Maybe the windows were tinted," Lauren pitched in.

"Grant, remember how you accidently turned the dash lights off of dad's truck and we couldn't figure out how to turn them back on?" Gretchen asked her brother. "You remember how it was so dark inside the truck it was scary?" She turned to Sam. "Well, that's how dark it was, so maybe he'd turned them off."

They went inside to jot down the various descriptions of the truck. When they didn't have anything else to add, Sam walked over to Doug's with the list and the cigarette butt in a plastic bag, while Carrie and all four kids stayed at her place. Occasionally, she walked to the back door to make sure Toto was still playing the role of sentinel and guard dog to the family. He'd look up at her with his big brown eyes and thump his tail exuberantly but remained at his post just outside the back door. *Good dog.*

Sam returned from Doug's about fifteen minutes later. "Doug called in the incident as well as the description. He said since it's so quiet around here because of the holidays, he thinks it's likely the truck driver is our man. Grant, I told him what you said about recognizing that truck from either Gardiner or Lake Erin. It's just too bad there were no identifying decals or custom paint job to make the truck stand out. That's a popular truck, and navy blue and black are common colors. They'll beef up the patrol in this area and swing by with their spotlights. He said they'll let the Gardiner and Lake Erin PD's know about it, and that's about all they can do for now."

Carrie lifted her chin and smiled at the group. "I bet he stops, now that he knows we're not such easy targets."

"I still don't like it, Mom. Let me hide in a corner with a baseball bat," Grant remarked.

"Or a tire tool. We could take care of this guy for you," Nick added.

"Oh, yeah, sure y'all could," Gretchen teased as Lauren snorted with laughter.

"No one's hiding anywhere with anything." Carrie turned to Sam, who wore a troubled expression.

Once the kids had all entered the house, he pulled her aside. "I'm leaning toward Grant's suggestion. I've always had a hell of a swing."

"Calm down, slugger. It'll be fine." She patted his arm reassuringly and pulled him into the house. "Let's go see which movies they chose."

The five of them sat down to watch movies chosen by the four teenagers. Carrie kicked off her shoes and curled her feet up on the comfy couch, snuggling closely to Sam. When the first movie ended, Sam and Nick got up to leave. The kids all said their "good nights," and Nick walked on home. Carrie stood out on the porch with Sam.

"Smell anything?" he asked, as he watched her lift her nose to the air.

"Nope. He's gone, thanks to Toto."

Sam pulled her into his arms. "Look, I don't want to scare you, but just because Toto chased him away tonight doesn't mean he won't come back and try something later."

"Seriously, I doubt he'll think I'm worth that much trouble."

"He'd be wrong." He pulled her close to kiss her.

She allowed one kiss and nearly lost herself in it. Somehow, she found the strength to push gently away from him. "Sam, my kids."

"They already know I'm crazy about you."

"I can't stand out here on the porch making out with a guy they saw for the first time yesterday. I need to set a better example than that." She patted his chest as he nodded patiently, his jaws tightly clenched. "How about you come for breakfast tomorrow before I leave for work?"

"I'll be here, but keep that radio on," he said, pulling her toward him for another kiss.

He ended the kiss, leaving her weak-kneed and wanting more. "The radio—Yeah—I'll—I'll keep it turned on," she stammered as Sam touched his forehead to hers.

He muttered a low curse, before giving her another light kiss on the lips and then backing away from her. "Looks like the radios won't be the only things turned on tonight."

"Looks like it," she murmured, catching the grin on his face as he turned away from her to walk home.

Chapter Twenty

Carrie walked into the office the next morning at five minutes to seven. She sniffed appreciatively at the smell of fresh brewed coffee.

J.C. glanced up from his desk. "Hey, Carrie, did you have a good Christmas?"

She nodded and set her purse down on her desk. "I did, J.C. I got moved into my new place, so it was busy."

J.C. nodded. "You heard from Sam? I wonder what he's been up to?"

Carrie remained silent as she walked into the kitchen to pour herself a cup of coffee. J.C. followed closely on her heels.

"I mean, when the rest of us left here that last day of work, you two were still here. I just thought maybe y'all had a chance to talk."

She prepared her cup in silence and took the first swallow before finally turning to face him. "We talked, and—stuff." She gave him an innocent smile, wondering how long he'd last.

"What *kind* of stuff?" The poor man was obviously past the point of simple curiosity.

Carrie shook her head. "You are so sad. Just spit it out, Nosy Rosy. You know you're dying to."

"Are you two a couple now, or what?"

She paused briefly before nodding. "We're a couple."

"I *knew* it," he exploded. "Even when you were pissed off at him on your second day here, I had a feeling about you two." He pulled up a chair at the small table in the kitchen. "Tell me."

"It's a long story, J.C. You sure you want to hear it?"

"It's just you and me here today. We've got all day to talk." Once she'd filled him in on all the happenings over the holidays, he shook his head in awe. "Sam wasn't too afraid to leave you alone today?"

"I asked him to stay home and watch my place instead. My kids are there."

"And you have no idea who the guy is?"

"J.C., I have wracked my brain and I can't figure it out. Grant says he's seen that truck somewhere before, so we're thinking it's someone in Gardiner or Lake Erin. For the life of me, I can't imagine who or why. I don't get it."

"Hey, some guys are turned on by scrappy women."

"I'm not scrappy," she insisted.

He burst into laughter. "Oh, yeah, you are! You put Langley in his place and shoved your ex into a police car. You're scrappy! Now, as for myself, I like a woman I can control. Someone who says 'yes sir' and 'no sir', someone who runs my bathwater for me, serves my food to me, and meets my every need," he droned on.

Carrie laughed so hard, she choked on her coffee. "Am I going to have to call Tracie over here to kick your ass?" she sputtered.

J.C. shook his head and chuckled. "I said I *like* women like that, didn't say I *married* one."

Carrie smiled at the sight of Toto waiting for her, tail wagging excitedly, as she pulled her car into her driveway later that afternoon. She walked over to the fence to praise him then frowned as she opened the door to the unlocked, empty house. Starting to panic, she reached for the newly-installed telephone, only to have it ring before she got to it.

Sam's deep base carried through the lines. "Grant left about an hour ago, but your girls are over here watching TV with Nick."

"They left the house unlocked, and I asked them to lock up if they were going to leave for any length of time. They aren't being pests, are they, Sam?"

"Nah, I like having them here, but I have to admit, we seem to be getting an unusual amount of company since word got out about those two being in the neighborhood."

"Oh, God," Carrie groaned.

"Babe. It's inevitable. There are two of them, and they're both as pretty as their mama."

"Flatterer." Carrie bit her lower lip in worry. "Just send them home now, please. They need to pick up around here. I'm baking chicken for supper and you and Nick are invited."

"Sure, what can I bring?"

Carrie checked the fridge and made a face. "Ugh, I can't afford to support their addictions to canned drinks. They've cleaned me out already. It takes enough to keep them fed."

"Yep, I made a pop run earlier today. We're a Coke family, but I picked up some DP's since that's your kids' drink of preference. I'll bring some over."

Carrie placed the seasoned pan of chicken, potatoes, and onions in the oven and glanced up as her daughters walked in.

She pointed to Gretchen. "Just in time to fold some laundry." She swiveled around to address Lauren. "You can wash the dishes. I believe I asked the two of you not to leave the house unlocked, or in a mess, didn't I?"

"Oh, sorry, Mom." Lauren started to load the dishwasher.

"Yeah, sorry. Nick and Mr. Sam asked if we wanted to go watch some TV over there, since we don't have cable," Gretchen added.

"Lock up before you leave, that's all I'm asking. When y'all finish up, I want you to go straighten your rooms."

"Okay, Mom," the twins said, in unison.

Gretchen turned to her. "Can we watch Oprah when we're done? It's supposed to be pretty good today."

Carrie couldn't help but remember how Dave would fuss when he caught her and the girls watching the talk show in the afternoons. He claimed Oprah's 'men-hating' opinions were a bad influence. "We sure can. Nobody's going to tell us we can't watch some Oprah, if we want to. New house, new rules, and I make them."

Later that evening, Sam and Nick walked into a home filled with the delicious aroma of baked chicken and vegetables.

Carrie glanced up as she emptied two cans of green beans into a pan of sautéed onions and mushrooms. "Hey, guys."

Nick told her hello then met the girls in the living room. As Carrie stood at the stove, Sam walked up behind her and put his hands on her waist to pull her close to him. She leaned her head back against his chest then turned in his arms. "Hmm, I could get used to this set-up," she murmured against Sam's neck after a good, long kiss from him.

"It's wonderful having you and the kids so close," he whispered. "You wouldn't believe how much I missed you today."

"I think I would. I missed you, too."

He kissed her again. "Mm. Glad to hear it. I'd hate to think I was the only one in such dire need." He gave her one last peck and back off. "Who was at work today?"

"Only me and J.C. He said to tell you hello, by the way."

She headed to the back porch to tend to Toto. Carrie poured some fresh dog food into his dish, while Sam filled his water bowl. The dog alternated between eating and looking up at his mistress as though he adored her. Carrie knelt down to scratch him behind the ears.

"That dog sure seems to love you and those kids," Sam admitted.

Carrie smiled and gazed into the eyes of her faithful pet. "He's been in our family for nearly eight years."

"That's a pretty good stretch for a dog."

She nodded and gave Toto one last rub behind the ears, then stood up to let him eat.

After Carrie, Sam, and the kids finished a pleasant meal, interspersed with lively conversation, they watched a couple of one-hour programs on the tube. Nick walked home afterwards, and Carrie stepped out to the porch to talk quietly with Sam for a few minutes.

"No cigarettes out here tonight?" he asked.

She sniffed the air. "Nah, that guy won't bother with me now that I have a dog. You'll see. I can give you that radio back since my phone is connected."

"Hang on to it for a while longer, just until this thing is completely settled."

She hugged him tightly. "If you insist."

"Good night, *ma belle fille*. I love you."

She smiled and touched his face. "I know you do."

He smiled as he pulled himself away from her and headed home. She called out to him when he reached the street.

"Call me later, okay?"

"Yes, ma'am, I'll do that. Now go on in and lock those doors, will you?"

He watched as Carrie stood out there on her porch with *Sam,* hanging on to him as though he was the last man on earth. He found it increasingly difficult to control his feelings: hatred toward Sam for being where he didn't belong, and disappointment toward Carrie for allowing Sam's presence. He breathed a sigh of relief when Sam finally left her, nearly laughed at their requests. A locked door would be about as much help as that phone line would be tonight.

By nine thirty, Carrie and her girls were showered and in their rooms for the night. Quiet murmurs came from Gretchen's room as her girls talked and listened to music on a low volume. Carrie picked up her latest read from the nightstand, while she waited for Sam to call. The fast paced, romantic suspense demanded her attention, and after a good half hour of reading, she yawned and checked her alarm clock. "Well, hell Sam," she muttered, slightly annoyed. "I thought you'd have called by now."

She picked up the phone and frowned, as dead silence greeted her from the earpiece. Carrie got up to check the other phones in the house, with the same results. She stood stock-still and felt a moment of panic before remembering the radios. Crawling back into bed, she pulled the radio out of the drawer. When she pressed the button, nothing happened. She took the back off and changed out the batteries with new ones. Still nothing.

"Dammit!" Trying not to panic, she dropped it on the bed and put her hands to her face. *Now what the hell am I going to do?*

She took a deep breath and rechecked the radio to see if she'd inserted the batteries correctly. When she noticed the switch was off, she flipped it on. Her radio emitted a shrill screech, indicating a page. She raised it to her mouth and hit the button. "Sam?"

"Carrie! I was about to walk over there." Her own panic was reflected in his voice. "Who's been on the phone all night long? Over."

"Nobody," she answered. "I've been waiting for you to call, and I finally picked it up to call you. All three of my phones are dead. Over."

"I'm calling Doug, and I'll be there in a minute. Hang tight, Babe."

Carrie watched Sam's departure from her window, amazed that the mere sight of him comforted her. She opened up the door for him. "Don't upset yourself for nothing, Sam. I bet it's just a short in the wiring or something."

He placed his hands on her shoulders. "Carrie, you don't know how bad I hope you're right. Where's that flashlight?"

By the time she walked out on the porch with it, Doug was also there with his own light. The three of them walked over to the box that fed the phone line into the house. Nothing looked amiss, until Sam reached down and pulled on a wire that came loose much too easily. The two men directed both flashlight beams on the wire and groaned, as Carrie's breath caught in her chest.

"That's a cut," Doug said.

"Son of a bitch! That's all it takes," Sam said.

Carrie's hand flew to her mouth. "Oh—God!" She turned to Sam, resisting the urge to vomit. "He did this! He cut the line."

Sam leveled a serious gaze on her. "Are your girls sleeping yet?"

She lifted her gaze to the shadows surrounding them before nodding.

"I'm getting Nick, Carrie. We're staying here tonight."

She continued to stare blankly into the darkness, her eyes fixed on a particular spot. Then she turned toward the neighbor's house and gazed at the spot they'd found the first cigarette butt. She pivoted slowly, adjusting her stare in the direction of the intersection where the truck nearly plowed into their children. She jumped back with a sharp gasp as a large hand landed on her shoulder.

"Carrie, did you hear me?"

"Wh—What?"

"I said Nick and I are spending the night here," Sam repeated.

Carrie fixed her terrified gaze on him and spoke in a shaky voice. "Okay—I'm—Thank you," she stammered.

"We'll bunk down on the couch and the chair."

She turned to walk into the house. "One of you can sleep in Lauren's bed. When I checked the girls' phone lines I saw them both asleep in Gretchen's room. Grant's futon is available, too."

"Doug, can you stay here while I go get Nick and pick up a few things?"

"Sure thing, do what you have to do."

In Sam's absence, Doug called the police station for some backup, then explained the plan to Carrie. "We'll keep somebody posted outside for tonight. Between that, and having Sam here, you should feel safe."

Carrie put a hand to her belly. "The only thing I feel right now is sick." She excused herself and went to her medicine cabinet to peruse its contents before popping the top on a liquid antacid. After a couple of good size gulps, she lowered the bottle and shuddered.

Feeling vulnerable in her pajamas and robe, she retreated into her bedroom to change. She shed her robe and flannel pajama bottoms, and pulled on some faded jeans. Carrie stared at the windows, knowing he couldn't see from out there. It didn't stop her from turning her back to the window, just in case. She slipped out of her shirt, shivering as frigid air nipped at bare skin. Carrie rushed putting on her bra, wincing, sucking in, as cold fabric met with warm mid-section. She hooked it then pulled the sweater over her head to ward off the chill.

Carrie looked toward the door, hearing Sam and Nick's arrival. She threw her pajamas on the chair and stepped into her wool-lined slippers, before turning off the bedroom light to get the boys situated.

He watched her undress from the comfort of his spot, regretting the all-too-soon end of the free peep show. He mourned the loss as she covered her long legs with denim. But he'd damn near groaned aloud when those full, pale breasts disappeared from his sight. He smiled, thinking of the Special Forces slogan tattooed across his shoulders...so fitting in this situation. *De Oppresso Liber...*To Liberate the Oppressed. His mouth watered at the thought of liberating that pair of thirty-six D's.

This situation was tricky, but as any adrenaline junkie would admit, the bigger the risk, the higher the pleasure factor. Besides, that dog of hers had wounded his pride. Before the night was over, he'd even up the score with that shaggy mutt.

He settled back into a comfortable position, knowing he'd have to spend the next few hours waiting for his opportunity to watch her. Now that he'd seen a little of what he'd be sampling, would he be able to resist touching her? Time would tell. Should he hold off since Sam and his boy would be spending the night in the same house with her? In his cocoon of darkness, he welcomed the added challenge. If the opportunity presented itself, he'd be more than happy to take care of Sam, as well as the son. For that matter, he could take care of everyone in the house, as well as the cop he heard them say would be posted outside, and all without making a sound. *Carrie wouldn't realize a thing was wrong until morning.*

⚜

When Carrie rejoined the others in the living room, Sam watched her try to shake off her obvious uneasiness. He saw her send Nick a look of apology.

"Sorry about this, buddy."

The teenager shrugged. "It's not a problem."

She pointed to a bedroom door. "Somebody can stay in there since the girls both fell asleep in Gretchen's room."

Nick shook his head and laughed. "After griping about how they had to share a bedroom all those years?"

"That's my girls," Carrie said, trying to smile as she gave his shoulder a gentle pat.

Sam recognized her effort for what it was...effort without success. The smile hadn't reached her eyes, but he loved her more for trying.

He stepped up and spoke quietly to his son. "Nick, you go ahead and take the bed. I'll be on the sofa."

Nick nodded and lifted his hand. "Good night, everybody." He disappeared into the room and closed the door behind him.

Doug spoke from the front door. "I'm going on home too."

Sam handed him one of the two-way radios. "Carrie has one here, so you hang on to mine. Batteries are fresh, so it's good for the night."

Doug stepped through the door with the radio. "Y'all stay safe."

Sam locked the door behind him and faced Carrie, who stood, attempting to ease her tense shoulders and neck by rotating her head in a slow circle. He walked behind her and began to massage her neck. After a few minutes of thorough manipulating, he wrapped his arms around her from behind and held on tight. "Better?"

"Yeah, thanks."

He turned her around, saw tension and fear reflected in her face, and began to massage her tight shoulders. "Try to relax."

"I don't think that's going to happen tonight."

It wasn't the words, but her tone that worried him. Tight and hard. No trace of the independence she'd worked so hard to achieve. She'd always had to be the one left standing. *Not this time, dammit.*

"Let go, Carrie," he murmured softly into her ear.

"What?"

He leaned forward to search her eyes beneath the furrowed brow—eyes shadowed with concern. "I said let go, let me worry about it for a while. Let go."

One stubborn shake of her head had him repeating himself. "Go ahead, I'm here. Just this once, let somebody else do the worrying for you."

At the first sign of tears, she covered her mouth with one shaking hand. "Come on." He gave her shoulders a gentle shake. "You'll feel better for it."

Another forceful shake of her head, and she turned to face the wall.

He placed both hands gently on either side of her shoulders and turned her so she faced him. Felt the steel grip of her hands on his wrists, and watched her squeeze her eyes shut in denial. "I'm here, Baby. I'll always be."

Sam crooned words of comfort to her, sensing the tears were close. One quiet sob escaped, then another. She finally dropped her forehead onto his chest and let her emotions spill out like water over an overflowing levee, first a trickle, then gaining speed and strength with the rush of emotions.

Sam held the woman he loved, terrified for her, but so proud she had allowed herself this moment of weakness in his arms. He let her cry until she stopped on her own, all of two minutes later.

"Feel better?" He snapped two tissues from the box on the counter top and handed them to her.

She wiped her eyes and then her nose. "I think so."

"Good, let's sit here. Are you still going to work in the morning?"

Carrie released a groan. "I have to. I only have a few days of annual built up."

"Take a sick day."

"If I do that, sure as shit I'll get sick and need it."

"Then you need to get some sleep."

"Not right now, Sam. I need to be here, close to you."

Sam settled himself on the sofa and pulled her down next to him as they watched thirty minutes of the news with no sound. When her lids started to droop he pulled himself away from her and stood.

"Okay, that's it." He punched the remote's off button and drew Carrie to her feet. "It's time for bed. Give me a blanket and a pillow and I'll be fine."

"Grant's futon is empty in his room." Her tone was quiet and insincere.

"I don't want a wall between us tonight. The sofa will be fine." Her look of relief made him want to pull her in his arms again, but he restrained himself. Sam waited for her to gather the items from the linen closet and took them from her arms. He dropped them on the sofa, and walked her to her bedroom door.

"I'll tuck you in. You want to change into your pajamas again?" She shook her head, and he gently pushed her toward her bed, made her climb in so he could tuck the thick quilt around her. He kissed her forehead and then walked to the door.

"Leave it open, Sam."

"Definitely." He made up the couch and attempted to get comfortable, nearly impossible since it was shy a good foot in length to fit him. He turned this way and that, unable to stretch out. He heard Carrie in the bedroom, tossing and turning as she fought her own demons of insomnia. After fifteen minutes, she asked if he was awake.

He turned on his side one more time, trying to find a position that wouldn't leave his back screaming in pain by morning. "Oh, yeah."

"Come here." Her voice carried a note of pleading.

Sam rolled his six-foot-two-and-then-some frame off his pallet of torture, grateful to have a reason to stretch out his back. "Is something wrong?"

"I can't get past this awful feeling that he's close. I don't want to be alone in here, Sam." She pulled the covers aside, inviting him in her bed. "Please, stay with me?"

"I thought you'd never ask." The mattress creaked with his weight as they snuggled close, his arm around her shoulders and her head on his chest. "Better?"

She nodded and hooked her foot around his muscular calf, denim to denim. "Better, but I still can't shake the feeling we're being watched, like he's outside my window." She shuddered, releasing her breath. "I wonder if I'll ever be able to enjoy this place."

He pulled her closer. "Everything will work out, hon. Get some sleep."

He unfolded himself from the dark solitude of her bedroom closet. He'd had plenty of time to oil the door's hinges, and it opened without a sound

He stood at the foot of Carrie's bed, staring at the couple sleeping like the dead. No, not a couple. Carrie and *him*. The man who was totally unaware he was seconds away from death.

Carrie slept fitfully, looking far from peaceful. Her brow furrowed even in her sleep. He wondered if she dreamed of being watched. That would be the ultimate turn on: if, somehow, Carrie dreamed that he stood over her, watching her dream, as she watched him watch her. Like mirrors facing each other, never ending. That would be a nightmare of his making, with no hope of her waking. *I'm a damn poet.*

He almost felt like laughing. Almost. He hadn't laughed in a long time. Not since he'd stopped believing there was any good in this world or a God to deliver him from his personal hell.

He walked over to her side of the bed and reached his hand out to move a curl from her brow. She turned away as if she sensed his presence. He smiled, knowing how upset she'd be if she knew he watched from *inside* her room instead of outside, as she'd suspected. He grew hard remembering how he'd watched her undress earlier. Would it break her? *No*. She'd get angry before she let that happen. He'd known it when he'd chosen her.

He cocked his head slowly to one side then the other, cracking his neck both ways. Take a deep breath, and let the game begin—the one whose rules were known only to him. The Restrain Game, he called it. He enjoyed it—both loving and hating at the same time, the act of holding himself back from his victims.

He reached out his hands to touch her, stopping just short of contact. Slowly, he moved his open palms over her face and exposed arms, only a fraction of an inch from her skin. He leaned his face over hers, his lips a mere hairsbreadth away from touching hers. The v-style collar of her sweater stretched down and twisted so that and a good portion of her neck was exposed to his gaze. He brought his nose and mouth near, breathing in her scent. He straightened suddenly, frowned at the smell of some type of scented soap. That wasn't at all what he wanted to smell on her warm skin. Her perfume, that woodsy, spicy, almost musky scent—the one she kept on her vanity. That's what she should be wearing, always.

He allowed himself the extravagance of touching her hair. Amazed at its softness, he tucked his finger just inside a ringlet that formed on the end of her shoulder-length hair. He lightly brushed his fingertips over her tendrils, releasing the scent of her shampoo and conditioner. Lowering his face, he breathed in, looking forward to the moment he could bury his face in her hair.

He made his way into her private bath and picked up the small bottle of amber liquid, uncapped it, and inhaled. *That's it.* The smell made him *want* to lose control, the name . . . *Obsession* . . . perfect. One more sign she belonged with him. Suddenly inspired, he sprayed a good amount on his index finger, taking the bottle with him. He reached out with his fingertip and touched the skin in the area of her carotid pulse, then dipped it down to the lowest part of her neckline, just at the top of her breast. Lastly, he touched just behind the only ear exposed to him. He gave it a few moments to mix with her own scent, then lowered his face as near to her as he dared and breathed her in. *Oh, yeah, that's more like it.*

He watched Sam's reaction. The asshole took a deep breath, almost as though he sensed the change in Carrie's presence. Even fast asleep, Sam released a low moan as he pulled her closer.

He straightened to his full height, his entire body tensing with the effort it took *not* to snap Sam's neck like a twig. Carrie saved him the trouble by turning in her sleep to rest on her side facing away from the man in her bed.

After several minutes more of the game, he left Carrie to check out the other residents of the house. He entered one room and walked out quickly, uninterested in *his* teenage son. The next room held Carrie's twin daughters. They'd apparently fallen asleep while watching television. He saw their faces clearly from the light emitted by the small set and realized how potentially gorgeous they would be in a few short years. He reached down and touched their hair, curlier than their mother's soft tendrils. If things didn't work out with their mom, he could always turn his attentions toward one, or both, of her daughters.

He'd never had twins, and the thought intrigued him. It would be a first. Nevertheless, he wasn't into pedophilia. He backed carefully out of the bedroom. *Years from now perhaps—and after they'd matured.* For now, he wanted to savor everything he'd experienced tonight.

He placed the uncapped bottle of perfume on the kitchen counter, wondering if she'd catch on. It was all part of his plan to test her reserves. He peaked out the window to verify the cruiser's location and then crossed over, slipping out a window on the north side of Carrie's home.

Only one thing left to do before slipping back into the darkness.

Chapter Twenty-One

Carrie woke with the soft chirp of her alarm clock. She turned it off and stretched under the covers before rolling over to see Sam's semi-sleep gaze on her. "Don't get up yet, it's still too early for you." She stretched again. "But I need to."

Sam pulled her to him and buried his face in her neck. "Hmm babe, you smell so good."

She turned her face away from him as she spoke. "I hardly think dragon breath first thing in the morning can be that much of a turn on." She rolled out of bed, slipped her feet into her slippers, and wrapped herself in her robe. She padded into the kitchen and pushed the start button on the coffee maker before going to the back door to check on Toto. She pushed the blind open enough to see him sprawled out on his side just in front of the back door. *Good dog.*

Carrie went in to her bathroom with her work clothes and emerged thirty minutes later, dressed, made-up and ready for the day. She smiled at Sam, who stood there, sleepy-eyed and rumpled, looking as though he was unsure of what to do.

"Want some breakfast?" She kissed his cheek.

"Sure, are you buying?"

"Yep. Want to help?"

"Uh huh." She cracked eggs, one-handed, into a bowl. He moved up closer to watch over her shoulder. "Nice technique, babe. Not a shell in the bowl. Need any help?" he asked, wrapping his hands around her waist.

"You can toast some bread. I don't have time for biscuits."

"I'm on it." He grabbed the loaf of bread and inserted two slices in the toaster, then reached across and picked up the bottle of perfume sitting on the snack bar. He waved it slowly under his nose then pulled her hair aside and buried his face in her neck. "This stuff is good in the bottle, but it's delicious on you."

Carrie scrunched her shoulders, giggling, and pulled out of his embrace to start whisking the eggs for scrambling. What started as a brisk movement slowed to a halt as the fork fell into the bowl of yolks and whites. She pulled his hand around and stared at the bottle of perfume he held.

"Where'd you find that? I know it was on my vanity last night. I could smell it in my bathroom this morning, but I couldn't find the bottle."

"It was right here on the counter," he told her. "You must have left it there after you used it last night."

She frowned and shook her head. "I didn't use any after my shower." She turned to look at the counter top. "When we left the kitchen last night, the counter was completely cleaned off. Where the hell's the cap? I never leave it uncovered."

He frowned and leaned in toward her. "Babe, you're definitely wearing perfume, and it's this stuff. It's here . . ." He sniffed her neck, then checked behind both ears. "Not this one, but it is behind the other." He touched the back of one ear.

She raised both wrists and smelled. "This doesn't make sense, Sam. I always spray it on my wrists then touch my wrists to my neck." She held her wrists to his nose.

"There's nothing there." He shook his head. "Babe, you must have—"

"I *didn't!*" She tried to reason things out as a last resort to panic. "This doesn't make sense. When I took my shower, I didn't put any on. I *know* that."

Sam shoved his hands deep into his pockets. "Well, you're right. This doesn't make sense."

Her eyes fixed on the bedroom door. "Sam. Last night. Could he have—Did he—He couldn't have. Could he?" Her entire being filled with dread. She spun around toward the other bedrooms. "Dear, God. Was he in my home?"

They rushed forward to check on their children and found them all unharmed and asleep.

Far from relieved, Sam paced the living room, as Carrie searched the kitchen for other clues. He stopped in his tracks and met her troubled gaze. "Is this possible?"

Carrie stared into the bedroom where she and Sam spent the night. "It's the only answer." She made her way to the bed, terrified of finding proof that she was right. There, at the foot of the unmade bed, sat the familiar top to her bottle of perfume. Carrie clapped one hand over her mouth to keep from screaming, and continued to search for anything else out of place. She pulled open the closet door and stepped closer flipping on the interior light. Bile rose in her throat at the distinct odor of tobacco smoke. "No. No. I can't believe this could happen. How could that happen?" She spun to face Sam.

He shook his head in denial. "The cop outside—and your dog—"

Carrie rushed out of the bedroom to the back door, pulling it open. "You would have let us know, right boy?" Toto was still there, sprawled out in the same position as he'd been earlier. Carrie tensed at the sight, praying her suspicions were wrong. "Get up, Toto." She waited. Repeated the command, knowing in her gut he wouldn't obey—he couldn't obey—he'd never hear her again. She reached over with her shoe to nudge his stiff body—pulled it back. She dropped to her knees, strangling on the scream that lurked in the shadows, just out of reach.

Her heart shattered as she passed both hands over the deathly still body of the pet she, her children, and even Dave, had loved for eight years. Her mind replayed the day she saw a car stop and drop off the tiny white ball of fluff in the middle of a busy street in Lake Erin. She'd doubled back in her car, praying he wouldn't get hit before she got to him, and finally found him hiding in a ditch. She'd pulled over onto a side street, opened her door and called to him. He'd run straight to her and launched his tiny body into her car. The powder puff had scrambled up onto her lap and buried his nose under her arm, knowing immediately he'd found his niche, his home, his family. It had been love at first sight for both of them. His first bath, the trips to two kindergarten classrooms, then a second grade classroom to show the kids, nights of bringing him outside to do his business, and laughing as the winter wind made his backside flip right over his head because he was so tiny. Memories flooded, soon replaced with the acute ache over losing a pet so loved.

The room filled with a low moan that turned into a wail. Somewhat shocked to discover the sound was coming from her, she clamped both hands over her mouth. A steady stream of curses from Sam brought her out of it. "No. No. Don't wake the girls, Sam." She sobbed into her hands, trying to stifle her cries.

Heartbroken for her, Sam knelt behind Carrie, wrapped his arms around her and held on tight. What kind of man could do this? Not a man. A sadistic son of a bitch. He clenched his jaw so tightly it popped. All he could do was hold her as she mourned her pet. A gnawing awareness filled him with dread: anyone who could do this under these conditions, and so easily, was capable of much worse. Feeling helpless, he muttered a low curse and held her tighter as she sobbed. He cursed again when he thought how heartbroken her kids would be. He glared at the police officer on guard who came around the back of the house.

"Is everything all right here?" Cody asked.

Sam cleared his throat and pulled the sobbing woman closer. "We've seen signs he was in the house last night and—" He lowered his voice. "We suspect he killed the dog."

The officer swore quietly and shook his head. "I never saw a thing. I never left my post, and I didn't fall asleep, Sam. I swear I didn't. The second patrol car made regular passes with the search light on all sides at least every thirty minutes." He pulled out his radio and ran to his cruiser.

Sam listened as Cody called in the probable breaking and entering, then walked Carrie back inside the house and away from Toto.

After a few minutes, the officer came back and stood inside the doorway. He cleared his throat and shuffled his black-booted feet. "Ms. Jeansonne, I'm so sorry this happened, but the chief thinks we should perform an autopsy on the animal to discover the cause of death. He's sending the K-nine officer over to pick him up since Kenton doesn't have any full-time animal control personnel. That guy usually comes from the parish seat, but he's out of state for the holidays." He stared down at the floor, shifted, and repositioned his clipboard. "Did, uh, did he have any health threatening conditions?"

Carrie sniffed and wiped her nose with the tissue Sam handed her. She shook her head. "He just had all his shots. The vet said he was good."

The officer shook his head and groaned. "I'm so sorry, ma'am. I really am." He turned as the K-9 unit pulled into the driveway and left to meet the truck. He came back a few minutes later and introduced her to another young officer.

This officer spoke to her in a quiet and respectful tone. "I'm sorry for your loss, Ma'am." He pointed to the specially outfitted K-9 truck parked in her driveway. "My name is Officer Bertrand, and I applied for this position because I'm a dog lover too. What's his name, ma'am?"

She took a deep breath. "Toto."

The officer nodded. "From *The Wizard of Oz*, huh? It fits him perfectly. How old was Toto, ma'am?"

"He's eight years old." She faltered and cleared her throat to stem the tears. "We raised him from a puppy." She swallowed the lump in her throat. "Can you take him now, please? I don't want my girls to see him like this." She shook her head. "This is gonna break their hearts."

Officer Bertrand crouched next to Toto's lifeless body. "From here on out, he'll be treated with nothing but respect, I can promise you that."

She nodded but kept her silence.

Sam thanked the officer. "How soon do you think we'll know something, Heath?"

"If there are any toxins in his system, it could take a couple of days, depending on what k—what was used on him," he finished.

"Toxins." Carrie nearly choked on the word. "That's a pretty way to say 'poison' isn't it?" She dabbed at her eyes with a tissue again. "If you rule out natural causes, it won't matter what he used on him."

The officer got to his feet. "The identity of the poison may be used as evidence when we catch this guy. It could help us put him away or even link him to any other unsolved crimes."

Carrie nodded and crouched over her dog, giving his thick, white coat one last rub. "Good boy," she whispered. She straightened, then backed into the kitchen and closed the door. She turned to face the one officer remaining in her living room. "Did Sam tell you why we suspect he's been in the house?"

"No, ma'am, I was waiting until you were ready." He pulled out a pad to take notes as both Carrie and Sam explained her reason for suspecting the stalker had been in her home. When Cody asked if he could check out her bedroom, she and Sam led him there. He opened the closet door and studied the inside before leaning over to pick up something up against the edge of the wall. He straightened, holding out a single, un-smoked cigarette.

"You were right," Cody told them.

She nodded. "That's him, that's what he smokes."

They did a quick check of the other rooms in the house and ended up back in her living room. Cody made some notes, then tucked his notepad into his shirt pocket. "If this guy's got the nerve, as well as the ability to do this, he's one dangerous son of a gun. We'll need to call in the troops on this one." He walked to the front door, then paused and turned to Sam. "I wouldn't lose sight of her until we resolve this situation."

Sam closed the door, then pulled Carrie close for a hug.

"I should trust my instincts more, Sam. I knew something was wrong in that bedroom." She closed her eyes and remembered the feeling of being watched—of how she'd turned away from the windows and toward the closet. "Oh, God, I undressed in front of him, Sam." Carrie shuddered visibly, feeling violated and dirty.

"You want me to call the office for you?"

She turned to walk into her bathroom. "Yeah, go ahead and call for me. Report the cut line to the phone company, while you're at it."

Sam watched the door close, then heard the shower running. He stepped onto the front porch and went to Doug's place across the street. He asked him to keep an eye on Carrie's home while he made the phone calls.

Fifteen minutes later, he returned to Carrie's. She sat curled up on the sofa, wearing jeans and a different sweater from last night.

"I called the office, and J.C.'s the only one there. He said he hopes we catch the bastard and to give you this." He reached over and gave her a hug.

She hugged Sam back, imagining what her friend would have had to say. "I bet he said worse than that."

"He did," Sam agreed. "But I was trying not to be as vile as he was."

Carrie gave him a bleak smile, remembering the string of curses that had come from his mouth earlier. "I want you to sit and listen to something I came up with." She explained her plan in detail.

"You can't be serious." Sam's face revealed his horror. "It'll work, Babe." He stood and paced the floor. "It's too damned dangerous."

"No more dangerous than having him lurk around here while we're all asleep and completely defenseless," she argued. "This is bullshit, Sam, and you know it. I won't be his victim, and I damn sure won't sit back and let my kids, or your son, or you be his victims either." She pressed her hands to her stomach. "When I think what could have happened while I slept, totally clueless that he was walking around in here—" She shivered. "I get sick inside."

Sam dropped his head accepting the inevitable, knowing she'd do this regardless of what he said. "Okay," he finally agreed. "But I have a few suggestions—with your safety in mind."

She nodded when he finished speaking. "I have to admit, I'd feel better if you were a part of this."

By eight a.m., the phone company had reconnected Carrie's phone line. With Sam by her side, she called Dave and told him she'd bring their daughters home later that morning, then broke the news about Toto.

Dave was quiet for a moment. "Have you told the twins yet?"

"No." She covered her eyes with one hand. "And I dread it more than anything I've ever done in my life. Is Grant awake yet?"

"You're kidding, right? Don't worry, I'll wake his lazy butt up around ten and tell him."

Carrie cringed. "Look, when you tell him, do you think you could do it without being so insensitive? Our kids grew up with that dog, Dave. Grant's going to be hurting."

"Hey, I'm hurting too, you know," Dave huffed, sounding insulted. "I liked that dog as much as you did, even if he didn't earn his keep around here like *my* dog does."

"Toto was free. You paid big bucks for Lucas, and we spent another three hundred on his eye surgery—oh, forget it. It doesn't matter. I love your dog too—jerk."

Dave's voice broke unexpectedly. "Look, I'm sorry for taking it out on you." He paused, obviously trying to control his emotions. "I'm just pissed that he died that way."

"It's okay, I understand."

"No! No, it's not okay. I apologize for being a jerk. That son of a bitch needs to pay for doing that to our dog."

"I know he does." She nodded at Sam. "And I've got a plan that can make that happen. Sam is letting me use his truck to bring the girls home, because I need to borrow something from you. It's a lot to ask, I know, but I believe it may make the difference." After she explained what she need from him and how it fit into her plans, he balked at first, but finally agreed.

"Thanks, Dave. Are you sure you don't want me to tell Grant when I get there?"

"No, you'll have your hands full telling the girls. I'll be sensitive, I promise."

"Thank you, Dave. We'll be there in a couple of hours. Tell *no one* about this, okay? Not even Grant. It's important that we have the element of surprise on our side. We think he's someone from around that area."

Dave agreed, and she ended the call. She rubbed at her forehead and faced Sam. "It's time to tell the girls."

Sam nodded. "You want me to go in there with you?"

"I think I should do this by myself, but thanks for the offer anyway." She walked into the room where her daughters slept and closed the door behind her.

Carrie sat on Gretchen's bed and held her daughters to her, one in each arm. She cried along with them as they mourned the loss of their beloved Toto. "I'm sorry," she whispered. "I'm so very sorry." She rocked them, ached for them, while wishing she could take away their pain. Her eyes focused on a tiny spot on the bedroom door, as she told herself that Sam was out there and waiting to help if she needed him. That thought gave her the strength she needed to comfort her children.

Gretchen was the first to calm and pull away from her mother. She wiped her eyes on the sleeve of her pajama top and sniffed loudly. "If that stupid *cigarette man* poisoned our dog, I hope we get to meet up with him one day."

She narrowed her eyes at her mother. "I'd sure like to beat the crap out of him."

Carrie couldn't help but smile at her daughter's determination and drive. "Sweetie, everyone feels the same way, even the local police. Don't worry, we'll get him, but we'll always have good memories of Toto. He was such a character, wasn't he?"

Gretchen gave her mom a tearful smile. "You remember how we'd clean him up so he could stay in the house when it was cold outside?"

Lauren joined the conversation. "Remember how he'd fart and stink up the house?"

Carrie laughed through her tears. "The faces he'd make when we'd discover it was him—poor Toto would hang his head, almost like he was ashamed." Before long, all three of them were laughing over other memories of their beloved Toto.

Carrie reached out to smooth her daughters' curls. "He's not gone as long as we remember him."

"I'll always remember him, but he is gone," Gretchen groaned. "And I'd still like the chance to beat the crap of that guy."

"I'd like somebody to hold him down so we could all beat the crap out of him," Lauren added.

Carrie smiled, hugging her girls to her, and prayed they'd end up with men who wouldn't try to take that spark away from them. "I need to bring you back to your dad's this morning. Until this is settled, I have to know you're all safe. Are either of you hungry?"

She patted their hands when they said no. "Get your stuff together and make the bed, please."

Sam and Nick stood in the kitchen talking quietly when Carrie exited the bedroom.

Nick walked over to hug her and shook his head. "That's messed up, Carrie. I'm sorry."

"Thank you, Nick, and you're right, it is messed up."

The girls came out the bedroom, fully dressed, eyes red-rimmed from crying. Carrie sniffed, her heart bursting with gratefulness, as they migrated straight to Sam. She watched as he held her daughters, whispering words of comfort. They moved to Nick, who enveloped them both in a consoling hug.

"Nick," Sam spoke softly after giving them several moments. "Take the girls over to our place until we get back. Carrie and I have to make a run to the police station."

Nick nodded and herded the girls out the door, as Carrie and Sam prepared to leave.

Carrie sat with Sam in Charlie Walker's office, discussing her plan. It took another thirty minutes to work out the details. They rose to leave, and she extended her hand to the police chief. “I appreciate your help in this situation, Chief Walker.”

“You’re welcome, Ms. Jeansonne. We’ll get this guy.”

By nine thirty, the twins sat in Sam’s truck, waiting for Carrie.

Sam pulled her to the back of the truck for a talk. “I hate the idea of you going over there without me.”

She placed her hand on his face to calm him. “I’ll be fine, Sam. I’m going straight to Dave’s, and then coming back here. No pit stops, I promise. I’m fighting the urge to cower in a corner somewhere, so I need to do this alone. It’s like getting back on a horse when you fall off, you know?”

Sam frowned but gave her a hug, anyway. “Just because I understand, doesn’t mean I have to like it. I won’t relax until you’re back.”

She turned Sam’s truck into the driveway of her old home and pulled to a stop. Dave and Grant came out to meet them.

She stepped down from the truck and cupped her son’s head in her two hands to study his eyes, still filled with grief. Toto had accompanied her son everywhere until recently, when Grant’s truck had replaced exploring on foot or bicycle. She pulled him close for a hug. “I’m so sorry, Son.”

“This really sucks, Mom.”

“I know, but they’ll get this guy.” She allowed herself several more moments to console him, then gave both him and her girls a final hug. “Ya’ll go on in the house now, please. I need to talk to your dad.”

Dave waited until their children were inside before speaking. “Do they know about the plan tonight?”

“No, I don’t want them to worry.” She closed her eyes and shook her head. “When I think about him walking around my home with our kids—it makes my skin crawl.”

Dave nodded. “I know, I’m sick about it too, but they’re fine. Listen, Carrie, I want to apologize to you again for acting the ass those other times. I’m the last person to be pointing the finger at you for anything, especially since we’re divorced now.” He leaned an elbow on Sam’s truck and crossed one booted foot over the other. “I got the scoop on you and Sam last night at the club in Gardiner.”

“Oh, yeah? Who’d you speak to?”

“Your brother, Mack, was there performing with their band.” He gave her a sheepish grin. “He let me have it pretty good.”

Carrie kept her silence as Dave told her how Mack had come to her defense as well as Sam’s. She watched as he ran one hand through his thick hair.

“He said he’s a real nice guy and he makes you happy. I blew all my chances, and you gave me plenty, so who am I to complain?”

She gave him a slow nod, her eyes squinted in concentration. “What else is going on here?”

He gave her what she was sure he *thought* was an innocent look. "What do you mean?"

Her smile broadened. "I mean, I know you like the back of my hand, David James Jeansonne. You've met someone else."

Dave's eyes widened. "Who'd you talk to?"

Carrie's laughter rang out. "I didn't talk to anyone. I just know you too well, that's all."

He swore under his breath. "I guess you do, at that." He grinned, looking a little sheepish. "I have met someone."

"Does she know what a jerk you are?"

"Yeah, and she likes me anyway."

Carrie laughed and gave him a quick nod of approval. "Good, I'm glad."

"Why, because I'll quit bugging you now?"

"Of course," she added, before cringing at the laugh that had begun to grate on her nerves over the years. She shook it off and scanned the area. "Where is he, Dave? I really need to go home and put things in motion."

Dave whistled and called to his dog. Lucas lumbered in from a nearby field behind the house. He ran to his mistress when he saw her, his tail wagging in excitement. She leaned over to rub his ears and the scruff of his neck. "Hey, buddy, I've got a job for you. Think you can handle it?" Lucas greeted her with happy noises at having her around to show him affection again.

"He can handle it. Do you remember his commands?"

"Yep."

"Make sure you're around when strangers show up so he doesn't attack, okay?" He lowered the tailgate and told Lucas to jump in. "Good luck, Carrie, and be careful."

Carrie slipped in behind the steering wheel of Sam's truck and buckled her seatbelt.

"I almost forgot, let me get his toy." He came back a minute later with the brown leather welder's glove stuffed with feathers and sewn shut. He threw it in the back of the truck and Lucas jumped after it. Carrie grinned at the sight of the dog with the stuffed glove in his mouth. She could certainly see why unsuspecting drivers and passengers of other cars sometimes thought it was a real arm.

Dave pointed to the truck bed. "Sit, Lucas. Stay." He ducked his head to look inside Carrie's window. "Did you ever get your car window fixed?"

She nodded. "I got it fixed at a place in Kenton."

He hung his head. "It won't happen again." He took a deep breath and nodded toward the dog. "Keep him in practice for me, will you?"

"I will, and thanks." She put on her sunglasses and started the truck.

"You're welcome. Good luck with everything." After a pause, he continued. "It might be nice to be friends with you again."

She flashed him a big grin. "It's a possibility, if you keep acting like an adult."

Dave pursed his lips and stared off toward the house. “Damn, I hate that you’re always right.” He leveled a serious gaze on her. “Don’t you ever get tired of it?”

Carrie shrugged. “It doesn’t seem to matter. Nobody ever listens to me anyway.” She shifted the truck into reverse and slowly backed away from him. She cringed as Dave put his head back and laughed. “I hate that laugh, you know.”

“You do?”

“Yep. For years now.” When Dave laughed again, Carrie grinned at him. “See you later, asshole.”

Carrie parked Sam’s truck in her driveway and lowered the tailgate to release Lucas. While he was getting used to the yard, she called Sam and Nick to come over. She met them outside. “Come on back here guys, so I can introduce you to the other family pet.” As soon as they approached the gate, the large dog barreled up to them, growling at the two strange men standing near his mistress.

“It’s okay boy, they’re the good guys.” She scratched his head and he immediately calmed down. “Sam—Nick—come here and get acquainted with him.”

“I don’t know about that.” Nick rubbed one hand at the back of his neck. “That’s a big freaking dog, Carrie.”

Sam had to agree with his son. “I’ve seen a couple of Mastiffs and St. Bernard’s in my time. He’s nowhere near that size, but for any other breed, he’s near the top of my list.” Sam reached out slowly to let Lucas sniff his hand. “Look at that head and the size of those paws.”

“I’m too busy looking at his teeth,” Nick said.

Carrie waved him over. “Come on over here, Nick. He needs to be able to recognize friend from foe.”

Within ten minutes, Sam and Nick were petting Lucas like he was an old friend. The dog moaned, enjoying the attention. Carrie tossed the stuffed arm to Nick as Lucas wagged his tail expectantly. “Throw it for him, Nick. He’ll retrieve all day, as long as the weather’s cool or he’s in water.”

Sam and Carrie left Nick in the backyard with the dog and walked inside. Sam made one phone call to the police department, and within minutes, Kenton police officers started showing up in unmarked vehicles. Carrie made sure she was present for all arrivals of officers, detectives, patrolmen, and even a few curious Sheriff’s deputies. She laughed at Lucas, who was clearly enjoying all the unaccustomed attention.

Sam never left her side, and by three p.m., Lucas and the entire police department were all best of buddies. It was a necessary step to protect the officers, so they could have the freedom to protect Carrie and her family in the future.

Chapter Twenty-Two

By seven p.m., Carrie had called Lucas to the back porch, and commanded him to *sit* and *stay*. She entered her kitchen and peeked through the window, comforted by the sight of him, then made adjustments to her blinds.

She showered, her vanity chair jammed securely under the doorknob for security. After changing into her pajamas, she prepared a ham sandwich and ate her supper watching television. By nine p.m., she could almost feel the change in the atmosphere. She forced herself to walk up to the window on the northeast corner of the house, and peek out toward the street. *He's out there.* The street lamp kept part of the area well lit, but a strip between the window and ditch was black as India ink. She shivered as prickles of warning caused the hair to stand up on the back of her neck.

She ignored the nausea caused by her nervous stomach and picked up her ringing phone. "Hey, Sam."

"Hey, Carrie," the deep voice resounded over the line.

"Listen, I'm tired and I'm not feeling all that well. I'm going to take something to sleep and go to bed early. Poor Toto, I still can't believe he's gone."

"Yeah, but you had to expect that with a dog his age."

"I know, and those damn heart worms… I guess the excitement of a new place was too much for him."

"I guess so. You sure you're okay?"

"Oh, yeah. I'll be fine, now that I have my phone back. The phone company said it was faulty wiring."

"They replaced the wire rather than repaired it, right?"

"They said they did. You want to come over for breakfast in the morning?"

"I'll be there."

"Good, I'll see you then. Good night Sam."

He watched through small slits in her blinds, as she walked around her house. By some twist of fate or fortune, they weren't shut tight tonight. She walked right up to the window and stared out onto the street. No way could she see him in the dark. The thick cloud coverage obliterated any chance of moonlight illumination. It was the perfect night to take Carrie away from this place—away from *him*.

He listened in to her call with Sam, able to hear both ends of the conversation clearly with the wireless device he'd acquired recently. As simple as this mission was, he had no need for anything more high tech than this.

She ended the call and popped what looked like some kind of sleep aid medication before disappearing into her bedroom. No Sam, no kids, no shaggy white mutt to blow his cover—*and* she's drugged? A frown tugged at his mouth. No challenge at all, actually, and a little too easy for his taste. He'd watch her sleep first. Play the game for a while before he let his urges overcome his will power. Only then would he allow himself to touch. Control. Possess. *Tonight.* He'd make her his tonight.

He reached into his pocket to feel the tools of his obsession. His zip pouch contained a few basics, plus a syringe full of Ketaset. He'd need her nice and quiet for transfer. All part of the plan, though he drew the line when it came to weapons. No guns or knives. A real soldier didn't need weapons against civilians. He preferred to rely solely on his other strengths to make women succumb to his will.

He could hardly wait to see how Carrie, by far the strongest of any of his targets, would react to him. He knew she wouldn't plead for her life, but would she show fear? Maybe at first, but then he'd see the one thing that separated her from the others—her determination not to show it.

Sleep, my girl, so I can wake you up. In my own way.

That Friday evening had all the signs of being a long, slow night on the job for Rob Ledoux. He sat at his desk, working, short-handed because of officers taking vacation leave. It was either take it before January 1st or lose it, but why did his people save it for the end of the year, every year, without fail? Being chief didn't mean squat in a town the size of Gardiner, especially when seventy-five percent of your force was either taking vacation time or on sick leave.

Rob couldn't fault Tim for calling in sick for the first time in a year. The man never took time off, never complained about the hours he worked. He was a model employee.

So, why can't I get myself to like the son of a bitch?

That very morning he'd told Mona there were two things about Tim Hardin that irritated the hell out of him. First, he never cussed, not even the occasional damn or hell. He could handle it if the guy didn't seem to look down his nose at anyone else who *did*. He shook his head, wondering for the six-hundredth time how a man who puffed his way through two packs of cigarettes a day didn't cuss. Just didn't seem natural.

Second, he printed everything. What the hell was wrong with longhand? It wasn't even normal printing—it was neat, precise block letters that would have made Rob's first grade teacher, Miss Madeline, do the eff-ing halleluiah dance. Regardless, it didn't make Tim a bad employee, and he sure as hell couldn't fire him for either of those things.

Rob stretched back in his chair, bored shitless. He glanced at his dispatcher. One year on the job, Henrietta was older than Rob by fifteen years and feisty as hell.

"Henri, did I get anything from Charlie Walker at Kenton P.D.? He called me at home today asking about a fax he sent. Something about a picture of a message scratched onto Carrie Jeansonne's windshield. When I said I hadn't seen any fax, he told me he'd resend it. I guess it got lost."

Henrietta looked up from her romance novel of the week. "I put two faxes in the incoming tray. One is that picture you mentioned, but it's the first I've seen of it."

"I just checked, and there's nothing but old payro—"

"The new, clear one I put on the wall."

"The wall?"

"Yep, so it doesn't get covered up from all the crap on that un-natural disaster you call a desk."

Rob turned to the wall, spotted the tray and grunted. "I guess that is better." He reached for the messages, scanned the message from Charlie. Info on the truck that almost hit the kids wasn't much help. Gardiner was a farming community, full of trucks with that description. Hell, two of his officers drove them.

He threw the message on his desk and flipped the fax, a black and white picture. Rob leaned forward to get a better look, and then cussed up a blue streak that made his dispatcher come running.

"What the hell's wrong with you?"

He pulled one particular personnel file and checked for comparisons, just to make sure he wasn't jumping to conclusion. Rob's gut clenched as he held the fax up to the neatly printed text on the original application and everything the man had touched since then. He ran quickly through the file. Army, Special Forces. Adept at hand to hand combat. Every reason he'd hired that man—suddenly a liability. A trained killer. "Son of a bitch!" He reached for his phone.

He checked his watch one last time. Eleven o'clock and no sign of movement anywhere in the quiet neighborhood. No cruiser tonight, no need to use a window. He crept silently to the door, knowing the unlit area and his dark clothing kept him hidden from sight. Once he'd lubricated the door's hardware, he picked the lock and walked through the portal. His palms itched with anticipation as he took several steps toward Carrie's bedroom. He paused, sensing their presence before he heard the warning.

"Hold it right there."

He turned slowly, seeing two guns on him, and smiled, a little surprised to be out-maneuvered by a handful of small-town cops. He could kill them all—easily—far too easily—but that would risk blowing his cover. Luckily, he'd been the only one in the office when that fax came in. His reputation was pure as the conscience of a newborn baby. Nope, better to escape tonight and have a better shot at Carrie another night, even if it meant letting these fools live. A third man came out of Carrie's bedroom, while someone from inside the room shut and locked the door. One by one, he stared them down, giving himself the time he needed to map his escape. "Never underestimate a small-town, red-neck cop." He didn't worry about his voice, muffled by the full face mask.

"Face down on the floor with your hands behind your back," one commanded.

He nodded slowly. "That'd be one option."

"Don't do anything stupi—" the man on the right began, just before the single kick dislocated his jaw.

He lunged through the door with two remaining officers hot on his trail, skidding to a halt as he saw two more officers blocking his path. He spun around and ran for the backyard, jumping the fence even as he heard Carrie's command to something named Lucas.

He'd seen a Bull Mastiff once, a monster of an animal that out-weighed most men. That dog may have been the largest he'd ever seen, but the one that came barreling out of nowhere and tackled him to the ground was a close second. The huge animal pinned him on his back in a split second, as two large, front paws, and a thick, heavy body covered his own. He froze, as sharp incisors pushed into skin, and massive jaws covered his neck and jugular. He knew the dog held back just enough to prevent him from doing lethal damage. Regardless, as that beast emitted a low growl, one that sent vibrations rumbling through his throat and head, the man realized one thing. As a soldier, he'd fought the unseen evils and threats that lurked around every corner, but since becoming a man, he'd never really known fear—until now.

Carrie and Sam watched from the relative safety of her bedroom window. Spotlights flooded the area, revealing a man completely covered from head to toe in black. Doug walked slowly to where Lucas had the man pinned to the ground. "Good boy, Lucas," Carrie murmured.

Doug commanded Lucas to "Hold," as he pulled out his handcuffs in the slow, steady movements she'd told him to use. The four other officers circled with their guns, as he spoke to the dog. "Lucas, release," Doug said to the dog. Nothing. "Lucas, let go, boy." Lucas didn't budge, but continued to hold the man's throat, his rumbling growl low and menacing.

"He's not listening to them, Sam." Carrie pushed away from the open window and ran to the porch. She walked slowly down the steps and stopped. The men grew quiet, the only sound coming from the dog. "Are you ready?"

Doug nodded.

"Lucas. Release. Watch." Her commands sharp and quick, the dog obeyed. He released his captive's neck but stood on alert, only inches away, every muscle in his large body tensed and ready to recapture if the need arose—the ominous growl still dangerously present.

Doug rolled the man onto his stomach and handcuffed him. As he did he spoke slowly, his voice lowered an octave to keep Lucas from over-reacting. "Don't go doing anything stupid, because there's not one of us here who can keep that dog off your ass." He pulled the man's wool mask from his face, before jerking him roughly up to his feet. He handed him off to two more men ready to walk him to the police cruiser pulling up to the front of the house.

Two steps from the cruiser, Carrie watched the man in black head butt one officer and jerk free.

Lucas bolted after the escapee, even as a second patrol car sped up to the scene.

Carrie's scream cut through the night air followed by the screech of tires and the thud of automobile coming into contact with not one, but two living, breathing animals.

Chapter Twenty-Three

The car skidded to a halt, and everyone ran to where it had thrown the body—all the way to the intersection. Chief Charlie Walker jumped out of the cruiser. "They came out of nowhere!"

Carrie ran up to stand beside the man's twisted body, searching the darkness. "Where's my dog? Lucas!" Nobody said a word as flashlights pierced the black night, searching for the dog.

Carrie held her breath, listening, waiting for some sign that she hadn't lost another member of her family. Her pleading call to him broke the silence. "Lucas. Come here boy, please!"

A faint, uneven cadence of paws hitting roadway and heavy panting had her pivoting toward the sound. Carrie ran to her limping dog, while every person there released a collective sigh.

The K-9 officer ran to meet her. "I need some light over here!" he called, dropping to his knees next to the dog. "Good boy." He began feeling for breaks and other injuries.

"Please tell me he's okay," Carrie groaned.

"I'll put him in my unit to bring him over to the local vet. He needs to give Lucas a good going over, but I believe your dog will be fine. It looks like the perp here got the brunt of the hit. I think Lucas only has a sprain."

"I was coming to let y'all know this was no ordinary peeping tom," Chief Walker said to the other officers. "His name's Tim Hardin, and he's an officer with Gardiner P.D. He's ex-military, too."

"He made a run for it, but if you hadn't stopped him, I'm sure that dog would have. Looks like more than just his neck is broken.

"I sure as hell didn't mean to do that," Charlie admitted.

One of the other officers walked up holding a black zip pouch. "I found this on the road."

Charlie Walker unzipped the pouch and gave a disgusted grunt. Carrie and Sam joined the others as Charlie spread the pouch wide enough for everyone to see.

A shiver ran through Carrie as she studied its contents—wire, rope, duct tape, hypodermic full of a clear substance, and regulation handcuffs.

Doug pointed to the pouch. "He's done this sort of thing before."

"I don't think he planned on leaving here without her," a second officer commented.

Heath brought the K-9 truck over and loaded Lucas inside. After convincing Carrie her dog would be fine with him, he left for an emergency meeting with the local veterinarian.

Carrie watched the truck drive away, turned to gaze at her stalker's recently revealed face. "I know him. That's Tim Hardin."

Something else clicked about the oh-so-considerate house call, and she cursed under her breath. He'd stayed a while after she'd left the room to bathe. She could just imagine him sweet talking Christie, coaxing information from her about Carrie's move to Kenton.

She shuddered, remembering his innocent flirtations with her sister. Dear God, he'd even seen and spoken to Max. Carrie's stomach turned as an image flashed in her mind, one of Tim Hardin shaking her precious nephew's hand.

Sam's gut clenched at the sight before him. A cop. The guy was a cop. Sworn to serve and protect. *Son of a bitch!* Rather than being horrified by the man's twisted, dead body, he felt nothing but intense relief. Finally, Carrie was safe. He turned to her, pulled her close enough to feel her violent trembling. "Come on, Babe. You don't need to see any more of this." He led her inside.

Ten minutes later, Carrie still convulsed in violent shivering, despite the mound of quilts piled on top of her. "Why am I s-st-still s-so c-c-cold?" She barely managed to speak through chattering teeth.

Sam went into her bathroom and came back with two aspirin and a glass of water. "Here, take these." She did as she was told and lay back with a violent shiver. He stretched himself out alongside her in her bed and held her until the trembling lessened. Her breathing evened out, as an exhausted sleep finally took control of the situation. He left the bedroom, closing the door softly behind him.

Sam spent the next hour making necessary phone calls to Carrie's family members, Dave and the children first, then Elaine. Next, he called his family, then their co-workers. Exhausted, and sick at heart from telling and retelling the terrifying story, Sam walked outside for a dose of fresh air.

He stepped onto the front porch to check on Lucas. The vet had cleared the dog and sent him home, saying he'd recover from the sprain, his only injury. The Chesapeake sat there with his wrapped leg, vigilant as a great stone lion guarding the palace gates. He stared up at Sam with large, trusting brown eyes and thumped his tail at Sam's approach.

"You did good, boy." Sam reached out to scratch the beast's large head, as man and dog watched the scene on the street unfold. The department finished taking their photos, freeing the coroner's office to leave with the body. Sam followed the flash of lights until the vehicle turned at the highway and disappeared from his sight. After a few more minutes, the street cleared completely.

Sam took Lucas to the back porch, turned as Nick met up with him.

"How's Carrie, Dad?"

"Sleeping. I don't think she let herself think about how dangerous this whole mess was. God almighty, he came close." Father and son talked a few minutes more before Nick stood up to leave.

"I'll be here, Son. I don't want her to wake up alone, but you're welcome to stay and keep me company."

Nick shook his head and stepped off the porch. "Naw, I'll go on home."

Sam went inside to lock up. He stared at the time on the microwave. Not even one a.m. He washed up in the bathroom before heading back to Carrie's bed. Settling himself beside her, he lay on top of the quilts so that layers of fabric separated them. When the drop in temperature convinced him to get up for another blanket, a soft touch on his arm stopped him in his tracks.

"Where do you think you're going?"

"I was just going to get an extra blanket."

Carrie lifted the covers. "It's warm under here."

Sam did as he was told, snuggling up to her under the mound of quilts and bedspreads. "How you feeling? Better?"

"Yeah, I am. I don't know what happened."

"Probably a mild case of shock. You've been through a lot."

She wiped at a stray tear with the palm of her hand and nodded. "But I didn't have to go through any of it alone. It's meant a lot to me that you've been here for me."

He gave her a light kiss. "Glad to be of service."

"How long have I been sleeping?"

"Not even two hours, not long enough."

She struggled to rise from the bed. "I need to call my kids and my mom before they hear it from someone else."

He placed a hand on shoulder. "I took care of it. They all said to tell you how proud they are of you and how much they love you. Grant and the girls will be here tomorrow morning, and your mom said she was glad to hear something before Kathleen Ledoux, for a change."

She closed her eyes in exhaustion and sighed, too emotionally drained to see the humor. Her head fell heavily against the pillow. "Is Lucas okay?"

"He's fine. He's as happy as a bundle of one-dollar bills in a club full of pole dancers. That dog is famous, fed, and fast asleep on the back porch." The heated gaze she sent him warmed him to his toes.

"You really do know how to take care of me, don't you?"

His chest rumbled with laughter. "It's a little difficult for *me* to do that when you're doing such a fine job of taking care of yourself." He fluffed her pillow and covered her with the extra blanket. "Try to sleep, hon. I'll be here."

She woke to low voices and a sudden knock on the side of the house. Carrie cracked one eye open, sensing she'd slept later than normal. Another knock, then another made her jerk upright in her bed and struggle to crawl out from under the mound of quilts and blankets.

"What the hell?" Her foot tangled in the sheet and sent her tumbling to the floor, only half-freed from the multiple bed coverings.

The door flew open and Sam stood there, his face a road map of concern until he saw the tangled mess hanging off the bed. “Hey, Babe. Looks like you’re going’ nowhere fast.”

“Dammit!” She raised one arm toward him as her head fell forward. “Help me.” It was more of a command than a request.

His laughter reached her before he did. “I will, as soon as I figure out where the quilts end and you begin.” He reached under her arms and hauled her up off the floor.

Carrie stood cautiously, assuring herself there was something solid under her feet before stepping free from the tangle. “Where’d you get the blankets?”

“Two other beds and a futon.”

She looked up, still trying to adjust to the brightly lit room, and noticed his sunbeam of a smile. “Don’t laugh at me. I can’t take it right now.”

“I’m not laughing,” he confessed. “Even with puffy eyes, rumpled clothes, and wild hair, I *know* I’ve never loved you more than I do right now.”

She sniffed. “Thanks for not saying I’m still beautiful.”

“Did you want me to lie?”

“If you did, I may have to shoot you. What time is it?”

“Almost eleven.”

“Half the day’s gone,” she groaned, and froze when she heard the distinctive wall-knocking sound again. “That!” She pointed to a spot on the exterior wall of her bedroom. “What is that knocking?”

“It’s your dog. He’s happy.”

She pictured that big tail of his wagging, knocking on the wall. “Oh. I get it now.” She stumbled to the bathroom to survey the damage to her face.

Carrie groaned at her reflection. She splashed cold water on her face, ran a brush through her hair, and started brushing her teeth. “Wait!” She stood in the doorway of the bathroom, toothbrush in hand. “Why’s Lucas so happy?”

“His kids are here. Didn’t you hear them outside?”

She rinsed her mouth, gave Sam a quick kiss, and rushed out through the front door, suddenly desperate to see them.

Carrie called for her kids and they came running. She pulled them close, needing the contact of her babies, even if they weren’t babies anymore. Then she hugged each one separately as her silent tears fell. About that time, Lucas barreled through his kids to get to Carrie. She hugged the dog, praising him for his courage, as he wagged that huge tail hard enough to hurt whomever it contacted. They made their way into the warmth of the house. Carrie stopped to wave at Sam, as he stood on his own steps. He raised his hand slowly, and she blew him a kiss before closing her door.

Carrie turned to her kids. “God, I’m glad to see y’all.”

Grant leaned forward on the couch. “Was it dangerous, Mom?”

She wondered how much he knew. “Did Sam tell you what happened?”

“Yeah.”

“Then you know that I was never in any danger.”

“Something could have gone wrong.”

"But it didn't, and Tim Hardin isn't a threat anymore." She sat across from the couch where she could see all three of them. "Maybe now I can start to enjoy this place."

Gretchen spoke first. "I can never live here, Mom."

Her daughter's words had her bolting upright. "Gretch, nobody's asking you to make a decision now."

"I don't want to stay here, either," Lauren added.

Carrie's breath hitched as she tried to come up with compromises. "You could all finish your school years in Gardiner. Girls, you could start your sophomore years in Kenton. And Grant, I'm still convinced you should graduate from here."

Grant shook his head but kept his silence.

Carrie sighed and turned to Lauren. "By next year you—"

"I don't ever want to see this place again."

"I don't ever want to see this town again," Gretchen added.

"Do you understand that *Officer* Hardin lived in Gardiner, and that he was the one making the phone calls?"

This time Grant spoke up. "We don't care, Mom. Toto was killed *here*. That guy tried to get to you *here*."

"Sometimes things happen that we can't contr—"

"Don't you think this place has, like, bad mojo or something?"

Carrie stared at Gretchen, felt a miniscule crack in the foundation of her brave, new, independent world. "Bad mojo?"

"Toto died here. I can't live here," Lauren tag teamed with her sister.

Carrie refused to give in. "We've had pets die in our home before. Heck, we had two die in one day, but we stayed, because it was our home."

Lauren stood suddenly. "But they weren't murdered!" Her large brown eyes pooled with tears. "That man murdered Toto! Our dog died right there, on the back porch."

Gretchen pointed to the street. "And then *that man* died, right there in the street. In front of the house."

Carrie's heart pounded, trying to pump blood back into the half of her body that felt drained. "This is my life, girls. This is my future. Our future. Someplace better for me."

Lauren shook her head. "Different doesn't mean better, Mom."

"And even if it's better for you, that doesn't mean it's better for us," Gretchen added.

"I have legal guardianship of the both of you." Carrie resorted to her big gun. "You will live with me. End. Of. Story."

Gretchen's chin lifted. "Dad said we can choose, because we're old enough now, and we all choose Gardiner."

Lauren's eyes welled with tears. "You promised me. You said if things didn't work out, you'd stop seeing Mr. Sam."

Carrie felt the color drain from her face, imagined the small crack in the foundation widening. "This is not a matter of things not working out with Sam.

He was with me through all of this. He never let me down. You three like Sam, as well as Nick and Amanda and Joe. Don't try to tell me you don't."

Tears slid down Lauren's cheeks. "I *believed* you when you said you wouldn't choose your boyfriend over us. I should have known better."

"Lauren—"

Grant shifted his stance. "Mom, if you hadn't moved here, Toto might still be alive."

"He *would* be alive," Gretchen finished for him.

Carrie collapsed into the nearest chair as Lauren's quiet sobs filled the space. The crack opened fully, engulfing everything in its path until any future with Sam crumbled into dust. She let her head fall back against her shoulders and pressed the heel of her hands to both eyes. She couldn't find the words to argue her children's theory. How could she blame them for feeling this way, when everything they said was true?

She stood, walked to the back porch, realizing she'd never be able to see it without seeing Toto's dead body lying there. It had been torture to leave Lucas there the previous night. He'd sniffed the floor where Toto had died and gazed up at her with those sad eyes, almost as if he'd known. At the time, it had felt as though he blamed her for Toto's death.

Now she knew her kids did, too.

She turned back, her eyes pleading, and made one last ditch effort to change their minds. "Please, kids. This is so important. I'm begging you to give this a chance."

The teenagers exchanged looks before facing her, shaking their heads.

Carrie took a deep shaky breath and released it. She ran her hands through her hair, suddenly resigned to the fact that no matter what she did, she'd have to do it alone. "All right, then. No more Kenton. No more Sam." She suddenly felt much older, and a lot less independent. "Pack your things. Everything you'll need for the weekend. We're going back to Gardiner tonight." She walked to the front door, reached for the handle and paused, filled with anger. Anger at the situation, at them, at herself for falling for Sam when her life was one, big question mark. Anger was good. Anger would help her get through the next five minutes.

"Make damn sure your stuff's packed by the time I get back. I'll only be a few minutes."

"Where are you goi—" Lauren began.

"Shut up, dumb ass!" Grant's hiss cut off his sister's question.

Carrie tensed and threw open the door, stared out toward Sam standing on his porch—waiting for her. "Whatever's not in the car or truck by the time I get back will stay here until everything else gets moved." She stormed out, slamming the door behind her.

Sam's stomach tightened, knotting with tension at Carrie's approach, knowing damn well he wouldn't like what she had to say. She walked up the sidewalk, determined in her purpose, her jaw tight with anger and hurt. "Ah hell, here it comes," he murmured softly to himself.

She marched up his steps and stopped in front of him. "We have to talk."

He nodded, reaching for her shoulder. "Let's go inside where it's warm."

"No." She pulled away, avoiding his touch.

"Carrie—"

"I'm moving back to Gardiner."

"Talk to me."

"They don't want anything to do with this place, Sam. Not the house, or the school, or the town or—" She faltered suddenly but caught her stride again as she finished, her tone hard and cold. "Or anyone in it."

He wasn't surprised, especially after speaking to her kids when they'd first arrived. He didn't like it, but at least he'd had time to think of alternative methods of keeping their relationship intact. "Babe." He placed his hands firmly on her shoulders. "It'll be okay. I'd rather have you here, but I understand. At least we'll see each other every day at work. We'll survive until the weekends get here."

"I made them a promise, Sam. If things didn't work out between us—all of us—I'd walk away."

"It's not that big of a deal, Carrie. It's only an hour drive. I'll take it."

"No, Sam."

He paused when he caught her meaning. "What are you saying?"

"I'm saying . . . I . . . I can't choose you over my children. It's over."

His breath rushed out at the two words capable of blowing his world apart. He'd been through this before, and damned if he wasn't going through it again. "You can't be serious." He nearly laughed at the lameness of his reaction, knowing she was dead serious.

"I am. And if you were in my shoes, you'd do the same thing, you know you would."

"I would stop to consider what I'd be giving up, I can promise *you* that." His shock morphed into indignation, then fury—fury that deflated when he saw the tremble of her chin.

"You don't think I know what I'm giving up?" She turned her gaze on him. "I'm giving up everything. I've done it once before for my kids, and I guess I'll have to do it again. It'll hurt like hell, but we've both been through worse than this and lived through it. I am sorry. I don't want to do this." She covered her mouth with her hand, before attempting to turn away from him.

Sam caught her by the arm and turned her back to face him. "Then don't, Carrie. Come on, Baby."

"Sam, stop it." Her gaze dropped to the floor as she pushed away from him, her hands fisted and unyielding. She stopped then, opened her hands as she raised her gaze to meet his, and then placed one hand on his face. "If you had to choose between me and your children, you would choose your children, don't tell me you wouldn't."

He caught her hand in both of his. "It doesn't sound much like a choice. It sounds like an ultimatum, bordering on blackmail."

"Maybe it is, but my children's feelings are no less important than ours. I have to go, Sam." She pulled her hand free and turned away from him.

"Carrie, please don't do this."

Ignoring his tortured plea she walked-ran back to her place before she changed her mind. Throwing the door open, she barked at her children. "Girls, get in my car. Grant! I want Lucas riding inside the truck cab with you."

"He's gonna smell up my truck."

"Too bad. His leg's hurt and he won't be able to keep his balance back there." She stopped in front of her girls. "Didn't I tell you two to get in the car?"

"I need my—"

"Now!" She pointed to the doorway.

As her kids scrambled to the door, Carrie rushed to her bedroom closet. She threw two pair of jeans and some blouses in a shoulder tote, along with her makeup kit and a few other items. Hoping to avoid a confrontation with Sam, she locked up and jumped inside her car.

"Can we ride with Grant while Lucas rides with you?"

Not bothering to look at the twin who'd asked the insensitive question, she ground out a reply through clenched teeth. "Sit your butts down and buckle up."

Carrie drove in silence, gripping the steering wheel so hard her hands turned numb. Every mile that took her further from Sam made the gnawing pain in her chest grow worse. Every minute away from him weakened her resolve not to cry. By the time she pulled into Dave's driveway, her heart ached, knowing how badly she'd left Sam hurting.

She pulled the trunk latch and got out to help her girls with luggage, only to find it empty. Remembering how she'd rushed them, she turned to the twins. They stood with their magenta and pink duffle bags, looking hesitant.

"I guess that's all you had time to pack. Sorry, but I had to get out of there."

"Mom—"

"Love you." She embraced Gretchen as she cut her off. She released her and pulled Lauren close for the same kind of hug. "Love you, too."

Carrie walked over to meet Grant, who'd pulled up seconds after her. "Love you, Son." Her voice tight with the need to cry, she hugged him also.

"Mom—"

She raised her hand to shush him and turned to give Lucas a grateful scratch behind the ears. "Good boy." She turned toward her still running car. "Be sure and tell your dad I said thanks, and that Lucas will be fine in a few days."

She peeled out onto the roadway, suspecting her kids watched her leave. They wouldn't understand how badly she didn't want to cry in front of them. She didn't want them to see how much their rejection of Sam hurt her.

Chapter Twenty-Four

Sam awoke to the ringing telephone. A double dose of nighttime pain reliever had cured his headache, but hadn't done a thing for the hollow ache in his chest. He'd slept fitfully, dreaming and waking several times during the night. He rubbed his hands over his eyes, willing the damn ringing to stop. The only person he cared to talk to wouldn't be calling him. She'd been ignoring his calls for over twenty-four hours.

The ringing quit and Nick pushed through his bedroom door. Sam lifted his head from the pillow. "If it's not Carrie, I'm not here."

Nick's eyes widened as he shoved the phone at his father. "*I'm* not telling her that. It's Carrie's Mom."

Sam sat up and reached for the phone. "Ms. Elaine?"

"Well, thank God somebody is answering their phone. Carrie sure won't. Is it out of service again?" Elaine sounded more annoyed than frantic.

"No, ma'am, it's working. She's not there."

A moment of quiet preceded her next comment. "Look, Sam, I know my daughter is all grown up, but if your intentions toward her aren't honorable, I may have to go slap you around a little."

Sam frowned, confused until her meaning dawned on him. "She's not here, if that's what you're thinking."

"She's not?"

"No, ma'am. I expect she's back at her sister's place."

Another pause before she spoke again. "What's going on with you two?"

"Not a thing, ma'am, and you'll have to talk to her to find out why. This wasn't my choice. If I read her right, she wasn't thrilled about it, either."

"Well, dammit. Now I'm really confused."

"Yes, ma'am, I imagine you are. All I can tell you is that shortly after her kids' arrival yesterday morning she walked over and broke it off. She said something about a promise she made them. The whole bunch of them left town before I could collect my thoughts and ask her to reconsider."

"Did you say a promise? What promise?"

Sam passed a hand over sleep-crusted eyes. "Like I said, you'll have to ask her."

"I'll do that. Are you all right?"

"Far from it, Ms. Elaine, but I'll live." He waited through her long pause.

"Well, you keep the faith, Sam."

"I'll try, Ms. Elaine, but . . ." He paused to swallow the catch in his voice. "I'll try," he repeated, before ending the call.

Elaine hit the button and dialed Christie's number.

"Ha-wo."

"Hey Max, my good boy. It's Maw Maw."

Max yelled for Christie. "Mom, it'th Maw Maw Lain!"

"Maxie, is Aunt Carrie at your house?"

"Aunt Cawee thwept in my bed."

"She did? Is she still sleeping?"

"Yeah. She—she cwied."

"Uh huh," Elaine said. Within a few seconds, Max handed the phone to Christie.

"Mom?"

"What's going on with Carrie? Sam said she broke it off because of some promise she made the kids."

"Christ, is that what happened? I haven't been able to get a word out of her about why. She goes to work, but when she comes in, she goes straight to the bedroom and cries. All she said was that it was all her fault and she should have known better."

"Oh my goodness, Sam's as upset about this as she is."

"I figured as much, but this is out of our hands, Mom."

Carrie's New Year's Eve held all the excitement and promise of a yearly physical, with a pap smear thrown in for kicks. She and Christie spent the evening with Dick Clark, watching the ball drop, along with millions of other Americans. They'd splurged on a bottle of cheap wine and a quart of Blue Bell Heavenly Hash ice cream, and although Carrie drank her share of the wine, she was too depressed to eat any ice cream. She seriously missed talking to Sam, but couldn't decide what was worse; not seeing him or seeing him. By the time she met her ride to work in early January, she'd dropped ten pounds and couldn't seem to get more than a few hours of sleep a night.

She stared out the window, hungry for the first sight of Sam as he waited at the designated pick up area. He looked just as good as she remembered, leaning casually against his truck with his arms crossed against his chest. Carrie shifted her gaze to the pages of her book as he settled into the passenger seat, directly in front of her.

"Good morning everybody!" His voice was an exuberant boom in the truck's previously quiet interior.

She mumbled a return greeting, hoping he wouldn't address her directly.

"How was everyone's Christmas? Mine was great."

"Ours was fair, but not long enough," Craig replied.

"No kiddin'," Cory agreed. "I could have used another couple of days off. What'd you do for New Years, Langley? Did you go out?"

She lifted her gaze as Sam gave them an exuberant nod.

"Yeah, I did, as a matter of fact. My daughter and son-in-law dragged me to the local Knights of Columbus New Year's Eve party. I have to admit I had a nice time."

"Oh, yeah? Did you cut a rug with the ladies, Big Boy?" Craig's shoulders moved as he mimicked dance moves.

Carrie waited for his answer, certain the thud of her heart could be heard by everyone in the double cab truck. She stared at the back of Sam's head as he nodded and cleared his throat.

"I danced with a couple."

Craig looked away from the roadway long enough to beam at his boss. "Yeah? Big Boy's still got it, huh?"

Sam nodded and gave a quiet grunt, then looked out the side window.

"What about you, Carrie?" Craig asked loudly. "Did you happen to be at the same party?"

"Nope." Dear God, let him drop it. He didn't.

"No? What'd you do, then?"

"My sister and I watched Dick Clark at her place." She turned to stare out the rear window. "That's it." His casual talk of attending a dance left her with equally humiliating feelings of hurt and betrayal. She couldn't blame him for moving on, but did he have to do it so quickly? She turned back to her novel, determined not to let it bother her.

Remarkably, she survived that first day around him without exchanging one word with Sam. Then another, as his survey crew hit the road early in the morning and didn't return until fifteen minutes before it was time to leave. Her luck ran out on day three.

She turned from pouring herself a mug of coffee to find him leaning casually against the kitchen's doorway. Slightly surprised, she faltered and paid for it by sloshing coffee onto the floor. She stared into blue eyes filled with anything but humor.

"You look tired, Carrie."

"I'm fine." She set her mug on the table, pulled two sheets from the paper towel dispenser, hoping he'd use that opportunity to leave. No such luck. She dropped the towels on the floor and bent over to wipe up the liquid. Maybe if she ignored him long enough, he'd leave. She deposited the towels in the trash and rinsed her hands. She turned to find he hadn't moved.

"Uh huh," he said. "I'm still here."

She lifted her mug from the counter, used a dampened towel to wipe the coffee ring. She walked to the door and stopped for a moment, staring straight ahead, refusing to meet the gaze he had pinned to her.

"I need to get by," she said.

"Looks like that's about all you're doing, is barely getting by."

She closed her eyes and turned her head away from him. Sensing a shift in the air, she glanced forward to find he'd walked away from her. He had to be angry, and disappointed in her decision to end their relationship.

Carrie set her coffee on her desk then picked up a photo. A trio of hinged school photos of her kids—each one posed before a different fall background. Using her cuff, she wiped a fine layer of dust from the glass and placed the frame back in its place. She sighed, pinching the bridge of her nose. It was easy for him, but who could she be angry with? She loved her kids and they had a right to be happy, too. Her phone rang and she reached over to pick it up.

"B & L Engineering. Carrie speaking."

"Is this the only way I can get you to speak to me?"

She looked toward Sam's office, but couldn't see him seated at his desk. Jeff had called in sick, so he had the room to himself.

"I'm worried about you, Carrie."

"Don't be." She bit down on her lower lip to keep from crying. She wouldn't be able to take it if he turned all sweet and understanding on her. She needn't have worried.

"All right, then," he said, then hung up. She set the phone softly in its cradle and stared at it. Was he *trying* to make her miserable? She was barely hanging on as it was.

Her head fell forward, cradled in one hand as she covered a yawn with her other. What she needed was a good night's sleep, minus the nightmares that plagued her. Every night she closed her eyes, praying she wouldn't see Tim Hardin looming over her, reaching out to touch her as she slept. Every night she woke up terrified, and twisting away from his grasp. Christie insisted she may need to see someone, a doctor who could prescribe something to get her through her rough patch. Had they invented a pill that could take the place of having Sam in her life?

Three torturous days at the office melded into four then five, as she was forced to watch Sam carry on as if nothing had happened between them. Did he have to act so freaking well-adjusted? She'd catch herself wanting to scream at him, and then remember that he had every right to move on. They spoke only of matters pertaining to work, and she made it a point never to be alone with him in the same room. They were back to acting as they had her first weeks on the job.

Every day, Carrie dissolved into tears as soon as she was alone in her car. Every day, she walked into Christie's, eyes puffy and red-rimmed from crying. Every day, she told Christie she didn't want to talk about it.

By the end of the week, she decided to look for another job. Jennings was only a thirty-minute drive from Gardiner, and it was a good-size city. She scoured the paper every afternoon, searched the internet, made calls, and asked around. Problem was, no company in Jennings had openings for anyone with a degree in drafting technology. She'd have to concentrate on something in Lake Coburn or Lafayette if she was going to stay in her field. There again, hanging over her like a twenty-pound weight swinging by a thread, was the same problem of high mileage and low starting salary. Frustrated, depressed, and running out of time, it was all she could do to keep her head up.

Thankfully, Len had agreed to let her keep everything in the rental in Kenton until January fifteenth, when she could move into the place in Gardiner. That was just a few days away.

Sam stepped out of Craig's truck on Friday afternoon, dreading the weekend. He waved his co-workers off, noticing that Carrie didn't look up from the book she was pretending to read. He knew that, because he sneaked a peek at it every chance he got and her marker stayed in the same spot. She looked exhausted, and he doubted she was getting much sleep. She barely ate anything at the office, and drank coffee all day to keep from falling asleep at her desk. Roxie and J.C. said she'd been too quiet, and wasn't talking about anything. Worry for her ate at him.

He'd attempted to speak with her one day, but her pitiful effort at holding it together had nearly done him in. So he tried to act as if he was okay with her decision, when he was far from it. He'd take seeing her every day at work, even if they weren't together, over not seeing her at all. But weekends sucked. Big time.

By six p.m., he'd been sitting in his recliner for two hours already. Sam powered off the television and dropped the remote on the couch. He went to the sink, poured himself a glass of water, but didn't drink it. Picked up the weekly newspaper but didn't read it. He paced the living room floor, pausing occasionally to check for lights at Carrie's place. He'd spoken to Len already, and knew she'd asked to hang on to it until the fifteenth. That was three days away, and he figured if she was going to move out, she'd have to do it by this weekend. He'd hoped to get her alone before then and try to talk some sense into her, but the more he thought about it, the less likely that seemed. When she did show, she'd probably be surrounded by family and friends. He'd play hell to get her alone for one second, much less in enough time to get her to reconsider.

"Son of a bitch." He reached for the phone, punched a number into the keypad, a number he'd looked at so many times over the week, he had the damn thing memorized. He heard it ring and took a deep breath, waiting to hear a familiar voice.

"Ha-wo."

Sam grinned, despite his foul mood. "Hello Max."

"Mommy wanth to know who thith ith."

"It's Sam, Max. Remember me?"

"Yeth. Aunt Cawee-th Tham."

"That's right. Can I talk to her please?"

"She'th not he-ah. Mommy can't find her."

It took a moment for Sam to process the child's statement, but when he did, the breath left his lungs in a rush. "Max, let me talk to your mama."

"Okay."

Sam heard the phone hit the floor, prayed the child had gone off to get his mother. A prolonged wait had him ready to hang up and drive over there. Christie answered, sounding breathless.

"Hello, Sam?"

"Yeah, what's going on, Christie?"

"Please tell me she's with you."

"No. No, damn it, she's not."

"You were my last hope. I don't know where the hell she could be. I called all her friends in Lake Erin, and even Dave's family. I thought maybe she'd be visiting with Ruby."

"Who?"

"Dave's mom, Ms. Ruby; she and Carrie are very close."

"Okay, yeah, I remember now. Well, if you hear from her tell her to call me, and if she doesn't want to talk to me you call."

"I will, Sam, as soon as I finish chewing her out for making me worry."

Sam paced his empty house for five minutes before pulling on his boots, and grabbing his coat and keys on the way out. His truck's engine barely had time to turn over before he threw it into reverse and pulled onto the rain-dampened street. He shifted into drive, skidding on the wet street until the tires bit, trying to ignore the sick feeling in the pit of his stomach.

He knocked on Christie's door, grumbling and cursing under his breath. Her car's absence and the dark house told him she wasn't home. "Dumbass!" he said, thinking back to how he'd told Craig that very day he had no use for a cell phone. Damn if he wouldn't give his left nut for one right now.

Within seconds, he was in his truck and headed for Elaine's place. He made it in less than five minutes and breathed a sigh of relief when he saw her car in the drive. He knocked on the door, and waited, praying all this worrying was for nothing. He knocked again, and peeked through the window. No sign of life, no television, just the one light on over her kitchen sink.

"Aw come on!" He took a step back and let his head drop back against his shoulders, wondering what else he could do, when he heard someone call his name. He left the porch and searched the darkness. "Hello?"

"Is that you, Sam?" Mack called out from next door.

"Yeah! What's going on, Mack? I'm looking for Carrie."

"She ran off the road and they brought her to the Jennings hospital to get checked out. Sharon drove Mom to meet her. I think Christie's there too."

"How bad?" Sam's gut clenched at the thought of losing her.

"I don't know, man. She fell asleep at the wheel."

"What the hell?"

"Apparently, she hasn't been sleeping much."

Sam nodded while backing away. “Thanks, Mack. If anyone asks, I’m headed to the Jennings hospital.”

He’d missed her by fifteen minutes. Relieved, but no less frustrated as hell, Sam walked to his truck then stood there, debating whether to go home or head back to Christie’s place. Consideration for Carrie’s injuries, even though the nurse had assured him they were minor, convinced him to head back towards Kenton. He drove by Carrie’s, hoping to see some sign of life, but got only darkened windows.

Sam walked inside and collapsed in his recliner, too drained to kick off his boots. He grabbed the phone and sat there, praying it would ring. Mack would tell her he’d gone by to look for her. Surely, she’d call him.

Sam sat there, wishing for some relief from the ache in his chest, and feeling about as useless as a bikini at the North Pole.

Chapter Twenty-Five

Sam's ringing telephone woke him from a fitful sleep, jarring him so badly it fell from his lap to the floor with a loud clatter. He sat up, blinking, and wiped the drool from his face. He reached for the phone while squinting at the wall clock. Nine-thirty—how the hell had he managed to sleep for an hour? He finally caught the phone and hit the talk button. "Hello?"

"I'd about given up on you answering. I figured you'd gone to bed already."

He sat up straight as Carrie's voice washed over him like a soothing balm. "Are you all right, Carrie?"

"Yeah, I'm fine. I've got a bump on my head. My car slipped in the ditch, but that's it. I was embarrassed to go to the hospital, but Mom insisted."

"It was the right thing to do."

"I guess." She paused, giving him the sense she was choosing her words carefully. "Christie said you called, and Mack told me you drove all the way to Mom's."

"Yeah, I-I wanted to talk to you."

"About what?"

No matter how minor her injuries, she was probably sore and achey. He wouldn't push her into an argument tonight. "Aw, it was nothing, just wanted to check up on you. Are you sure you're okay?"

"Well, if you're that worried, you could come on over here and check me out for yourself," she drawled.

He took a deep breath, released it slowly, teetering on the brink of annoyance. "You want me to drive back to Gardiner tonight to see if you're okay?"

"I didn't say anything about driving."

His spine stiffened. "Where are you, Carrie?"

She chuckled seductively into the phone. "I'm here in my house, Sam. Are you coming over, or what?"

He leaned over to pull the curtain aside and saw a soft glow coming from her house on the corner. "Are you packing up?"

Carrie lit another candle and placed it on the end table. "Nah, decided I'd stay for a while."

"Oh, yeah? What brought that on?"

"It seems Maw Maw Elaine had a pow wow with my kids at the hospital."

"Oh, yeah? What'd she say to them?"

"Don't know, exactly. No one's talking. All I heard was that she wasn't too happy with them."

"I bet she wasn't."

"Whatever she said, it worked. Grant and the twins walked into my hospital room and admitted they over reacted to the whole move situation. Grant still wants to graduate from Gardiner, and the girls asked to stay with Dave until they could finish out the school year. I agreed. But, it sounds as if they're willing to give Kenton a chance, as well as you."

"That's good news."

"I thought so, too."

"I knew I liked your Mom."

Carrie grinned at his comment. "Yeah, I guess I'll keep her."

"And I like you."

"I kind of like you too."

"I hear you've been having some issues with nightmares keeping you from sleeping at night."

One glance at her bedroom, also glowing with candlelight, had her heart pounding. "At Christie's, I dream that Tim Hardin is standing over me while I sleep. I decided to come here to face my fears. I've worked too hard to let a ghost keep me from being independent."

"I agree. Is there any way I could help you out with that?"

She smoothed down her red and black silk blouse, and half-turned, causing the black skirt to twirl gracefully and settle against her legs. "You mean by keeping me company? Talking me through my first night back here?"

"I was thinking more along the lines of being there to hold you during the night if you have another nightmare, or better yet, keeping you from having one at all."

"And how do you propose to do that?"

"Oh, I can think of several ways."

She heard a knock on the door and walked over to answer it. She tensed, momentarily forgetting that Tim Hardin was no longer a threat.

"Hey, Carrie?" Sam's tone was low and seductive.

"Yeah?" She reached for the switch and flipped on the porch light.

"Open the damn door."

Carrie opened the blind, and her breath caught at the more than welcome sight of him standing there with his cordless phone to his ear. She dropped her hand to her side and pulled open the door. "Hey."

He hit the end call button and lifted the cordless phone. "I'm as surprised as you are that I had a signal all the way over here." He stepped slowly across the threshold to meet her. Closing the door behind him, he took one deliberate step closer. "Look, lady. We're gonna get something straight here and now."

She nodded, keeping her silence.

"Don't ask me to stay unless you want more than friendship from me. I mean it. I can't take anymore goodbyes."

She shook her head. "I won't."

Sam's brow rose warily. "You won't *what*?"

"I mean, I want you to stay."

He nodded, and took a step closer. "How long have you been here?"

Carrie looked at her watch. "About forty-five minutes."

Sam shook his head slowly, clucking his tongue. "You should have called me sooner, Baby. Think of all the time we wasted."

"A girl needs time to fix herself up when she's about to plead her case to the man she loves.

"Yeah? Did I just hear you say you loved me?"

She nodded. "You did."

"You do, huh?"

She nodded again. "I do, Sam. The thought of not having you in my life made me realize how much."

"Glad to see you came to your senses."

"Glad my kids came to theirs."

"God bless Maw Maw Elaine."

She smiled. "Yep, God bless her. And Sam?" She reached out for him.

"Yeah?" He slipped his arms around her waist, pulled her close.

She lifted to her toes, brushed her lips against his before pausing. "I still love it when you call me Baby."

Carrie woke slowly, kept her eyes closed as she became totally aware of her surroundings. The steady *thump-thump-thump* of a heart reverberated in her right ear. Her head rested against a broad chest.

Sam's chest. Sam's heart.

The heart of the man who claims to love her.

Did she believe him?

Absolutely.

Would he love her enough to forsake all others?

If she didn't believe that, she wouldn't be here.

Carrie passed her finger softly along the side of his face. She smiled at the twitch of his nose while he slept peacefully, his arms wrapped protectively around her.

Could she grow to love this man as much as he claimed to love her?

She hooked her foot around his bare calf, pulled him closer. She slid the arch of her foot along the muscular length of it until he released a low, pleasurable moan. Still sleeping, he tightened his hold on her, strengthening the skin-to-skin contact—all inhibitions vanished after their first beautiful experience at love-making. Her lids lowered as she settled further into his warmth.

Could she?

Hell, she already did.

Epilogue

Late summer of 2013

Carrie Langley dusted the credenza, lifting the latest family photo—her and Sam sitting on a porch swing, surrounded by all five of their children with the addition of several grandchildren.

For whatever reason, she and Sam had clicked, and she was as in love with her husband today as she'd been in their first year of marriage. All indications pointed to him feeling the same way. Sam was a wonderful husband, a doting stepdad, and a loving grandfather.

He slipped his arms around her from behind and hugged her tightly before whispering the words he'd repeated countless times to her over the years. "I love you, Carrie." He placed a gentle kiss on the side of her neck.

She smiled as she rested her head against her man—her rock—Sam.

"I love you, Sam. Always."

They had successfully built a life together, joined their two families into one. They were far from rich with material wealth, but always had enough to get by—while rich with something of much more importance.

She placed her hands over his and closed her eyes, thanking God for whatever troubles had eventually led her to this man. As far as she was concerned, God had come through for her and her children, and she owed him.

She owed him big.

Other books by
LORI LEGER

La Fleur de Love Series
Book 1: *Some Day Somebody*
Book 2: *Last First Kiss*
Book 2.5: *Hart's Desire* (Novella)
Book 3: *Brown Eyed Girl*
Book 4: *Heaven in Your Eyes*

Halos & Horns Series
Book 1: *Green Eyed Temptation*
Book 2: *Sarah Smile*
Book 3: *Meagan's Marine*
Book 4: *One Year to Forever*

Seasons of Love Series
Book 1: *Hearts, Hearths & Holidays*
Book 2: *Spring Promise*
Book 3: *Sweet Summertime Love*
Book 4: *Christmas by Candlelight*
Book 5: *It's a Summer Thing*

Full Circle Love: Combined short stories from Seasons of Love series (Books 2-5) involving Cathryn and Zachary. Their story is revisited in *Running Out of Rain,* a novel about Zach's father and grandfather, John Michael and John David (J.D.) Ferguson.

Prime of Love Series
Book 1: *Running Out of Rain*

ABOUT THE AUTHOR

Lori Leger is a wife, mother, doting grandmother, and Mistress of Procrastination. She lives in Louisiana with the love of her life, her very own Studley-do-Right. He's earned his spot in the Keeper Husband's Hall of Fame by allowing her to walk away from an eighteen year career as an Engineering Technician in Road Design to stay home and write.

She adores writing stories set in her beloved south Louisiana, where good Cajun cooking, helping your neighbors, and saying y'all is as normal as hurricanes, heat, and humidity. She figures as long as she's not tunneling through ten feet of snow to get to her car, it's a perfectly acceptable trade-off.

Lori has nine novels published in two series: La Fleur de Love and its spin-off, Halos & Horns series. She has also contributed to, as well as published, short stories in each of the five Seasons of Love anthologies, an author collaboration series. She's contributed to the Sweet & Savory Cookbook of Amazon Authors, published by Top Ten Press. Lori also has an article published in the non-fiction book Writing After Retirement: Tips From Retired Writers, published by Rowman and Littlefield Publishers, and edited and compiled by Carol Smallwood and Christine Redman-Waldeyer.

Her latest book, Running Out of Rain is the first book in her Prime of Love Series, novels dedicated to mature characters finding love and laughter through the everyday twists and turns of growing older. She has a second planned for a fall 2015 release date, and a third set for the summer of 2016.

Lori Leger
P.O. Box 641
Kinder, LA 70648
cajunflair@lorilegerauthor.com
www.lorilegerauthor.com
www.facebook.com/lorilegerauthor
www.facebook.com/llegerauthor
www.facebook.com/CajunflairPublishing
Twitter: @LoriLegerAuthor

www.ingramcontent.com/pod-product-compliance
Lightning Source LLC
LaVergne TN
LVHW020043110826
845155LV00029B/616

* 9 7 8 1 9 4 0 3 0 5 2 2 6 *